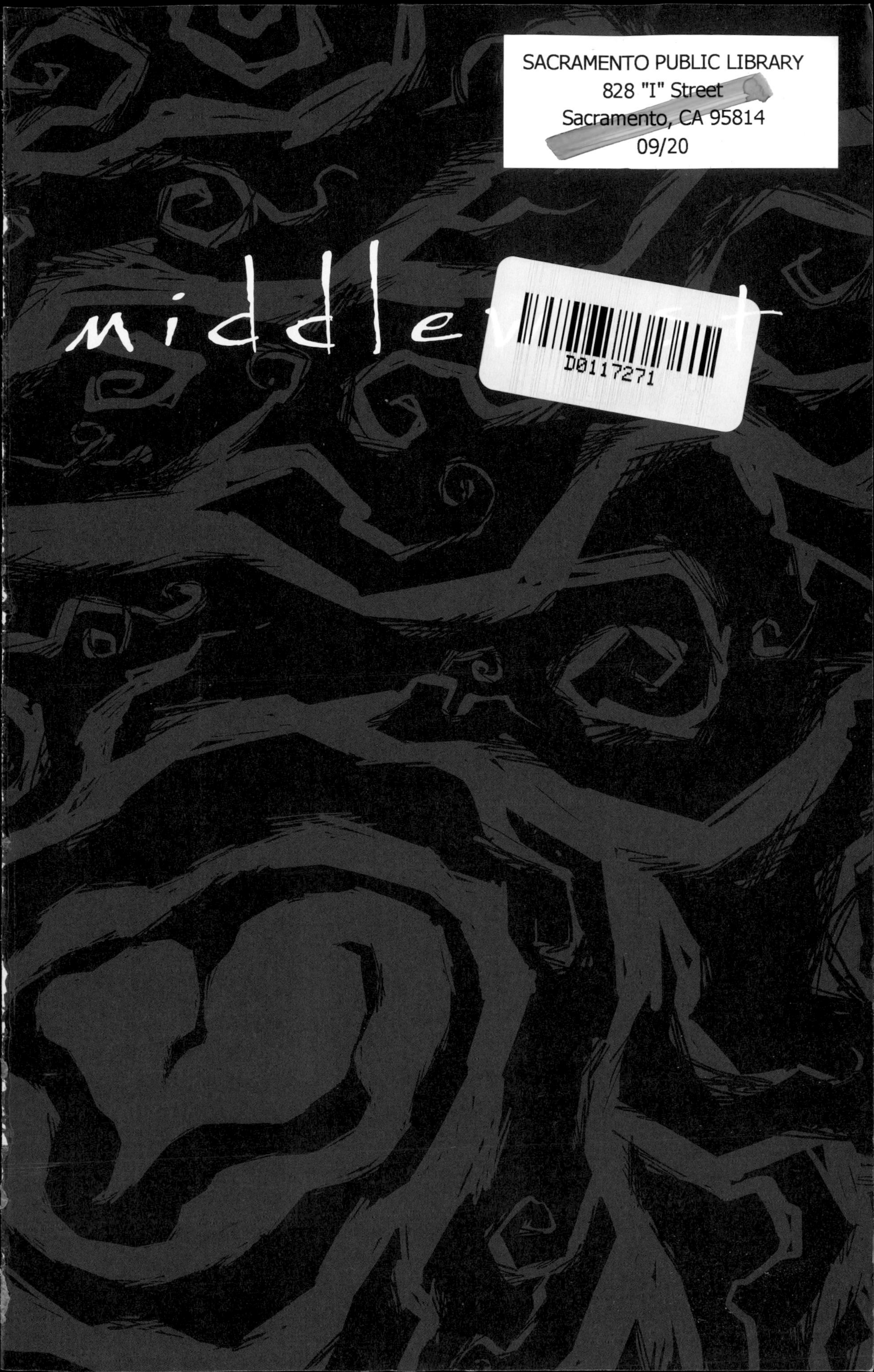

middlewest

IMAGE COMICS, INC. ROBERT KIRKMAN: Chief Operating Officer • ERIK LARSEN: Chief Financial Officer • TODD MCFARLANE: President • MARC SILVESTRI: Chief Executive Officer • JIM VALENTINO: Vice President • ERIC STEPHENSON: Publisher/Chief Creative Officer • JEFF BOISON: Director of Sales & Publishing Planning • JEFF STANG: Director of Direct Market Sales • KAT SALAZAR: Director of PR & Marketing • DREW GILL: Cover Editor • HEATHER DOORNINK: Production Director • NICOLE LAPALME: Controller **IMAGECOMICS.COM**

middlewest

STORY
SKOTTIE YOUNG

ART
JORGE CORONA

COLORS
JEAN-FRANCOIS BEAULIEU

LETTERING
NATE PIEKOS OF BLAMBOT®

COVER ART
JORGE CORONA &
JEAN-FRANCOIS BEAULIEU

EDITOR
KENT WAGENSCHUTZ

DESIGN
CAREY HALL

PRODUCTION
DEANNA PHELPS

CHAPTER

THIRTEEN

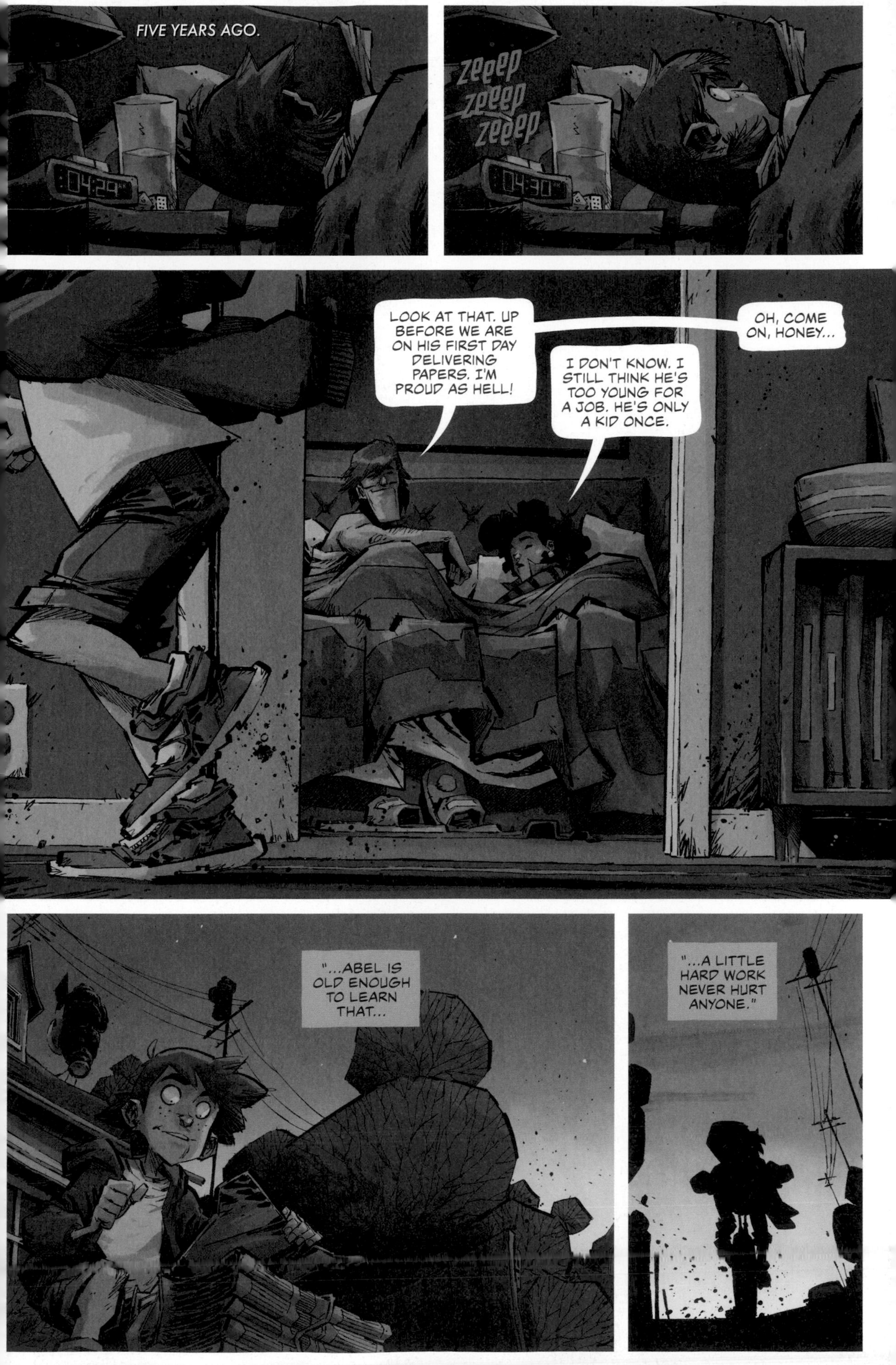
FIVE YEARS AGO.
ZEEEP ZEEEP ZEEEP
LOOK AT THAT. UP BEFORE WE ARE ON HIS FIRST DAY DELIVERING PAPERS. I'M PROUD AS HELL!
I DON'T KNOW. I STILL THINK HE'S TOO YOUNG FOR A JOB. HE'S ONLY A KID ONCE.
OH, COME ON, HONEY...
"...ABEL IS OLD ENOUGH TO LEARN THAT...
"...A LITTLE HARD WORK NEVER HURT ANYONE."

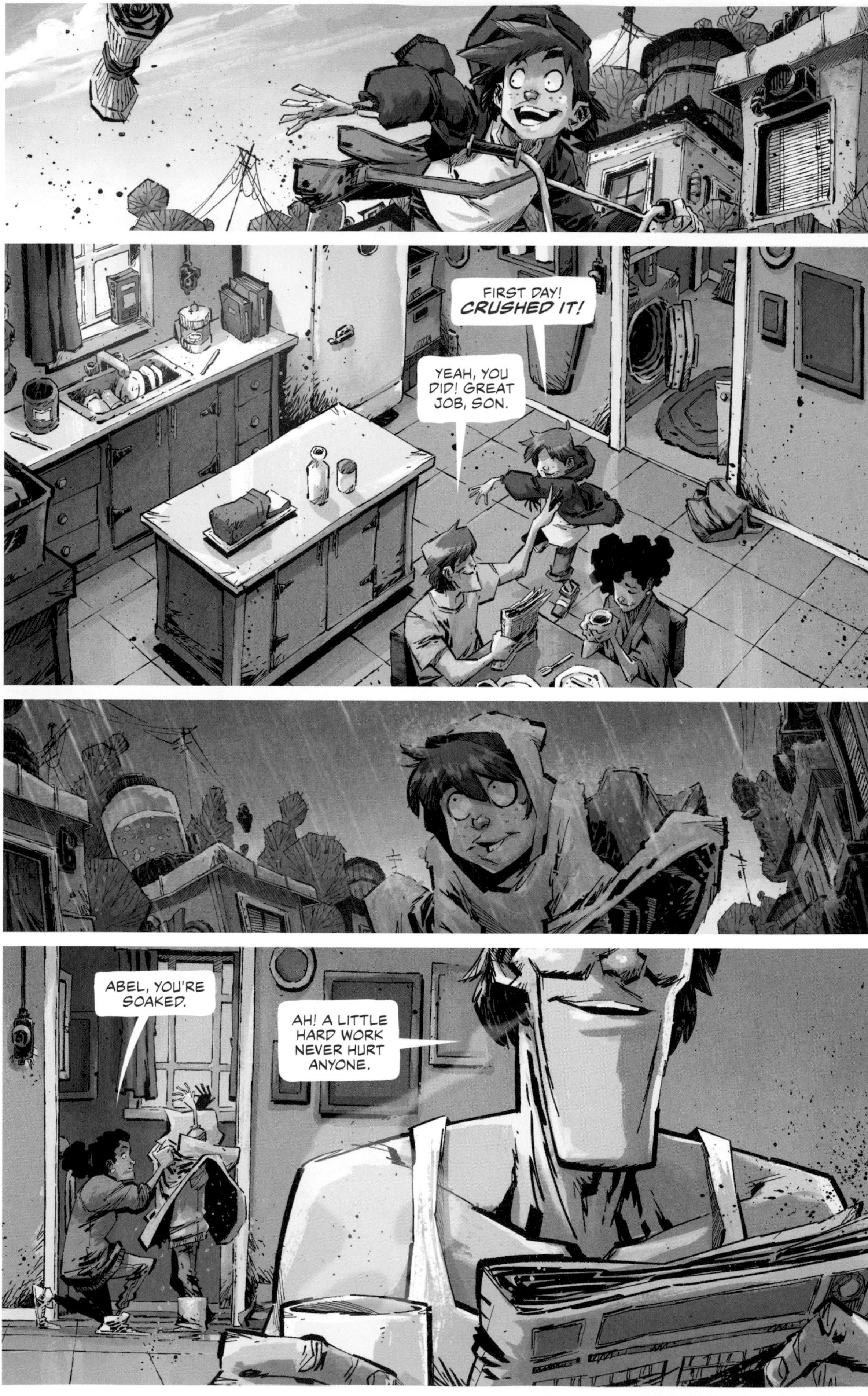
FIRST DAY! CRUSHED IT!
YEAH, YOU DID! GREAT JOB, SON.
ABEL, YOU'RE SOAKED.
AH! A LITTLE HARD WORK NEVER HURT ANYONE.

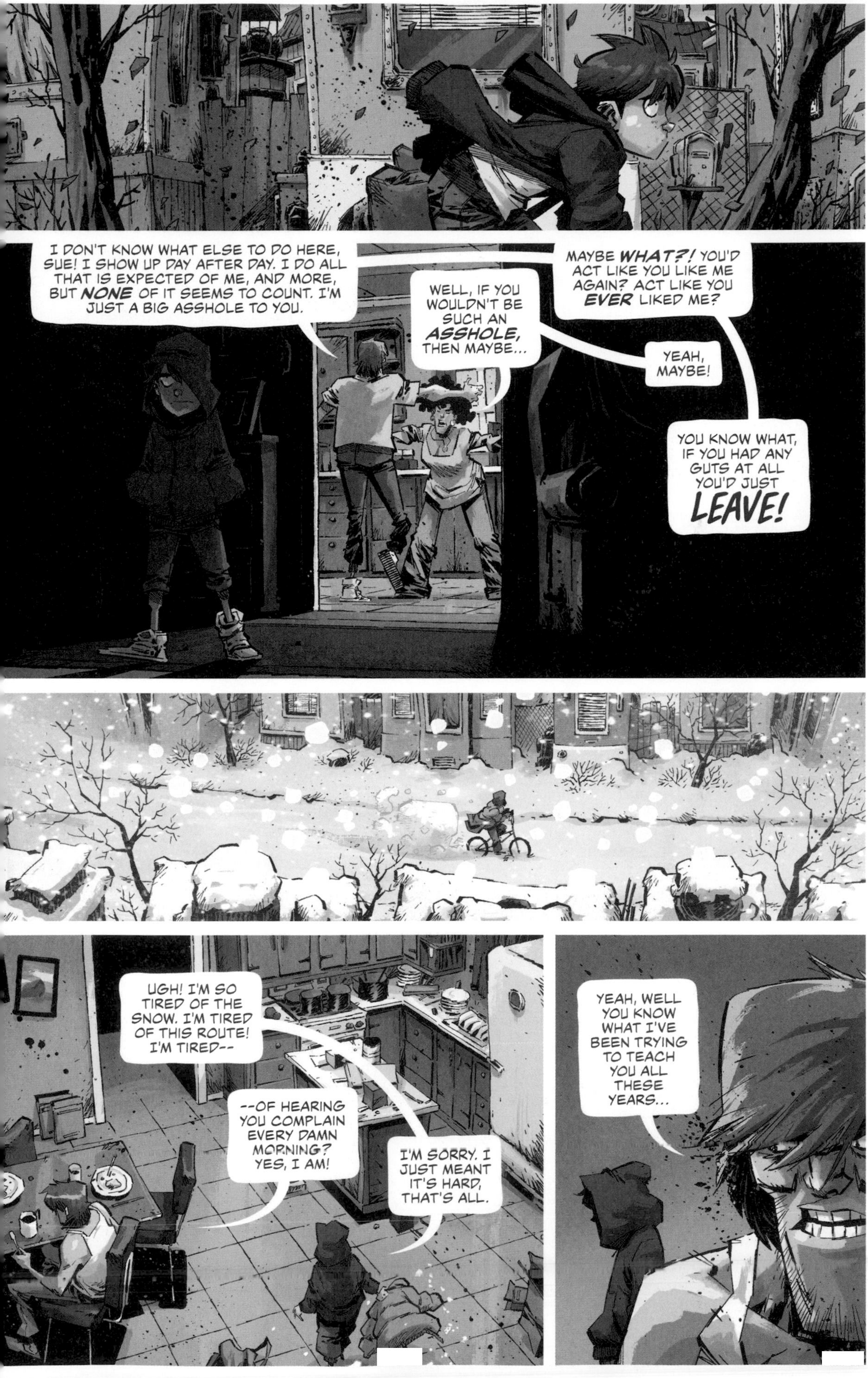

I DON'T KNOW WHAT ELSE TO DO HERE, SUE! I SHOW UP DAY AFTER DAY. I DO ALL THAT IS EXPECTED OF ME, AND MORE, BUT NONE OF IT SEEMS TO COUNT. I'M JUST A BIG ASSHOLE TO YOU.
WELL, IF YOU WOULDN'T BE SUCH AN ASSHOLE, THEN MAYBE...
MAYBE WHAT?! YOU'D ACT LIKE YOU LIKE ME AGAIN? ACT LIKE YOU EVER LIKED ME?
YEAH, MAYBE!
YOU KNOW WHAT, IF YOU HAD ANY GUTS AT ALL YOU'D JUST LEAVE!
UGH! I'M SO TIRED OF THE SNOW. I'M TIRED OF THIS ROUTE! I'M TIRED--
--OF HEARING YOU COMPLAIN EVERY DAMN MORNING? YES, I AM!
I'M SORRY. I JUST MEANT IT'S HARD, THAT'S ALL.
YEAH, WELL YOU KNOW WHAT I'VE BEEN TRYING TO TEACH YOU ALL THESE YEARS...

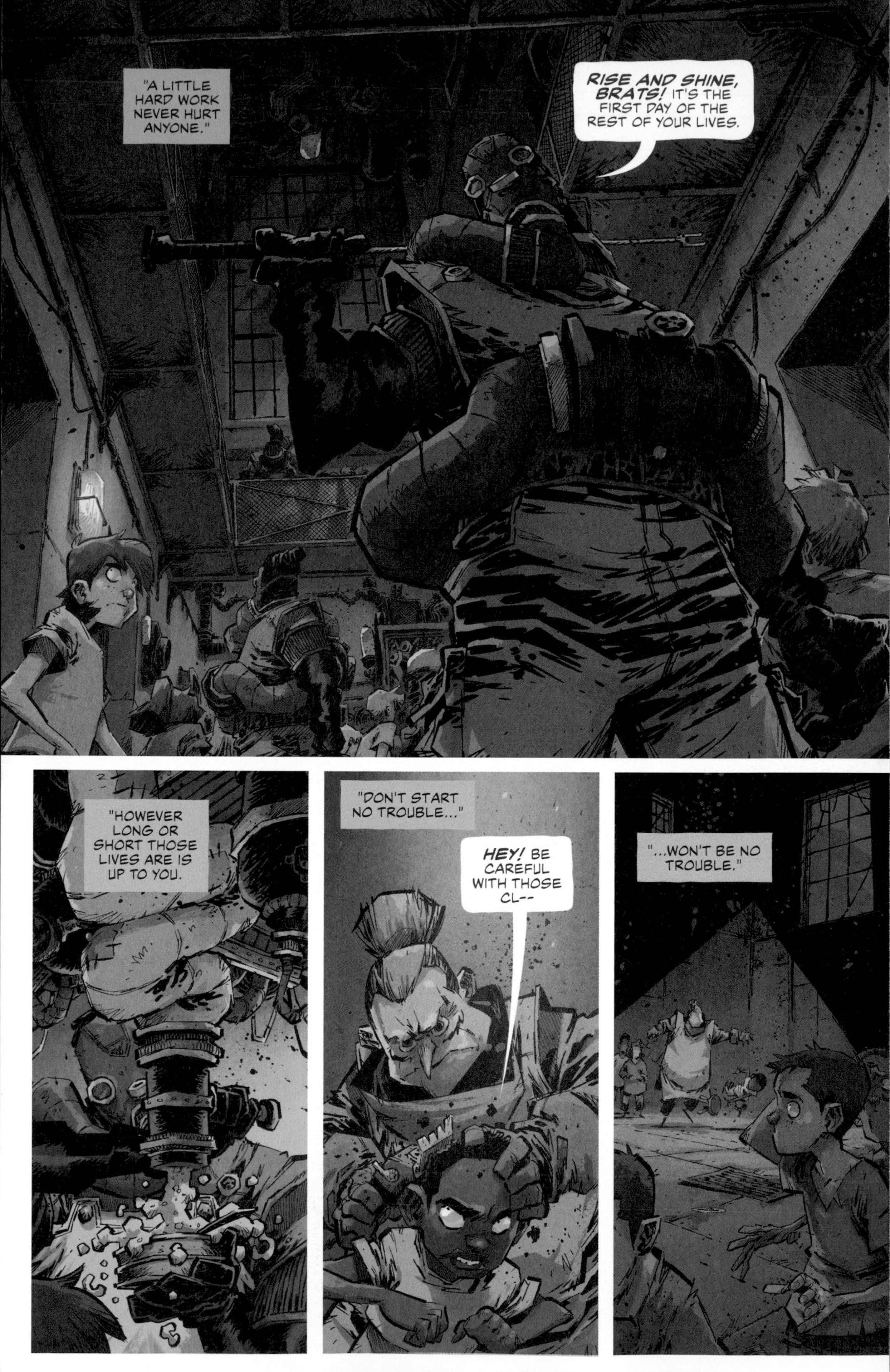
"A LITTLE HARD WORK NEVER HURT ANYONE."
RISE AND SHINE, BRATS! IT'S THE FIRST DAY OF THE REST OF YOUR LIVES.
"HOWEVER LONG OR SHORT THOSE LIVES ARE IS UP TO YOU.
"DON'T START NO TROUBLE..."
HEY! BE CAREFUL WITH THOSE CL--
"...WON'T BE NO TROUBLE."

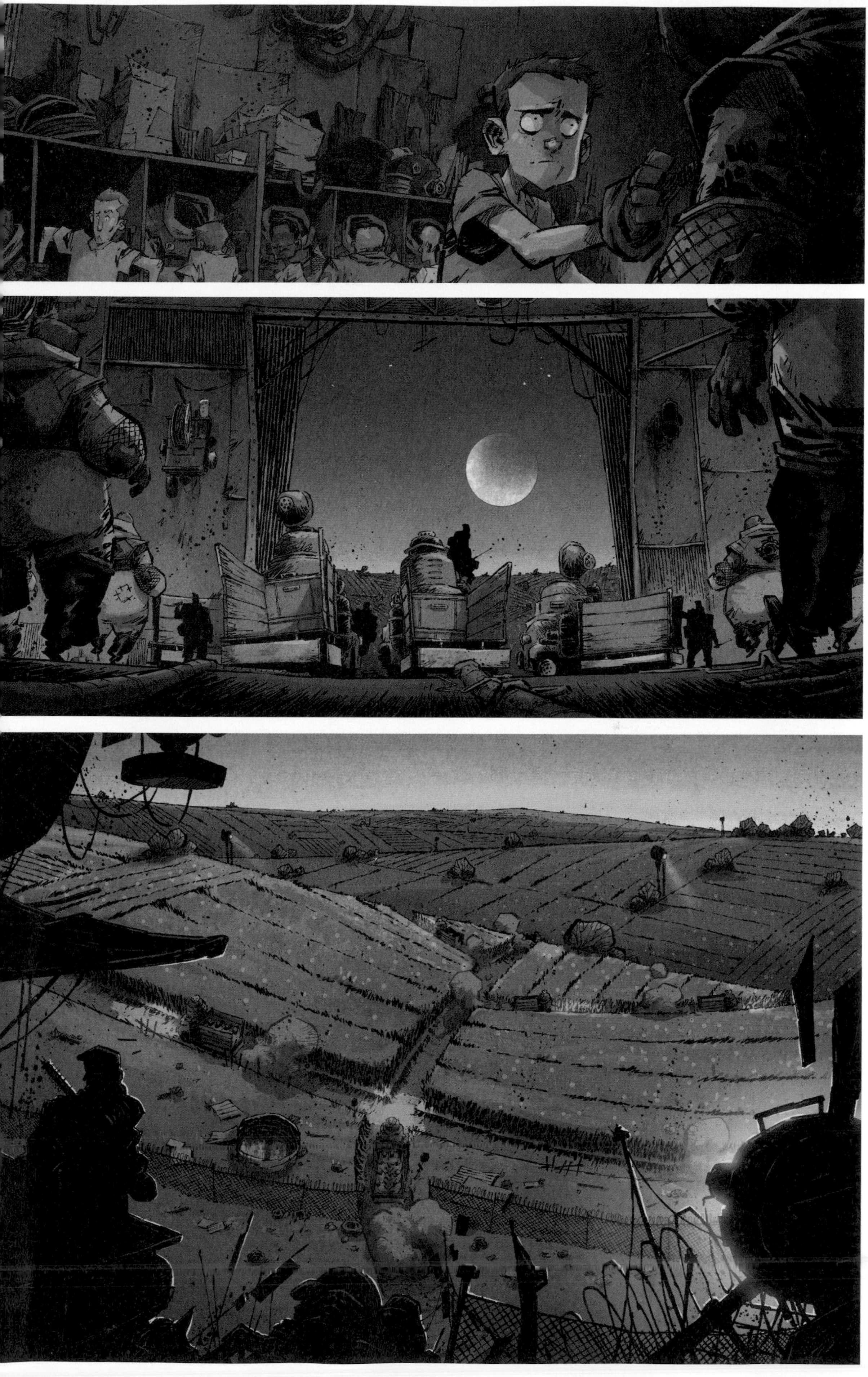

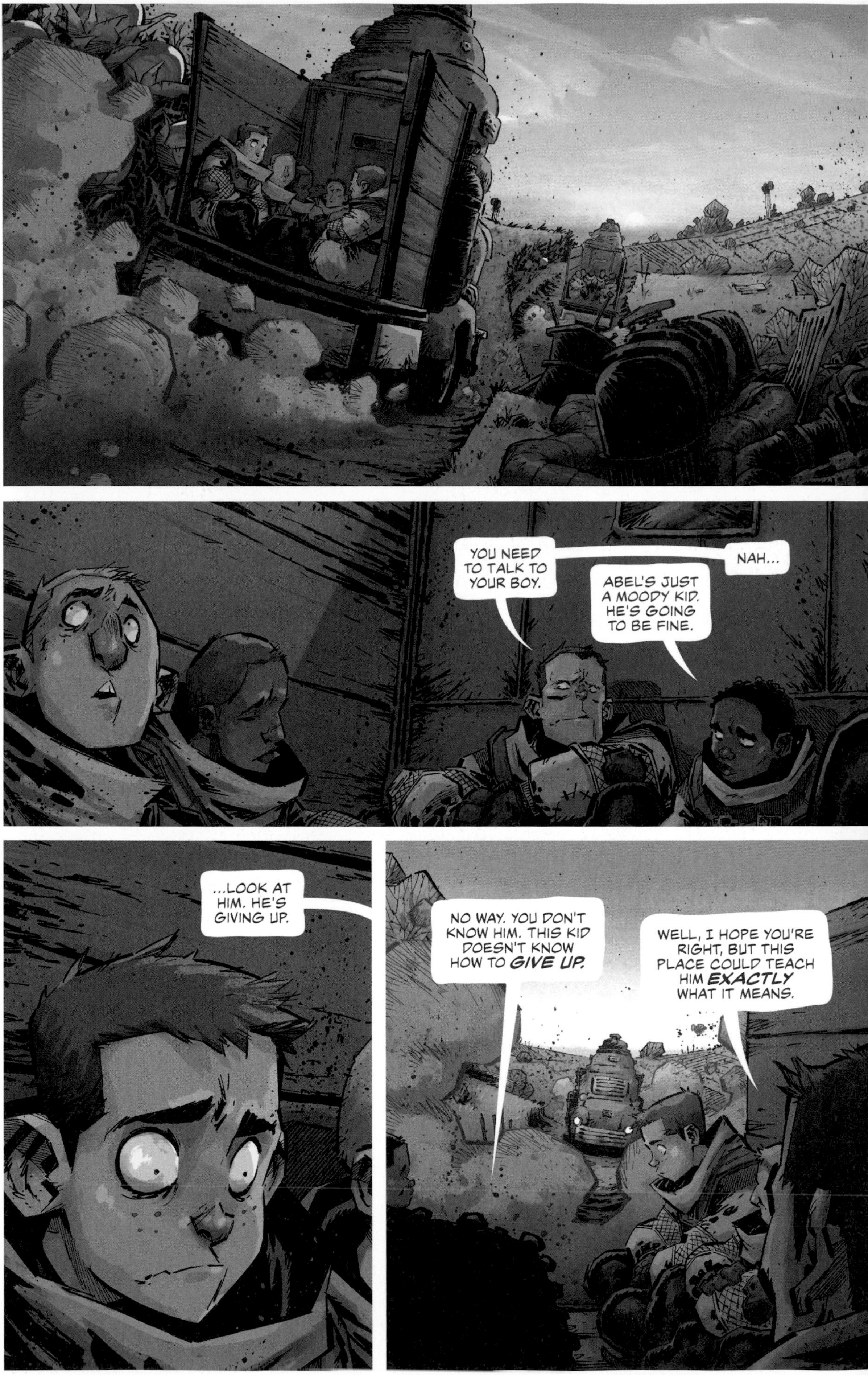

YOU NEED TO TALK TO YOUR BOY.
NAH...
ABEL'S JUST A MOODY KID. HE'S GOING TO BE FINE.
...LOOK AT HIM. HE'S GIVING UP.
NO WAY. YOU DON'T KNOW HIM. THIS KID DOESN'T KNOW HOW TO GIVE UP.
WELL, I HOPE YOU'RE RIGHT, BUT THIS PLACE COULD TEACH HIM EXACTLY WHAT IT MEANS.

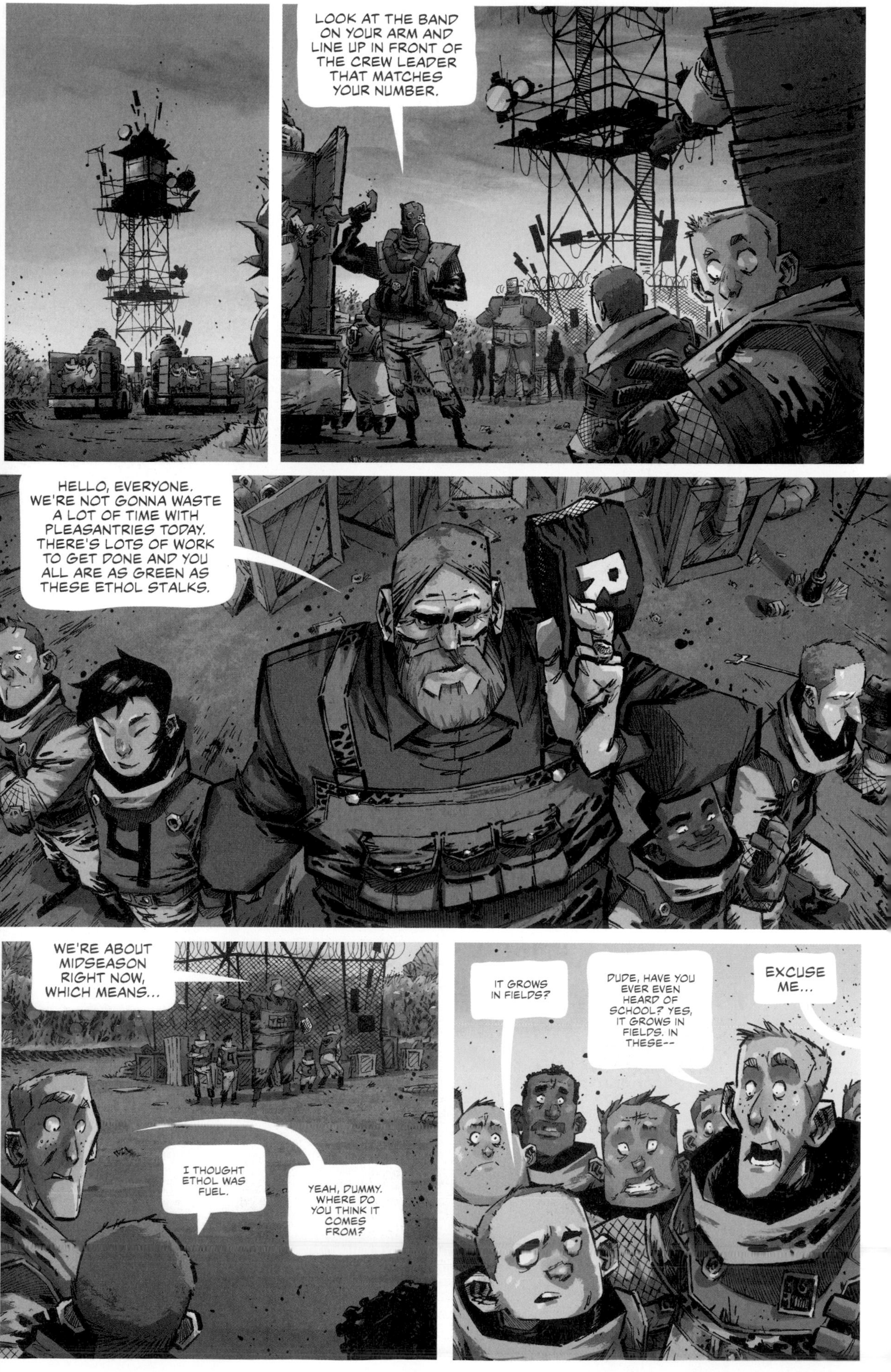

LOOK AT THE BAND ON YOUR ARM AND LINE UP IN FRONT OF THE CREW LEADER THAT MATCHES YOUR NUMBER.
HELLO, EVERYONE. WE'RE NOT GONNA WASTE A LOT OF TIME WITH PLEASANTRIES TODAY. THERE'S LOTS OF WORK TO GET DONE AND YOU ALL ARE AS GREEN AS THESE ETHOL STALKS.
WE'RE ABOUT MIDSEASON RIGHT NOW, WHICH MEANS...
I THOUGHT ETHOL WAS FUEL.
YEAH, DUMMY. WHERE DO YOU THINK IT COMES FROM?
IT GROWS IN FIELDS?
DUDE, HAVE YOU EVER EVEN HEARD OF SCHOOL? YES, IT GROWS IN FIELDS. IN THESE--
EXCUSE ME...

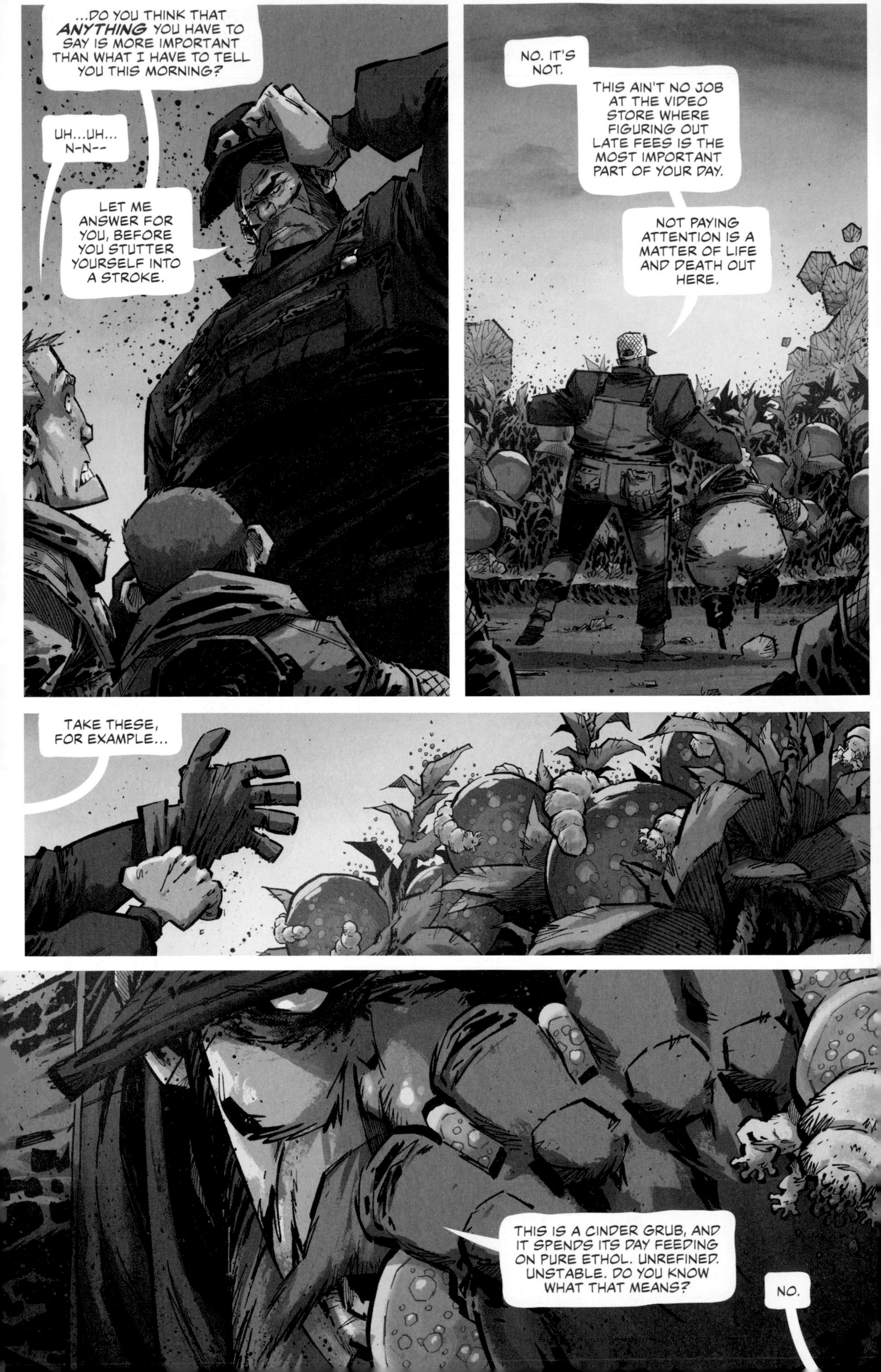
...DO YOU THINK THAT ANYTHING YOU HAVE TO SAY IS MORE IMPORTANT THAN WHAT I HAVE TO TELL YOU THIS MORNING?
UH...UH... N-N--
LET ME ANSWER FOR YOU, BEFORE YOU STUTTER YOURSELF INTO A STROKE.
NO. IT'S NOT.
THIS AIN'T NO JOB AT THE VIDEO STORE WHERE FIGURING OUT LATE FEES IS THE MOST IMPORTANT PART OF YOUR DAY.
NOT PAYING ATTENTION IS A MATTER OF LIFE AND DEATH OUT HERE.
TAKE THESE, FOR EXAMPLE...
THIS IS A CINDER GRUB, AND IT SPENDS ITS DAY FEEDING ON PURE ETHOL. UNREFINED. UNSTABLE. DO YOU KNOW WHAT THAT MEANS?
NO.

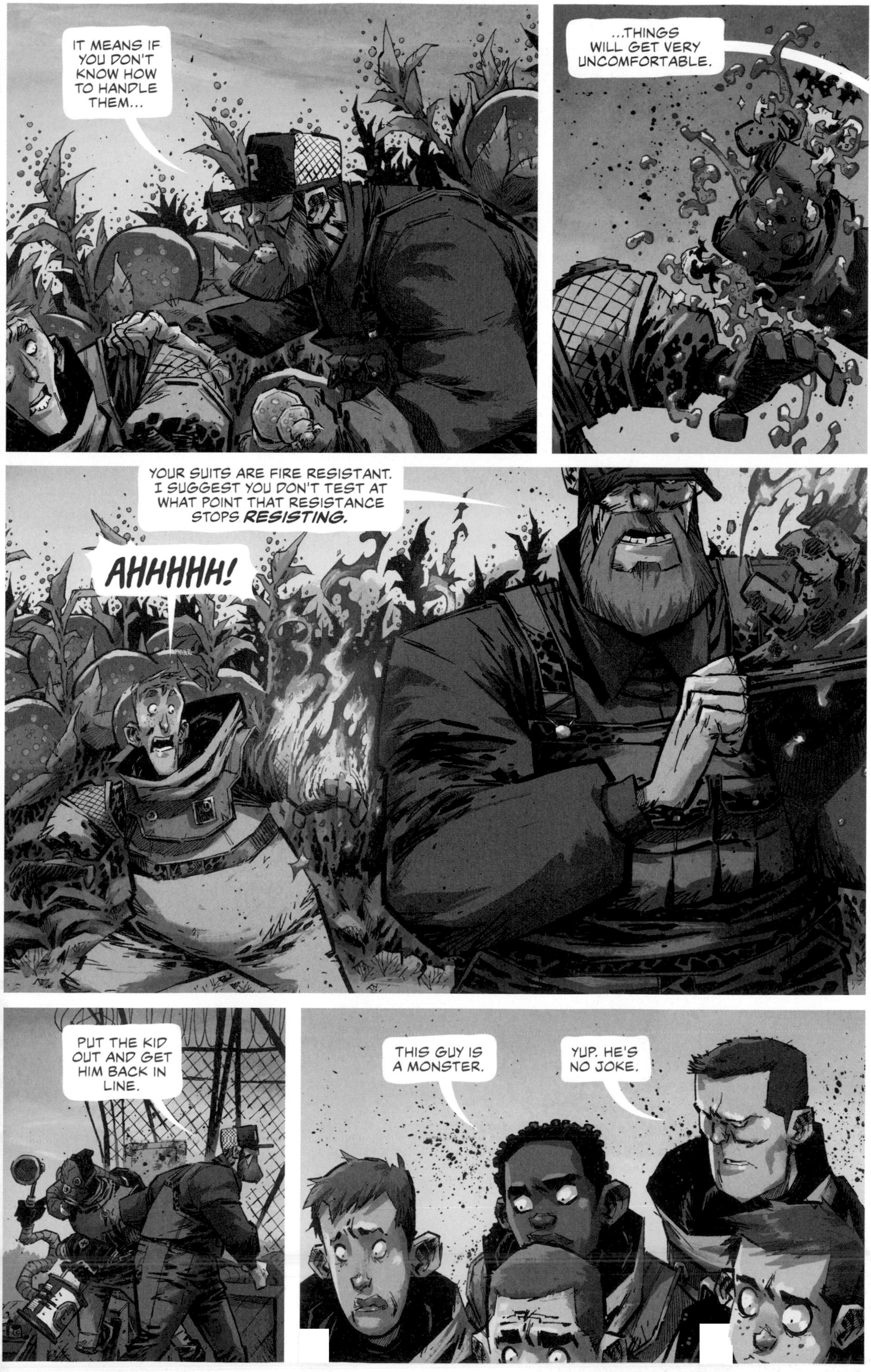
IT MEANS IF YOU DON'T KNOW HOW TO HANDLE THEM...
...THINGS WILL GET VERY UNCOMFORTABLE.
YOUR SUITS ARE FIRE RESISTANT. I SUGGEST YOU DON'T TEST AT WHAT POINT THAT RESISTANCE STOPS RESISTING.
AHHHHH!
PUT THE KID OUT AND GET HIM BACK IN LINE.
THIS GUY IS A MONSTER.
YUP. HE'S NO JOKE.

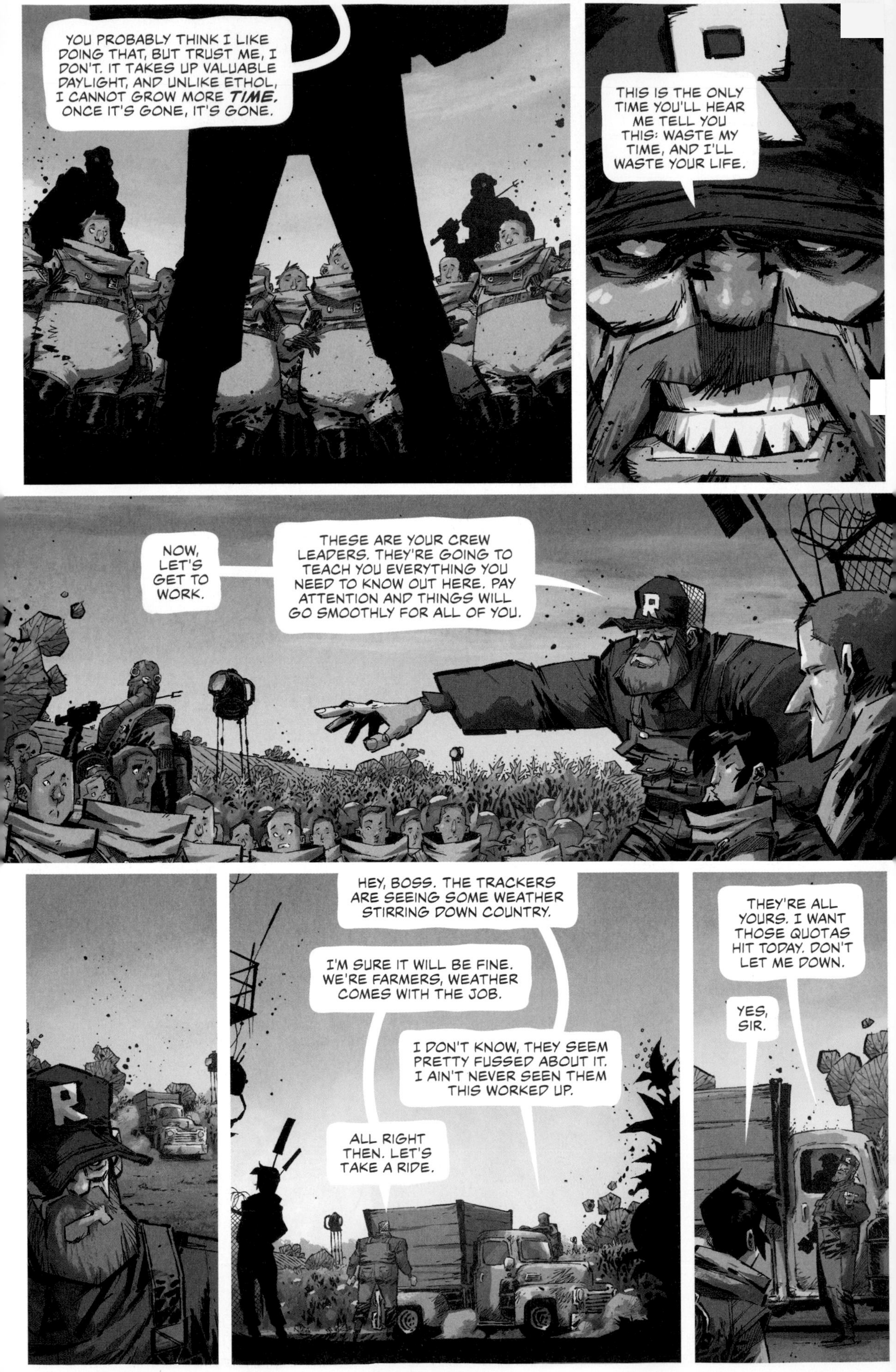
YOU PROBABLY THINK I LIKE DOING THAT, BUT TRUST ME, I DON'T. IT TAKES UP VALUABLE DAYLIGHT, AND UNLIKE ETHOL, I CANNOT GROW MORE TIME. ONCE IT'S GONE, IT'S GONE.
THIS IS THE ONLY TIME YOU'LL HEAR ME TELL YOU THIS: WASTE MY TIME, AND I'LL WASTE YOUR LIFE.
THESE ARE YOUR CREW LEADERS. THEY'RE GOING TO TEACH YOU EVERYTHING YOU NEED TO KNOW OUT HERE. PAY ATTENTION AND THINGS WILL GO SMOOTHLY FOR ALL OF YOU.
NOW, LET'S GET TO WORK.
HEY, BOSS. THE TRACKERS ARE SEEING SOME WEATHER STIRRING DOWN COUNTRY.
I'M SURE IT WILL BE FINE. WE'RE FARMERS, WEATHER COMES WITH THE JOB.
I DON'T KNOW, THEY SEEM PRETTY FUSSED ABOUT IT. I AIN'T NEVER SEEN THEM THIS WORKED UP.
ALL RIGHT THEN. LET'S TAKE A RIDE.
THEY'RE ALL YOURS. I WANT THOSE QUOTAS HIT TODAY. DON'T LET ME DOWN.
YES, SIR.

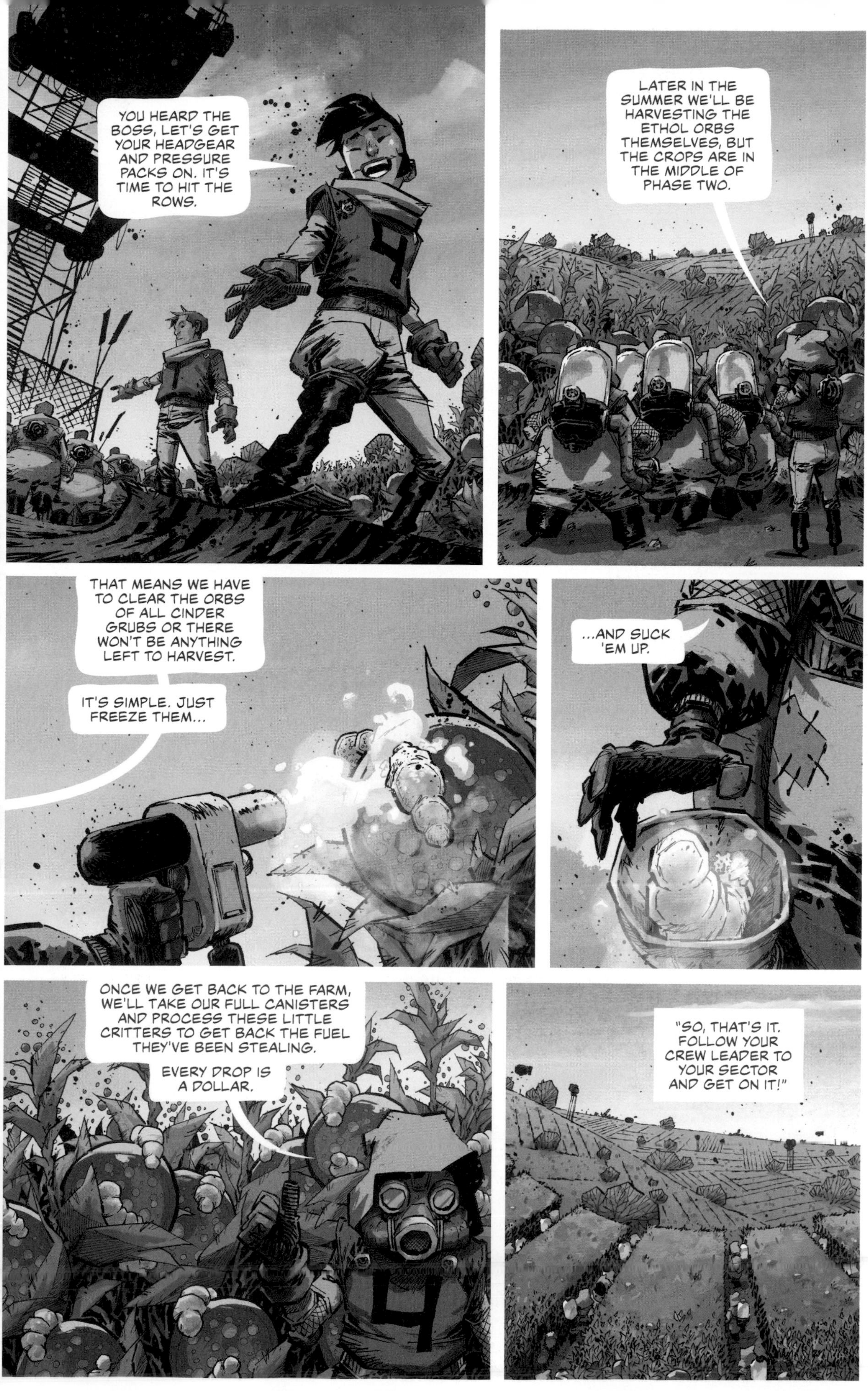
YOU HEARD THE BOSS, LET'S GET YOUR HEADGEAR AND PRESSURE PACKS ON. IT'S TIME TO HIT THE ROWS.
LATER IN THE SUMMER WE'LL BE HARVESTING THE ETHOL ORBS THEMSELVES, BUT THE CROPS ARE IN THE MIDDLE OF PHASE TWO.
THAT MEANS WE HAVE TO CLEAR THE ORBS OF ALL CINDER GRUBS OR THERE WON'T BE ANYTHING LEFT TO HARVEST.
IT'S SIMPLE. JUST FREEZE THEM...
...AND SUCK 'EM UP.
ONCE WE GET BACK TO THE FARM, WE'LL TAKE OUR FULL CANISTERS AND PROCESS THESE LITTLE CRITTERS TO GET BACK THE FUEL THEY'VE BEEN STEALING.
EVERY DROP IS A DOLLAR.
"SO, THAT'S IT. FOLLOW YOUR CREW LEADER TO YOUR SECTOR AND GET ON IT!"

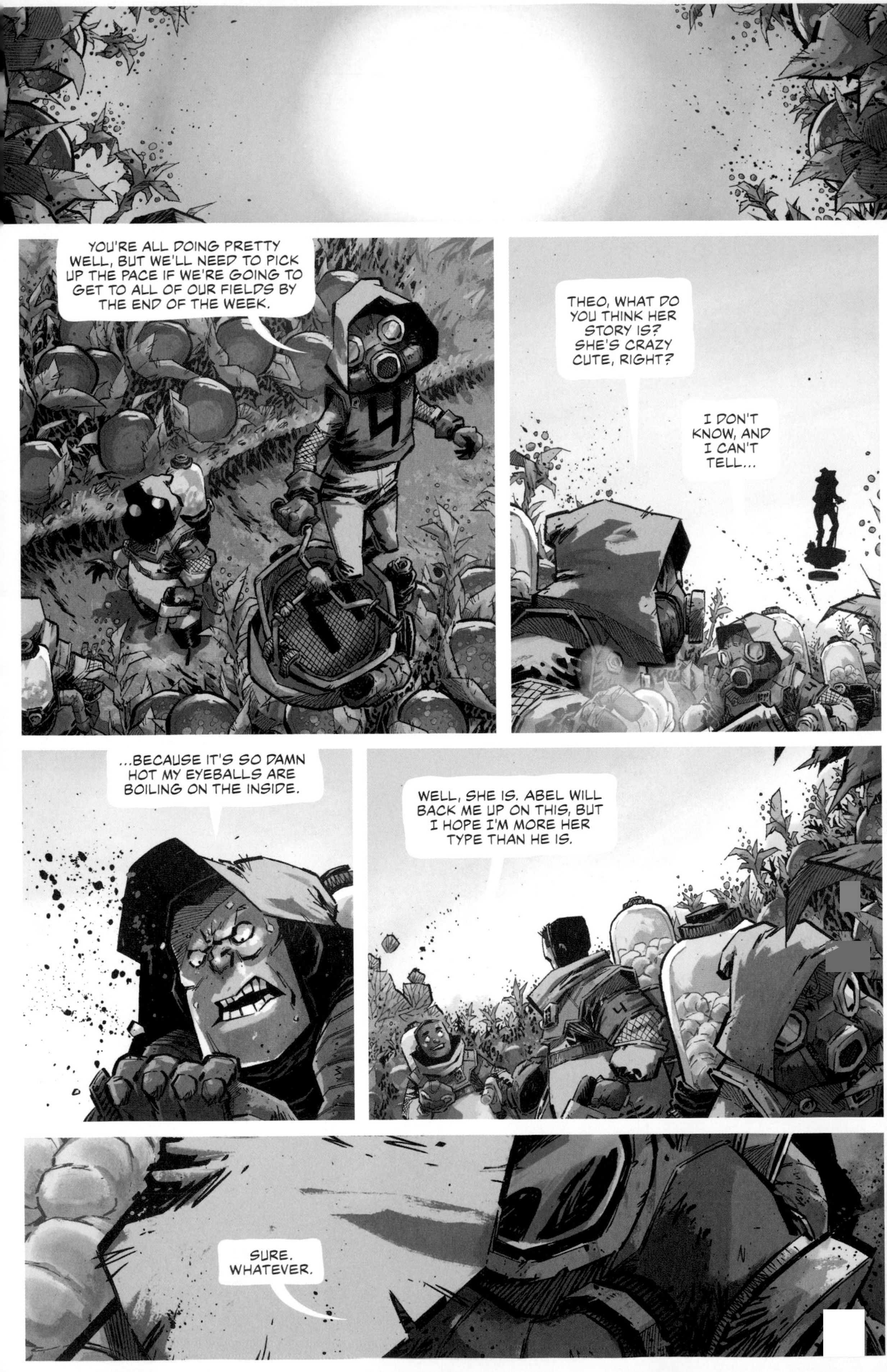
YOU'RE ALL DOING PRETTY WELL, BUT WE'LL NEED TO PICK UP THE PACE IF WE'RE GOING TO GET TO ALL OF OUR FIELDS BY THE END OF THE WEEK.
THEO, WHAT DO YOU THINK HER STORY IS? SHE'S CRAZY CUTE, RIGHT?
I DON'T KNOW, AND I CAN'T TELL...
...BECAUSE IT'S SO DAMN HOT MY EYEBALLS ARE BOILING ON THE INSIDE.
WELL, SHE IS. ABEL WILL BACK ME UP ON THIS, BUT I HOPE I'M MORE HER TYPE THAN HE IS.
SURE. WHATEVER.

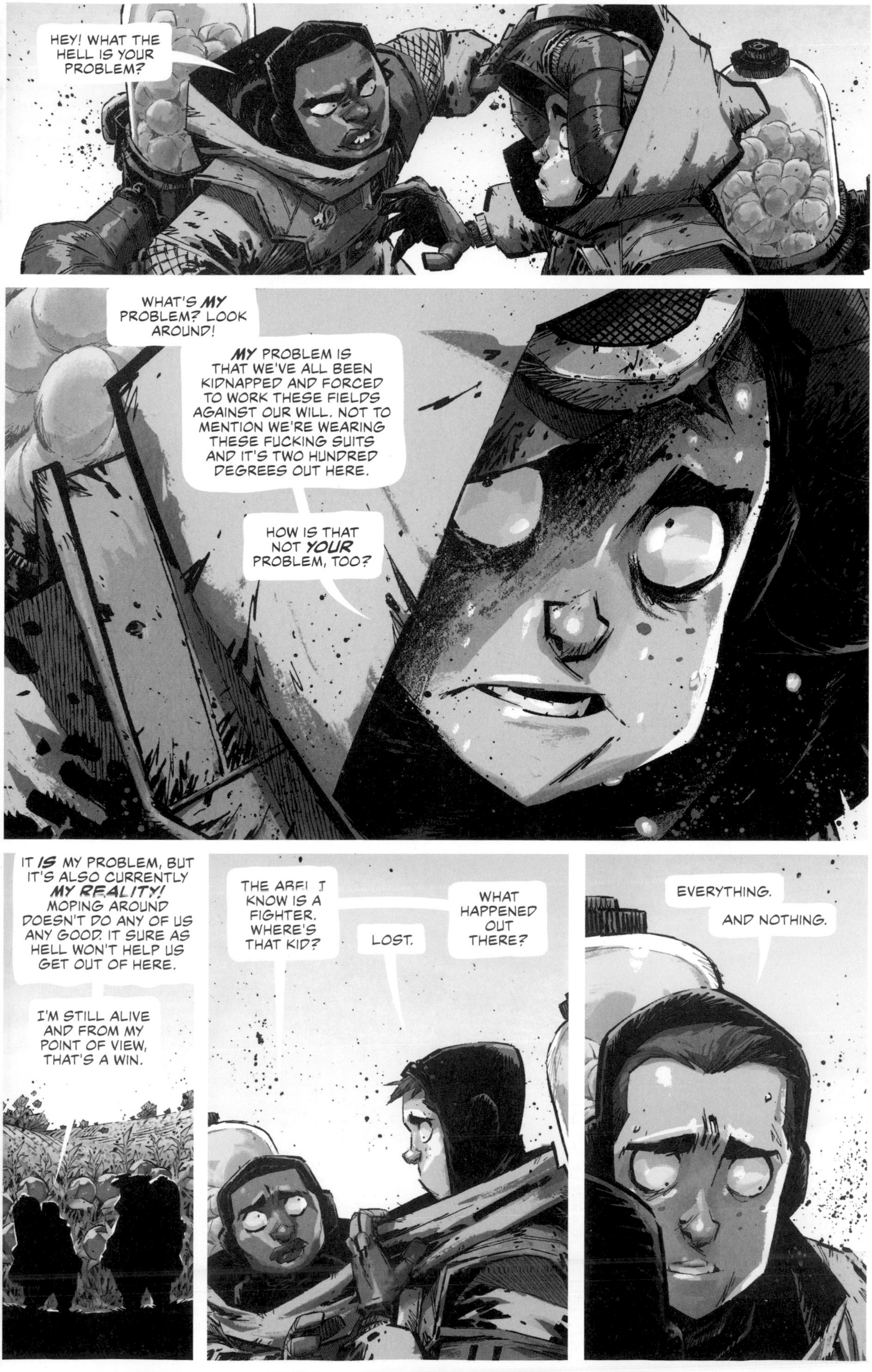
HEY! WHAT THE HELL IS YOUR PROBLEM?
WHAT'S *MY* PROBLEM? LOOK AROUND!
MY PROBLEM IS THAT WE'VE ALL BEEN KIDNAPPED AND FORCED TO WORK THESE FIELDS AGAINST OUR WILL. NOT TO MENTION WE'RE WEARING THESE FUCKING SUITS AND IT'S TWO HUNDRED DEGREES OUT HERE.
HOW IS THAT NOT *YOUR* PROBLEM, TOO?
IT *IS* MY PROBLEM, BUT IT'S ALSO CURRENTLY *MY REALITY!* MOPING AROUND DOESN'T DO ANY OF US ANY GOOD. IT SURE AS HELL WON'T HELP US GET OUT OF HERE.
I'M STILL ALIVE AND FROM MY POINT OF VIEW, THAT'S A WIN.
THE ABEL I KNOW IS A FIGHTER. WHERE'S THAT KID?
LOST.
WHAT HAPPENED OUT THERE?
EVERYTHING.
AND NOTHING.

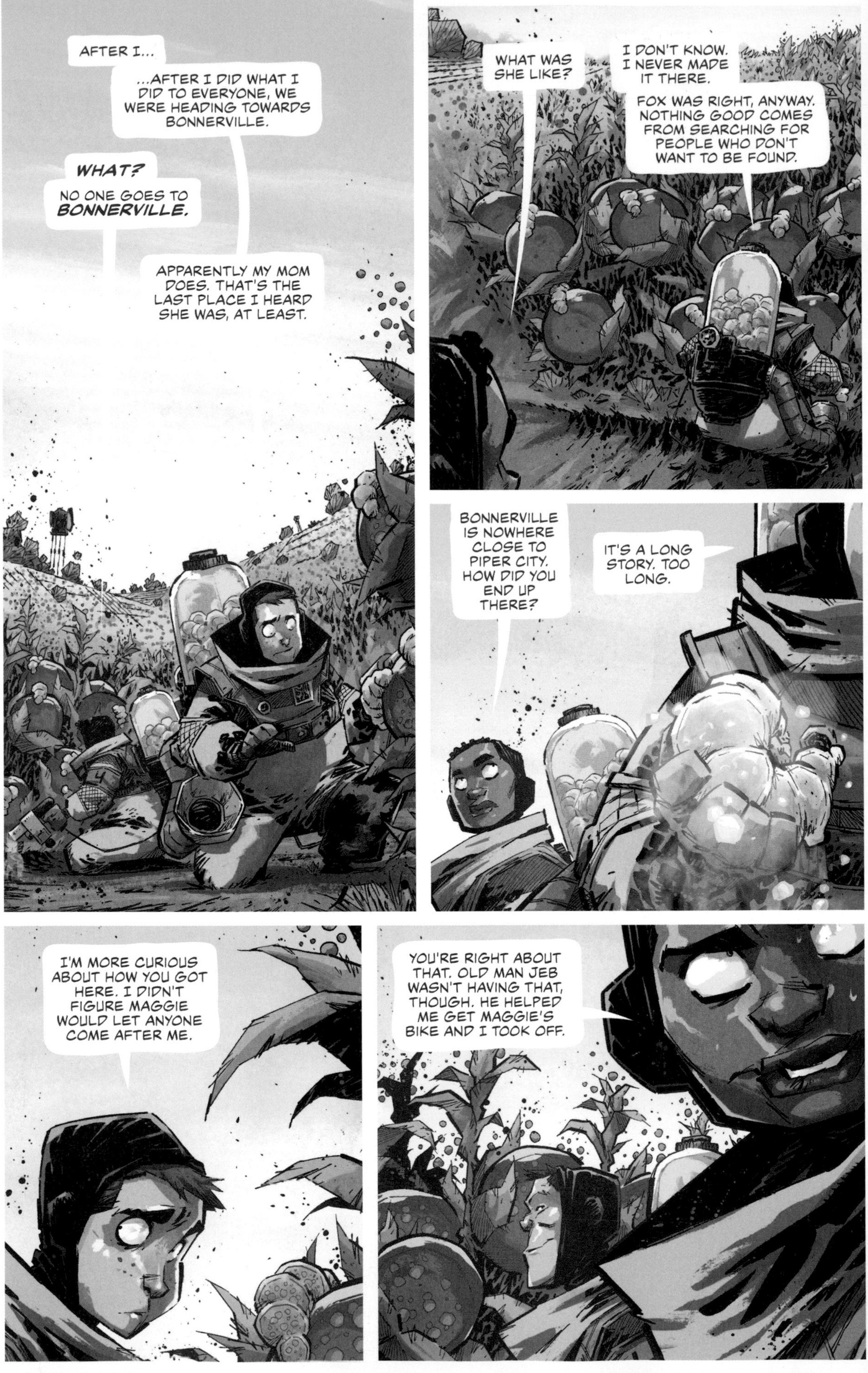
AFTER I...
...AFTER I DID WHAT I DID TO EVERYONE, WE WERE HEADING TOWARDS BONNERVILLE.
WHAT?
NO ONE GOES TO ***BONNERVILLE.***
APPARENTLY MY MOM DOES. THAT'S THE LAST PLACE I HEARD SHE WAS, AT LEAST.
WHAT WAS SHE LIKE?
I DON'T KNOW. I NEVER MADE IT THERE.
FOX WAS RIGHT, ANYWAY. NOTHING GOOD COMES FROM SEARCHING FOR PEOPLE WHO DON'T WANT TO BE FOUND.
BONNERVILLE IS NOWHERE CLOSE TO PIPER CITY. HOW DID YOU END UP THERE?
IT'S A LONG STORY. TOO LONG.
I'M MORE CURIOUS ABOUT HOW YOU GOT HERE. I DIDN'T FIGURE MAGGIE WOULD LET ANYONE COME AFTER ME.
YOU'RE RIGHT ABOUT THAT. OLD MAN JEB WASN'T HAVING THAT, THOUGH. HE HELPED ME GET MAGGIE'S BIKE AND I TOOK OFF.

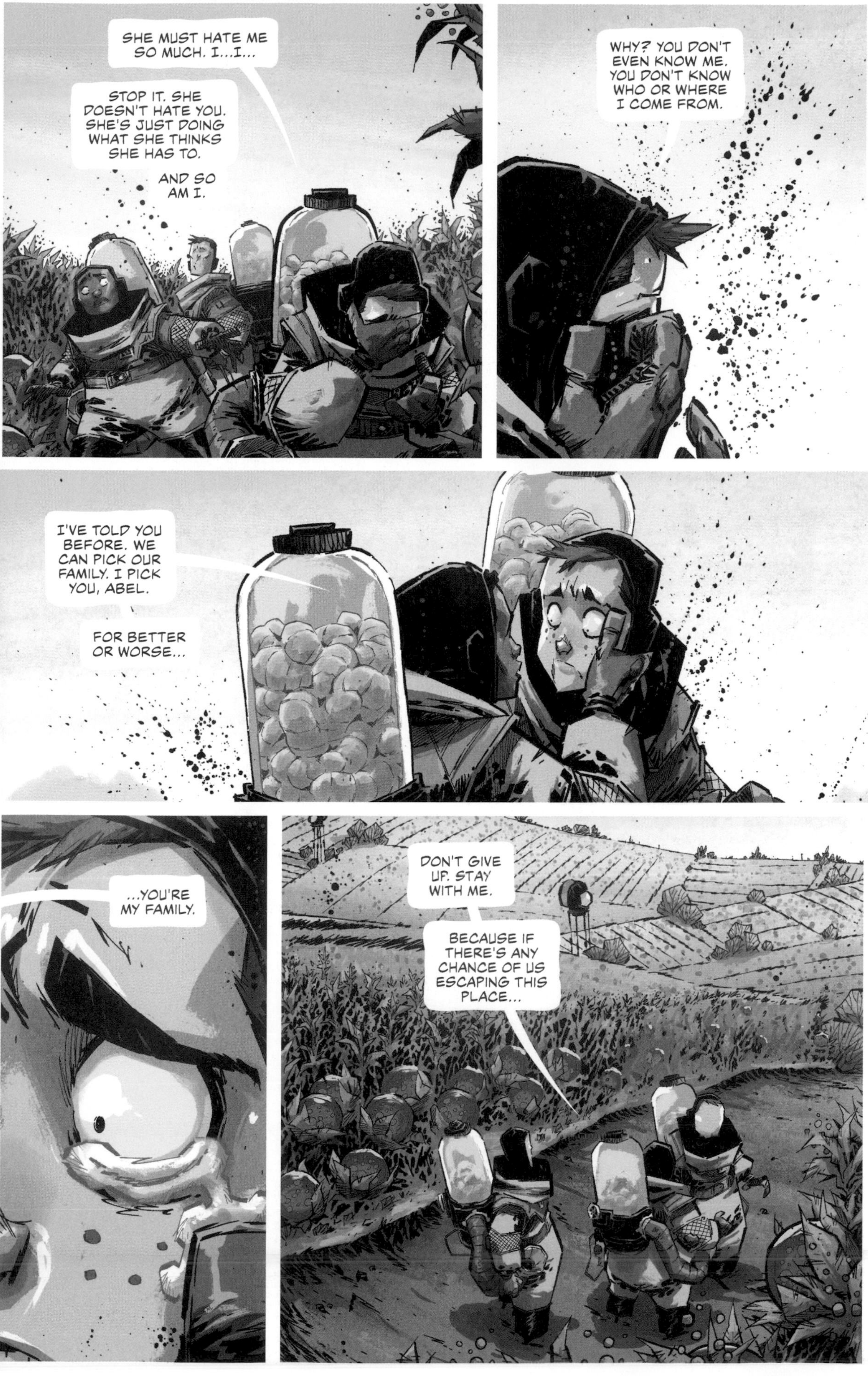
SHE MUST HATE ME SO MUCH. I...I...
STOP IT. SHE DOESN'T HATE YOU. SHE'S JUST DOING WHAT SHE THINKS SHE HAS TO.
AND SO AM I.
WHY? YOU DON'T EVEN KNOW ME. YOU DON'T KNOW WHO OR WHERE I COME FROM.
I'VE TOLD YOU BEFORE. WE CAN PICK OUR FAMILY. I PICK YOU, ABEL.
FOR BETTER OR WORSE...
...YOU'RE MY FAMILY.
DON'T GIVE UP. STAY WITH ME.
BECAUSE IF THERE'S ANY CHANCE OF US ESCAPING THIS PLACE...

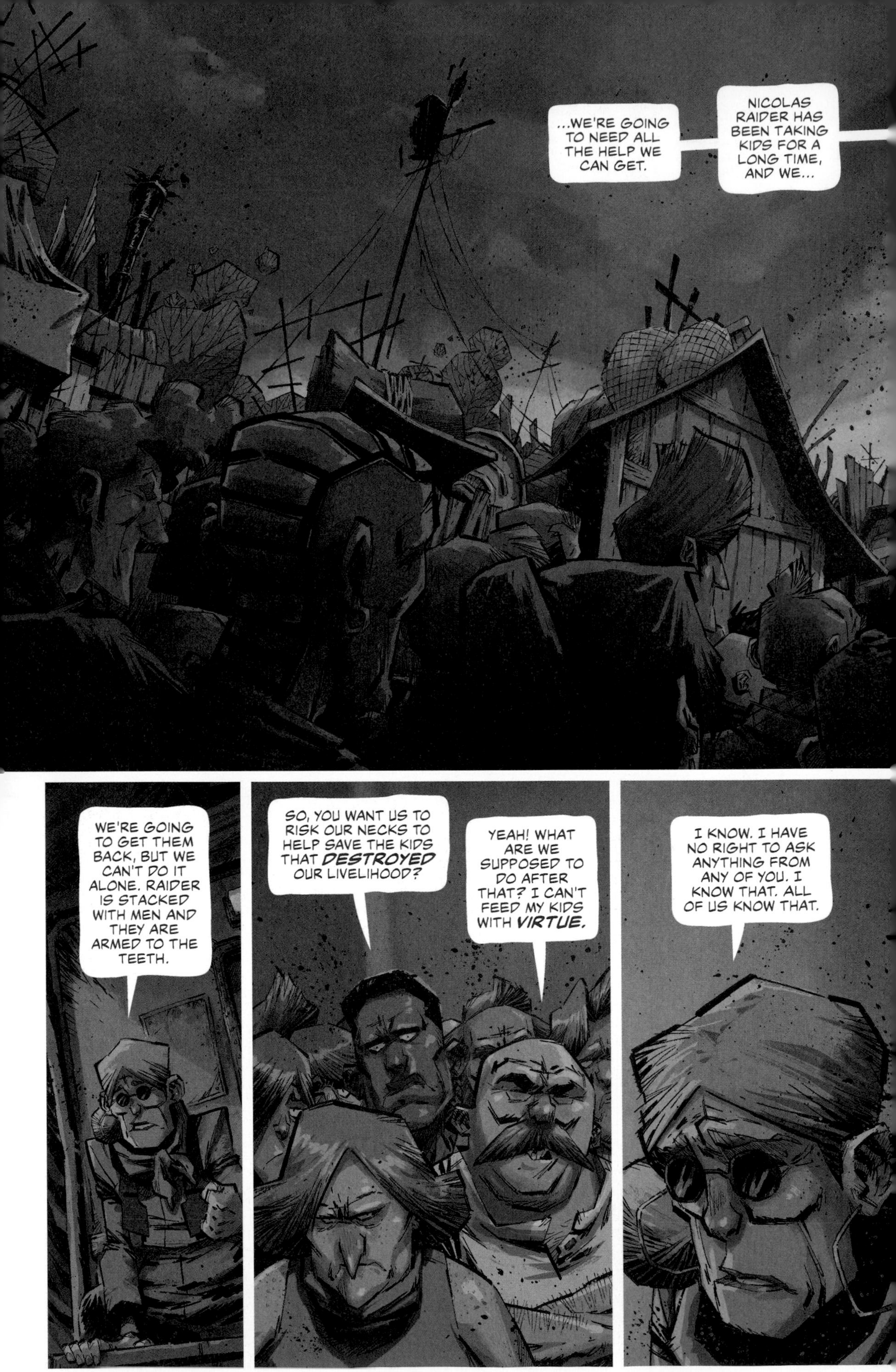
NICOLAS RAIDER HAS BEEN TAKING KIDS FOR A LONG TIME, AND WE...
...WE'RE GOING TO NEED ALL THE HELP WE CAN GET.
WE'RE GOING TO GET THEM BACK, BUT WE CAN'T DO IT ALONE. RAIDER IS STACKED WITH MEN AND THEY ARE ARMED TO THE TEETH.
SO, YOU WANT US TO RISK OUR NECKS TO HELP SAVE THE KIDS THAT **DESTROYED** OUR LIVELIHOOD?
YEAH! WHAT ARE WE SUPPOSED TO DO AFTER THAT? I CAN'T FEED MY KIDS WITH **VIRTUE.**
I KNOW. I HAVE NO RIGHT TO ASK ANYTHING FROM ANY OF YOU. I KNOW THAT. ALL OF US KNOW THAT.

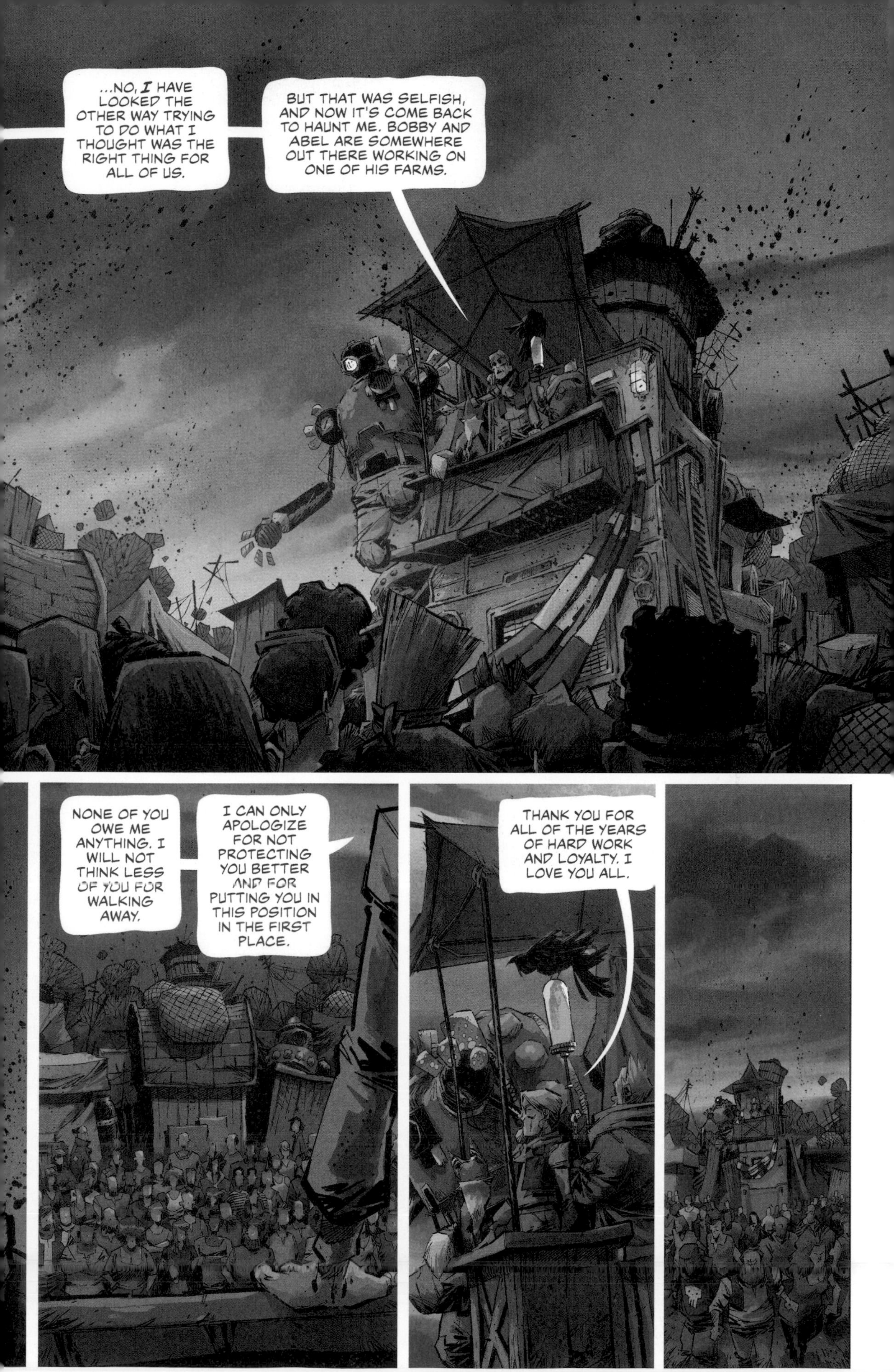
...NO, I HAVE LOOKED THE OTHER WAY TRYING TO DO WHAT I THOUGHT WAS THE RIGHT THING FOR ALL OF US.
BUT THAT WAS SELFISH, AND NOW IT'S COME BACK TO HAUNT ME. BOBBY AND ABEL ARE SOMEWHERE OUT THERE WORKING ON ONE OF HIS FARMS.
NONE OF YOU OWE ME ANYTHING. I WILL NOT THINK LESS OF YOU FOR WALKING AWAY.
I CAN ONLY APOLOGIZE FOR NOT PROTECTING YOU BETTER AND FOR PUTTING YOU IN THIS POSITION IN THE FIRST PLACE.
THANK YOU FOR ALL OF THE YEARS OF HARD WORK AND LOYALTY. I LOVE YOU ALL.

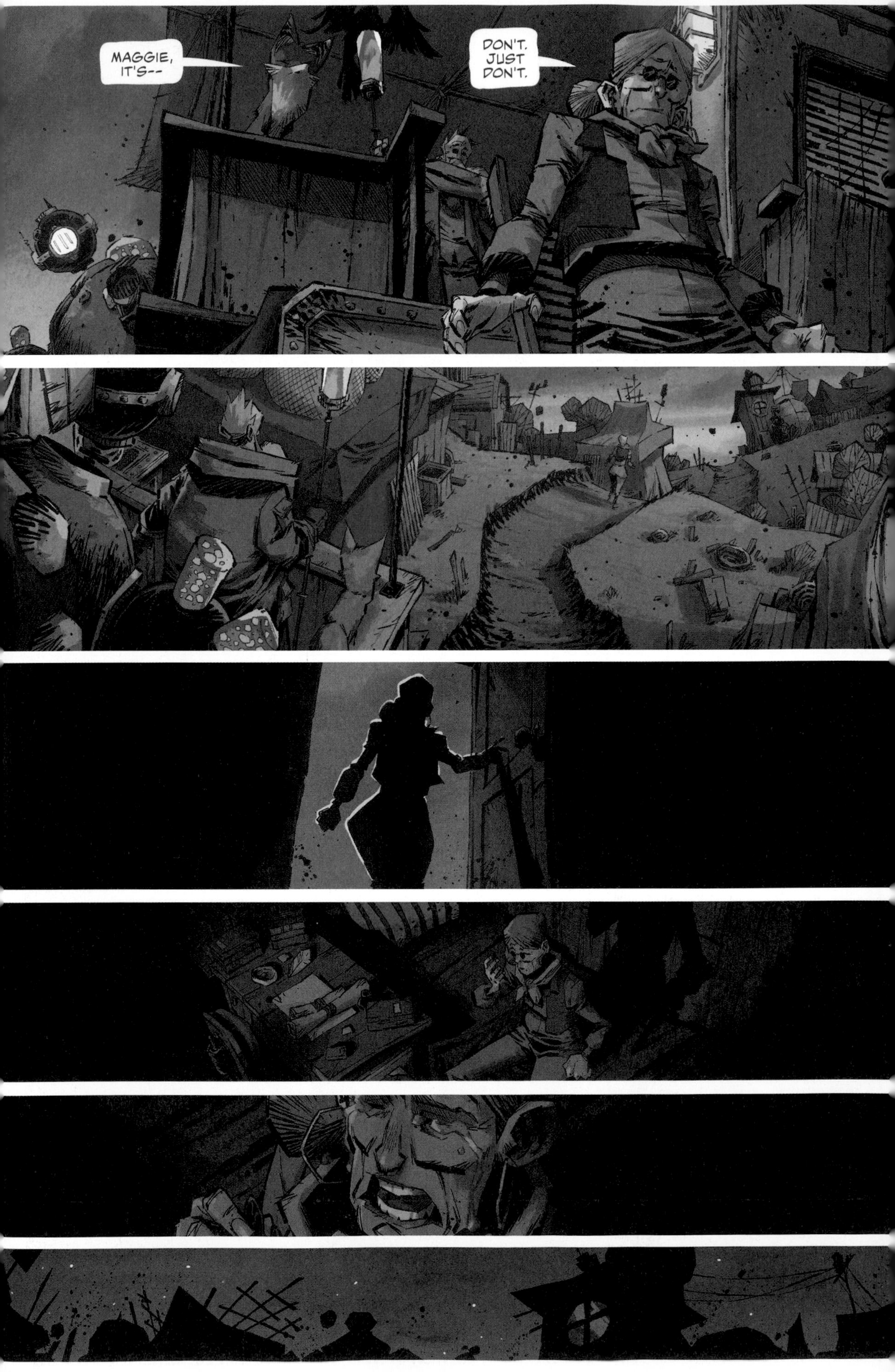
MAGGIE, IT'S--
DON'T. JUST DON'T.

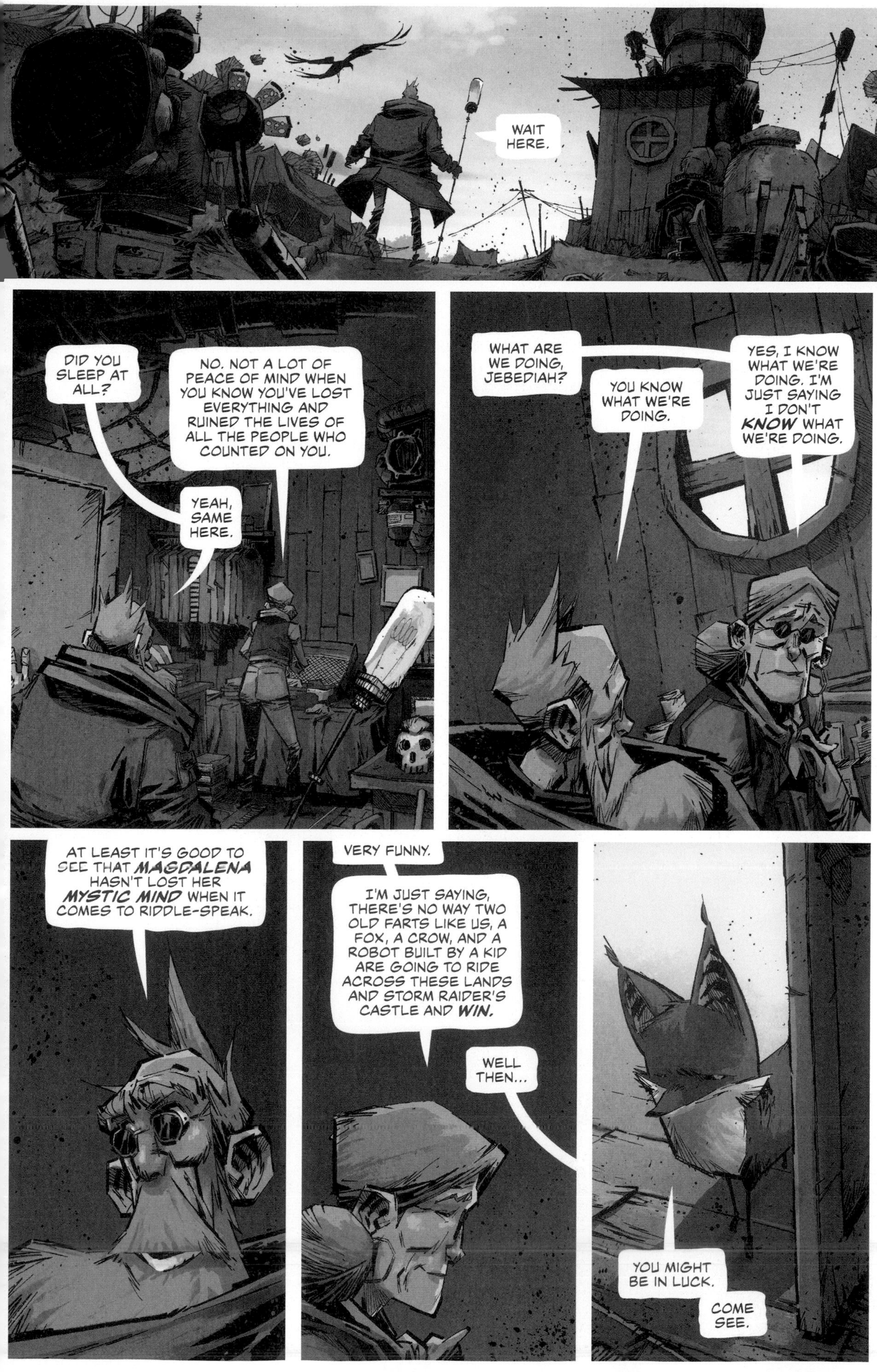
WAIT HERE.
DID YOU SLEEP AT ALL?
NO. NOT A LOT OF PEACE OF MIND WHEN YOU KNOW YOU'VE LOST EVERYTHING AND RUINED THE LIVES OF ALL THE PEOPLE WHO COUNTED ON YOU.
YEAH, SAME HERE.
WHAT ARE WE DOING, JEBEDIAH?
YOU KNOW WHAT WE'RE DOING.
YES, I KNOW WHAT WE'RE DOING. I'M JUST SAYING I DON'T KNOW WHAT WE'RE DOING.
AT LEAST IT'S GOOD TO SEE THAT MAGDALENA HASN'T LOST HER MYSTIC MIND WHEN IT COMES TO RIDDLE-SPEAK.
VERY FUNNY.
I'M JUST SAYING, THERE'S NO WAY TWO OLD FARTS LIKE US, A FOX, A CROW, AND A ROBOT BUILT BY A KID ARE GOING TO RIDE ACROSS THESE LANDS AND STORM RAIDER'S CASTLE AND WIN.
WELL THEN...
YOU MIGHT BE IN LUCK.
COME SEE.

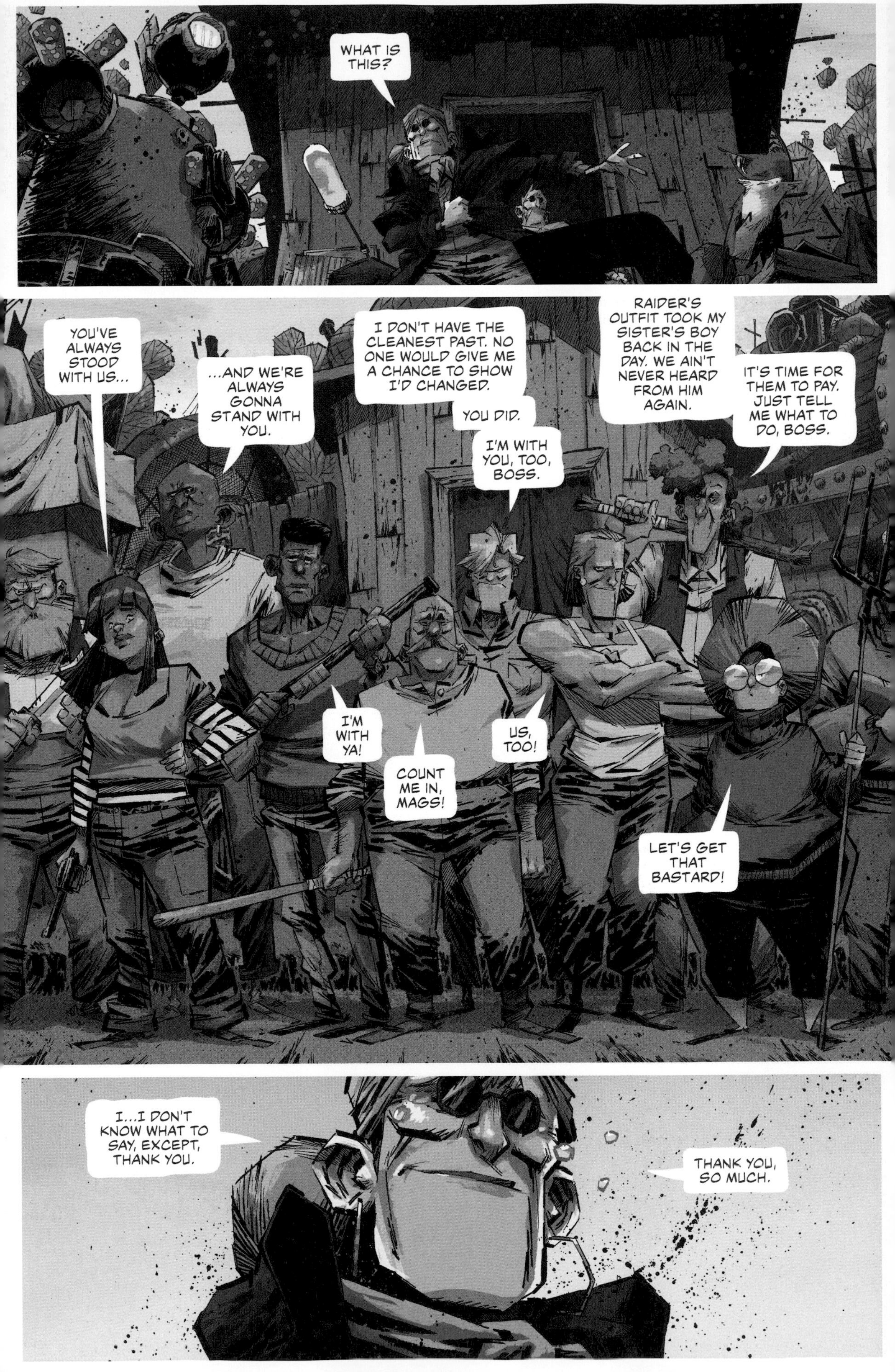
WHAT IS THIS?
YOU'VE ALWAYS STOOD WITH US...
...AND WE'RE ALWAYS GONNA STAND WITH YOU.
I DON'T HAVE THE CLEANEST PAST. NO ONE WOULD GIVE ME A CHANCE TO SHOW I'D CHANGED.
YOU DID.
I'M WITH YOU, TOO, BOSS.
RAIDER'S OUTFIT TOOK MY SISTER'S BOY BACK IN THE DAY. WE AIN'T NEVER HEARD FROM HIM AGAIN.
IT'S TIME FOR THEM TO PAY. JUST TELL ME WHAT TO DO, BOSS.
I'M WITH YA!
COUNT ME IN, MAGS!
US, TOO!
LET'S GET THAT BASTARD!
I...I DON'T KNOW WHAT TO SAY, EXCEPT, THANK YOU.
THANK YOU, SO MUCH.

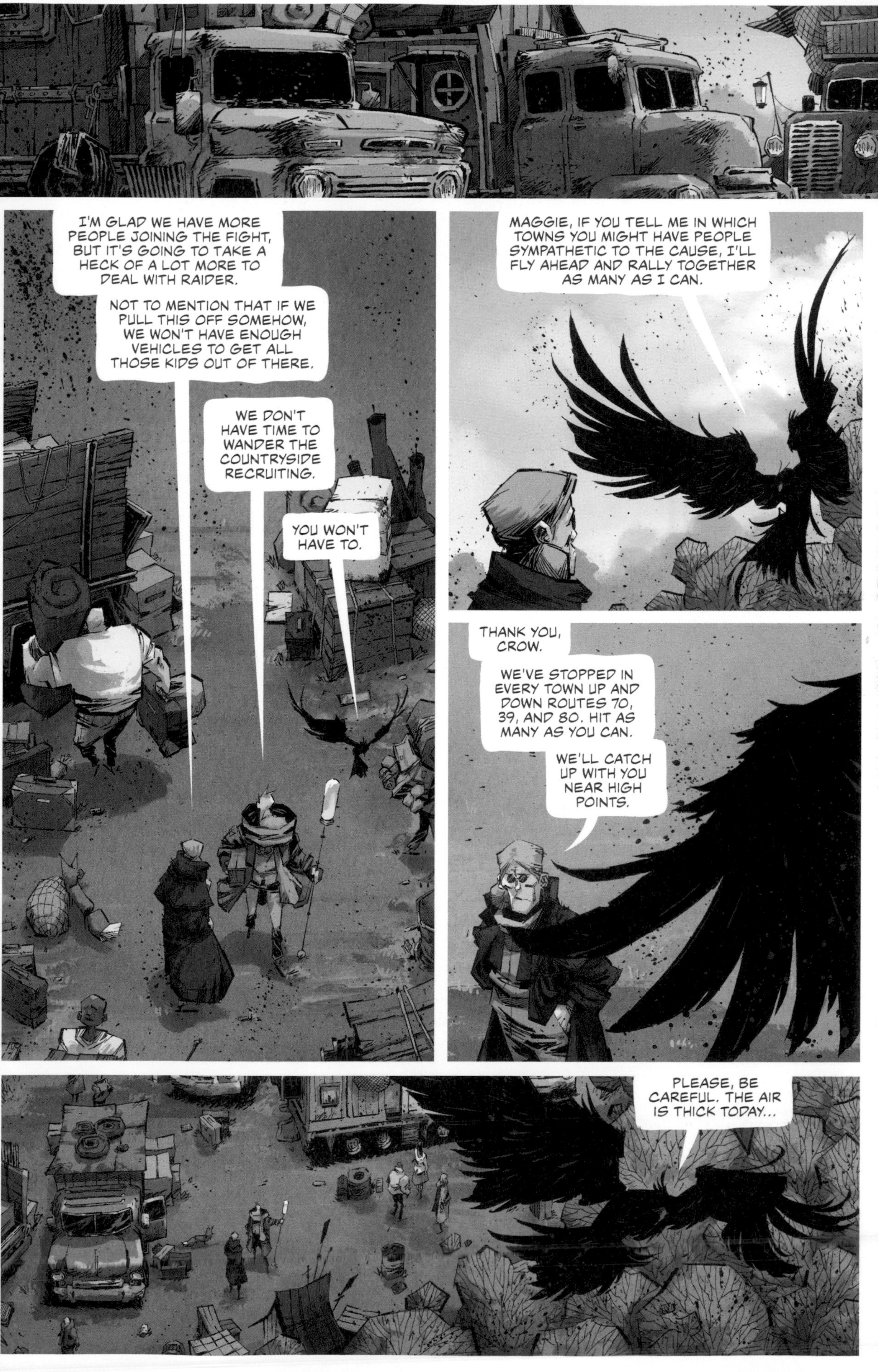
I'M GLAD WE HAVE MORE PEOPLE JOINING THE FIGHT, BUT IT'S GOING TO TAKE A HECK OF A LOT MORE TO DEAL WITH RAIDER.
NOT TO MENTION THAT IF WE PULL THIS OFF SOMEHOW, WE WON'T HAVE ENOUGH VEHICLES TO GET ALL THOSE KIDS OUT OF THERE.
WE DON'T HAVE TIME TO WANDER THE COUNTRYSIDE RECRUITING.
YOU WON'T HAVE TO.
MAGGIE, IF YOU TELL ME IN WHICH TOWNS YOU MIGHT HAVE PEOPLE SYMPATHETIC TO THE CAUSE, I'LL FLY AHEAD AND RALLY TOGETHER AS MANY AS I CAN.
THANK YOU, CROW.
WE'VE STOPPED IN EVERY TOWN UP AND DOWN ROUTES 70, 39, AND 80. HIT AS MANY AS YOU CAN.
WE'LL CATCH UP WITH YOU NEAR HIGH POINTS.
PLEASE, BE CAREFUL. THE AIR IS THICK TODAY...

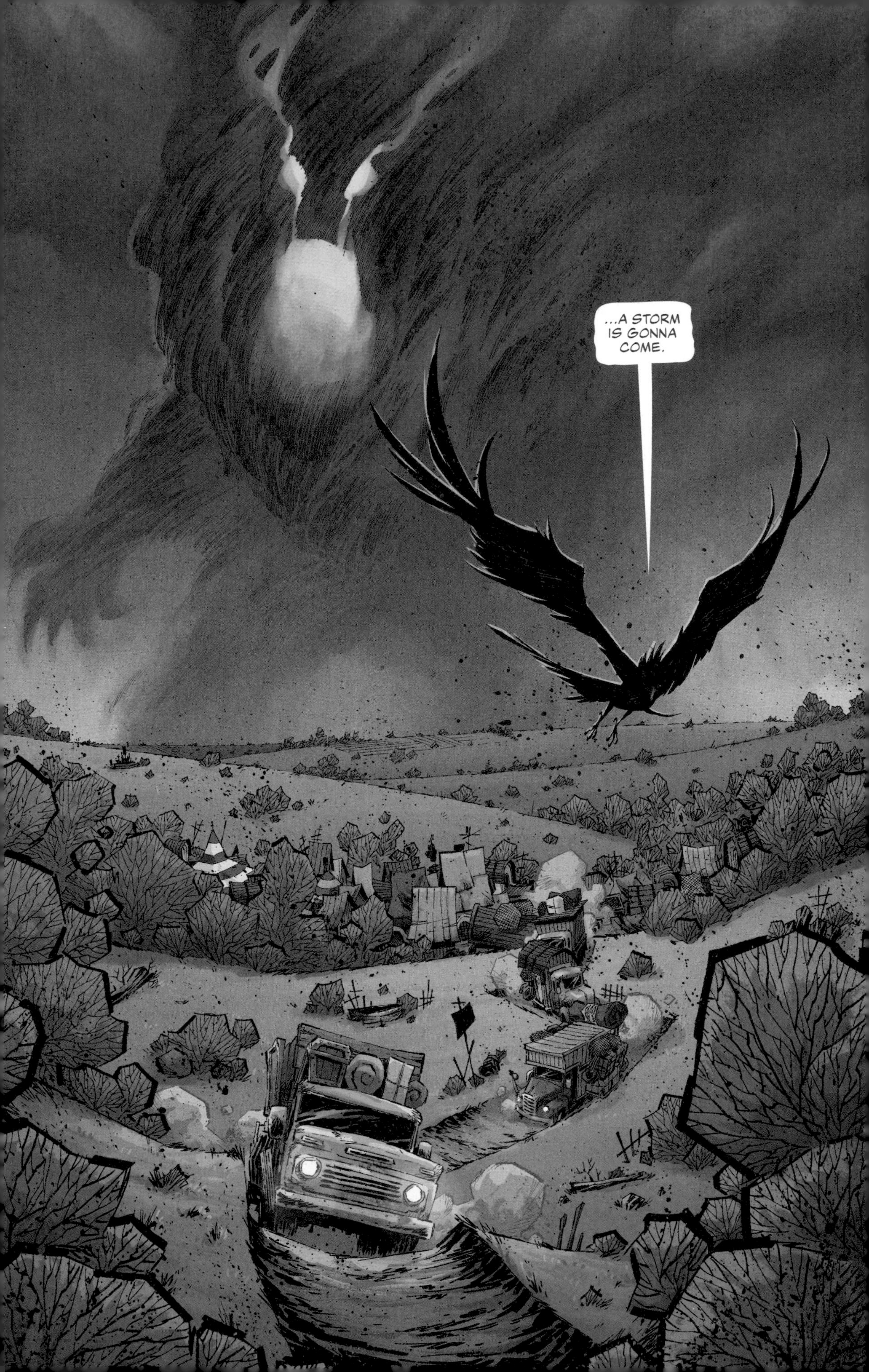
...A STORM IS GONNA COME.

CHAPTER
FOURTEEN

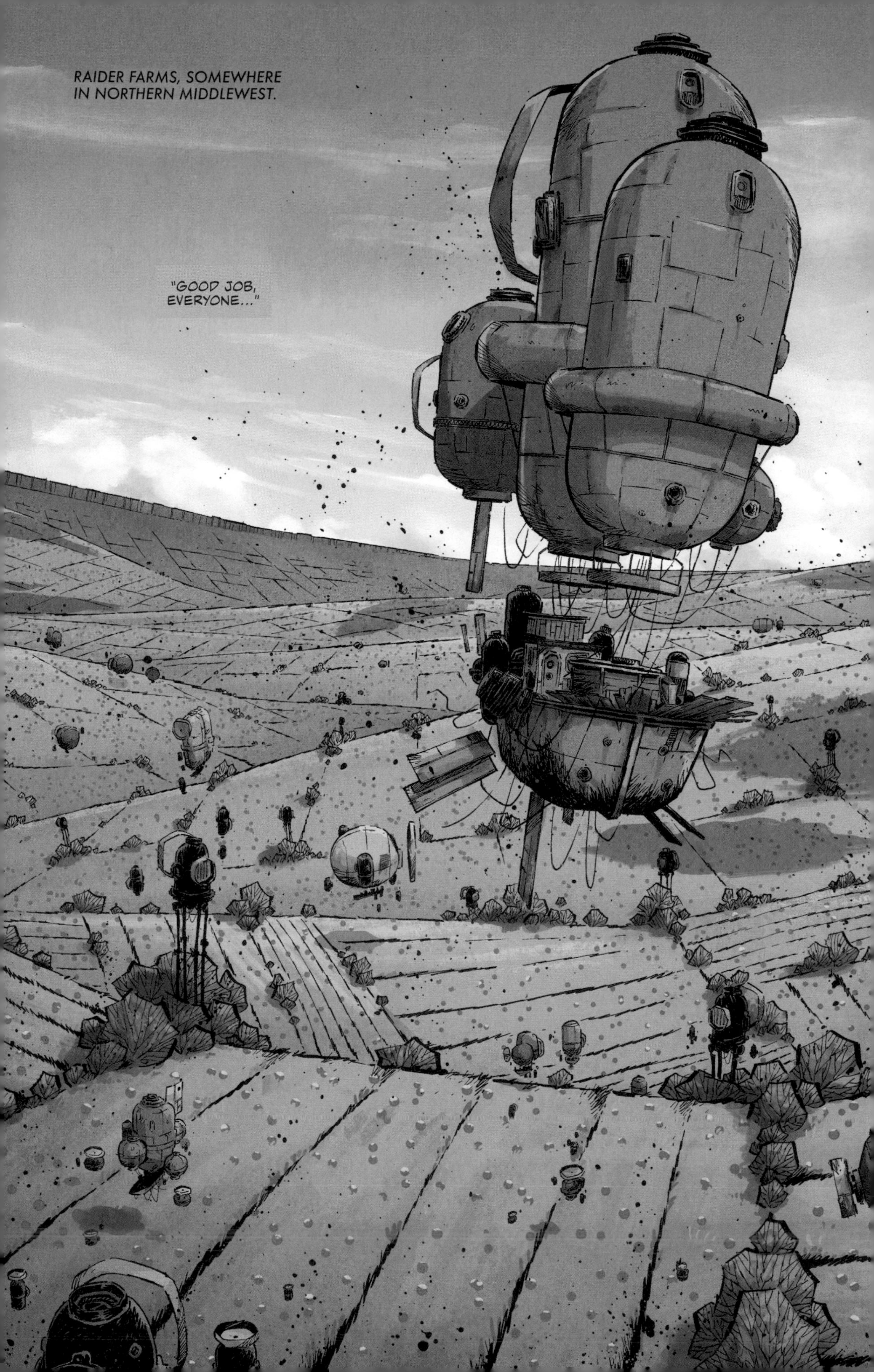
RAIDER FARMS, SOMEWHERE IN NORTHERN MIDDLEWEST.
"GOOD JOB, EVERYONE..."

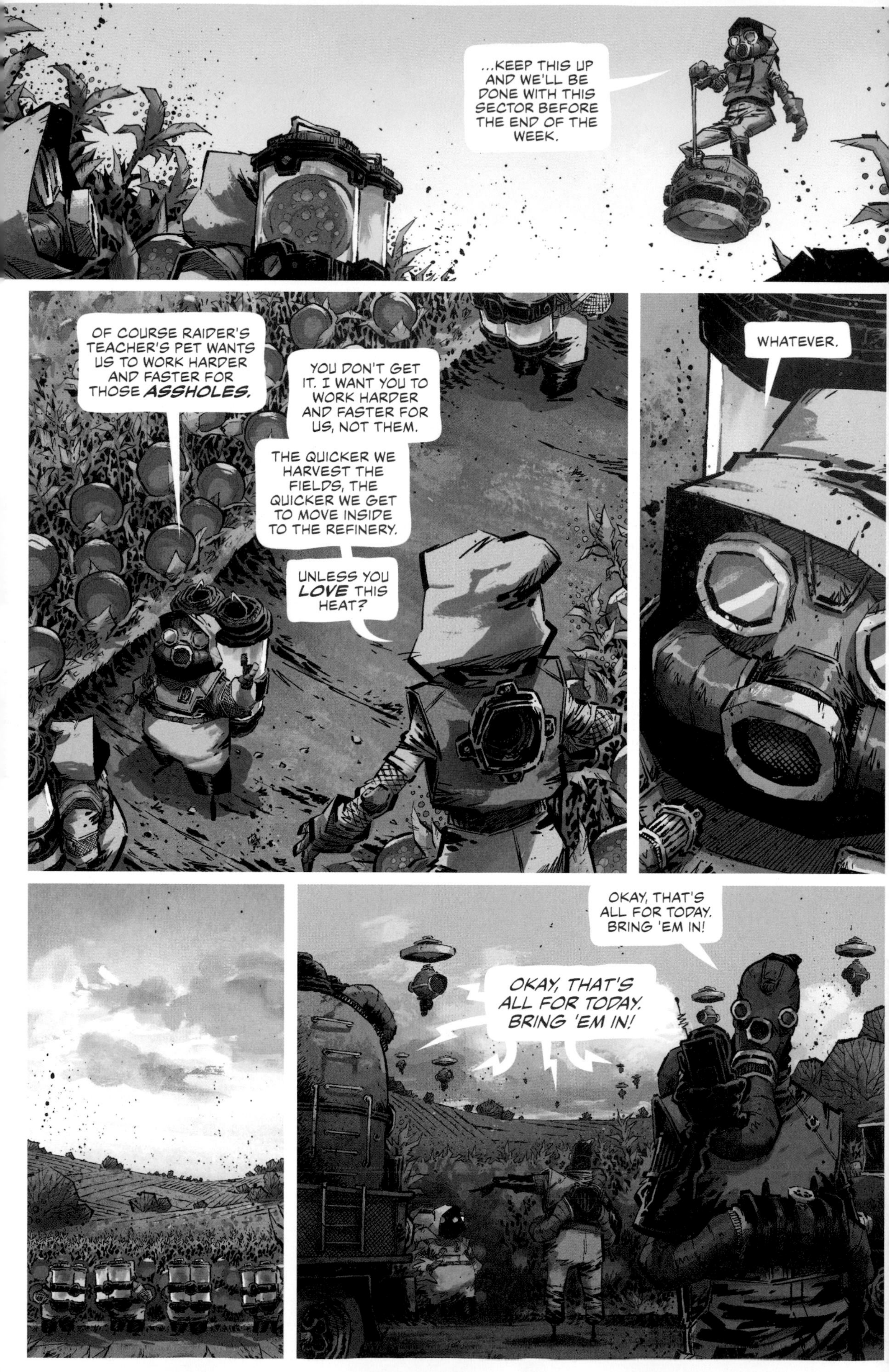
...KEEP THIS UP AND WE'LL BE DONE WITH THIS SECTOR BEFORE THE END OF THE WEEK.
OF COURSE RAIDER'S TEACHER'S PET WANTS US TO WORK HARDER AND FASTER FOR THOSE ***ASSHOLES.***
YOU DON'T GET IT. I WANT YOU TO WORK HARDER AND FASTER FOR US, NOT THEM.
THE QUICKER WE HARVEST THE FIELDS, THE QUICKER WE GET TO MOVE INSIDE TO THE REFINERY.
UNLESS YOU ***LOVE*** THIS HEAT?
WHATEVER.
OKAY, THAT'S ALL FOR TODAY. BRING 'EM IN!
OKAY, THAT'S ALL FOR TODAY. BRING 'EM IN!

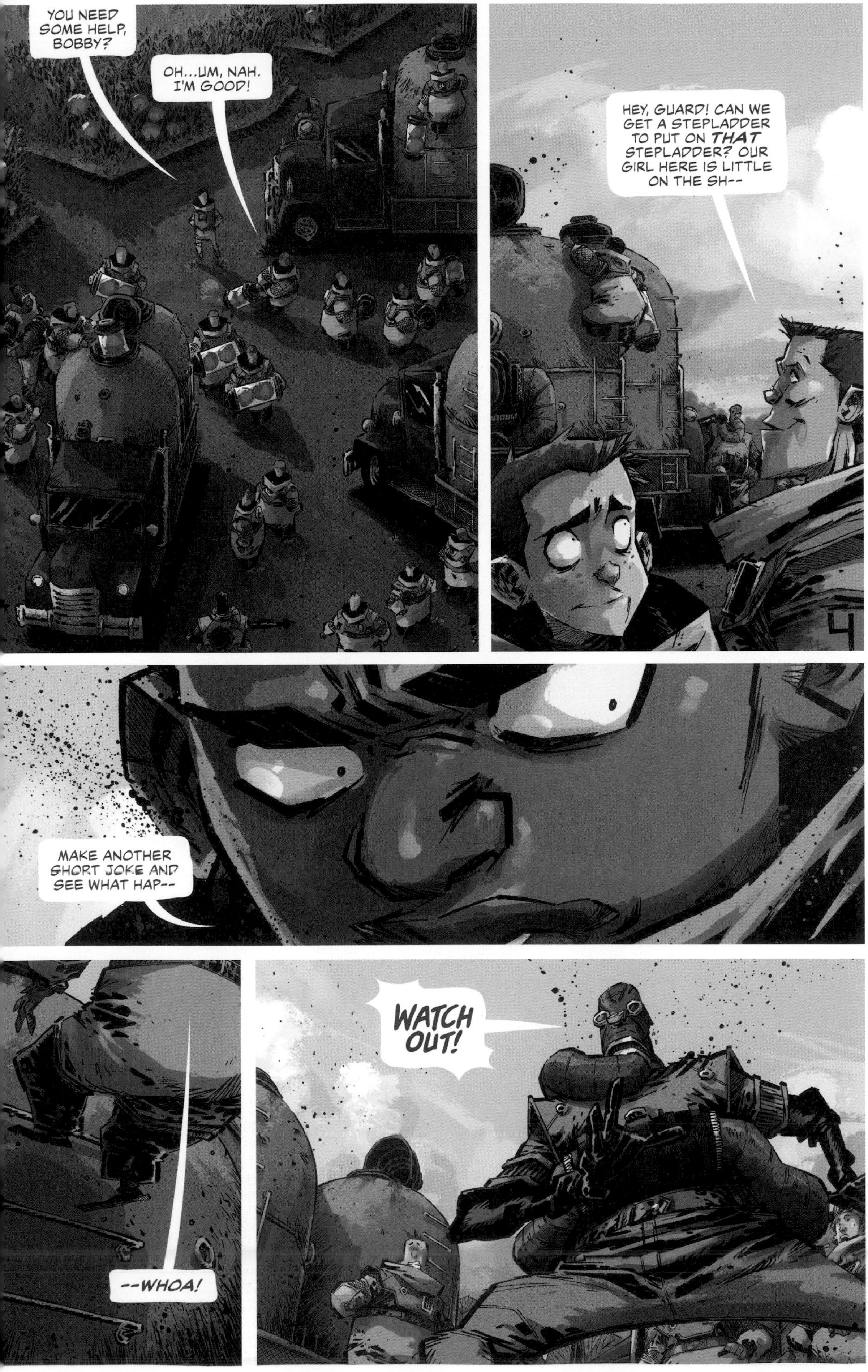
YOU NEED SOME HELP, BOBBY?
OH...UM, NAH. I'M GOOD!
HEY, GUARD! CAN WE GET A STEPLADDER TO PUT ON THAT STEPLADDER? OUR GIRL HERE IS LITTLE ON THE SH--
MAKE ANOTHER SHORT JOKE AND SEE WHAT HAP--
--WHOA!
WATCH OUT!

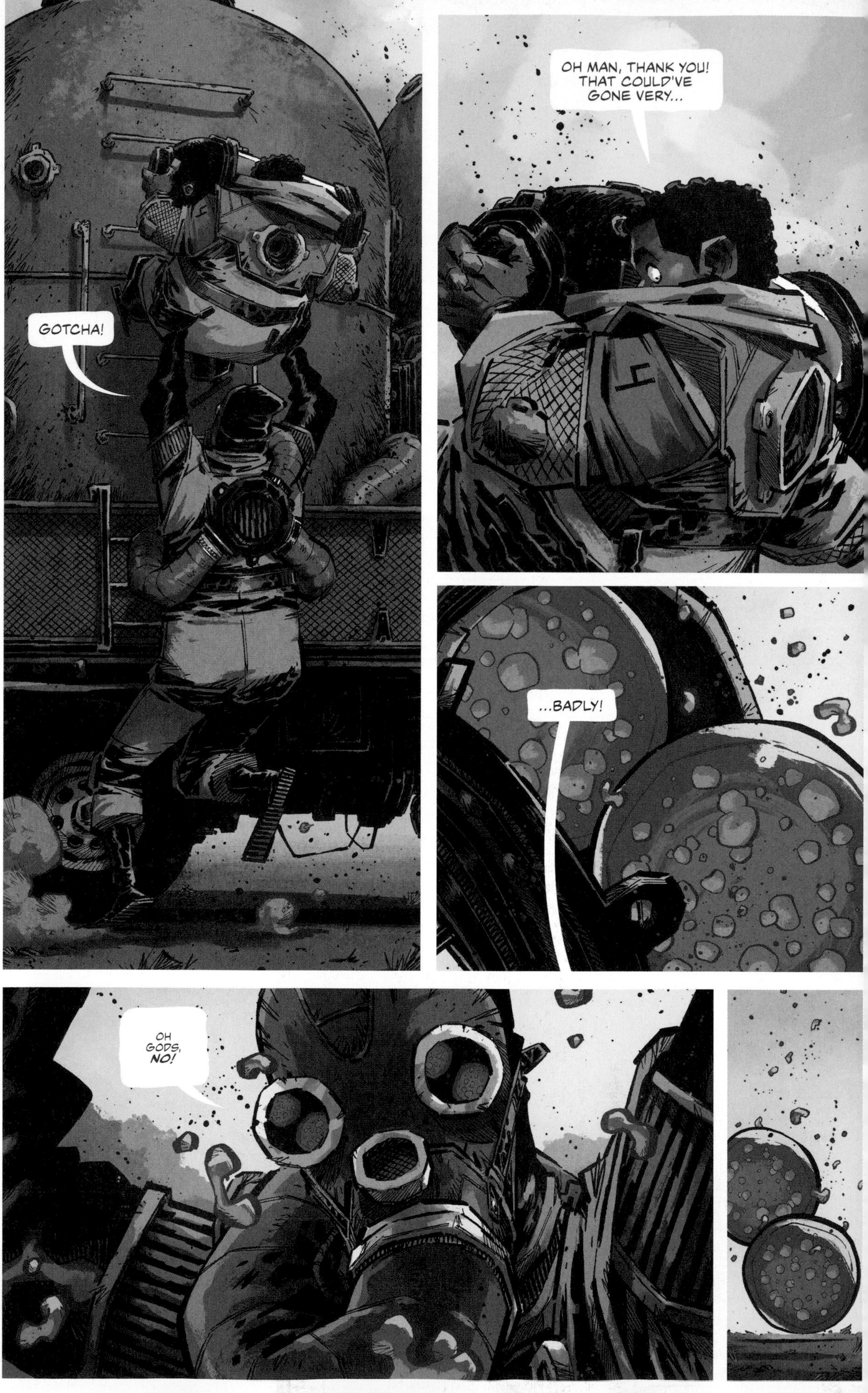
GOTCHA!
OH MAN, THANK YOU! THAT COULD'VE GONE VERY...
...BADLY!
OH GODS, NO!

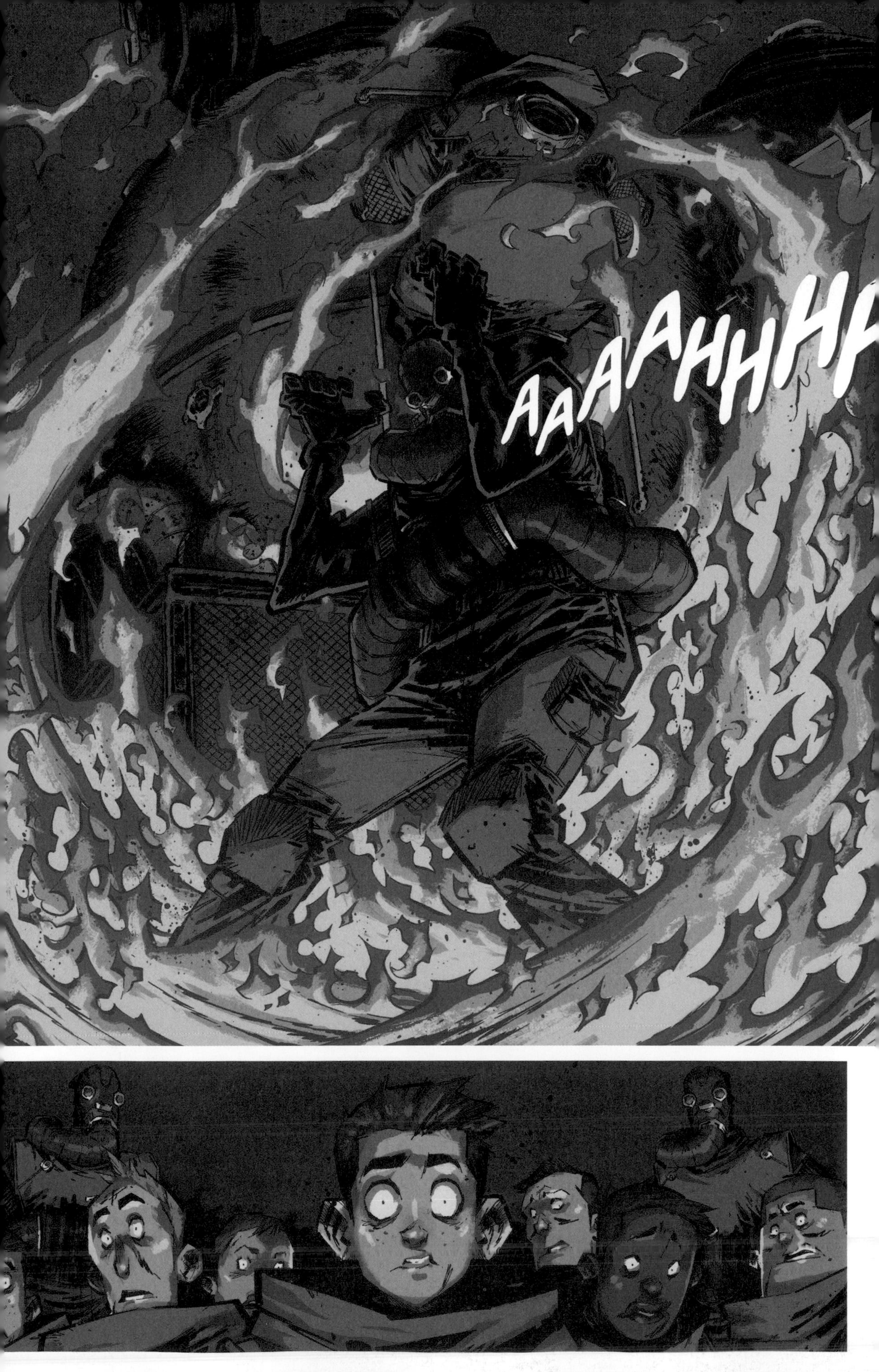
AAAAHHHH

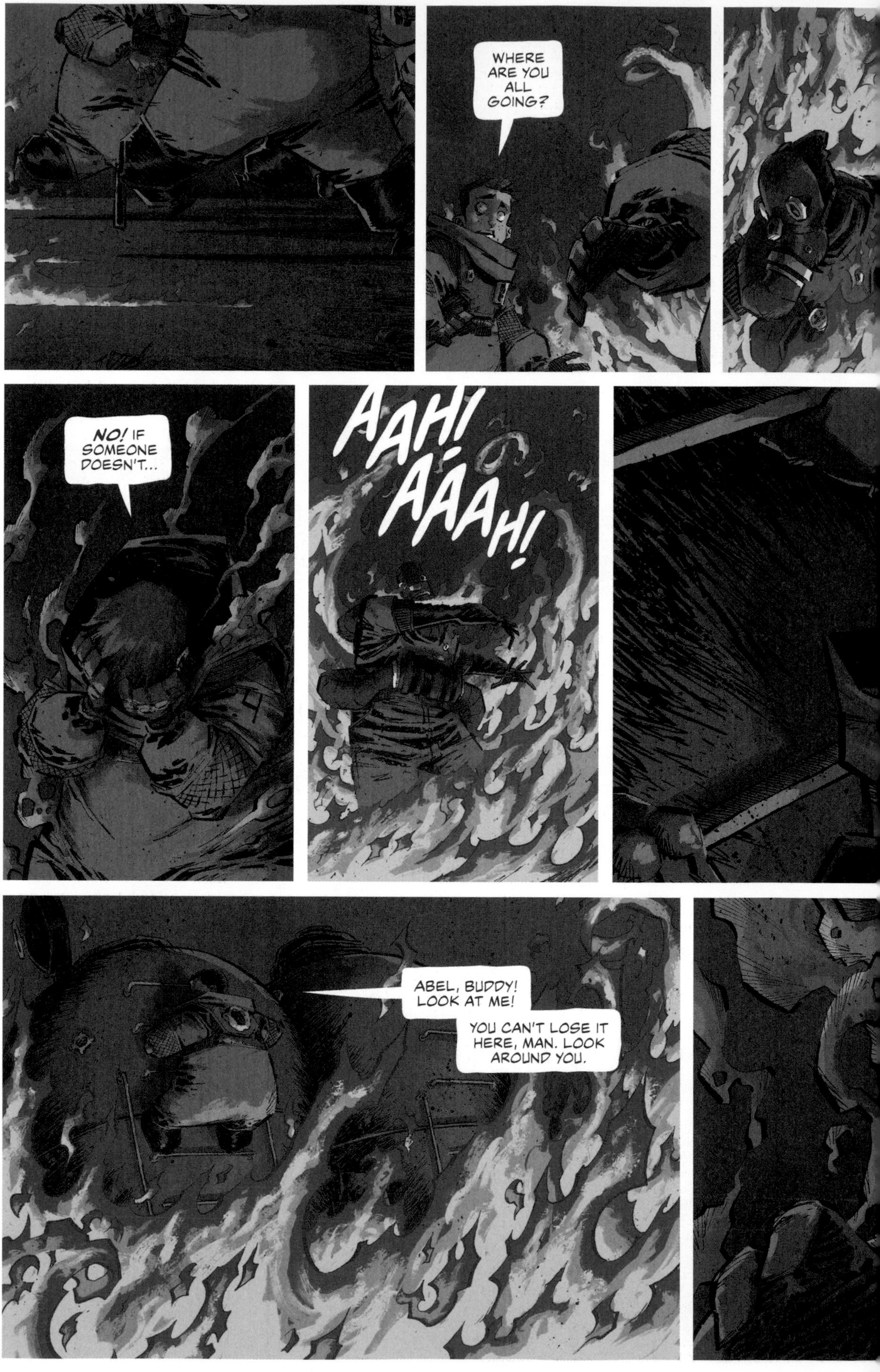
WHERE ARE YOU ALL GOING?
NO! IF SOMEONE DOESN'T...
AAH! AAAAH!
ABEL, BUDDY! LOOK AT ME!
YOU CAN'T LOSE IT HERE, MAN. LOOK AROUND YOU.

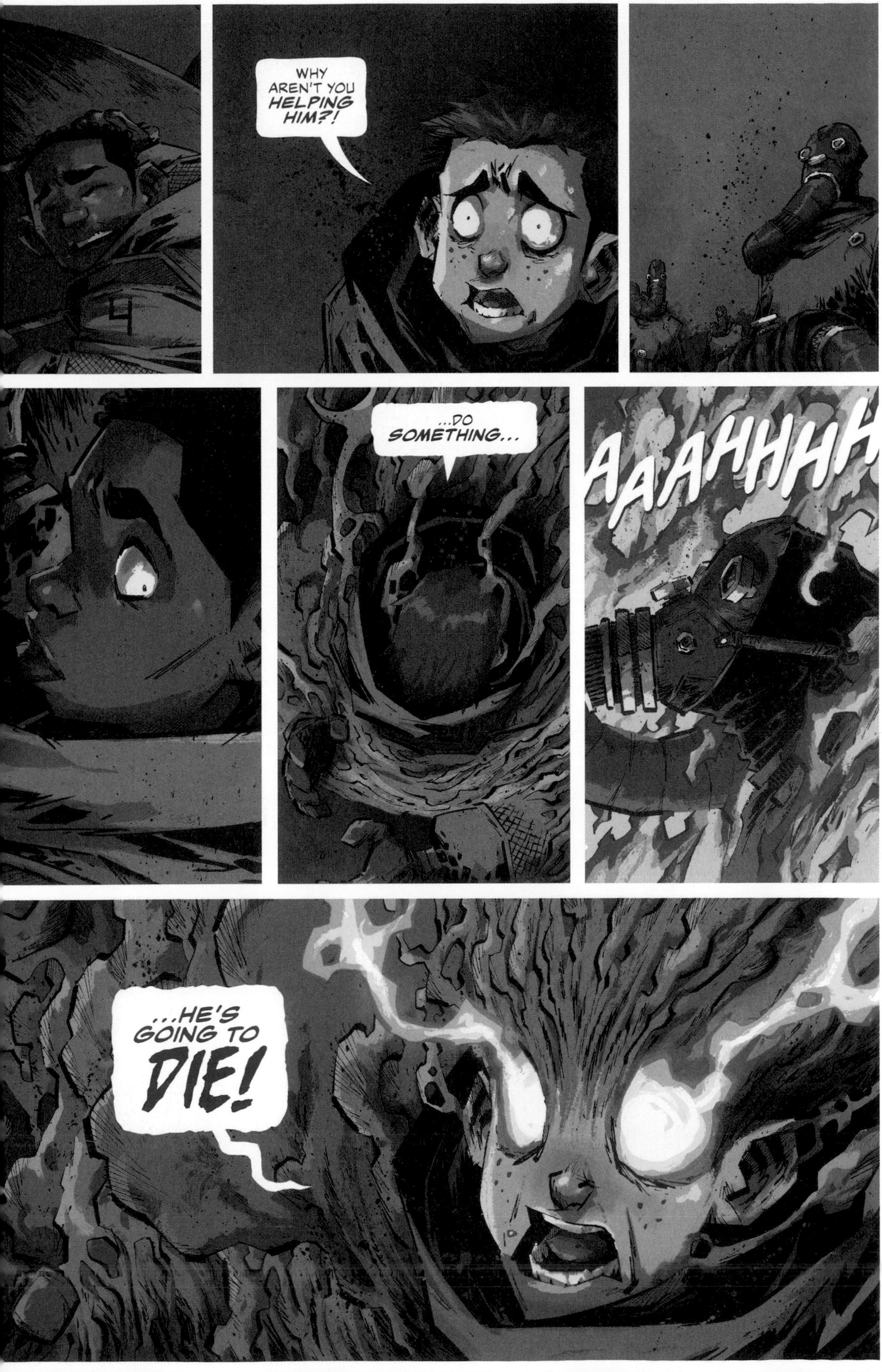

WHY AREN'T YOU HELPING HIM?!
...DO SOMETHING...
AAAHHHH
...HE'S GOING TO DIE!

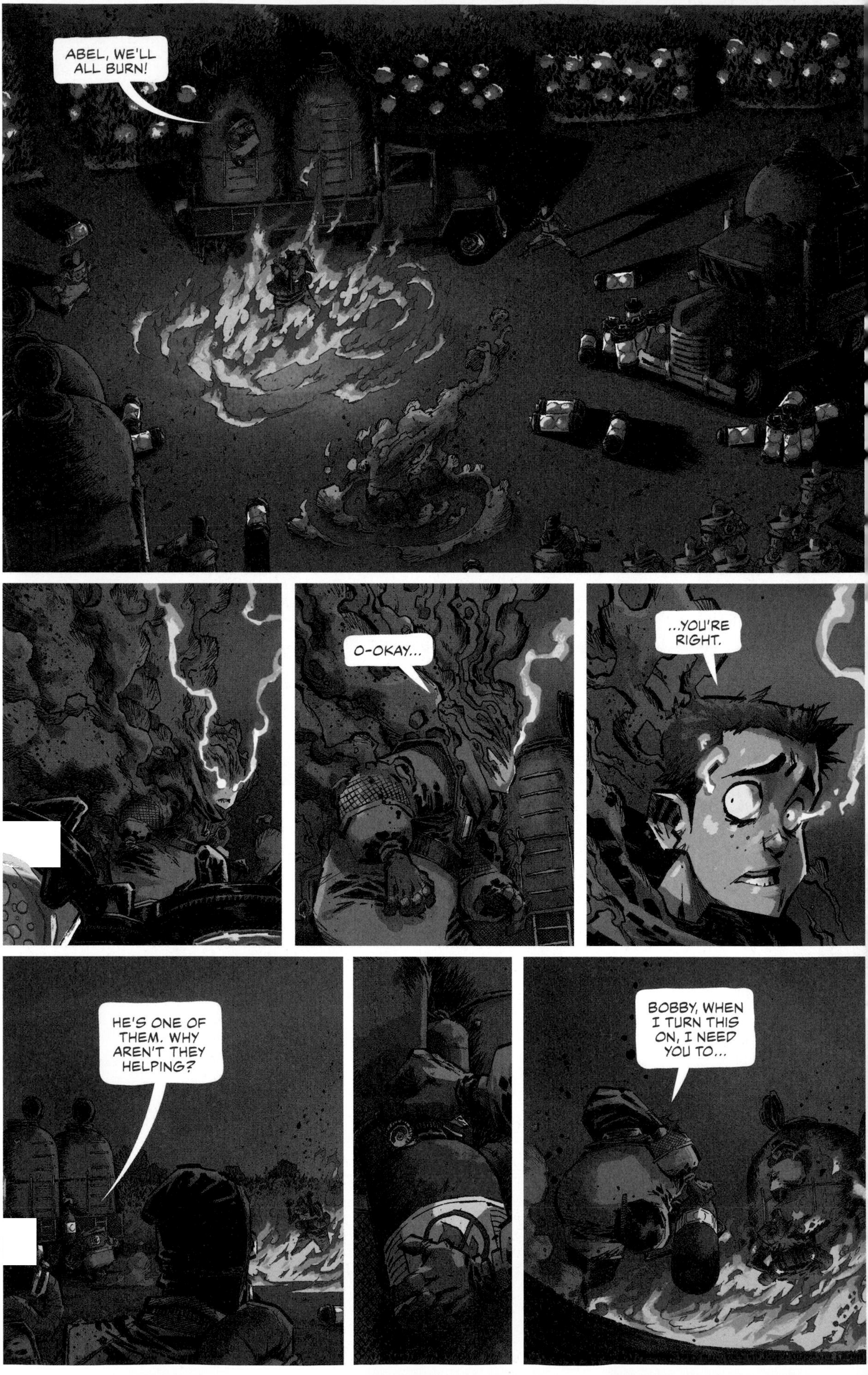
ABEL, WE'LL ALL BURN!
O-OKAY...
...YOU'RE RIGHT.
HE'S ONE OF THEM. WHY AREN'T THEY HELPING?
BOBBY, WHEN I TURN THIS ON, I NEED YOU TO...

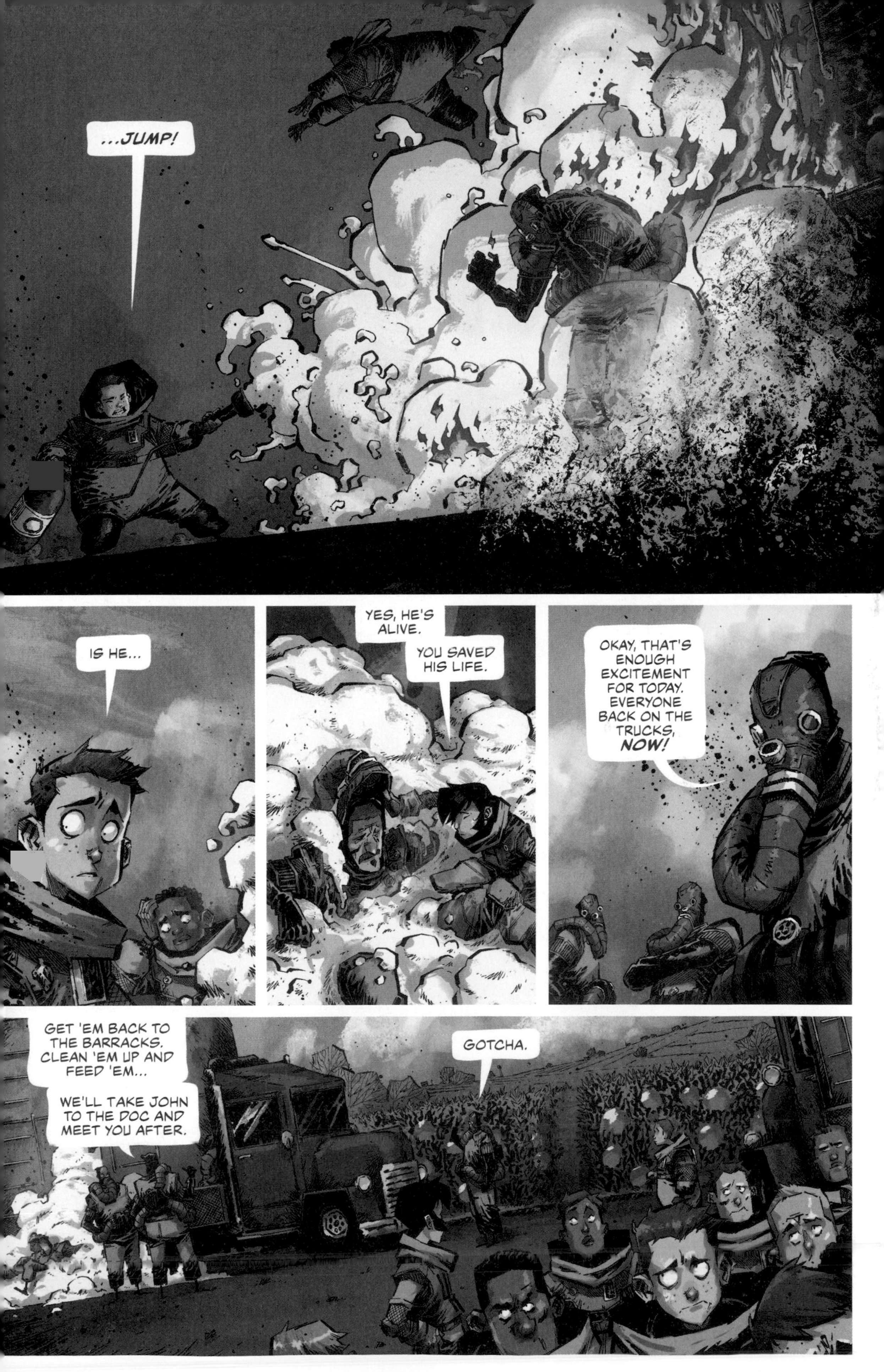
...JUMP!
IS HE...
YES, HE'S ALIVE.
YOU SAVED HIS LIFE.
OKAY, THAT'S ENOUGH EXCITEMENT FOR TODAY. EVERYONE BACK ON THE TRUCKS, NOW!
GET 'EM BACK TO THE BARRACKS. CLEAN 'EM UP AND FEED 'EM...
WE'LL TAKE JOHN TO THE DOC AND MEET YOU AFTER.
GOTCHA.

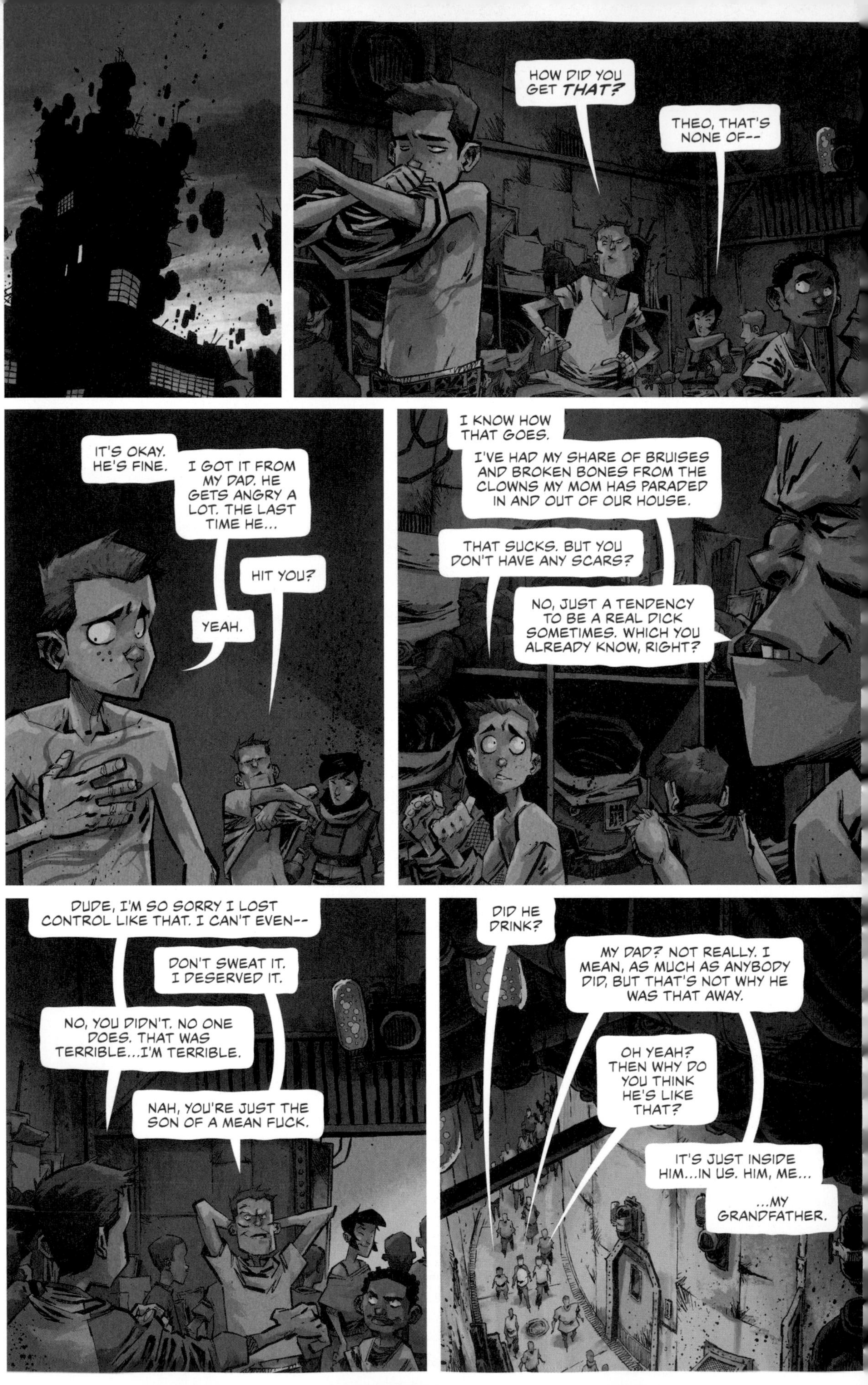
HOW DID YOU GET *THAT?*
THEO, THAT'S NONE OF--
IT'S OKAY. HE'S FINE.
I GOT IT FROM MY DAD. HE GETS ANGRY A LOT. THE LAST TIME HE...
HIT YOU?
YEAH.
I KNOW HOW THAT GOES.
I'VE HAD MY SHARE OF BRUISES AND BROKEN BONES FROM THE CLOWNS MY MOM HAS PARADED IN AND OUT OF OUR HOUSE.
THAT SUCKS. BUT YOU DON'T HAVE ANY SCARS?
NO, JUST A TENDENCY TO BE A REAL DICK SOMETIMES. WHICH YOU ALREADY KNOW, RIGHT?
DUDE, I'M SO SORRY I LOST CONTROL LIKE THAT. I CAN'T EVEN--
DON'T SWEAT IT. I DESERVED IT.
NO, YOU DIDN'T. NO ONE DOES. THAT WAS TERRIBLE...I'M TERRIBLE.
NAH, YOU'RE JUST THE SON OF A MEAN FUCK.
DID HE DRINK?
MY DAD? NOT REALLY. I MEAN, AS MUCH AS ANYBODY DID, BUT THAT'S NOT WHY HE WAS THAT AWAY.
OH YEAH? THEN WHY DO YOU THINK HE'S LIKE THAT?
IT'S JUST INSIDE HIM...IN US. HIM, ME...
...MY GRANDFATHER.

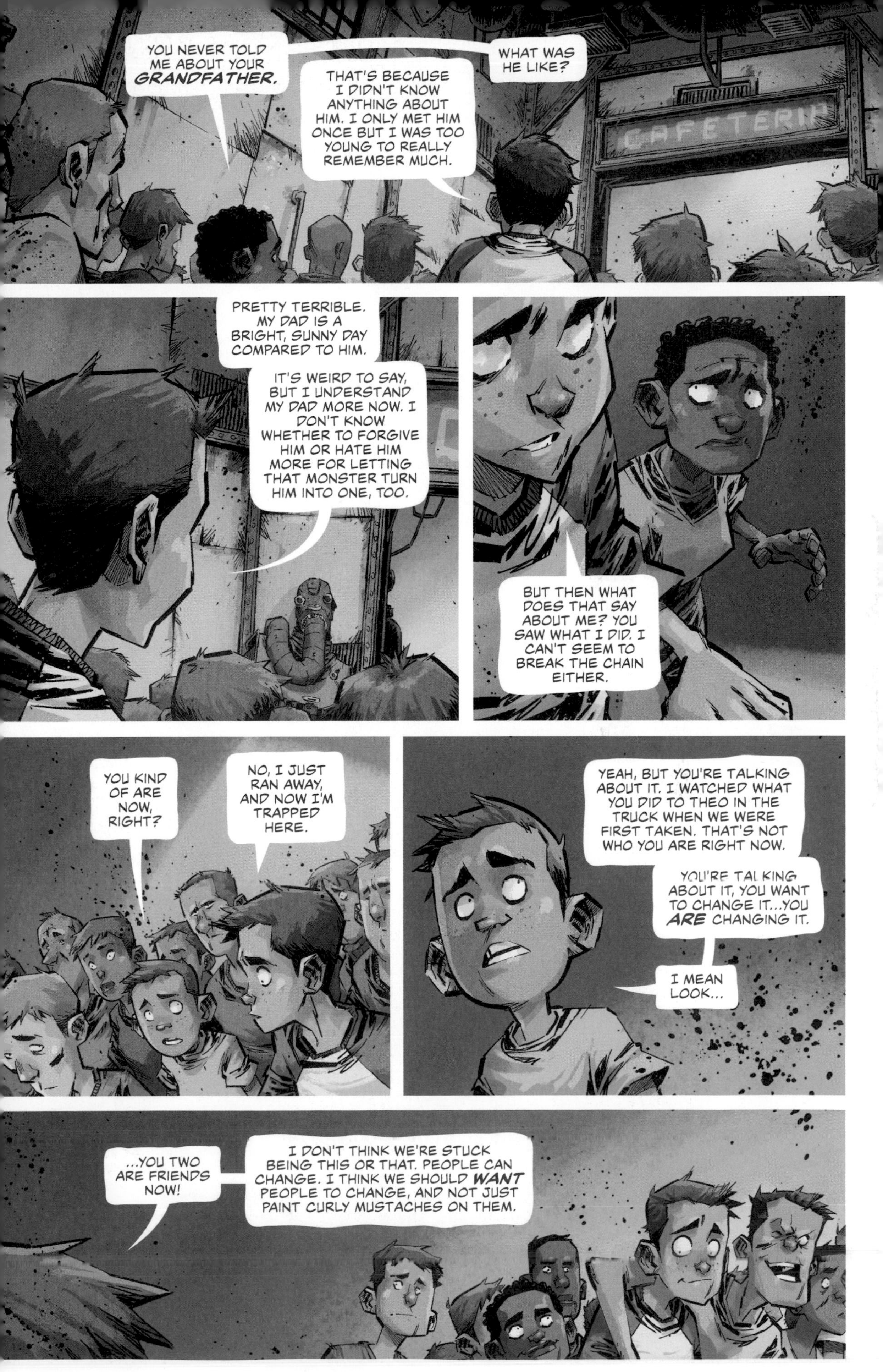
YOU NEVER TOLD ME ABOUT YOUR GRANDFATHER.
WHAT WAS HE LIKE?
THAT'S BECAUSE I DIDN'T KNOW ANYTHING ABOUT HIM. I ONLY MET HIM ONCE BUT I WAS TOO YOUNG TO REALLY REMEMBER MUCH.
CAFETERIA
PRETTY TERRIBLE. MY DAD IS A BRIGHT, SUNNY DAY COMPARED TO HIM.
IT'S WEIRD TO SAY, BUT I UNDERSTAND MY DAD MORE NOW. I DON'T KNOW WHETHER TO FORGIVE HIM OR HATE HIM MORE FOR LETTING THAT MONSTER TURN HIM INTO ONE, TOO.
BUT THEN WHAT DOES THAT SAY ABOUT ME? YOU SAW WHAT I DID. I CAN'T SEEM TO BREAK THE CHAIN EITHER.
YOU KIND OF ARE NOW, RIGHT?
NO, I JUST RAN AWAY, AND NOW I'M TRAPPED HERE.
YEAH, BUT YOU'RE TALKING ABOUT IT. I WATCHED WHAT YOU DID TO THEO IN THE TRUCK WHEN WE WERE FIRST TAKEN. THAT'S NOT WHO YOU ARE RIGHT NOW.
YOU'RE TALKING ABOUT IT, YOU WANT TO CHANGE IT...YOU ARE CHANGING IT.
I MEAN LOOK...
...YOU TWO ARE FRIENDS NOW!
I DON'T THINK WE'RE STUCK BEING THIS OR THAT. PEOPLE CAN CHANGE. I THINK WE SHOULD WANT PEOPLE TO CHANGE, AND NOT JUST PAINT CURLY MUSTACHES ON THEM.

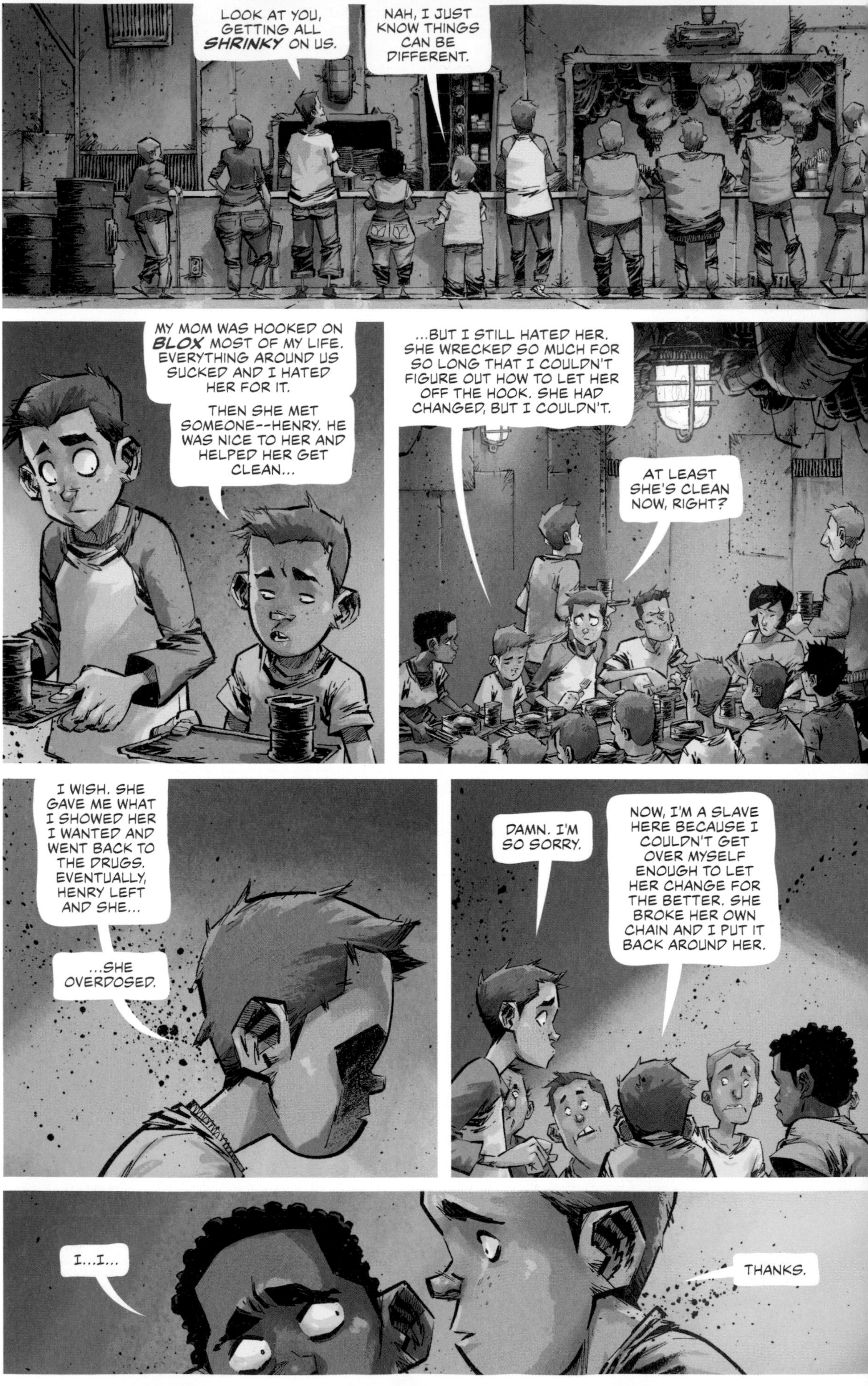

LOOK AT YOU, GETTING ALL SHRINKY ON US.
NAH, I JUST KNOW THINGS CAN BE DIFFERENT.
MY MOM WAS HOOKED ON BLOX MOST OF MY LIFE. EVERYTHING AROUND US SUCKED AND I HATED HER FOR IT.
THEN SHE MET SOMEONE--HENRY. HE WAS NICE TO HER AND HELPED HER GET CLEAN...
...BUT I STILL HATED HER. SHE WRECKED SO MUCH FOR SO LONG THAT I COULDN'T FIGURE OUT HOW TO LET HER OFF THE HOOK. SHE HAD CHANGED, BUT I COULDN'T.
AT LEAST SHE'S CLEAN NOW, RIGHT?
I WISH. SHE GAVE ME WHAT I SHOWED HER I WANTED AND WENT BACK TO THE DRUGS. EVENTUALLY, HENRY LEFT AND SHE...
...SHE OVERDOSED.
DAMN. I'M SO SORRY.
NOW, I'M A SLAVE HERE BECAUSE I COULDN'T GET OVER MYSELF ENOUGH TO LET HER CHANGE FOR THE BETTER. SHE BROKE HER OWN CHAIN AND I PUT IT BACK AROUND HER.
I...I...
THANKS.

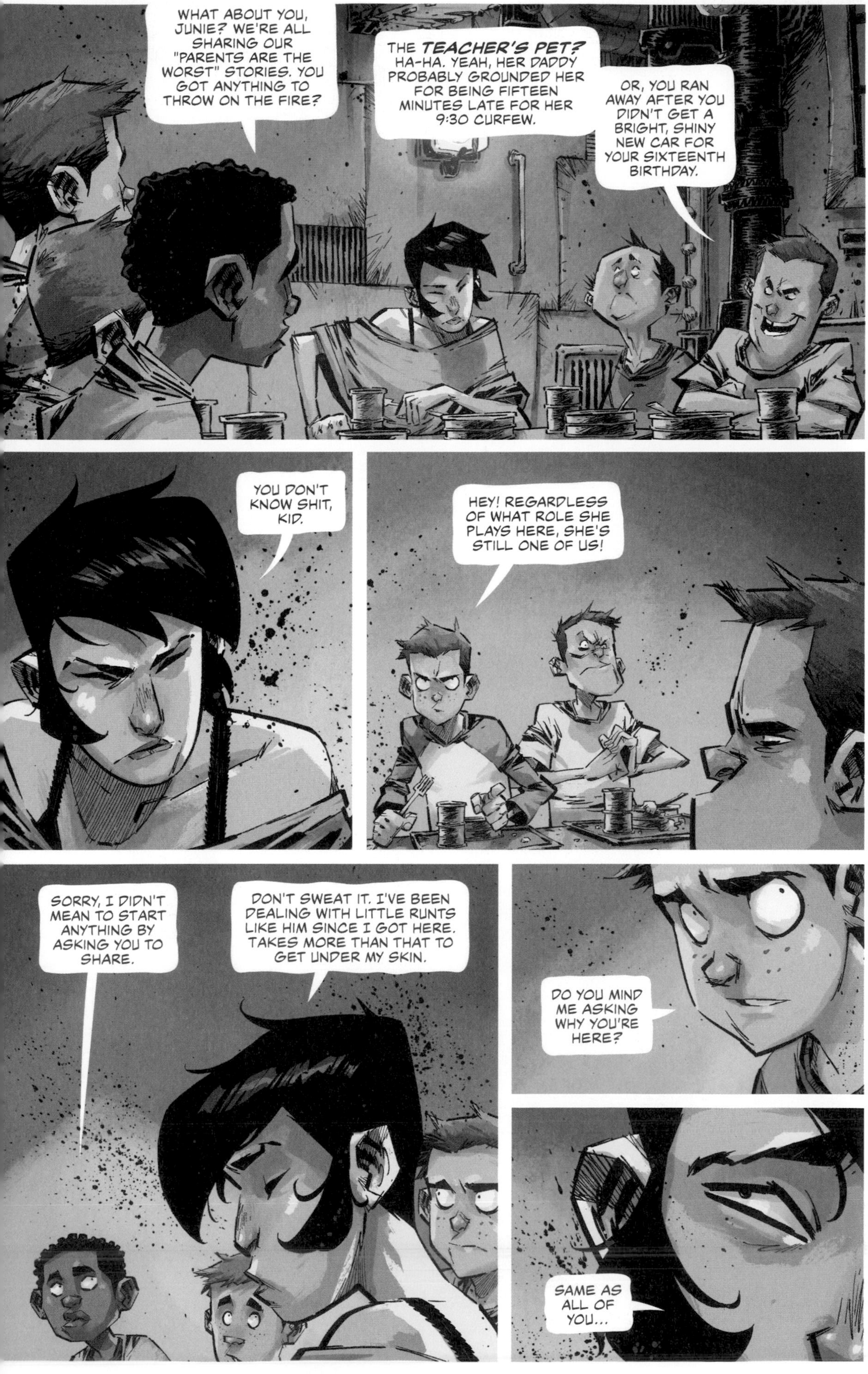
WHAT ABOUT YOU, JUNIE? WE'RE ALL SHARING OUR "PARENTS ARE THE WORST" STORIES. YOU GOT ANYTHING TO THROW ON THE FIRE?
THE **TEACHER'S PET?** HA-HA. YEAH, HER DADDY PROBABLY GROUNDED HER FOR BEING FIFTEEN MINUTES LATE FOR HER 9:30 CURFEW.
OR, YOU RAN AWAY AFTER YOU DIDN'T GET A BRIGHT, SHINY NEW CAR FOR YOUR SIXTEENTH BIRTHDAY.
YOU DON'T KNOW SHIT, KID.
HEY! REGARDLESS OF WHAT ROLE SHE PLAYS HERE, SHE'S STILL ONE OF US!
SORRY, I DIDN'T MEAN TO START ANYTHING BY ASKING YOU TO SHARE.
DON'T SWEAT IT. I'VE BEEN DEALING WITH LITTLE RUNTS LIKE HIM SINCE I GOT HERE. TAKES MORE THAN THAT TO GET UNDER MY SKIN.
DO YOU MIND ME ASKING WHY YOU'RE HERE?
SAME AS ALL OF YOU...

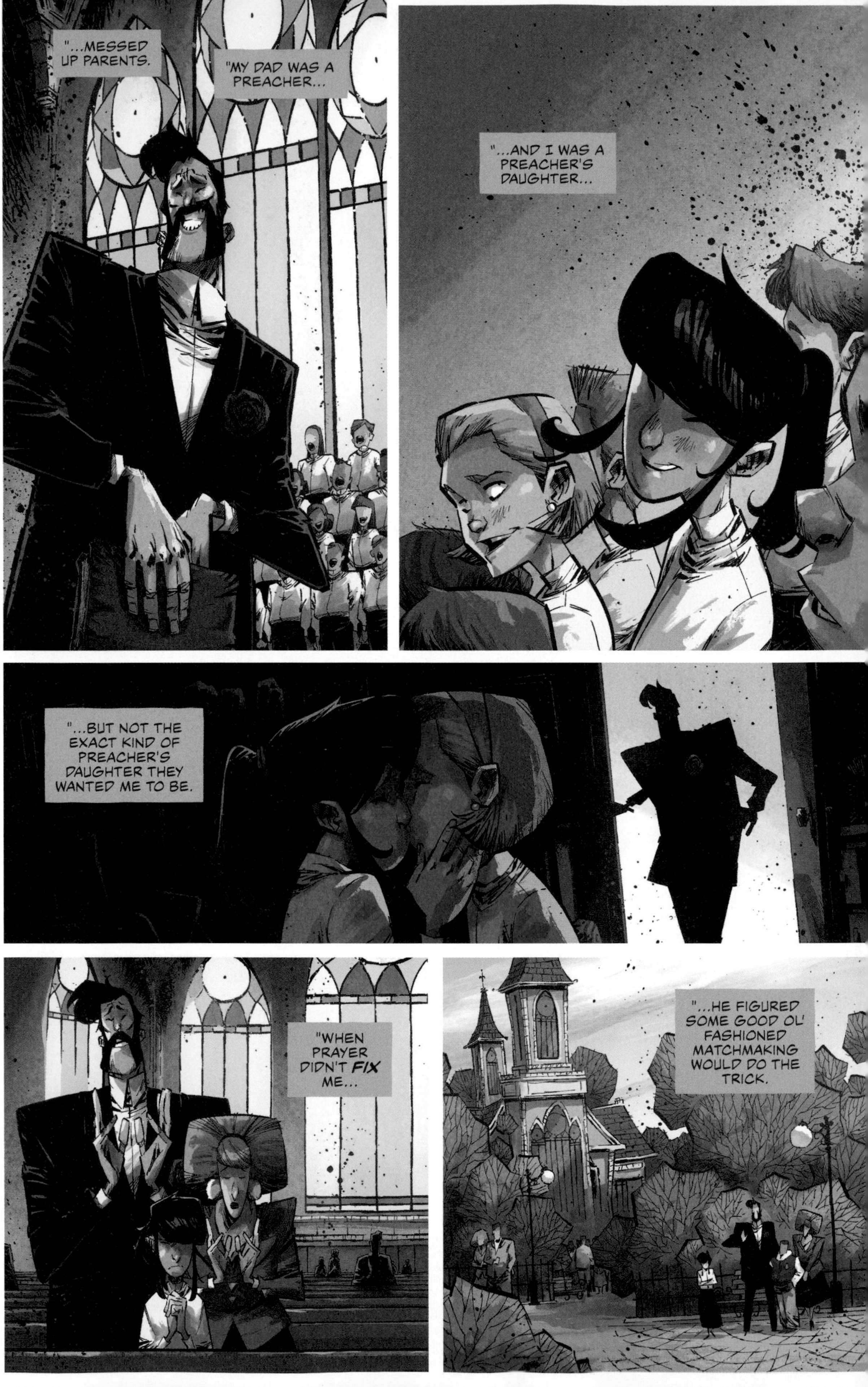
"...MESSED UP PARENTS.
"MY DAD WAS A PREACHER...
"...AND I WAS A PREACHER'S DAUGHTER...
"...BUT NOT THE EXACT KIND OF PREACHER'S DAUGHTER THEY WANTED ME TO BE.
"WHEN PRAYER DIDN'T *FIX* ME...
"...HE FIGURED SOME GOOD OL' FASHIONED MATCHMAKING WOULD DO THE TRICK.

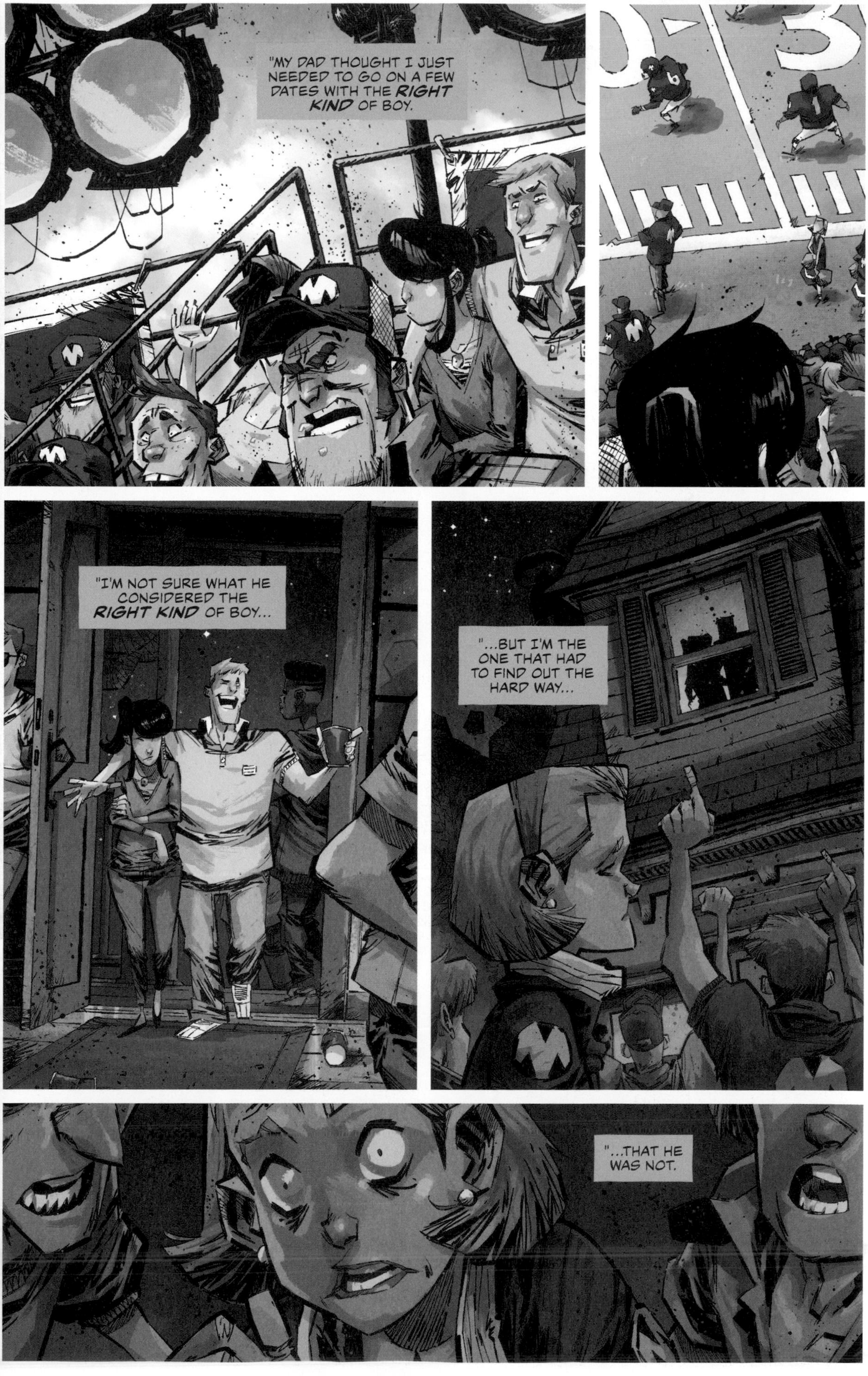
"MY DAD THOUGHT I JUST NEEDED TO GO ON A FEW DATES WITH THE RIGHT KIND OF BOY.
"I'M NOT SURE WHAT HE CONSIDERED THE RIGHT KIND OF BOY...
"...BUT I'M THE ONE THAT HAD TO FIND OUT THE HARD WAY...
"...THAT HE WAS NOT.

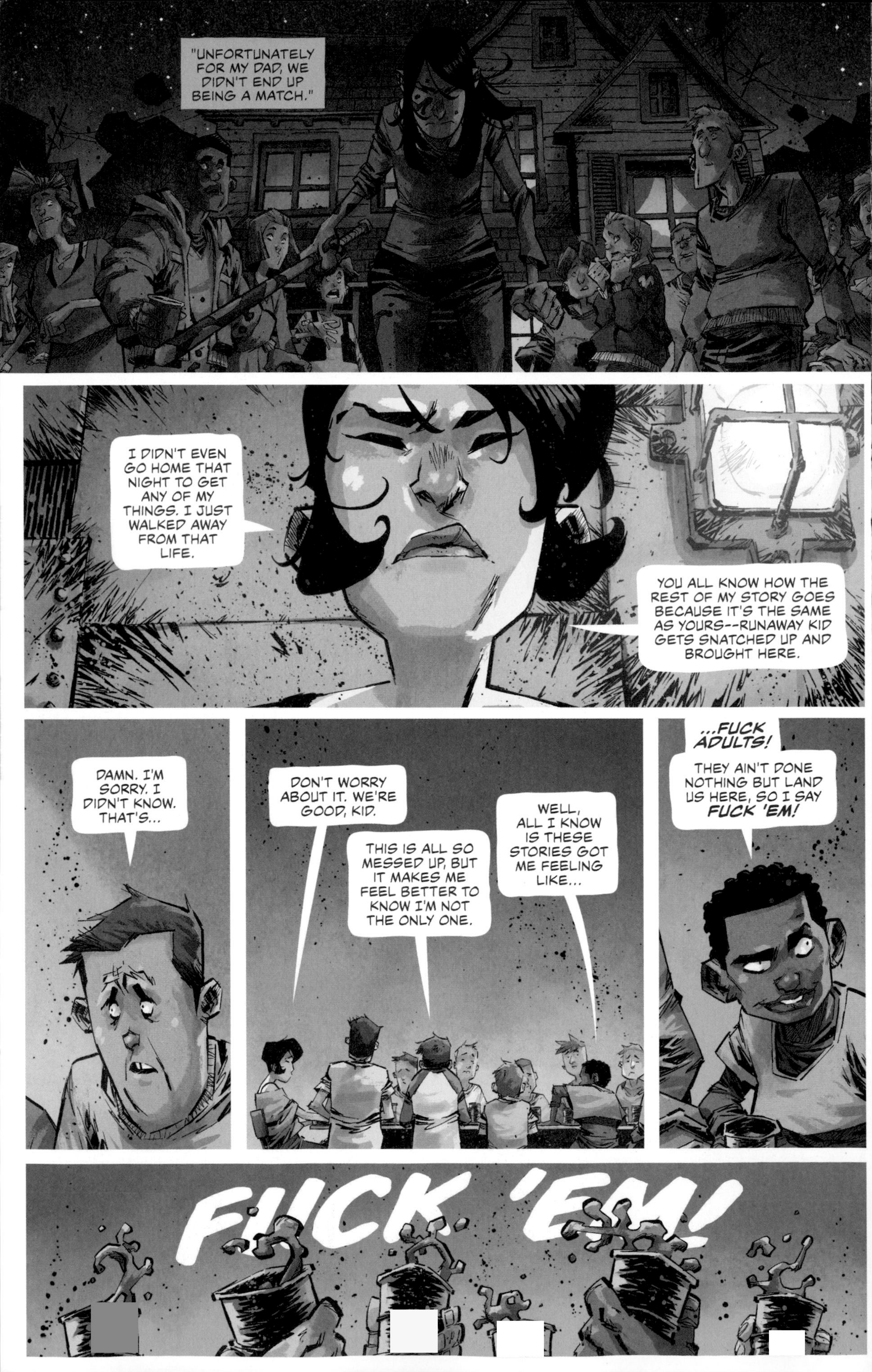
"UNFORTUNATELY FOR MY DAD, WE DIDN'T END UP BEING A MATCH."
I DIDN'T EVEN GO HOME THAT NIGHT TO GET ANY OF MY THINGS. I JUST WALKED AWAY FROM THAT LIFE.
YOU ALL KNOW HOW THE REST OF MY STORY GOES BECAUSE IT'S THE SAME AS YOURS--RUNAWAY KID GETS SNATCHED UP AND BROUGHT HERE.
DAMN. I'M SORRY. I DIDN'T KNOW. THAT'S...
DON'T WORRY ABOUT IT. WE'RE GOOD, KID.
THIS IS ALL SO MESSED UP, BUT IT MAKES ME FEEL BETTER TO KNOW I'M NOT THE ONLY ONE.
WELL, ALL I KNOW IS THESE STORIES GOT ME FEELING LIKE...
...FUCK ADULTS!
THEY AIN'T DONE NOTHING BUT LAND US HERE, SO I SAY FUCK 'EM!
FUCK 'EM!

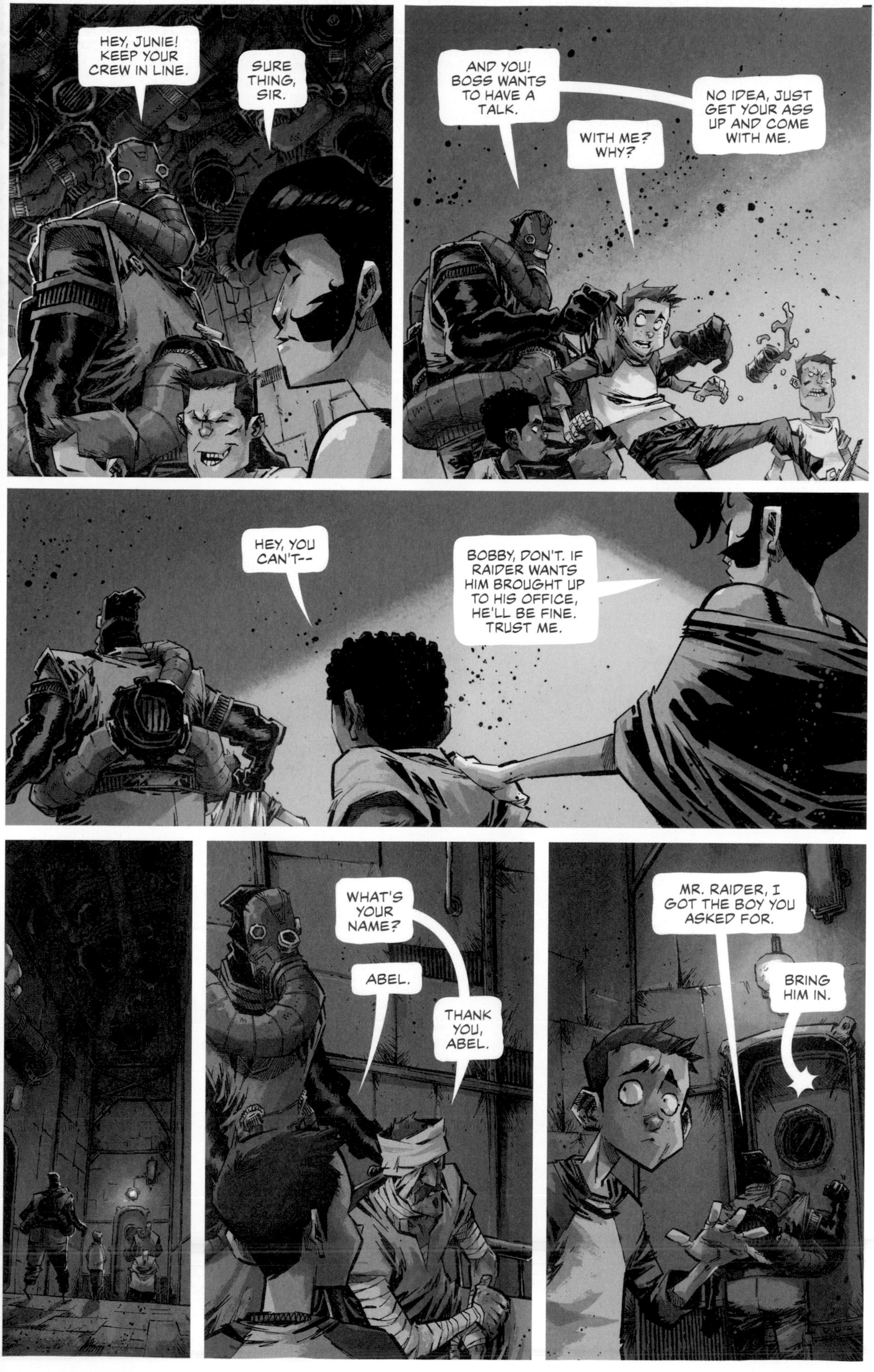
HEY, JUNIE! KEEP YOUR CREW IN LINE.
SURE THING, SIR.
AND YOU! BOSS WANTS TO HAVE A TALK.
WITH ME? WHY?
NO IDEA, JUST GET YOUR ASS UP AND COME WITH ME.
HEY, YOU CAN'T--
BOBBY, DON'T. IF RAIDER WANTS HIM BROUGHT UP TO HIS OFFICE, HE'LL BE FINE. TRUST ME.
WHAT'S YOUR NAME?
ABEL.
THANK YOU, ABEL.
MR. RAIDER, I GOT THE BOY YOU ASKED FOR.
BRING HIM IN.

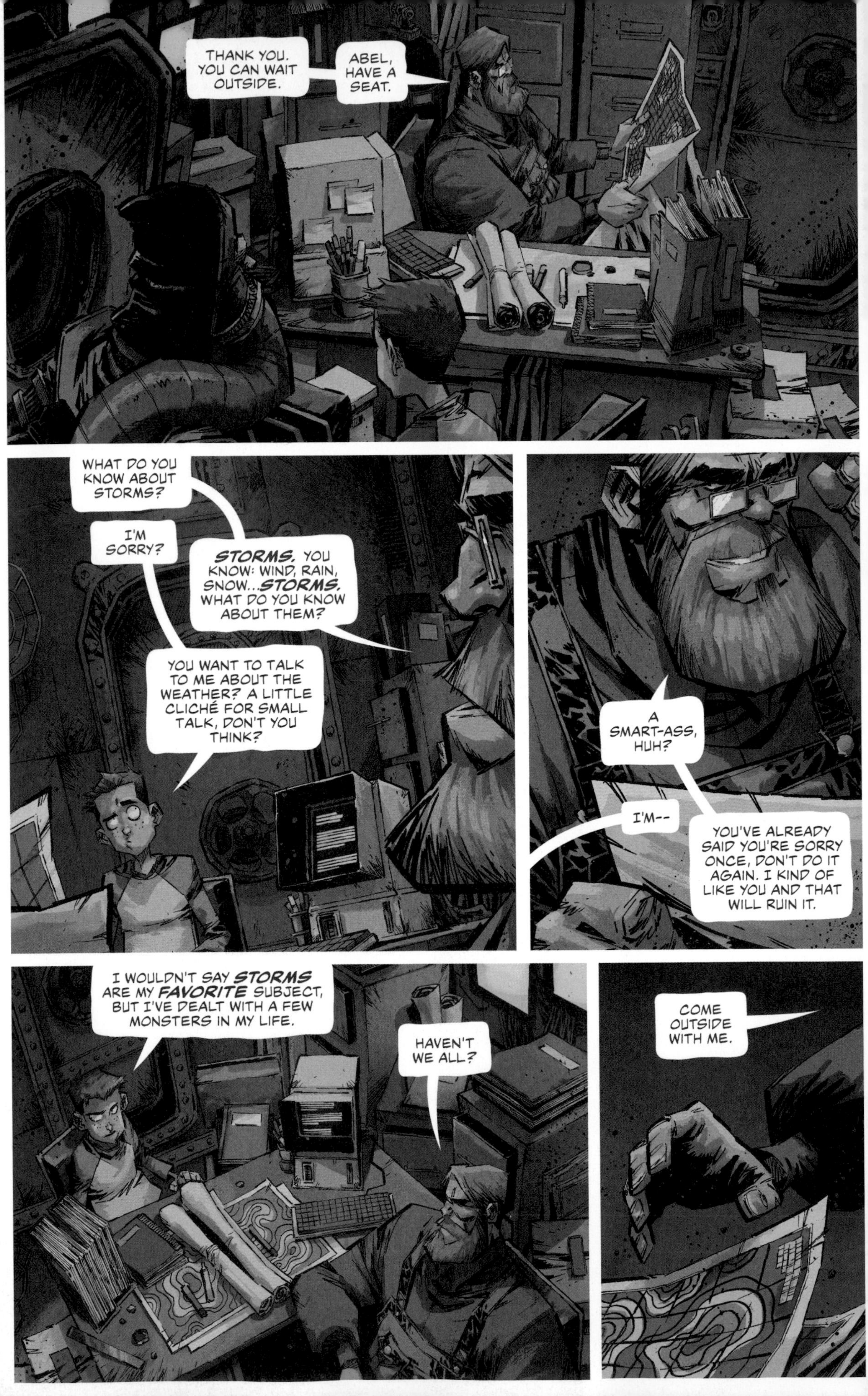
THANK YOU. YOU CAN WAIT OUTSIDE.
ABEL, HAVE A SEAT.
WHAT DO YOU KNOW ABOUT STORMS?
I'M SORRY?
STORMS. YOU KNOW: WIND, RAIN, SNOW...STORMS. WHAT DO YOU KNOW ABOUT THEM?
YOU WANT TO TALK TO ME ABOUT THE WEATHER? A LITTLE CLICHÉ FOR SMALL TALK, DON'T YOU THINK?
A SMART-ASS, HUH?
I'M--
YOU'VE ALREADY SAID YOU'RE SORRY ONCE, DON'T DO IT AGAIN. I KIND OF LIKE YOU AND THAT WILL RUIN IT.
I WOULDN'T SAY STORMS ARE MY FAVORITE SUBJECT, BUT I'VE DEALT WITH A FEW MONSTERS IN MY LIFE.
HAVEN'T WE ALL?
COME OUTSIDE WITH ME.

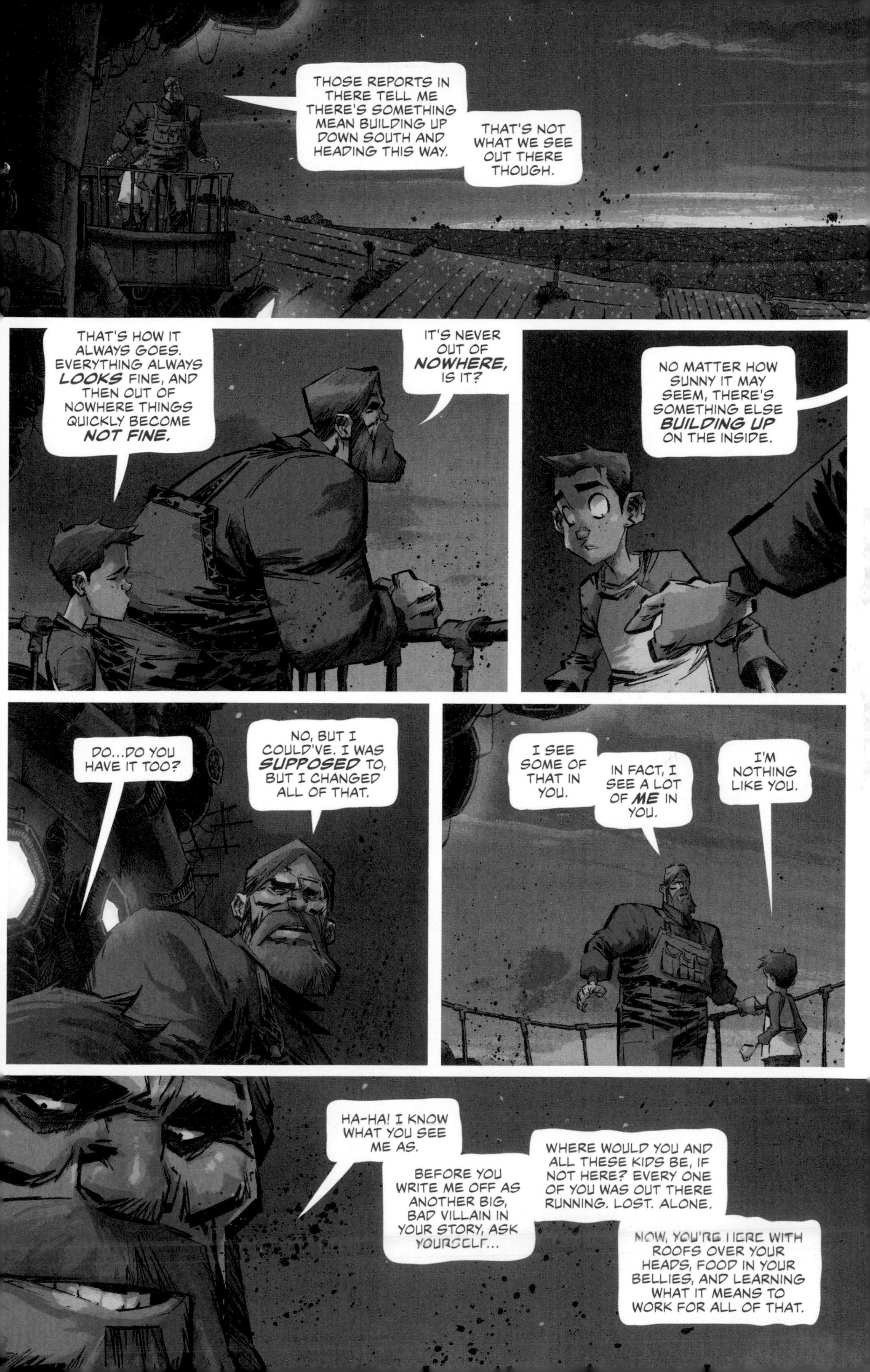
THOSE REPORTS IN THERE TELL ME THERE'S SOMETHING MEAN BUILDING UP DOWN SOUTH AND HEADING THIS WAY.
THAT'S NOT WHAT WE SEE OUT THERE THOUGH.
THAT'S HOW IT ALWAYS GOES. EVERYTHING ALWAYS LOOKS FINE, AND THEN OUT OF NOWHERE THINGS QUICKLY BECOME NOT FINE.
IT'S NEVER OUT OF NOWHERE, IS IT?
NO MATTER HOW SUNNY IT MAY SEEM, THERE'S SOMETHING ELSE BUILDING UP ON THE INSIDE.
DO...DO YOU HAVE IT TOO?
NO, BUT I COULD'VE. I WAS SUPPOSED TO, BUT I CHANGED ALL OF THAT.
I SEE SOME OF THAT IN YOU.
IN FACT, I SEE A LOT OF ME IN YOU.
I'M NOTHING LIKE YOU.
HA-HA! I KNOW WHAT YOU SEE ME AS.
BEFORE YOU WRITE ME OFF AS ANOTHER BIG, BAD VILLAIN IN YOUR STORY, ASK YOURSELF...
WHERE WOULD YOU AND ALL THESE KIDS BE, IF NOT HERE? EVERY ONE OF YOU WAS OUT THERE RUNNING. LOST. ALONE.
NOW, YOU'RE HERE WITH ROOFS OVER YOUR HEADS, FOOD IN YOUR BELLIES, AND LEARNING WHAT IT MEANS TO WORK FOR ALL OF THAT.

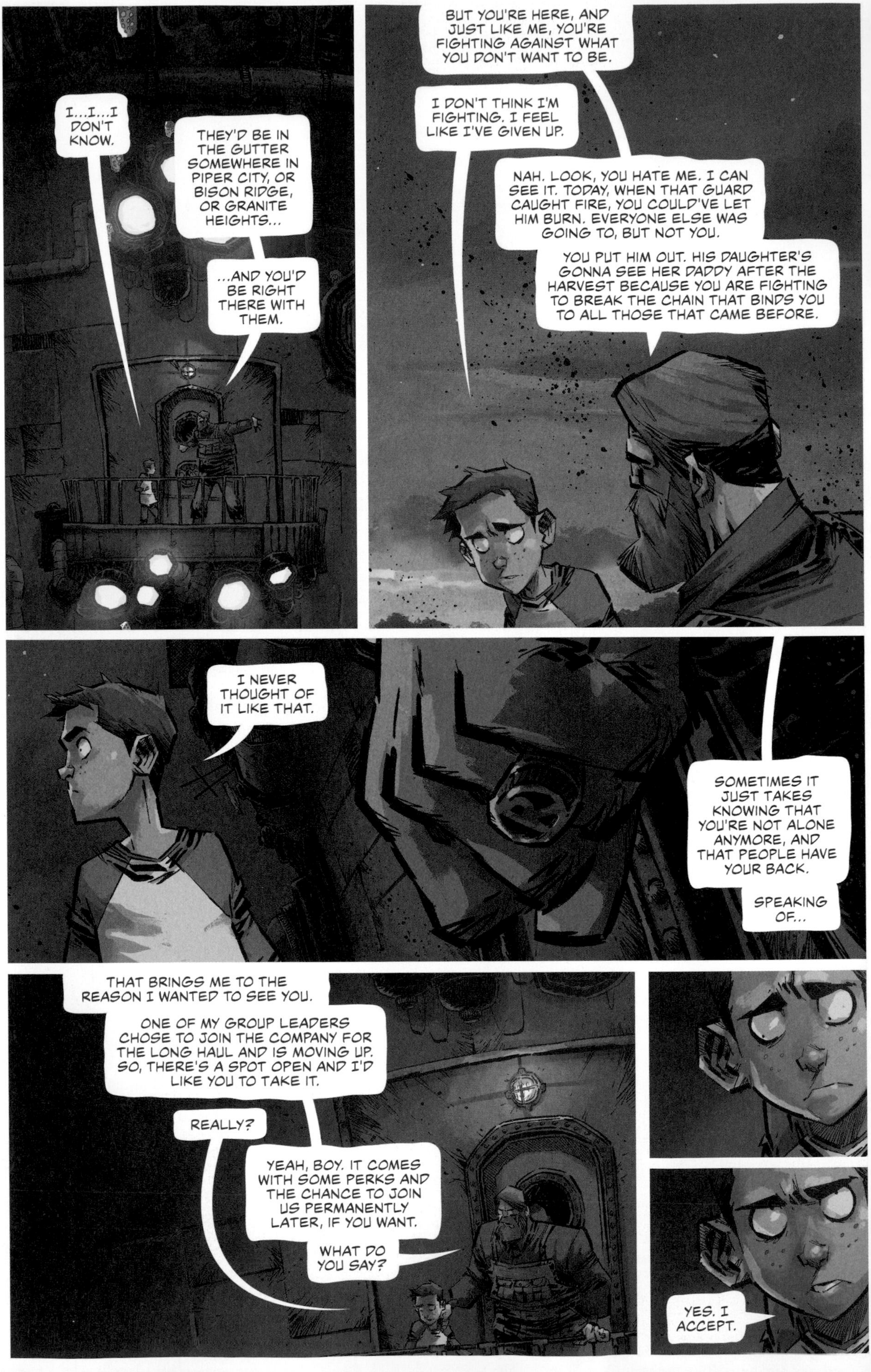
I...I...I DON'T KNOW.
THEY'D BE IN THE GUTTER SOMEWHERE IN PIPER CITY, OR BISON RIDGE, OR GRANITE HEIGHTS...
...AND YOU'D BE RIGHT THERE WITH THEM.
BUT YOU'RE HERE, AND JUST LIKE ME, YOU'RE FIGHTING AGAINST WHAT YOU DON'T WANT TO BE.
I DON'T THINK I'M FIGHTING. I FEEL LIKE I'VE GIVEN UP.
NAH. LOOK, YOU HATE ME. I CAN SEE IT. TODAY, WHEN THAT GUARD CAUGHT FIRE, YOU COULD'VE LET HIM BURN. EVERYONE ELSE WAS GOING TO, BUT NOT YOU.
YOU PUT HIM OUT. HIS DAUGHTER'S GONNA SEE HER DADDY AFTER THE HARVEST BECAUSE YOU ARE FIGHTING TO BREAK THE CHAIN THAT BINDS YOU TO ALL THOSE THAT CAME BEFORE.
I NEVER THOUGHT OF IT LIKE THAT.
SOMETIMES IT JUST TAKES KNOWING THAT YOU'RE NOT ALONE ANYMORE, AND THAT PEOPLE HAVE YOUR BACK.
SPEAKING OF...
THAT BRINGS ME TO THE REASON I WANTED TO SEE YOU.
ONE OF MY GROUP LEADERS CHOSE TO JOIN THE COMPANY FOR THE LONG HAUL AND IS MOVING UP. SO, THERE'S A SPOT OPEN AND I'D LIKE YOU TO TAKE IT.
REALLY?
YEAH, BOY. IT COMES WITH SOME PERKS AND THE CHANCE TO JOIN US PERMANENTLY LATER, IF YOU WANT.
WHAT DO YOU SAY?
YES. I ACCEPT.

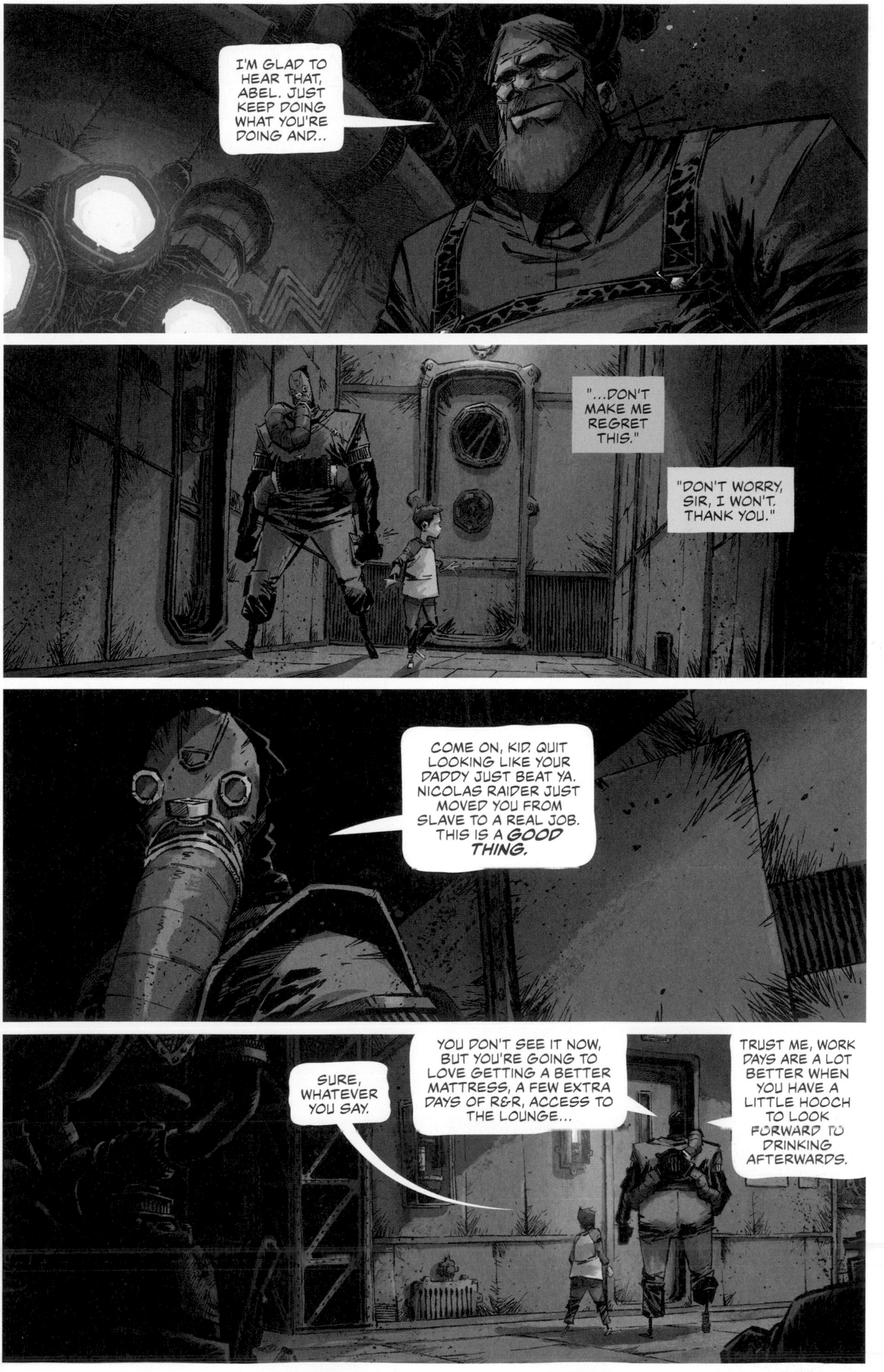

I'M GLAD TO HEAR THAT, ABEL. JUST KEEP DOING WHAT YOU'RE DOING AND...
"...DON'T MAKE ME REGRET THIS."
"DON'T WORRY, SIR, I WON'T. THANK YOU."
COME ON, KID. QUIT LOOKING LIKE YOUR DADDY JUST BEAT YA. NICOLAS RAIDER JUST MOVED YOU FROM SLAVE TO A REAL JOB. THIS IS A *GOOD THING.*
YOU DON'T SEE IT NOW, BUT YOU'RE GOING TO LOVE GETTING A BETTER MATTRESS, A FEW EXTRA DAYS OF R&R, ACCESS TO THE LOUNGE...
SURE, WHATEVER YOU SAY.
TRUST ME, WORK DAYS ARE A LOT BETTER WHEN YOU HAVE A LITTLE HOOCH TO LOOK FORWARD TO DRINKING AFTERWARDS.

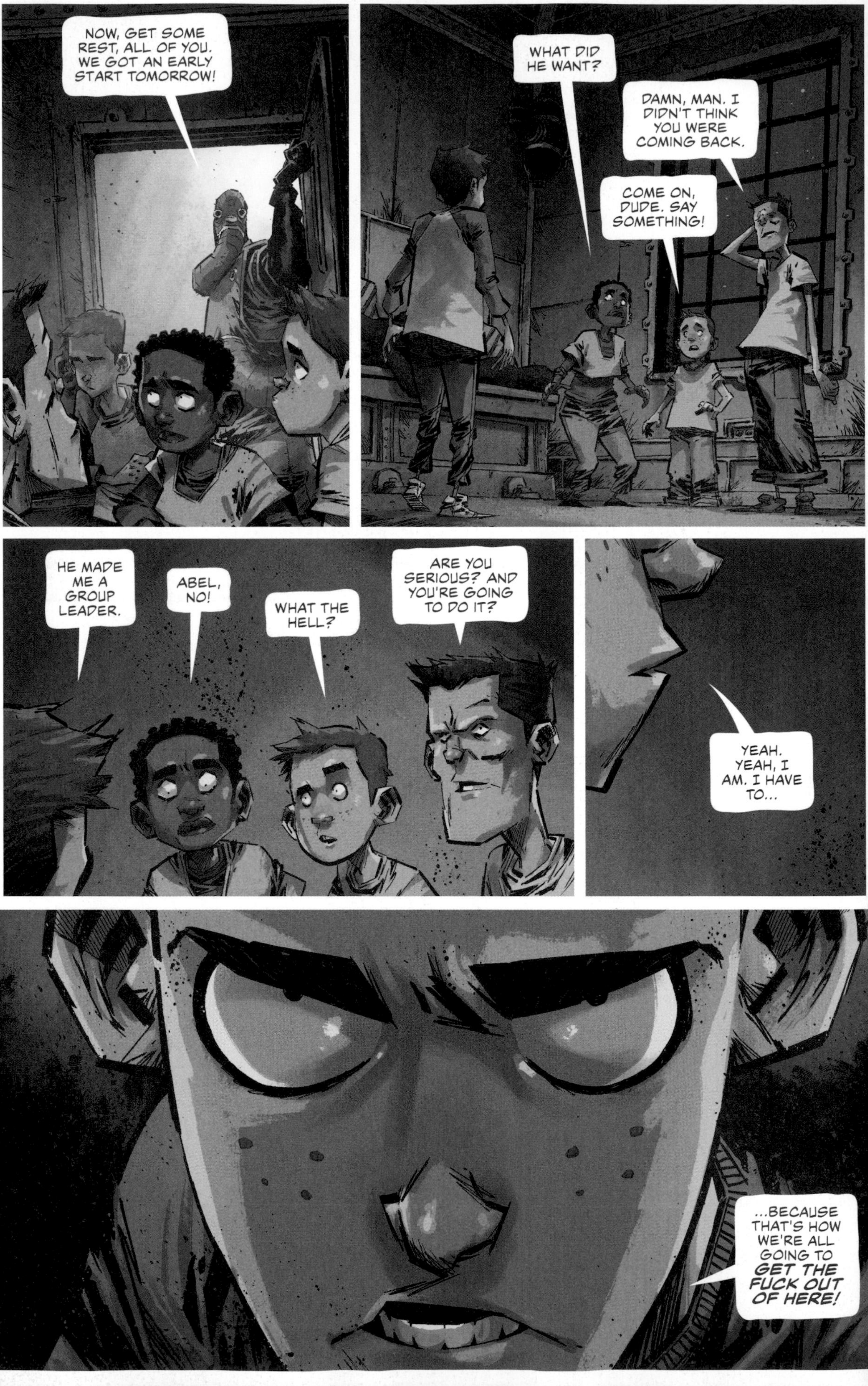
NOW, GET SOME REST, ALL OF YOU. WE GOT AN EARLY START TOMORROW!
WHAT DID HE WANT?
DAMN, MAN. I DIDN'T THINK YOU WERE COMING BACK.
COME ON, DUDE. SAY SOMETHING!
HE MADE ME A GROUP LEADER.
ABEL, NO!
WHAT THE HELL?
ARE YOU SERIOUS? AND YOU'RE GOING TO DO IT?
YEAH. YEAH, I AM. I HAVE TO...
...BECAUSE THAT'S HOW WE'RE ALL GOING TO GET THE FUCK OUT OF HERE!

CHAPTER

FIFTEEN

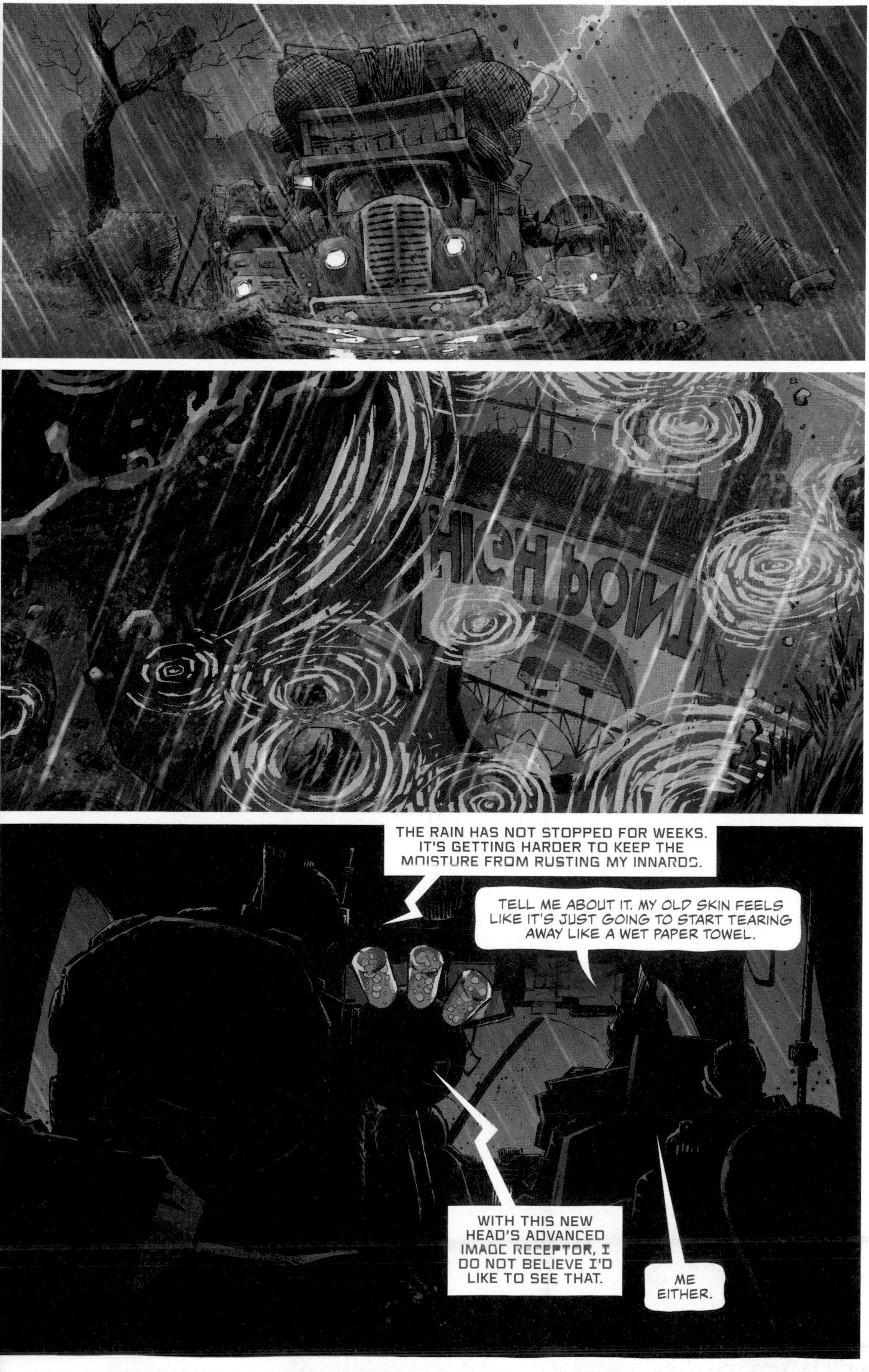
THE RAIN HAS NOT STOPPED FOR WEEKS. IT'S GETTING HARDER TO KEEP THE MOISTURE FROM RUSTING MY INNARDS.
TELL ME ABOUT IT. MY OLD SKIN FEELS LIKE IT'S JUST GOING TO START TEARING AWAY LIKE A WET PAPER TOWEL.
WITH THIS NEW HEAD'S ADVANCED IMAGE RECEPTOR, I DO NOT BELIEVE I'D LIKE TO SEE THAT.
ME EITHER.

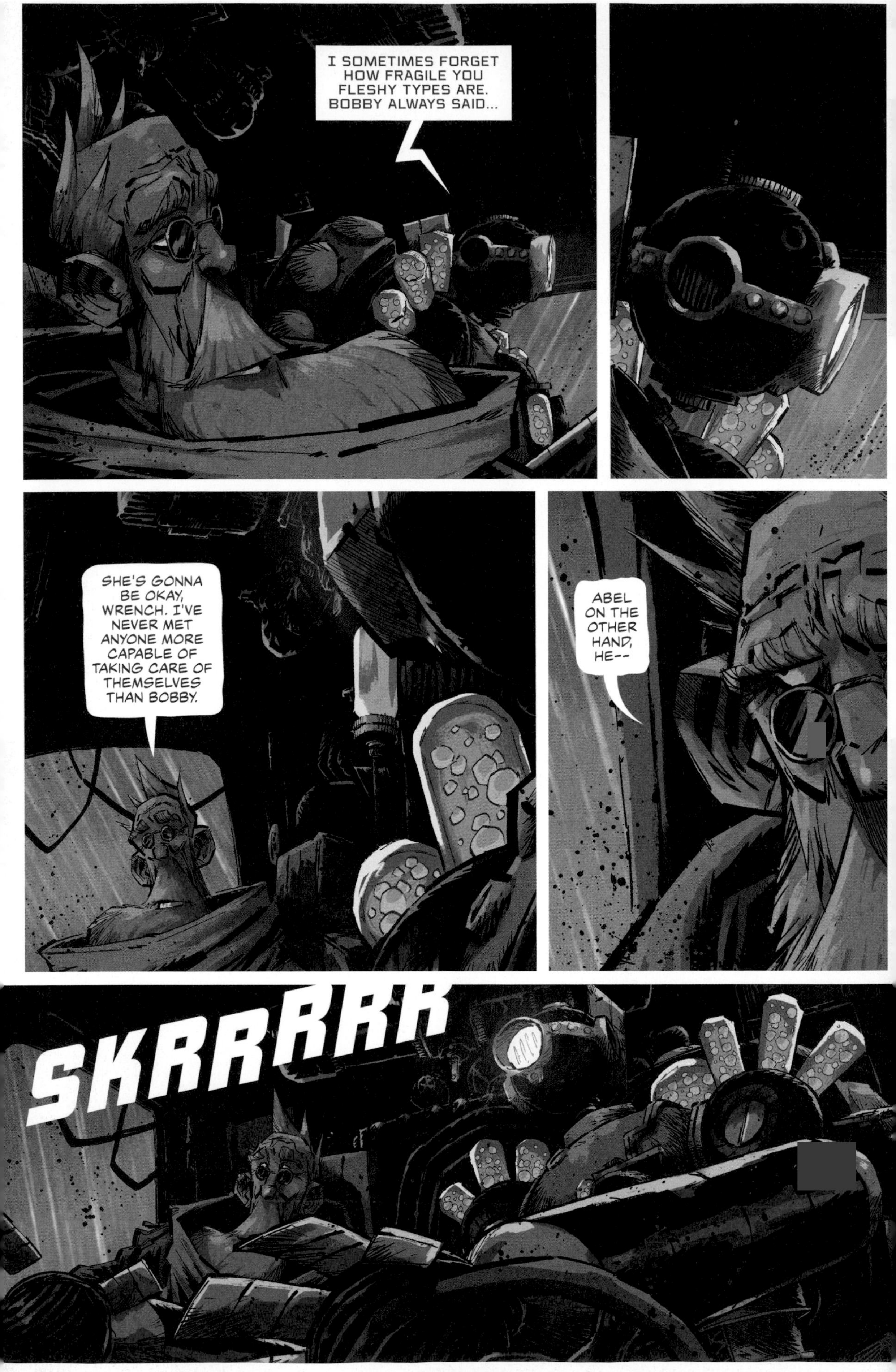
I SOMETIMES FORGET HOW FRAGILE YOU FLESHY TYPES ARE. BOBBY ALWAYS SAID...
SHE'S GONNA BE OKAY, WRENCH. I'VE NEVER MET ANYONE MORE CAPABLE OF TAKING CARE OF THEMSELVES THAN BOBBY.
ABEL ON THE OTHER HAND, HE--
SKRRRRR

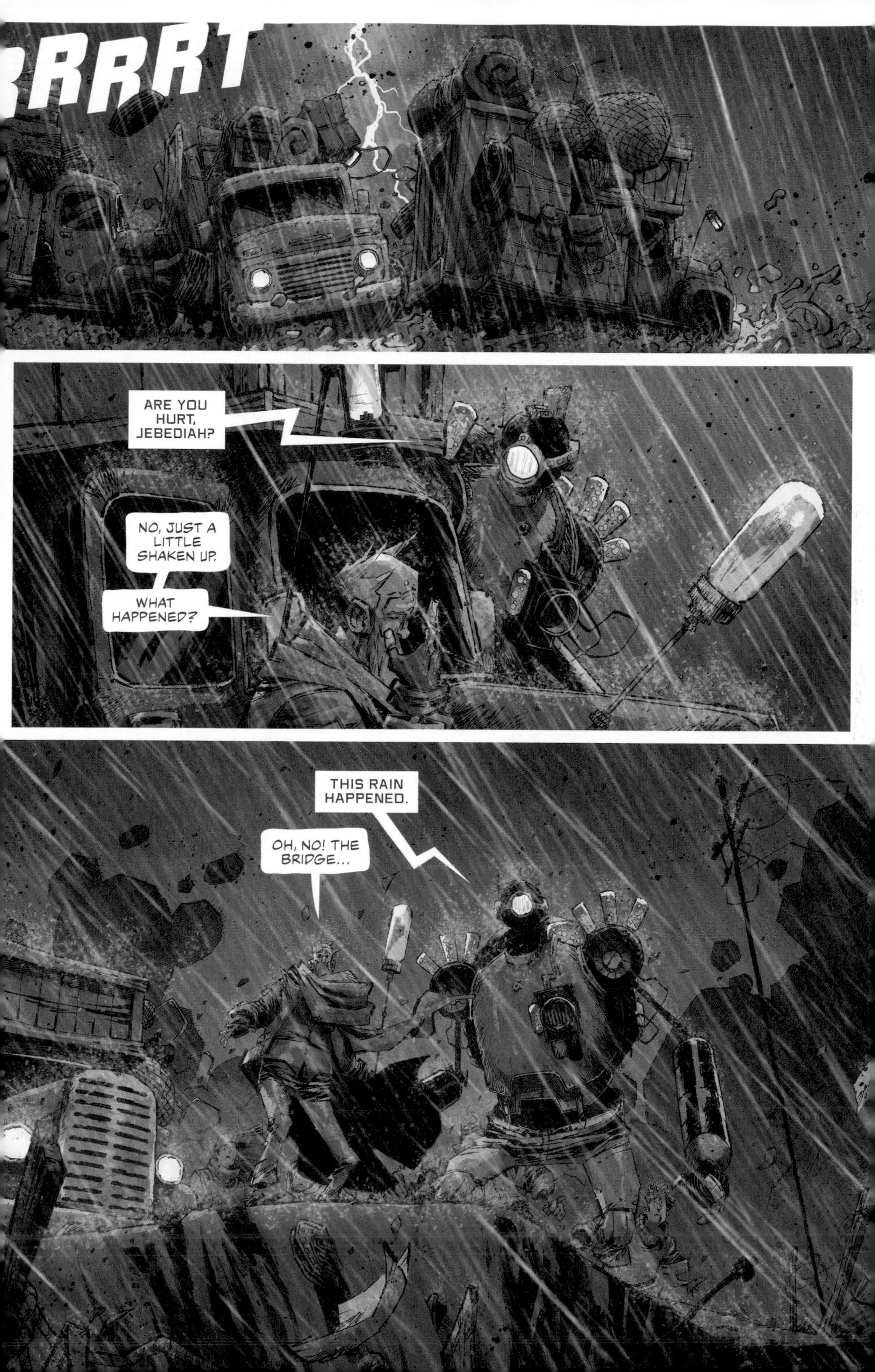
RRRT
ARE YOU HURT, JEBEDIAH?
NO, JUST A LITTLE SHAKEN UP.
WHAT HAPPENED?
THIS RAIN HAPPENED.
OH, NO! THE BRIDGE...

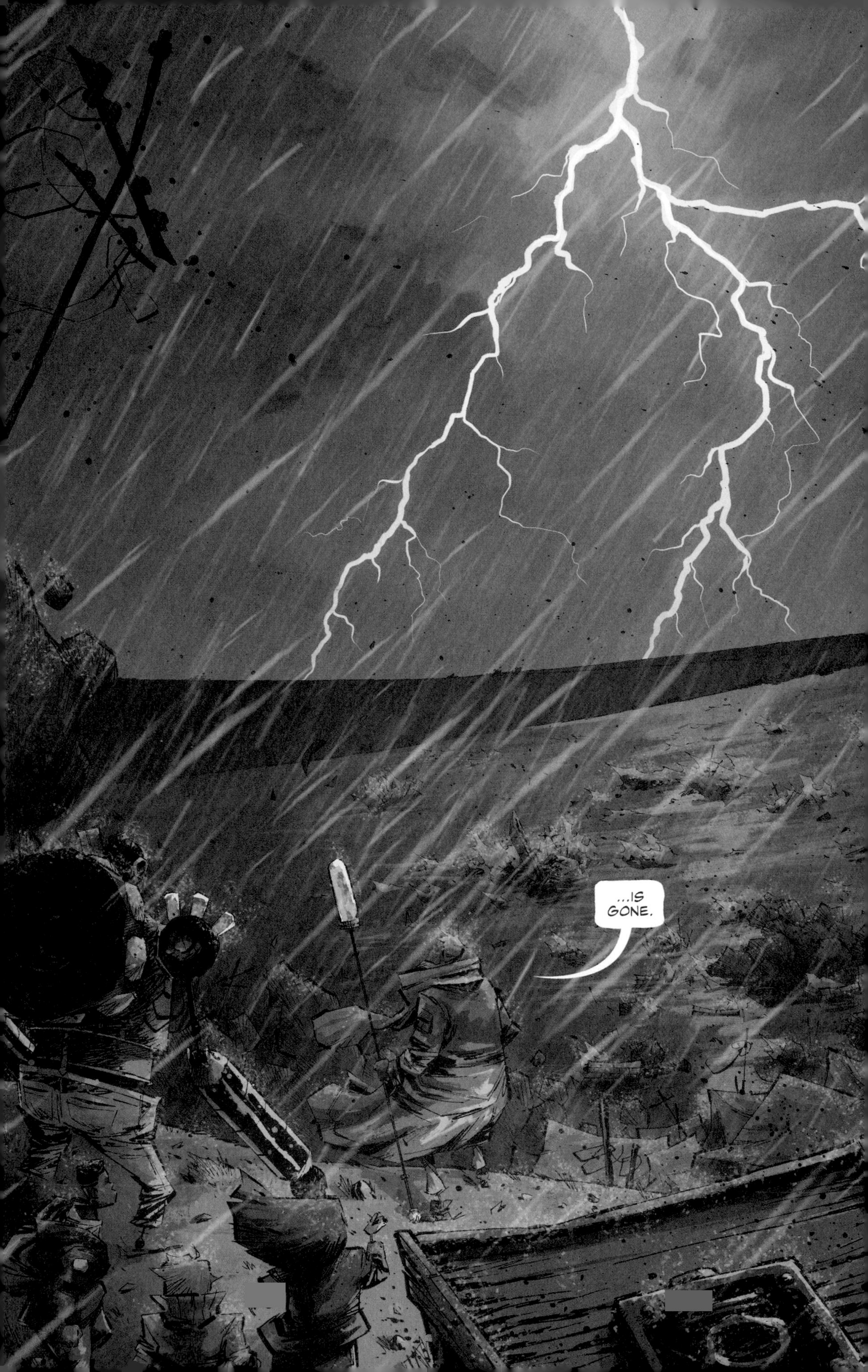
...IS GONE.

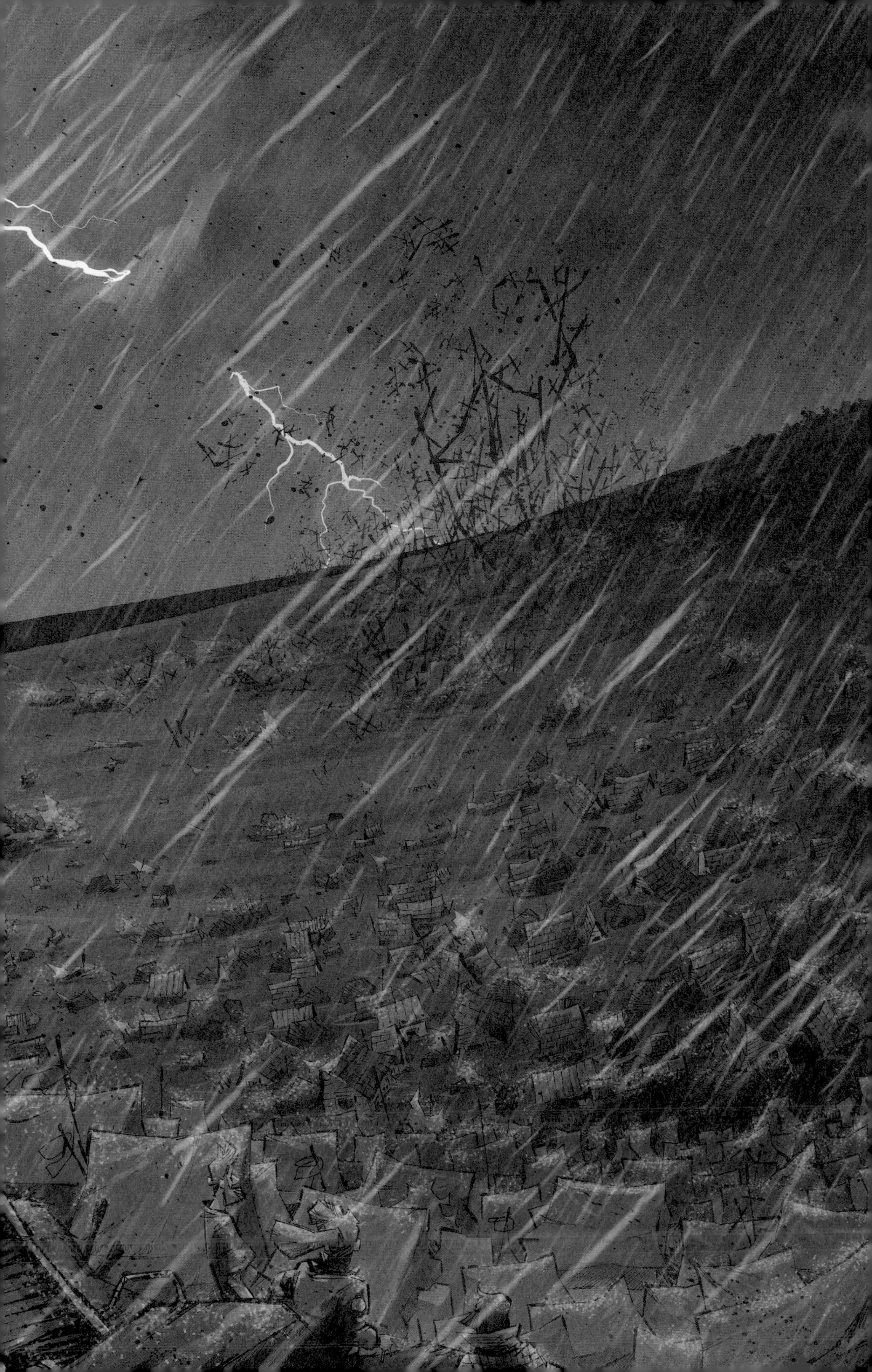

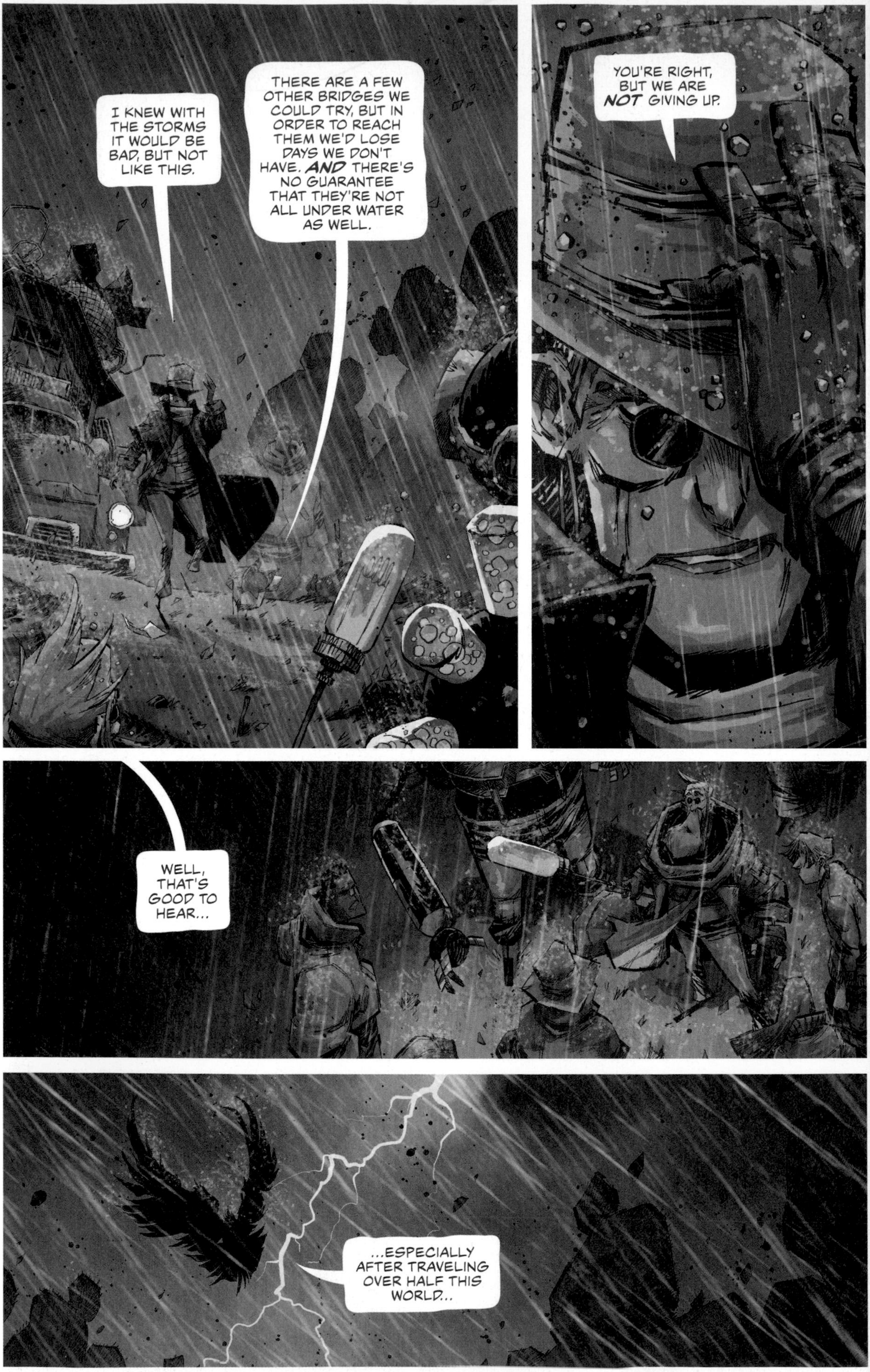
I KNEW WITH THE STORMS IT WOULD BE BAD, BUT NOT LIKE THIS.
THERE ARE A FEW OTHER BRIDGES WE COULD TRY, BUT IN ORDER TO REACH THEM WE'D LOSE DAYS WE DON'T HAVE. **AND** THERE'S NO GUARANTEE THAT THEY'RE NOT ALL UNDER WATER AS WELL.
YOU'RE RIGHT, BUT WE ARE **NOT** GIVING UP.
WELL, THAT'S GOOD TO HEAR...
...ESPECIALLY AFTER TRAVELING OVER HALF THIS WORLD...

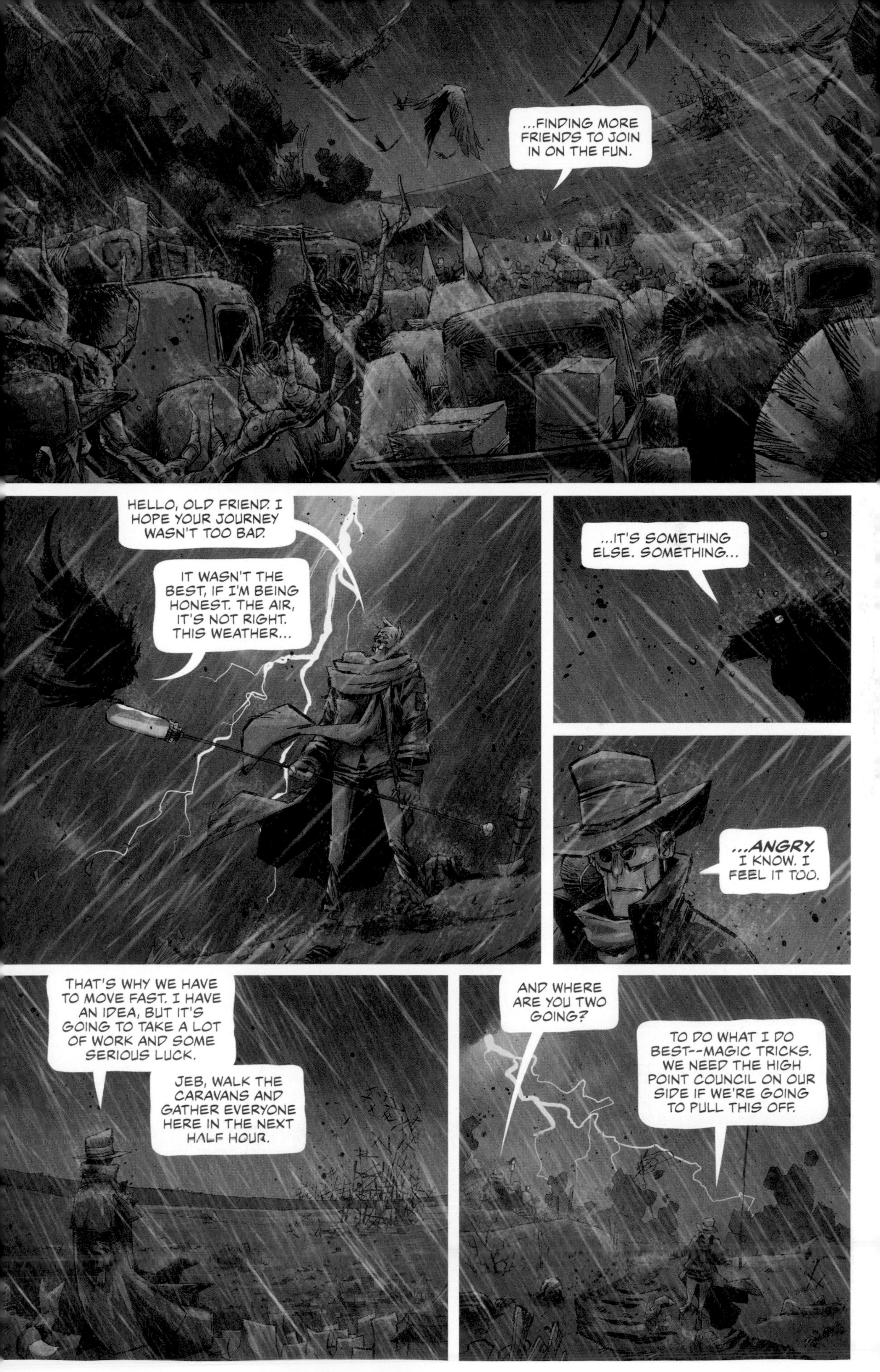
...FINDING MORE FRIENDS TO JOIN IN ON THE FUN.
HELLO, OLD FRIEND. I HOPE YOUR JOURNEY WASN'T TOO BAD.
IT WASN'T THE BEST, IF I'M BEING HONEST. THE AIR, IT'S NOT RIGHT. THIS WEATHER...
...IT'S SOMETHING ELSE. SOMETHING...
...ANGRY. I KNOW. I FEEL IT TOO.
THAT'S WHY WE HAVE TO MOVE FAST. I HAVE AN IDEA, BUT IT'S GOING TO TAKE A LOT OF WORK AND SOME SERIOUS LUCK.
JEB, WALK THE CARAVANS AND GATHER EVERYONE HERE IN THE NEXT HALF HOUR.
AND WHERE ARE YOU TWO GOING?
TO DO WHAT I DO BEST--MAGIC TRICKS. WE NEED THE HIGH POINT COUNCIL ON OUR SIDE IF WE'RE GOING TO PULL THIS OFF.

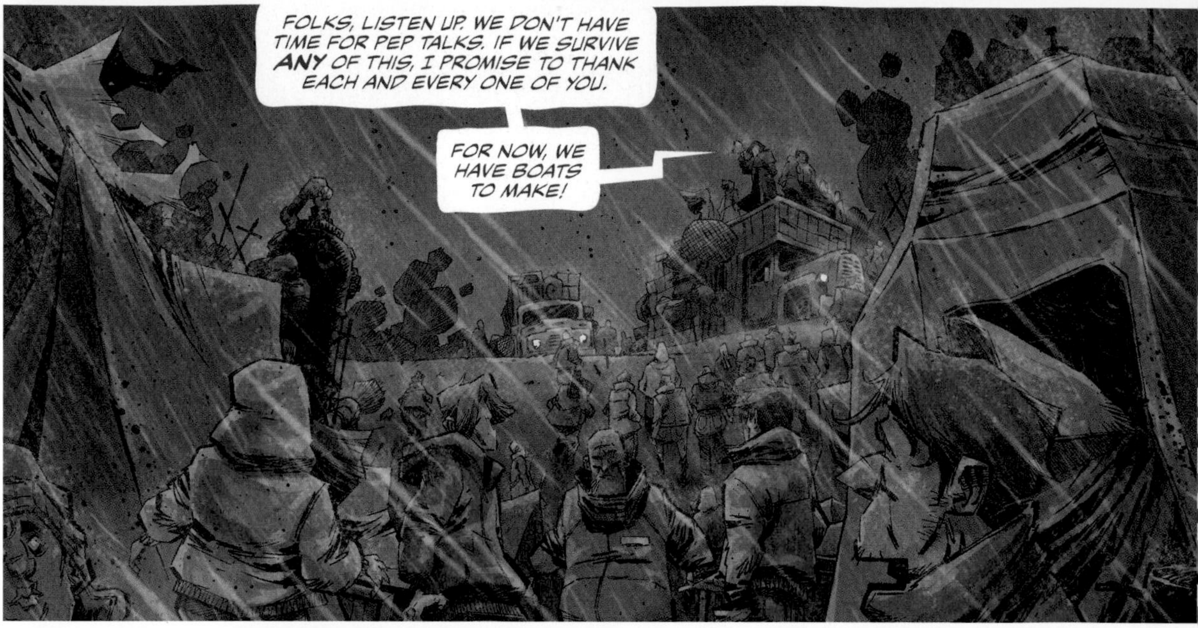
FOLKS, LISTEN UP. WE DON'T HAVE TIME FOR PEP TALKS. IF WE SURVIVE ANY OF THIS, I PROMISE TO THANK EACH AND EVERY ONE OF YOU.
FOR NOW, WE HAVE BOATS TO MAKE!

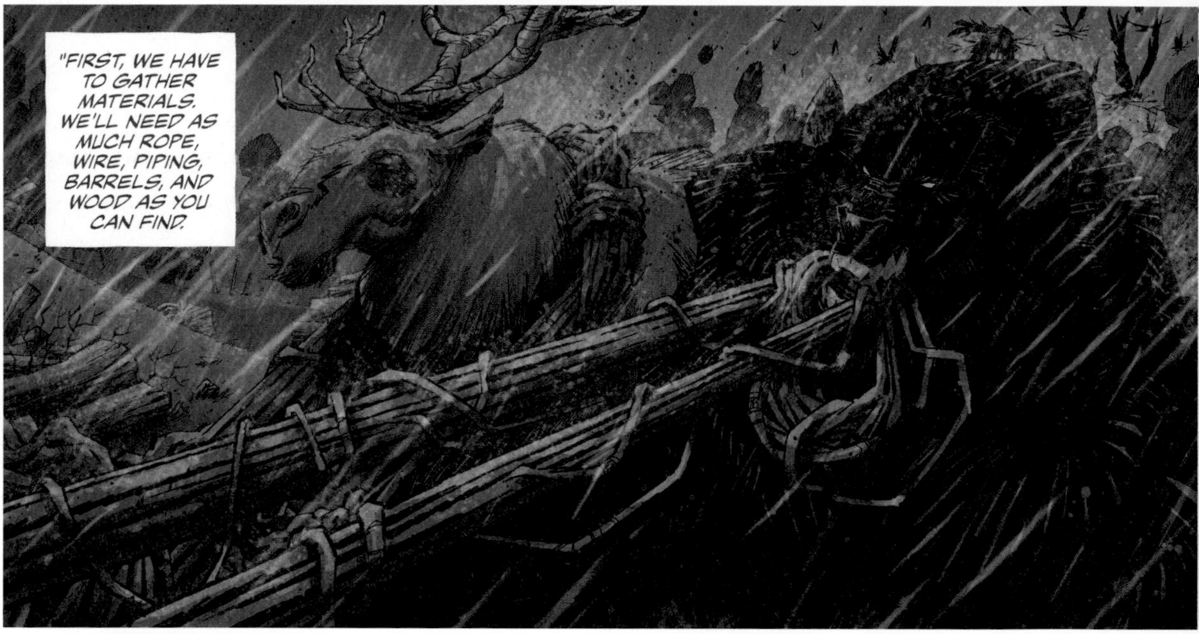
"FIRST, WE HAVE TO GATHER MATERIALS. WE'LL NEED AS MUCH ROPE, WIRE, PIPING, BARRELS, AND WOOD AS YOU CAN FIND.

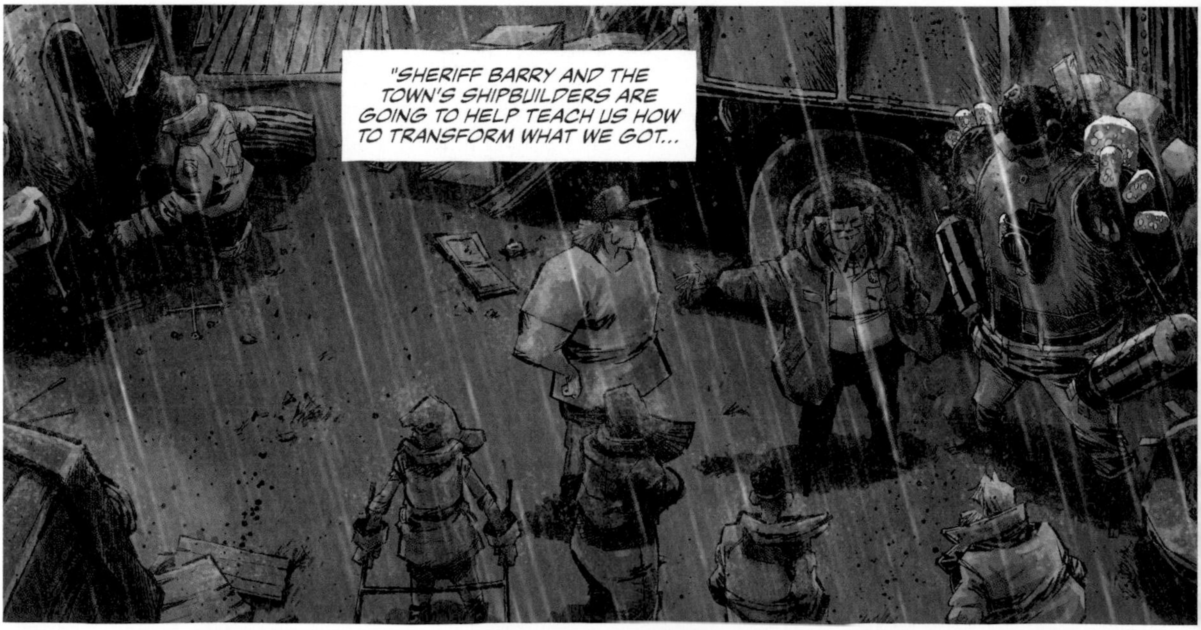
"SHERIFF BARRY AND THE TOWN'S SHIPBUILDERS ARE GOING TO HELP TEACH US HOW TO TRANSFORM WHAT WE GOT...

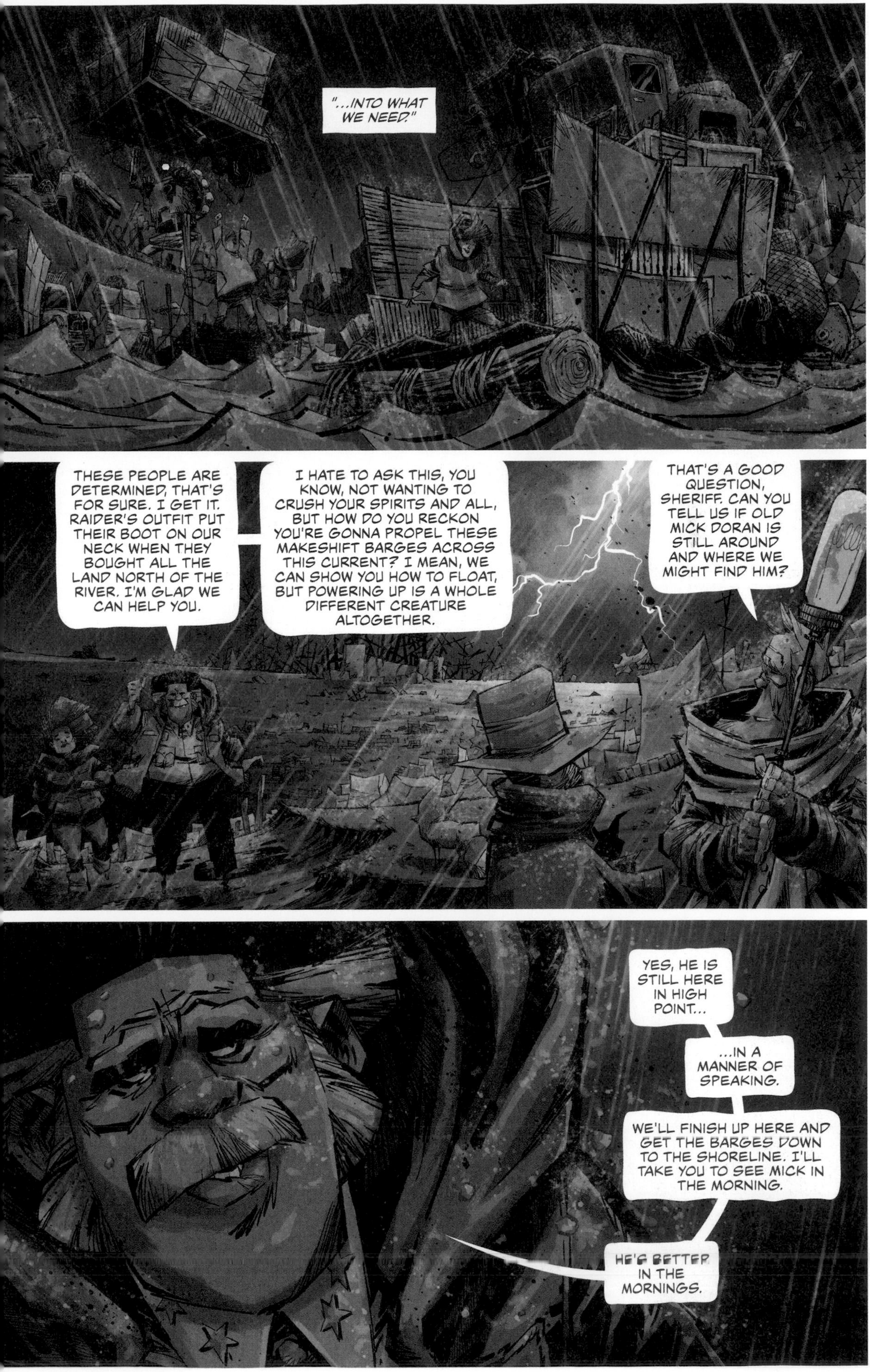
"...INTO WHAT WE NEED."
THESE PEOPLE ARE DETERMINED, THAT'S FOR SURE. I GET IT. RAIDER'S OUTFIT PUT THEIR BOOT ON OUR NECK WHEN THEY BOUGHT ALL THE LAND NORTH OF THE RIVER. I'M GLAD WE CAN HELP YOU.
I HATE TO ASK THIS, YOU KNOW, NOT WANTING TO CRUSH YOUR SPIRITS AND ALL, BUT HOW DO YOU RECKON YOU'RE GONNA PROPEL THESE MAKESHIFT BARGES ACROSS THIS CURRENT? I MEAN, WE CAN SHOW YOU HOW TO FLOAT, BUT POWERING UP IS A WHOLE DIFFERENT CREATURE ALTOGETHER.
THAT'S A GOOD QUESTION, SHERIFF. CAN YOU TELL US IF OLD MICK DORAN IS STILL AROUND AND WHERE WE MIGHT FIND HIM?
YES, HE IS STILL HERE IN HIGH POINT...
...IN A MANNER OF SPEAKING.
WE'LL FINISH UP HERE AND GET THE BARGES DOWN TO THE SHORELINE. I'LL TAKE YOU TO SEE MICK IN THE MORNING.
HE'S BETTER IN THE MORNINGS.

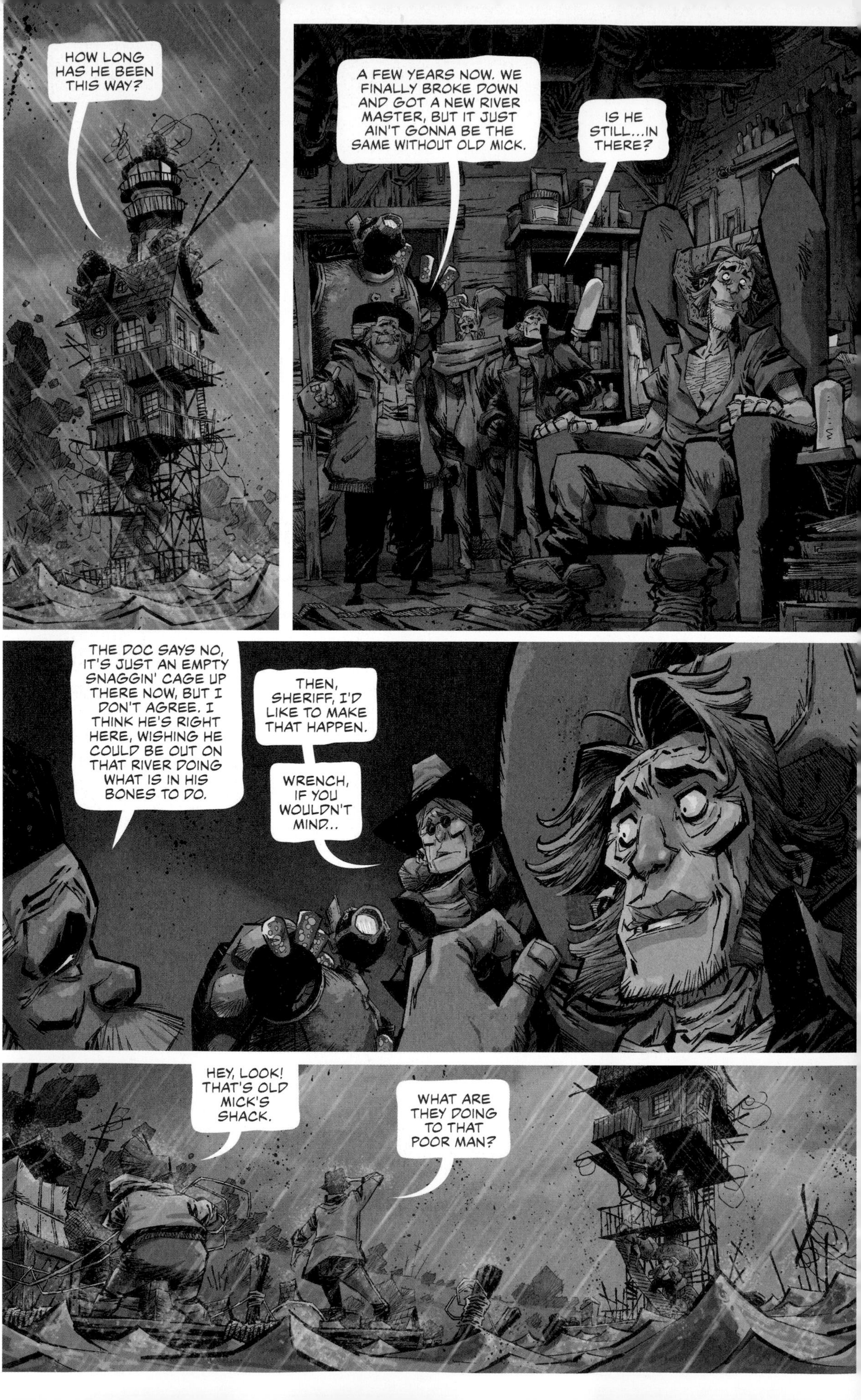
HOW LONG HAS HE BEEN THIS WAY?
A FEW YEARS NOW. WE FINALLY BROKE DOWN AND GOT A NEW RIVER MASTER, BUT IT JUST AIN'T GONNA BE THE SAME WITHOUT OLD MICK.
IS HE STILL...IN THERE?
THE DOC SAYS NO, IT'S JUST AN EMPTY SNAGGIN' CAGE UP THERE NOW, BUT I DON'T AGREE. I THINK HE'S RIGHT HERE, WISHING HE COULD BE OUT ON THAT RIVER DOING WHAT IS IN HIS BONES TO DO.
THEN, SHERIFF, I'D LIKE TO MAKE THAT HAPPEN.
WRENCH, IF YOU WOULDN'T MIND...
HEY, LOOK! THAT'S OLD MICK'S SHACK.
WHAT ARE THEY DOING TO THAT POOR MAN?

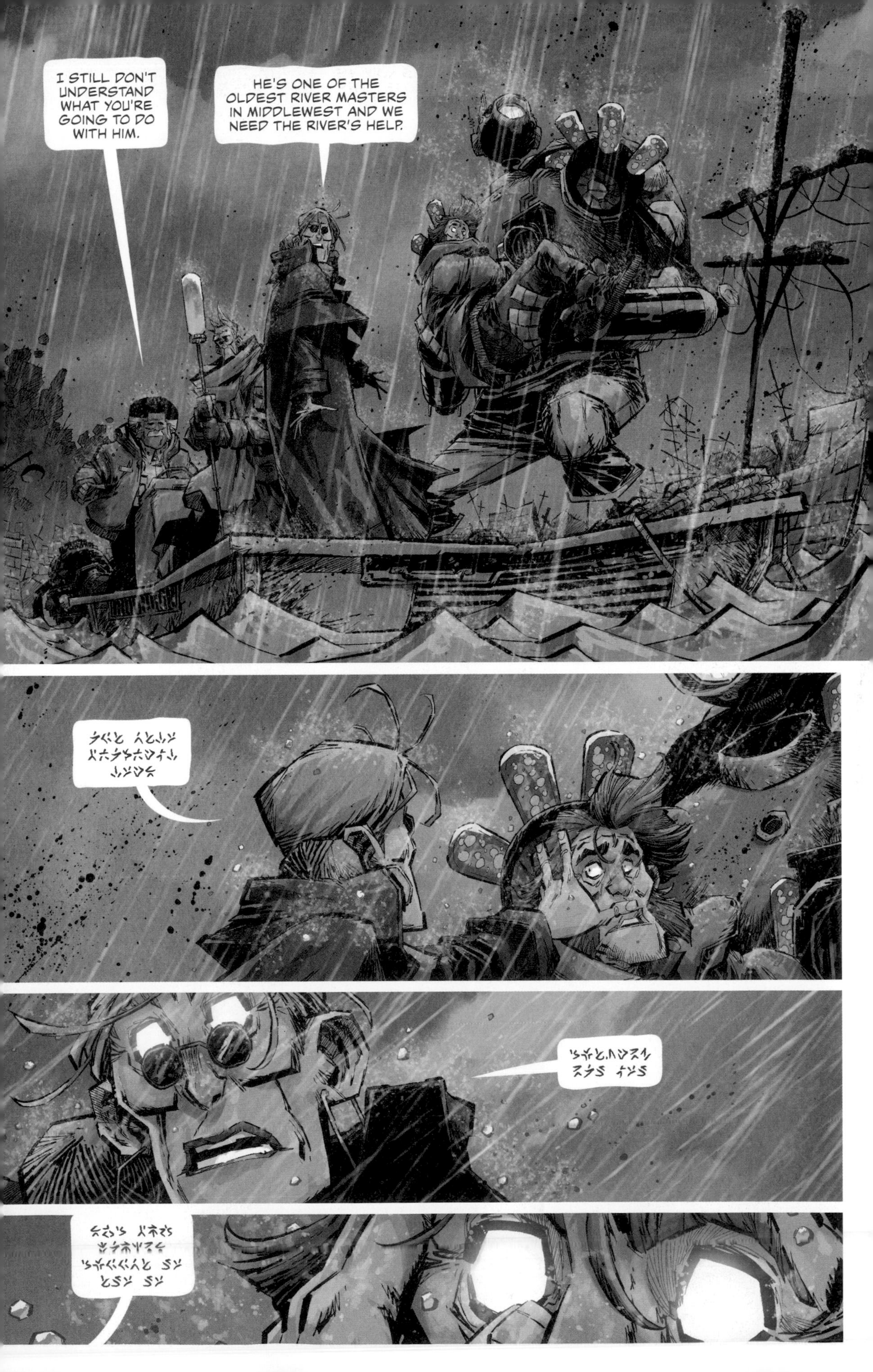
I STILL DON'T UNDERSTAND WHAT YOU'RE GOING TO DO WITH HIM.
HE'S ONE OF THE OLDEST RIVER MASTERS IN MIDDLEWEST AND WE NEED THE RIVER'S HELP.

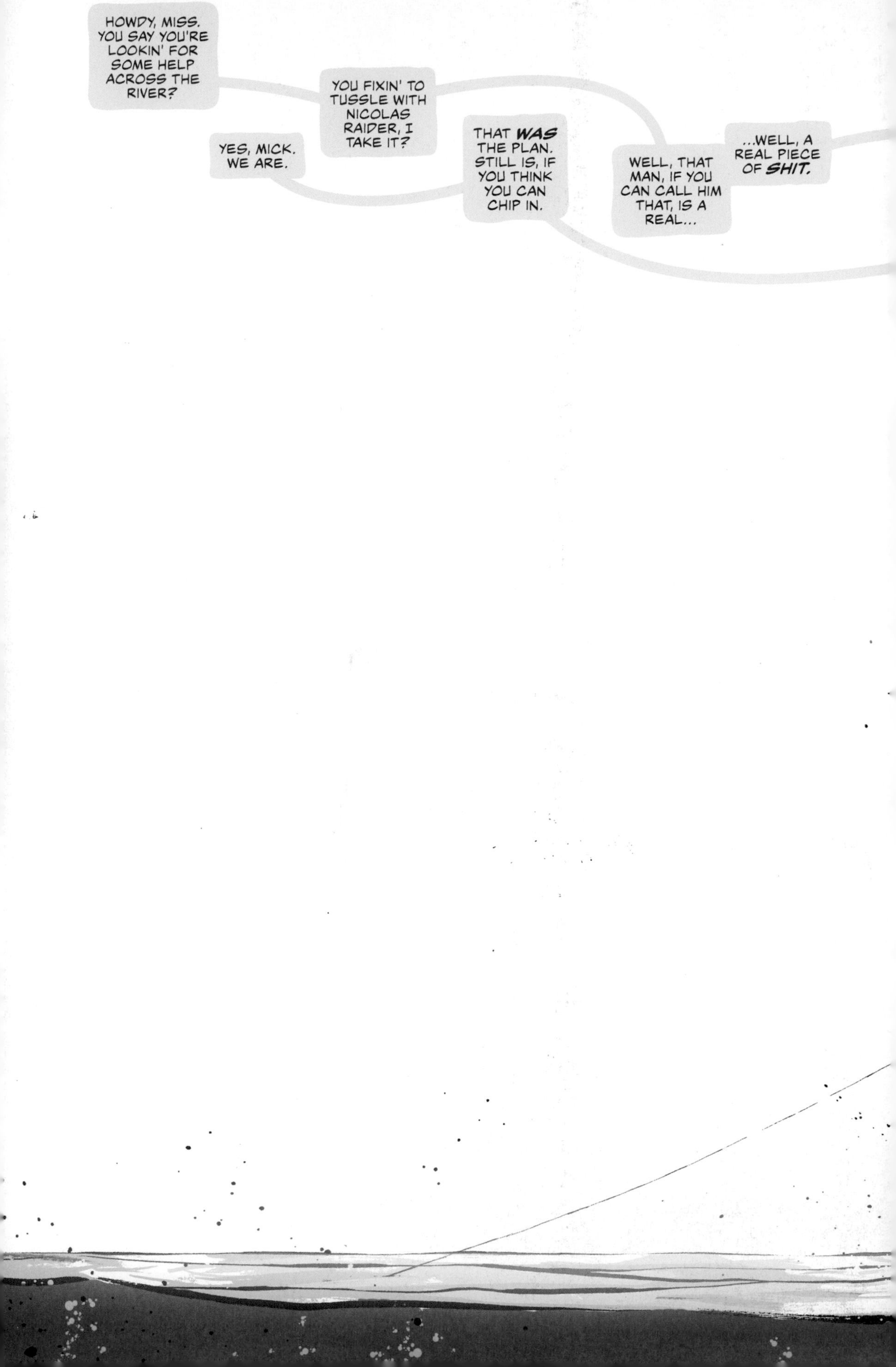
HOWDY, MISS. YOU SAY YOU'RE LOOKIN' FOR SOME HELP ACROSS THE RIVER?
YES, MICK. WE ARE.
YOU FIXIN' TO TUSSLE WITH NICOLAS RAIDER, I TAKE IT?
THAT WAS THE PLAN. STILL IS, IF YOU THINK YOU CAN CHIP IN.
WELL, THAT MAN, IF YOU CAN CALL HIM THAT, IS A REAL...
...WELL, A REAL PIECE OF SHIT.

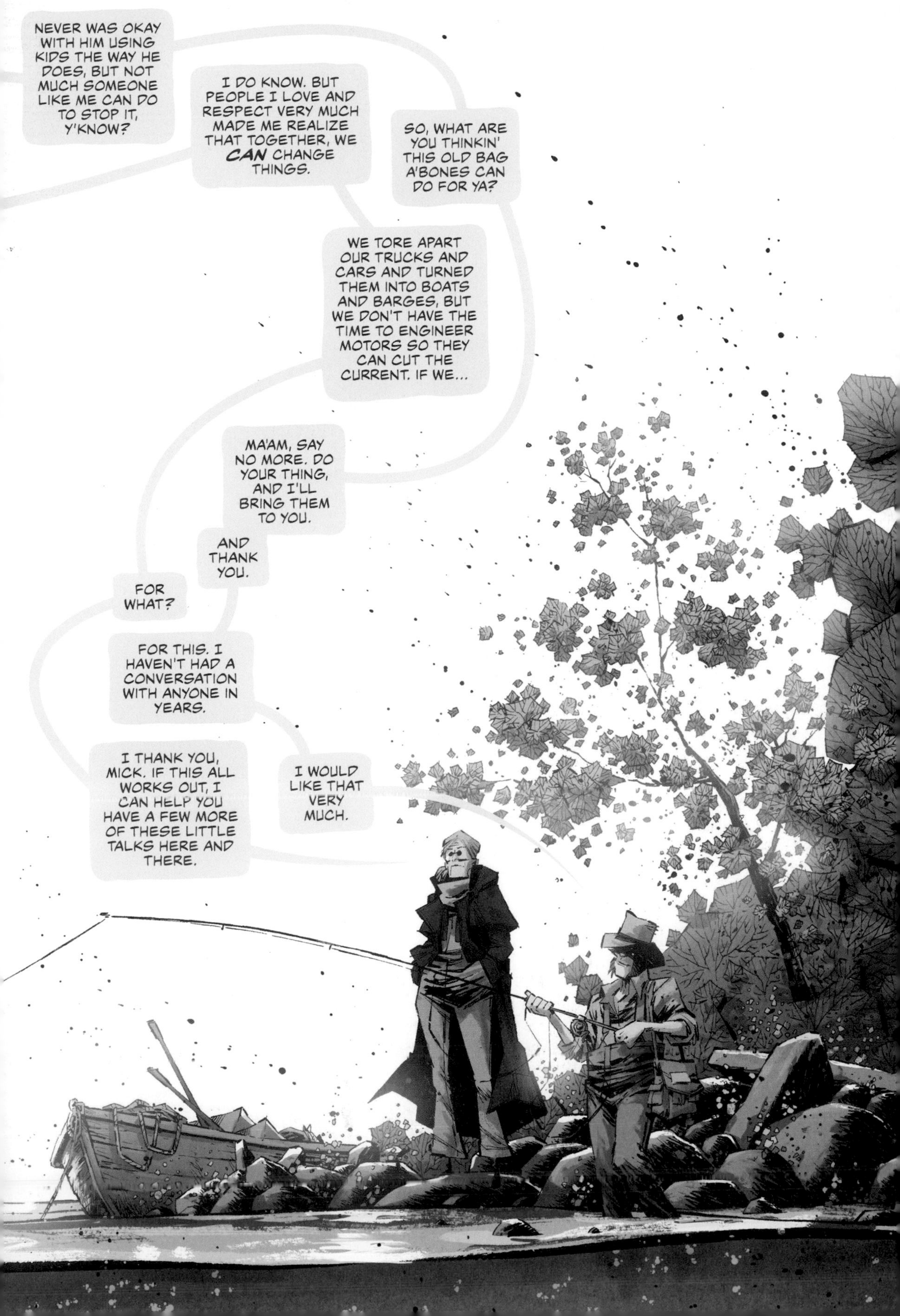
NEVER WAS OKAY WITH HIM USING KIDS THE WAY HE DOES, BUT NOT MUCH SOMEONE LIKE ME CAN DO TO STOP IT, Y'KNOW?
I DO KNOW. BUT PEOPLE I LOVE AND RESPECT VERY MUCH MADE ME REALIZE THAT TOGETHER, WE CAN CHANGE THINGS.
SO, WHAT ARE YOU THINKIN' THIS OLD BAG A'BONES CAN DO FOR YA?
WE TORE APART OUR TRUCKS AND CARS AND TURNED THEM INTO BOATS AND BARGES, BUT WE DON'T HAVE THE TIME TO ENGINEER MOTORS SO THEY CAN CUT THE CURRENT. IF WE...
MA'AM, SAY NO MORE. DO YOUR THING, AND I'LL BRING THEM TO YOU.
AND THANK YOU.
FOR WHAT?
FOR THIS. I HAVEN'T HAD A CONVERSATION WITH ANYONE IN YEARS.
I THANK YOU, MICK. IF THIS ALL WORKS OUT, I CAN HELP YOU HAVE A FEW MORE OF THESE LITTLE TALKS HERE AND THERE.
I WOULD LIKE THAT VERY MUCH.

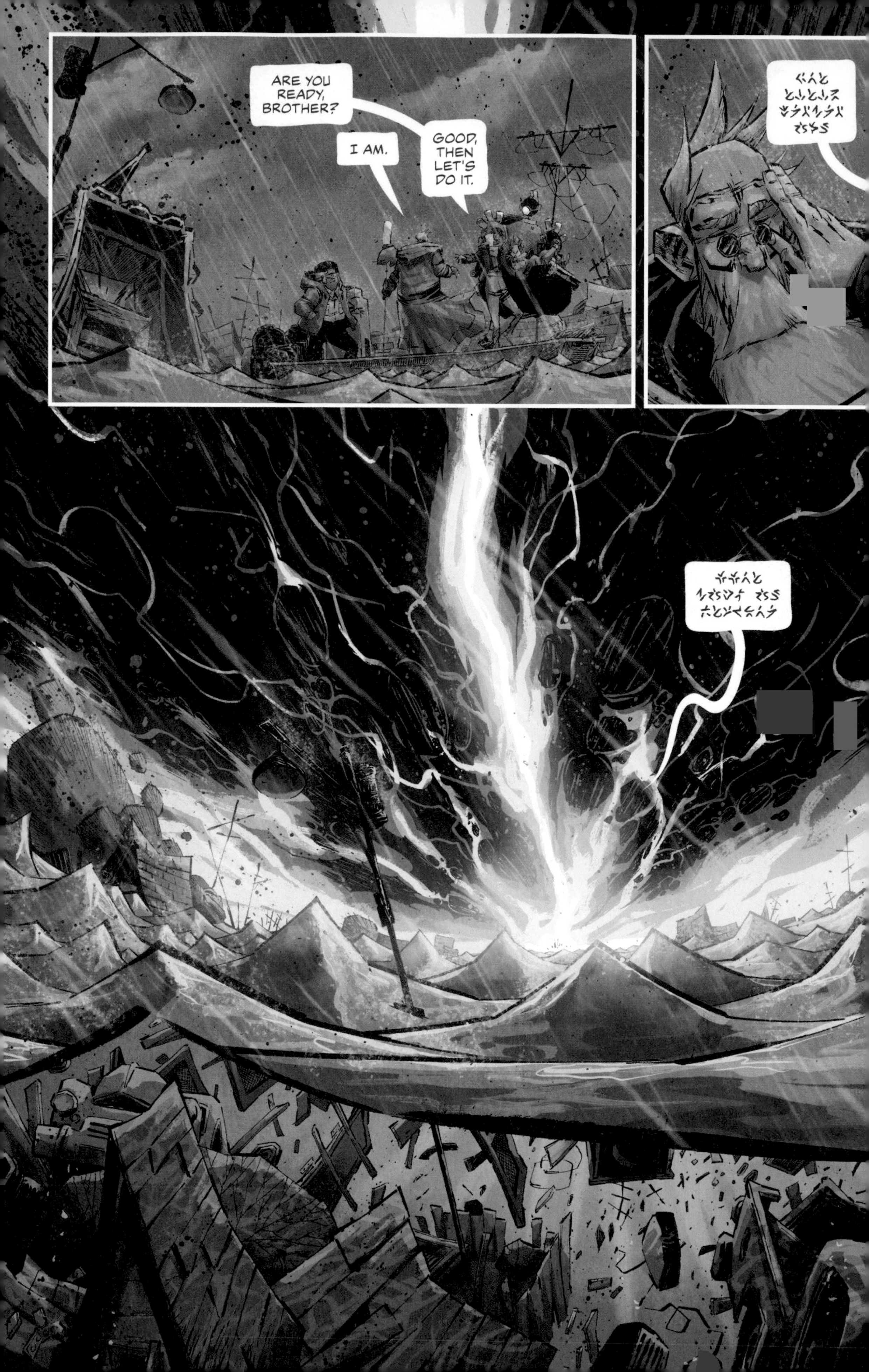
ARE YOU READY, BROTHER?
I AM.
GOOD, THEN LET'S DO IT.

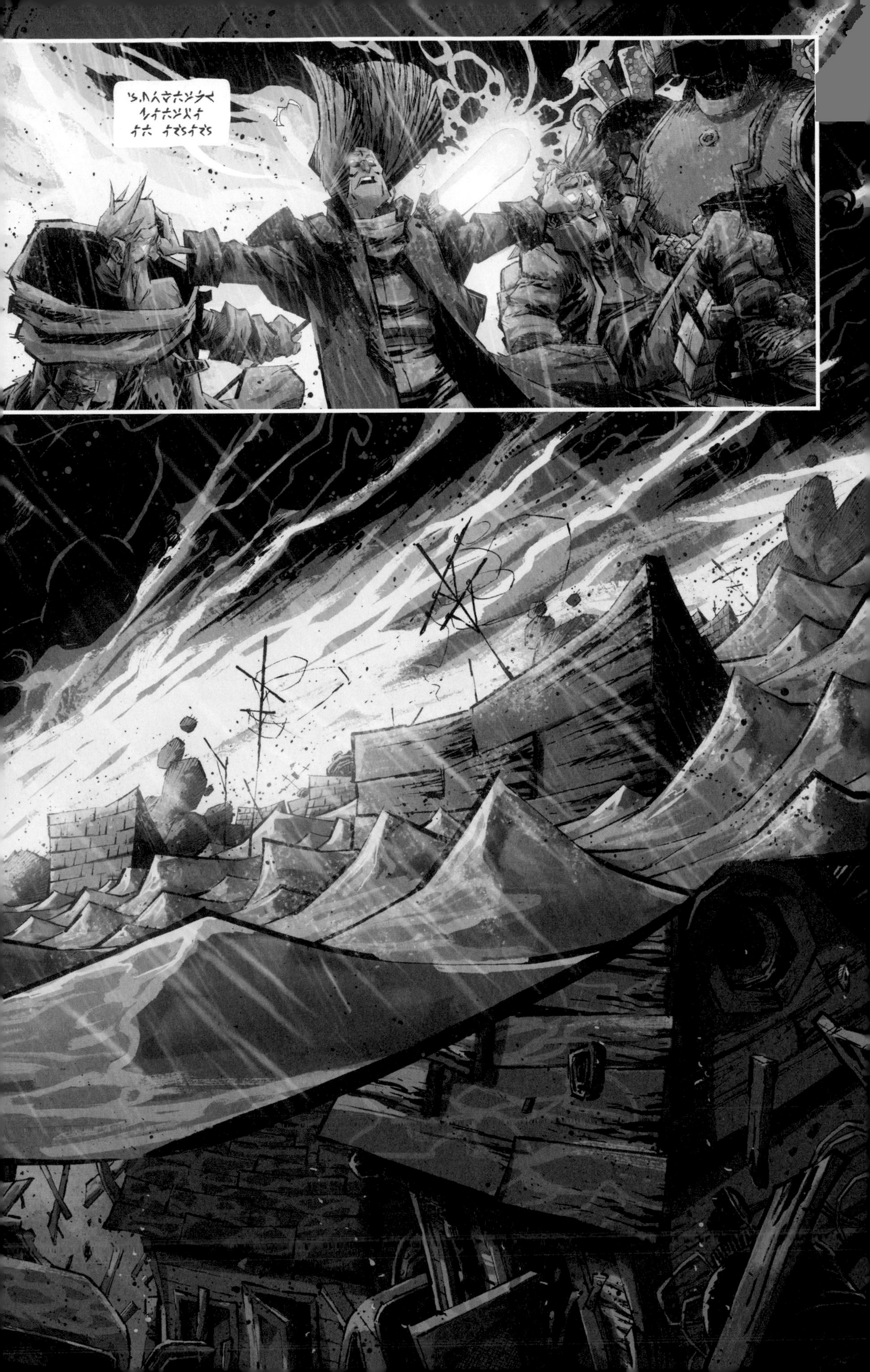

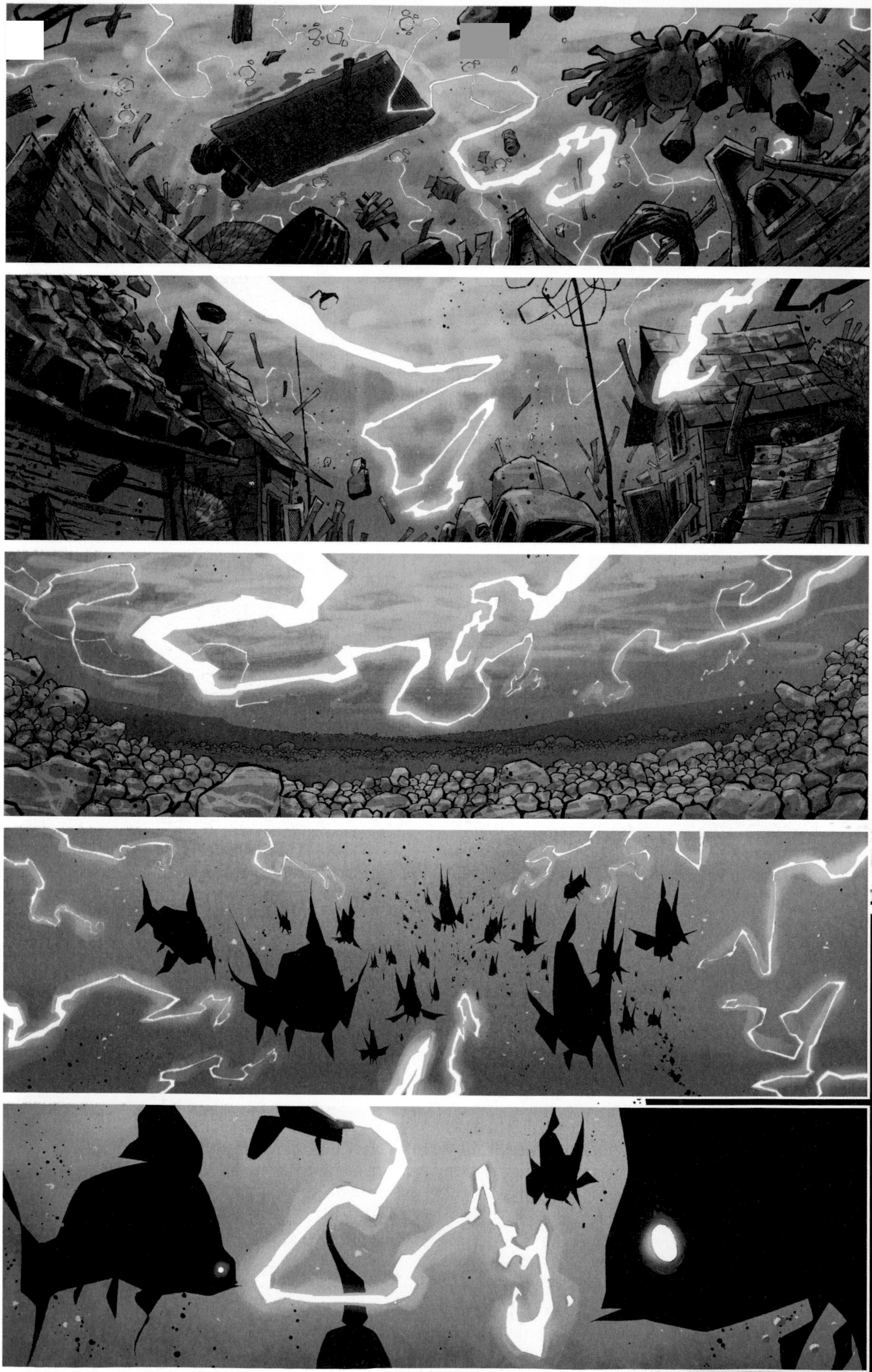

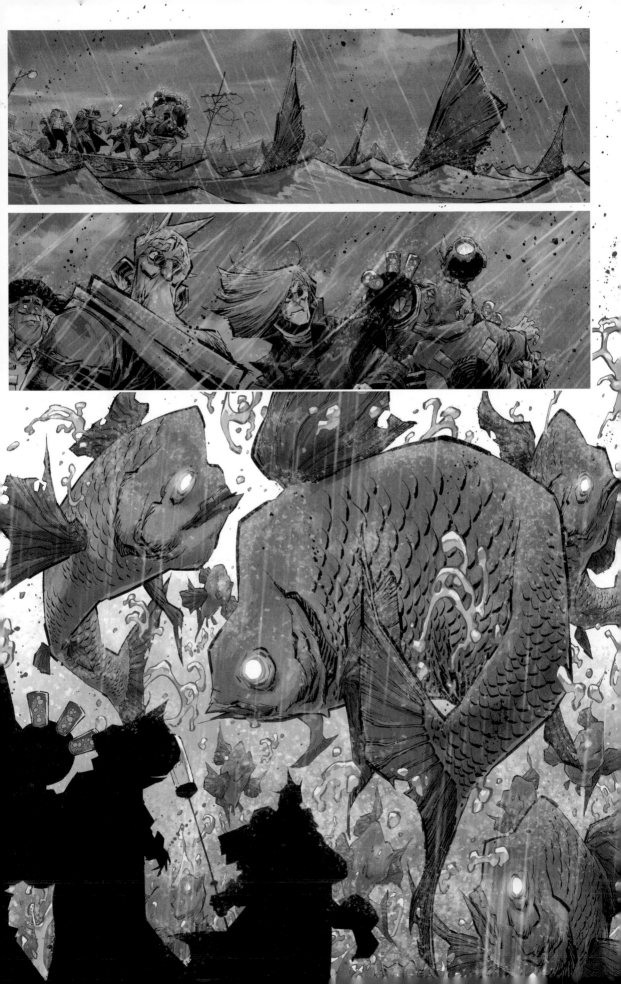

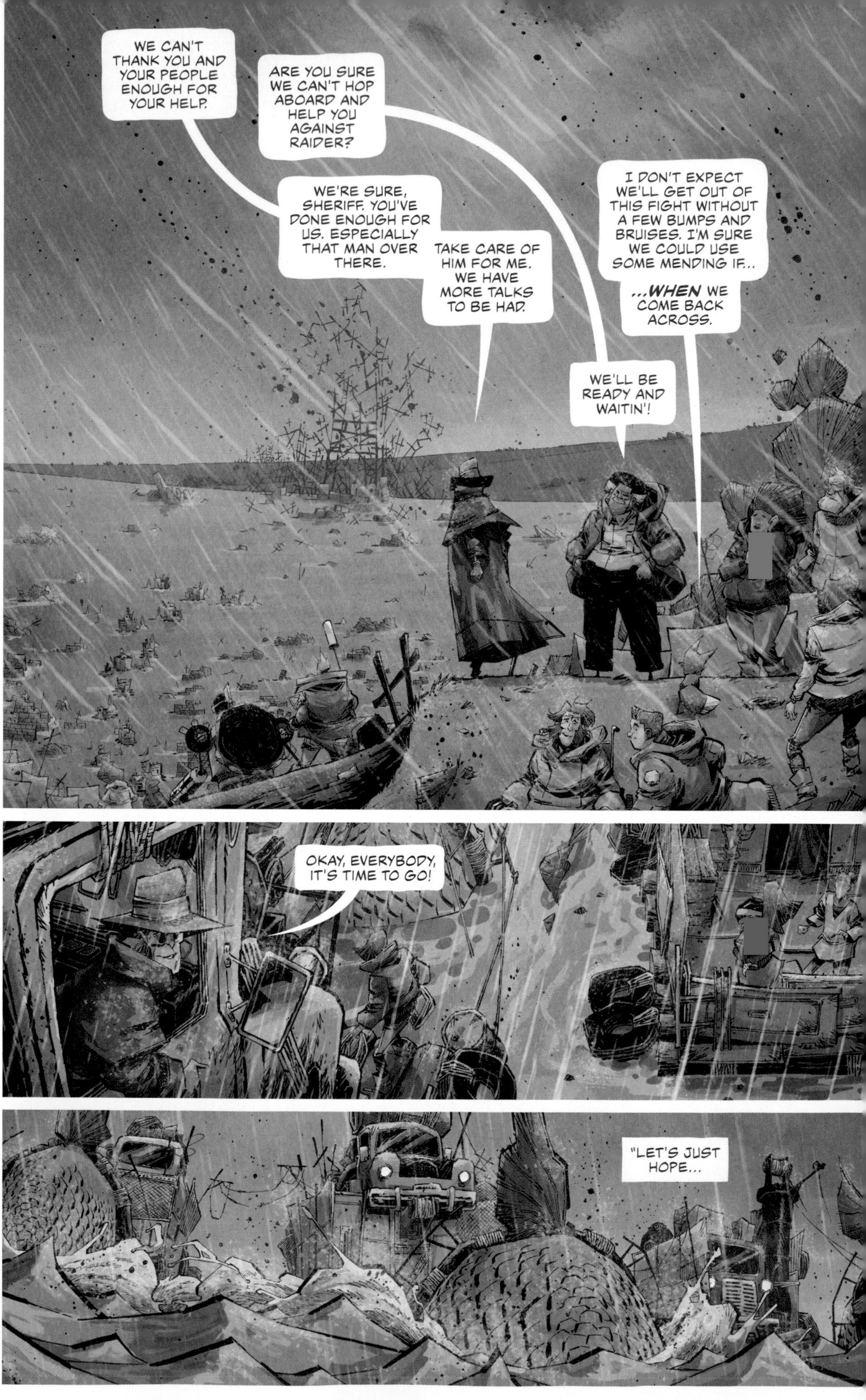

WE CAN'T THANK YOU AND YOUR PEOPLE ENOUGH FOR YOUR HELP.
ARE YOU SURE WE CAN'T HOP ABOARD AND HELP YOU AGAINST RAIDER?
WE'RE SURE, SHERIFF. YOU'VE DONE ENOUGH FOR US. ESPECIALLY THAT MAN OVER THERE.
TAKE CARE OF HIM FOR ME. WE HAVE MORE TALKS TO BE HAD.
I DON'T EXPECT WE'LL GET OUT OF THIS FIGHT WITHOUT A FEW BUMPS AND BRUISES. I'M SURE WE COULD USE SOME MENDING IF...
...WHEN WE COME BACK ACROSS.
WE'LL BE READY AND WAITIN'!
OKAY, EVERYBODY, IT'S TIME TO GO!
"LET'S JUST HOPE...

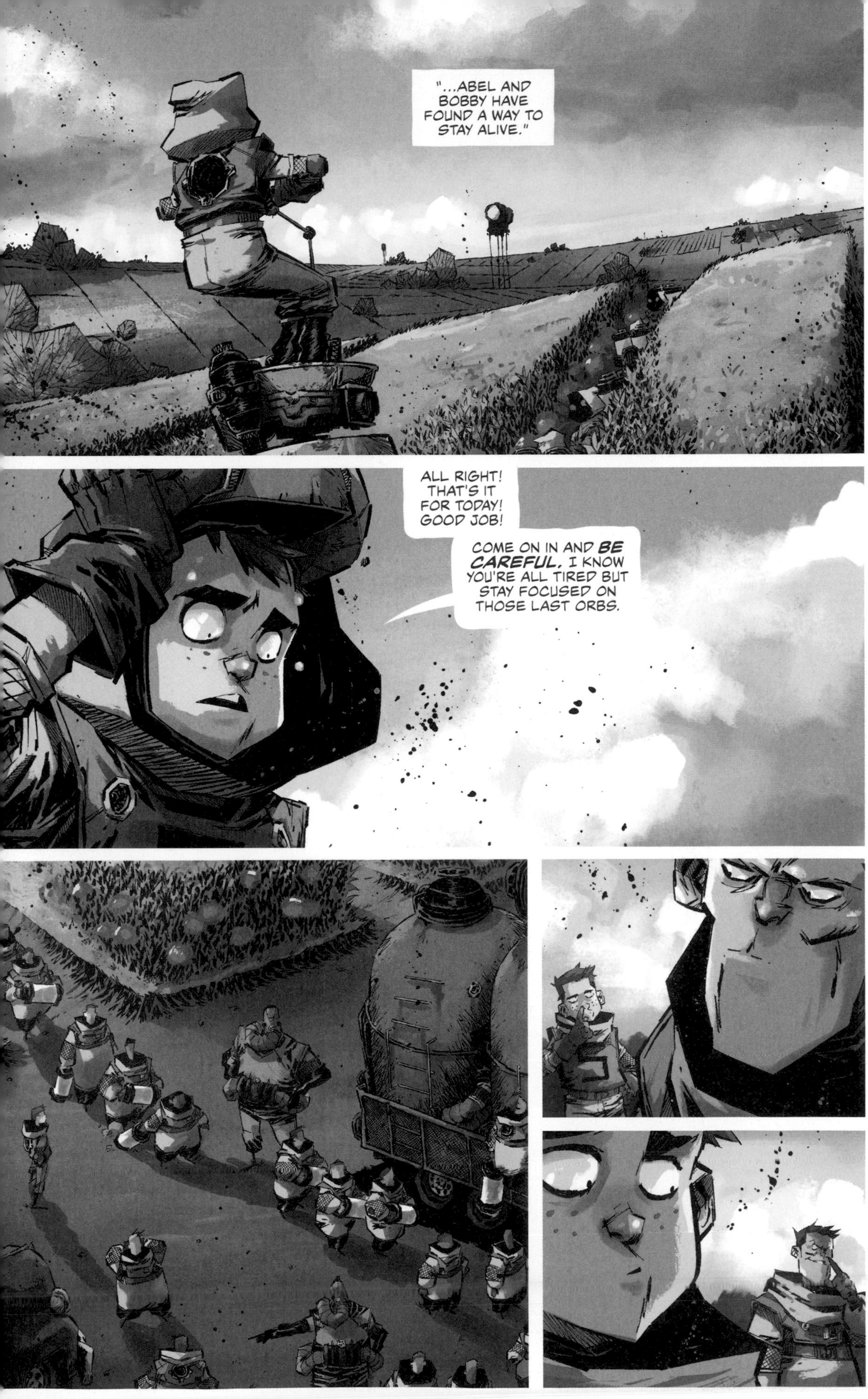
"...ABEL AND BOBBY HAVE FOUND A WAY TO STAY ALIVE."
ALL RIGHT! THAT'S IT FOR TODAY! GOOD JOB!
COME ON IN AND **BE CAREFUL.** I KNOW YOU'RE ALL TIRED BUT STAY FOCUSED ON THOSE LAST ORBS.

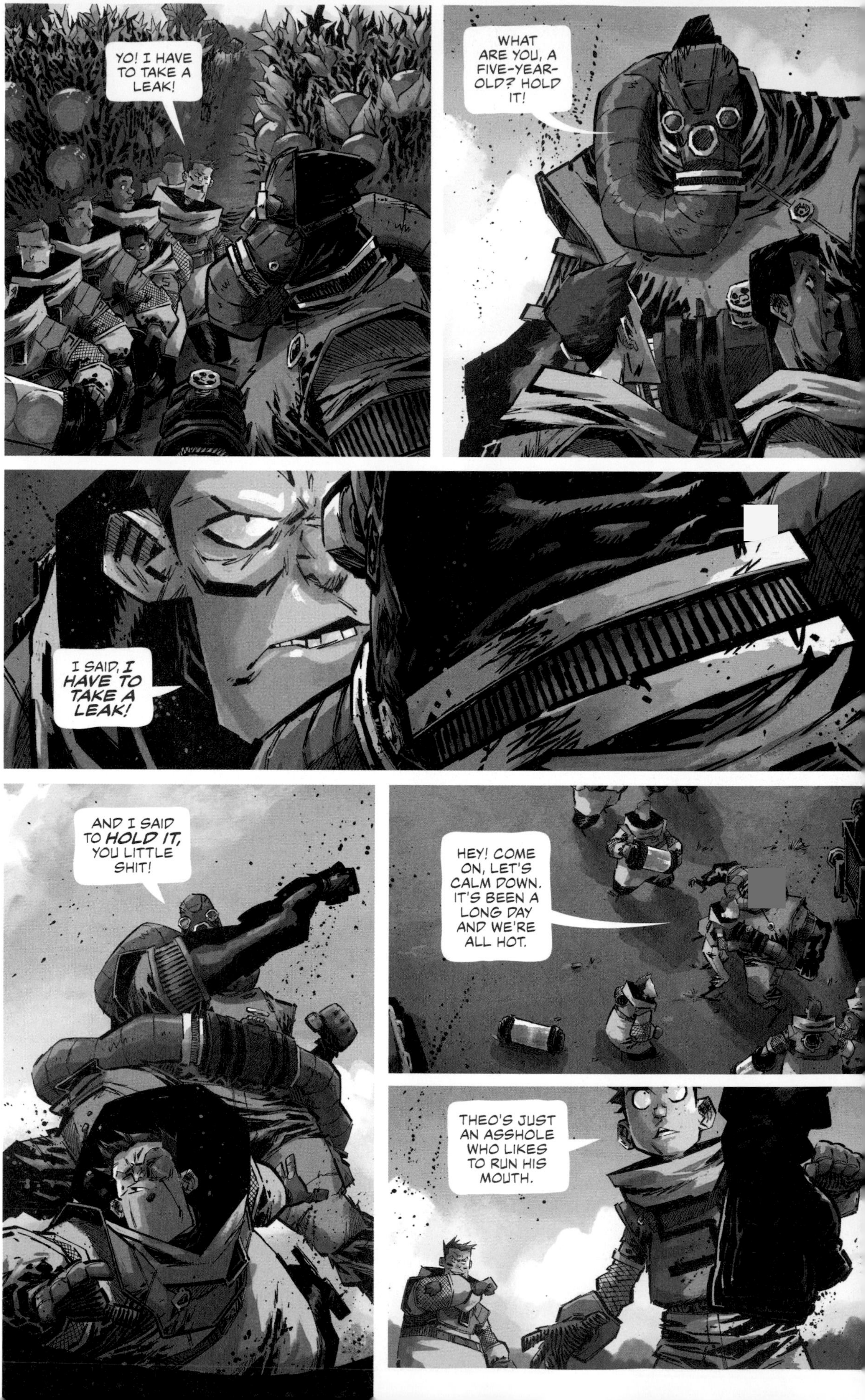
YO! I HAVE TO TAKE A LEAK!
WHAT ARE YOU, A FIVE-YEAR-OLD? HOLD IT!
I SAID, *I HAVE TO TAKE A LEAK!*
AND I SAID TO *HOLD IT,* YOU LITTLE SHIT!
HEY! COME ON, LET'S CALM DOWN. IT'S BEEN A LONG DAY AND WE'RE ALL HOT.
THEO'S JUST AN ASSHOLE WHO LIKES TO RUN HIS MOUTH.

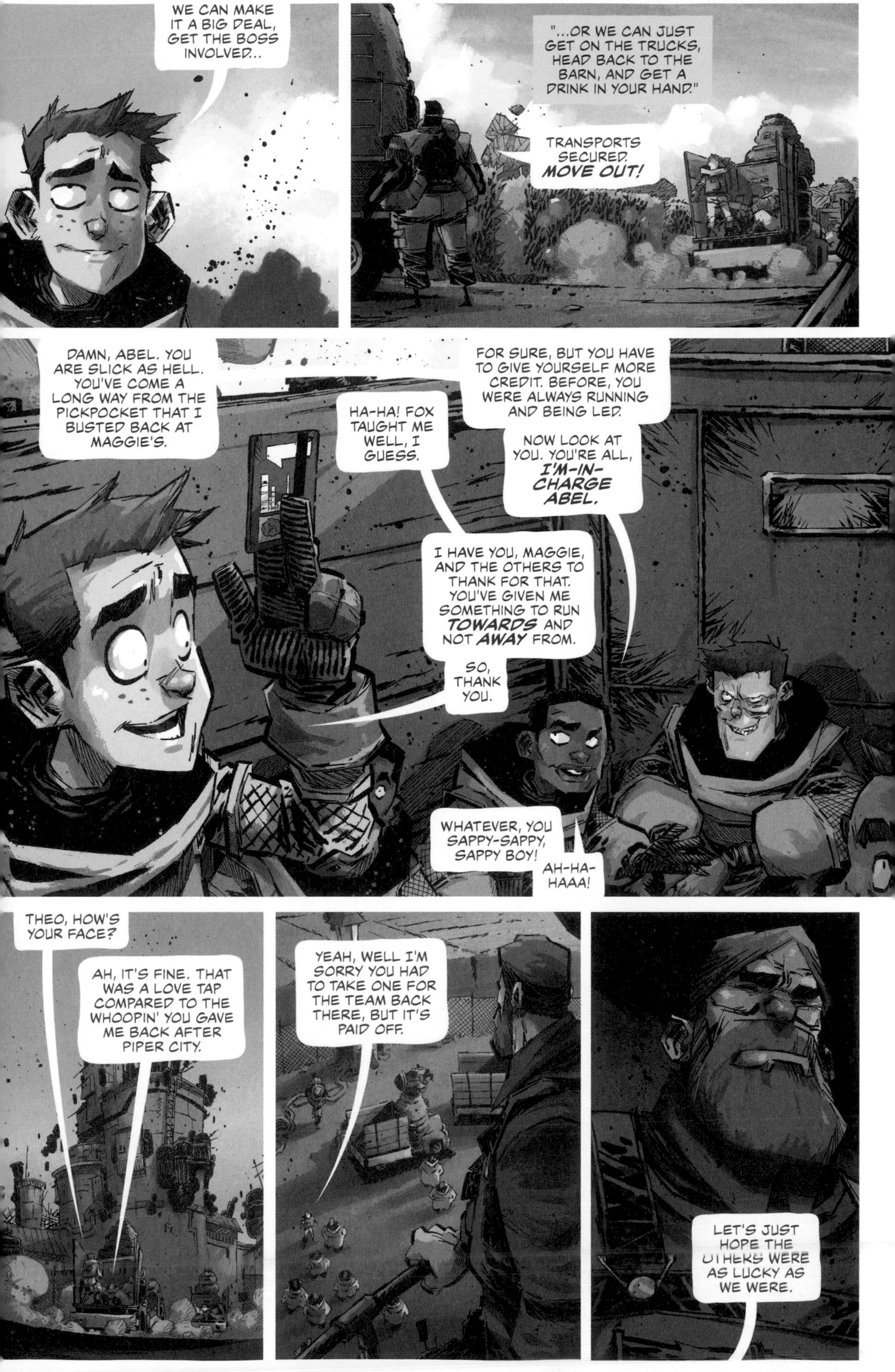
WE CAN MAKE IT A BIG DEAL, GET THE BOSS INVOLVED...
"...OR WE CAN JUST GET ON THE TRUCKS, HEAD BACK TO THE BARN, AND GET A DRINK IN YOUR HAND."
TRANSPORTS SECURED. MOVE OUT!
DAMN, ABEL. YOU ARE SLICK AS HELL. YOU'VE COME A LONG WAY FROM THE PICKPOCKET THAT I BUSTED BACK AT MAGGIE'S.
HA-HA! FOX TAUGHT ME WELL, I GUESS.
FOR SURE, BUT YOU HAVE TO GIVE YOURSELF MORE CREDIT. BEFORE, YOU WERE ALWAYS RUNNING AND BEING LED.
NOW LOOK AT YOU. YOU'RE ALL, I'M-IN-CHARGE ABEL.
I HAVE YOU, MAGGIE, AND THE OTHERS TO THANK FOR THAT. YOU'VE GIVEN ME SOMETHING TO RUN TOWARDS AND NOT AWAY FROM.
SO, THANK YOU.
WHATEVER, YOU SAPPY-SAPPY, SAPPY BOY!
AH-HA-HAAA!
THEO, HOW'S YOUR FACE?
AH, IT'S FINE. THAT WAS A LOVE TAP COMPARED TO THE WHOOPIN' YOU GAVE ME BACK AFTER PIPER CITY.
YEAH, WELL I'M SORRY YOU HAD TO TAKE ONE FOR THE TEAM BACK THERE, BUT IT'S PAID OFF.
LET'S JUST HOPE THE OTHERS WERE AS LUCKY AS WE WERE.

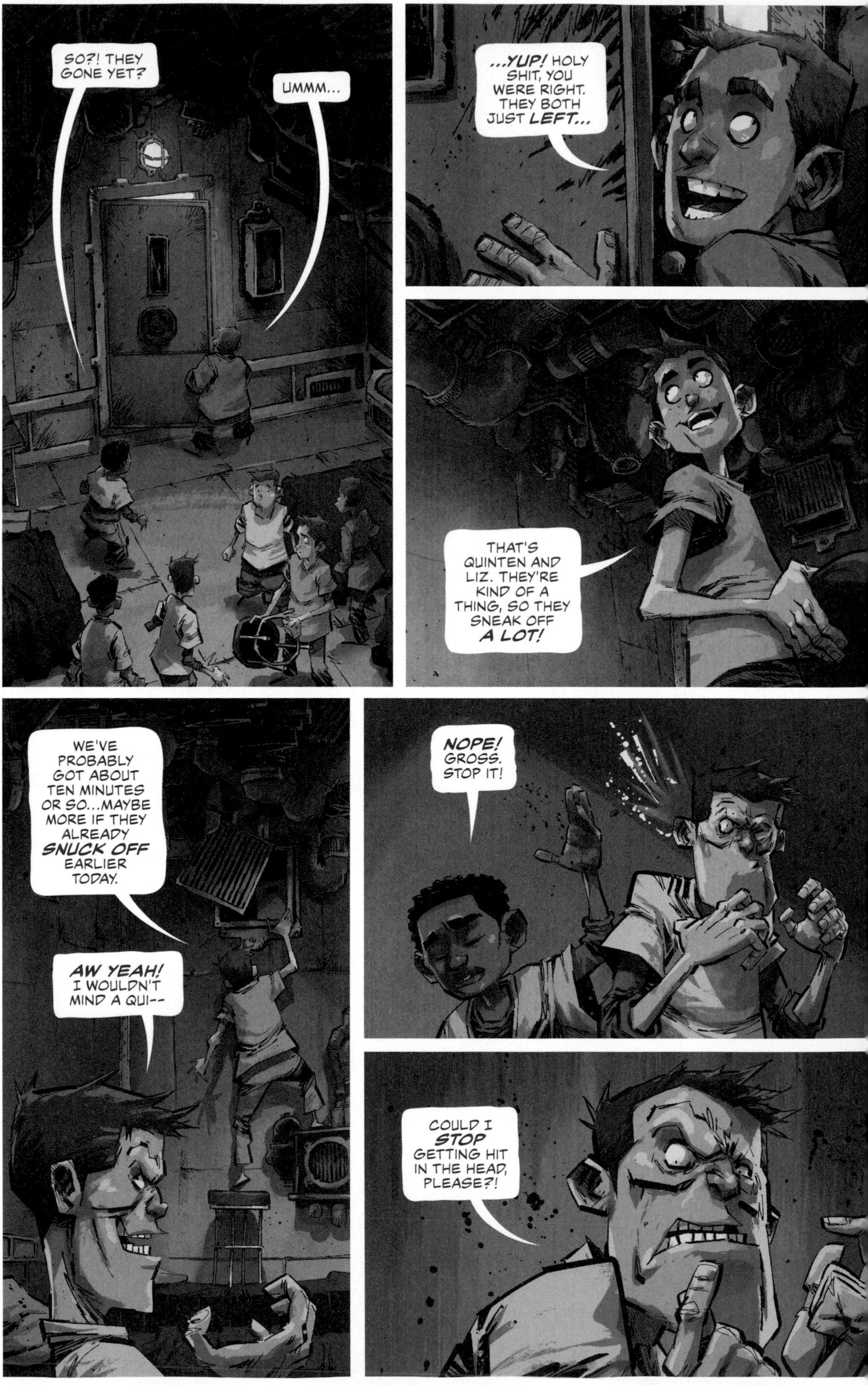
SO?! THEY GONE YET?
UMMM...
...YUP! HOLY SHIT, YOU WERE RIGHT. THEY BOTH JUST LEFT...
THAT'S QUINTEN AND LIZ. THEY'RE KIND OF A THING, SO THEY SNEAK OFF A LOT!
WE'VE PROBABLY GOT ABOUT TEN MINUTES OR SO...MAYBE MORE IF THEY ALREADY SNUCK OFF EARLIER TODAY.
AW YEAH! I WOULDN'T MIND A QUI--
NOPE! GROSS. STOP IT!
COULD I STOP GETTING HIT IN THE HEAD, PLEASE?!

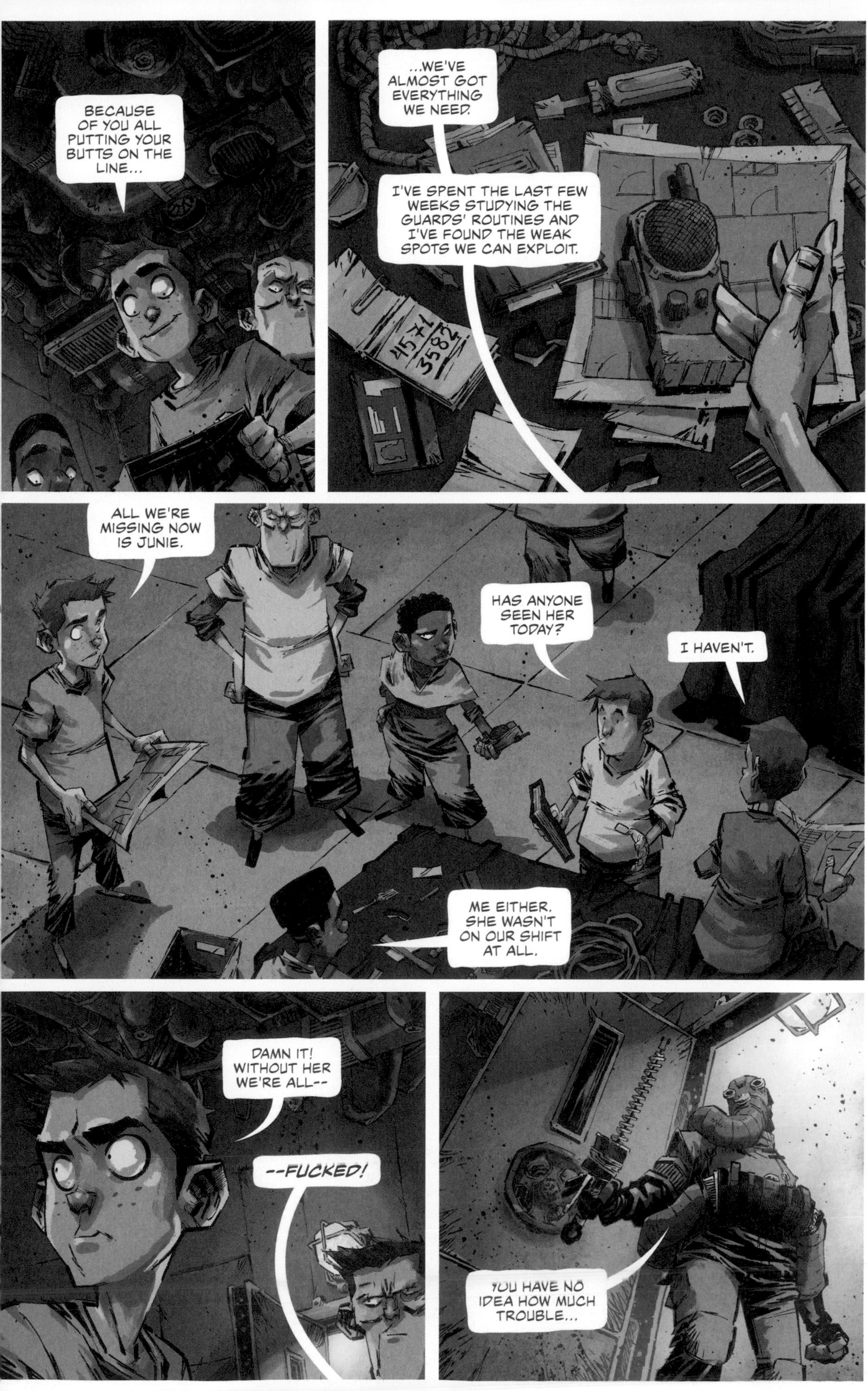
BECAUSE OF YOU ALL PUTTING YOUR BUTTS ON THE LINE...
...WE'VE ALMOST GOT EVERYTHING WE NEED.
I'VE SPENT THE LAST FEW WEEKS STUDYING THE GUARDS' ROUTINES AND I'VE FOUND THE WEAK SPOTS WE CAN EXPLOIT.
ALL WE'RE MISSING NOW IS JUNIE.
HAS ANYONE SEEN HER TODAY?
I HAVEN'T.
ME EITHER. SHE WASN'T ON OUR SHIFT AT ALL.
DAMN IT! WITHOUT HER WE'RE ALL--
--FUCKED!
YOU HAVE NO IDEA HOW MUCH TROUBLE...

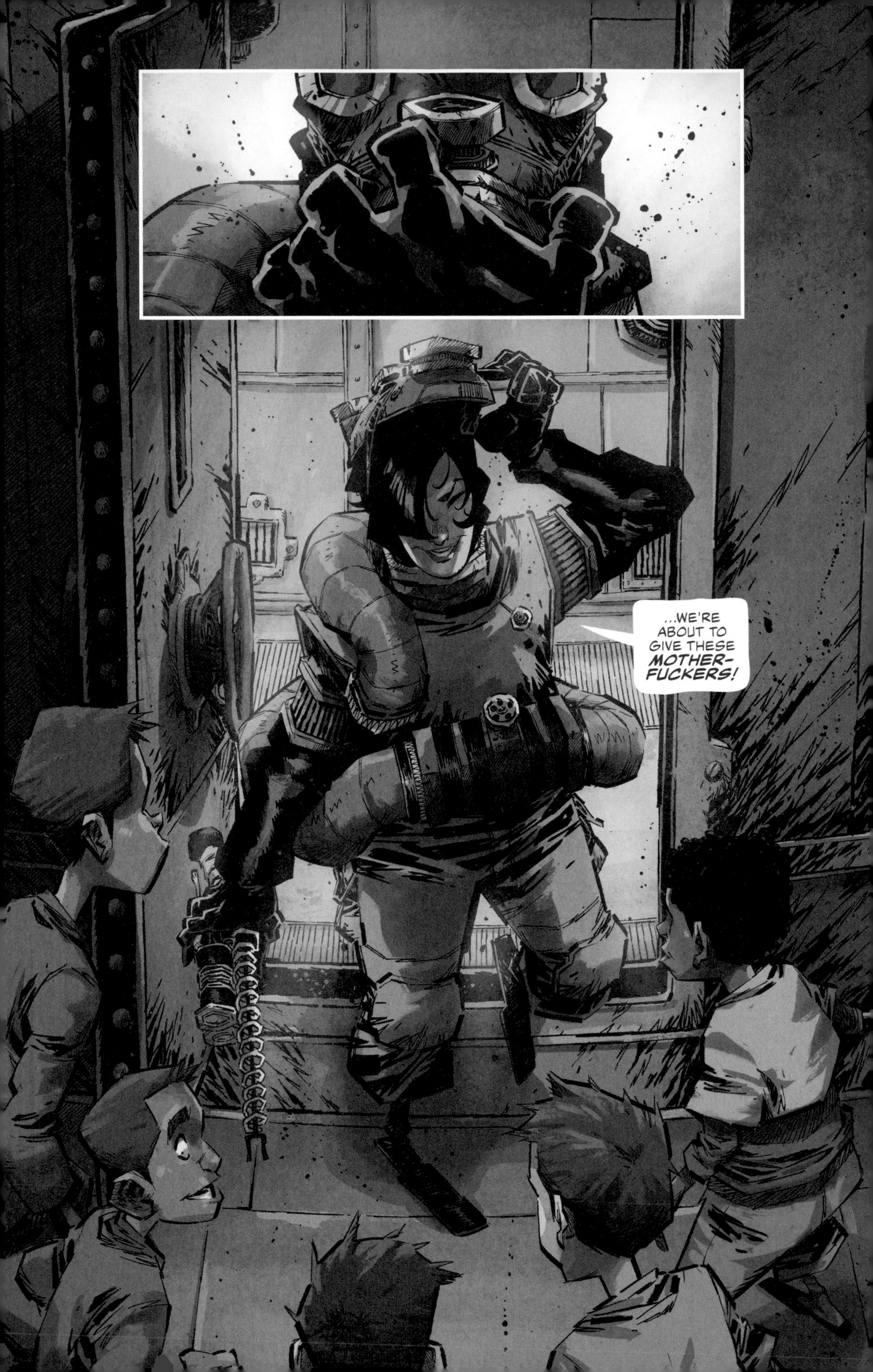
...WE'RE ABOUT TO GIVE THESE MOTHER-FUCKERS!

CHAPTER SIXTEEN

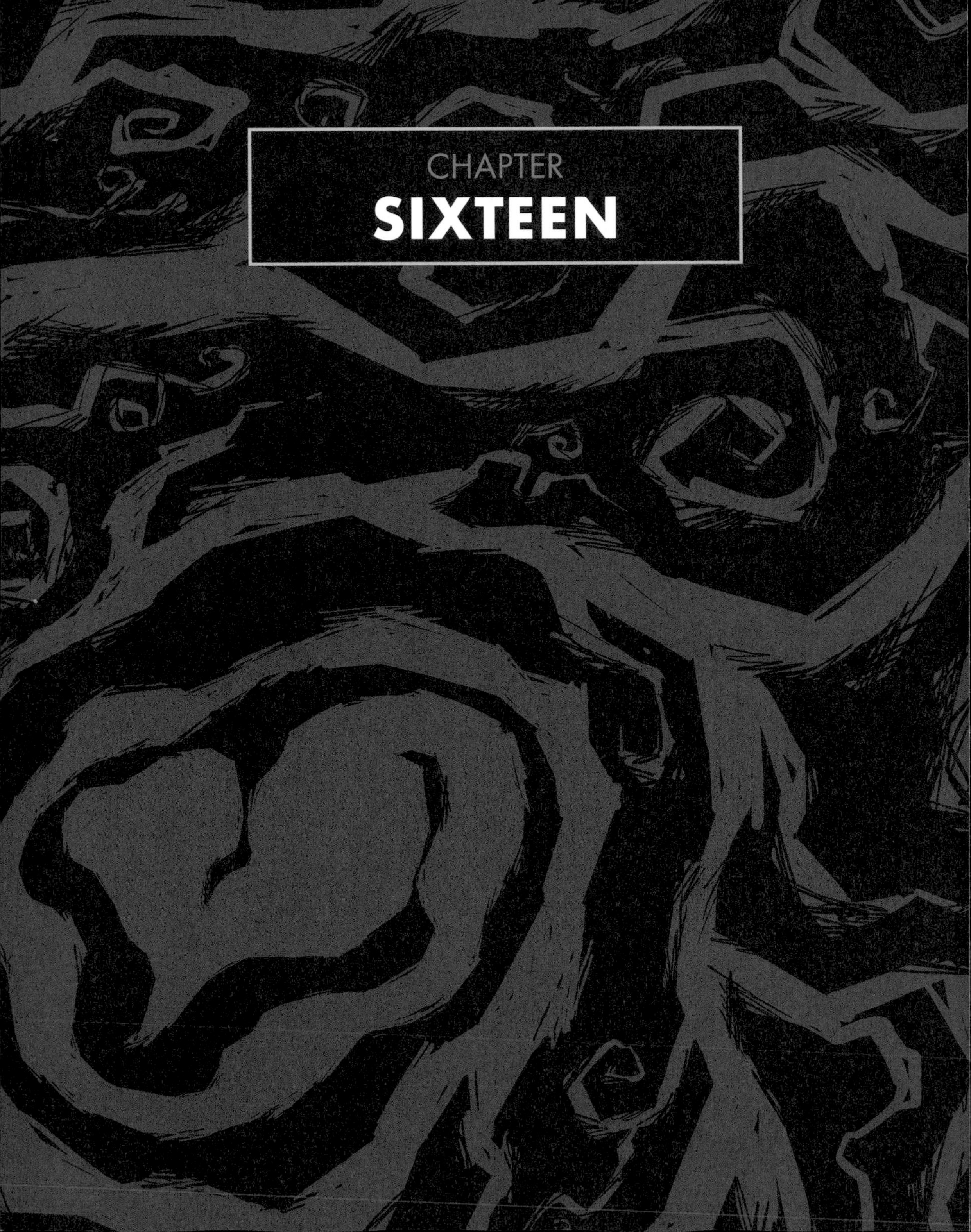

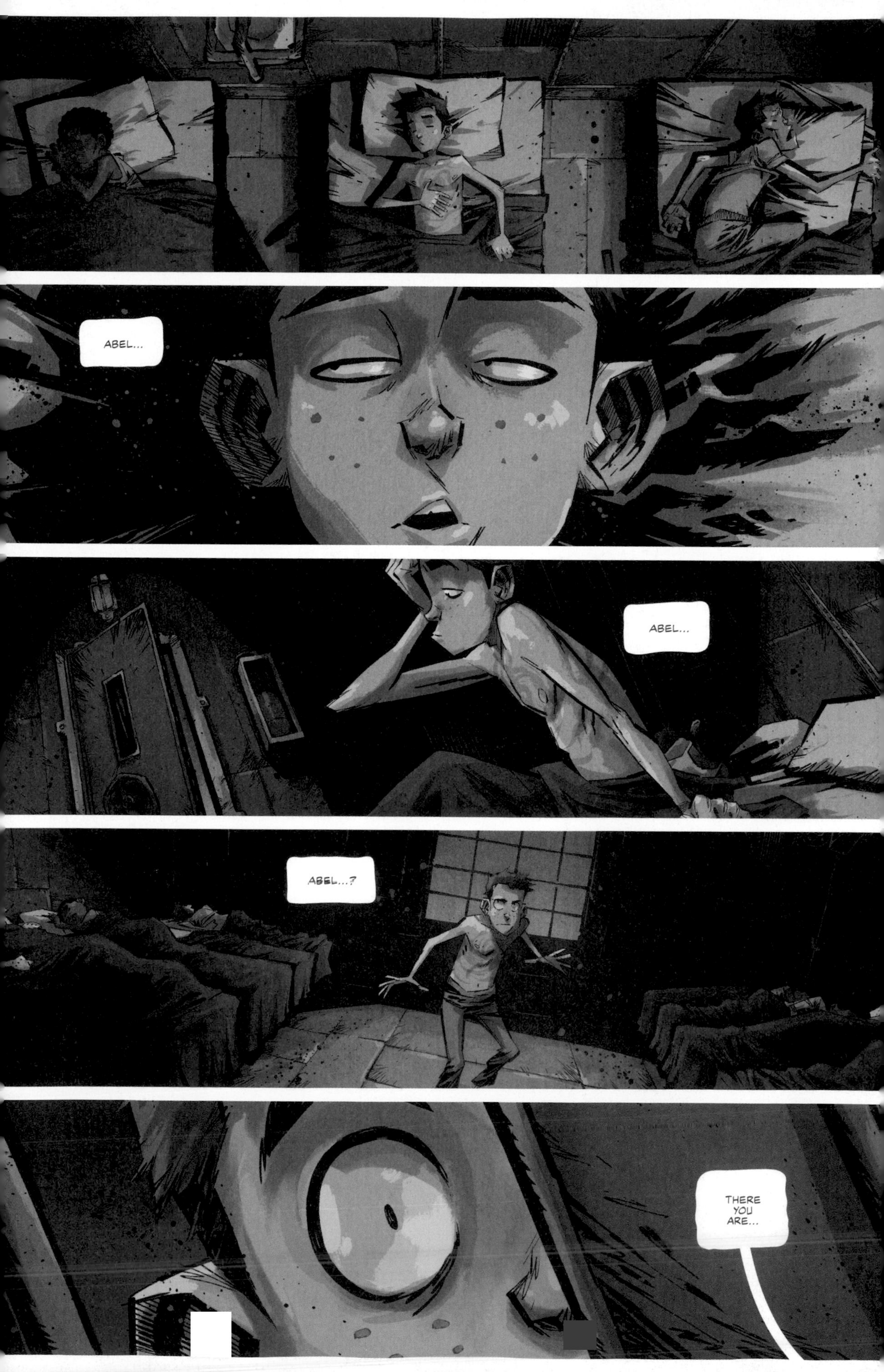
ABEL...
ABEL...
ABEL...?
THERE YOU ARE...

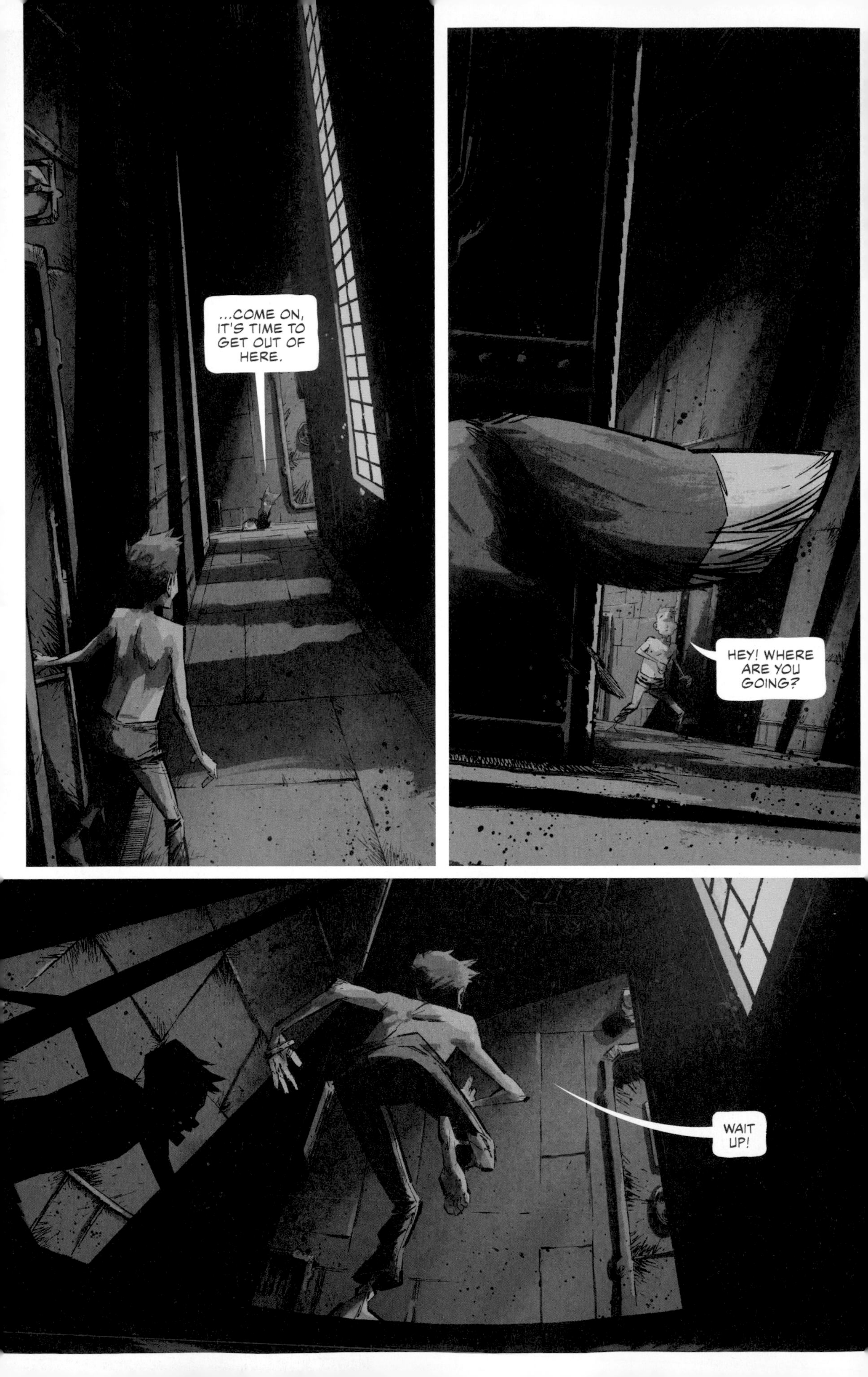
...COME ON, IT'S TIME TO GET OUT OF HERE.
HEY! WHERE ARE YOU GOING?
WAIT UP!

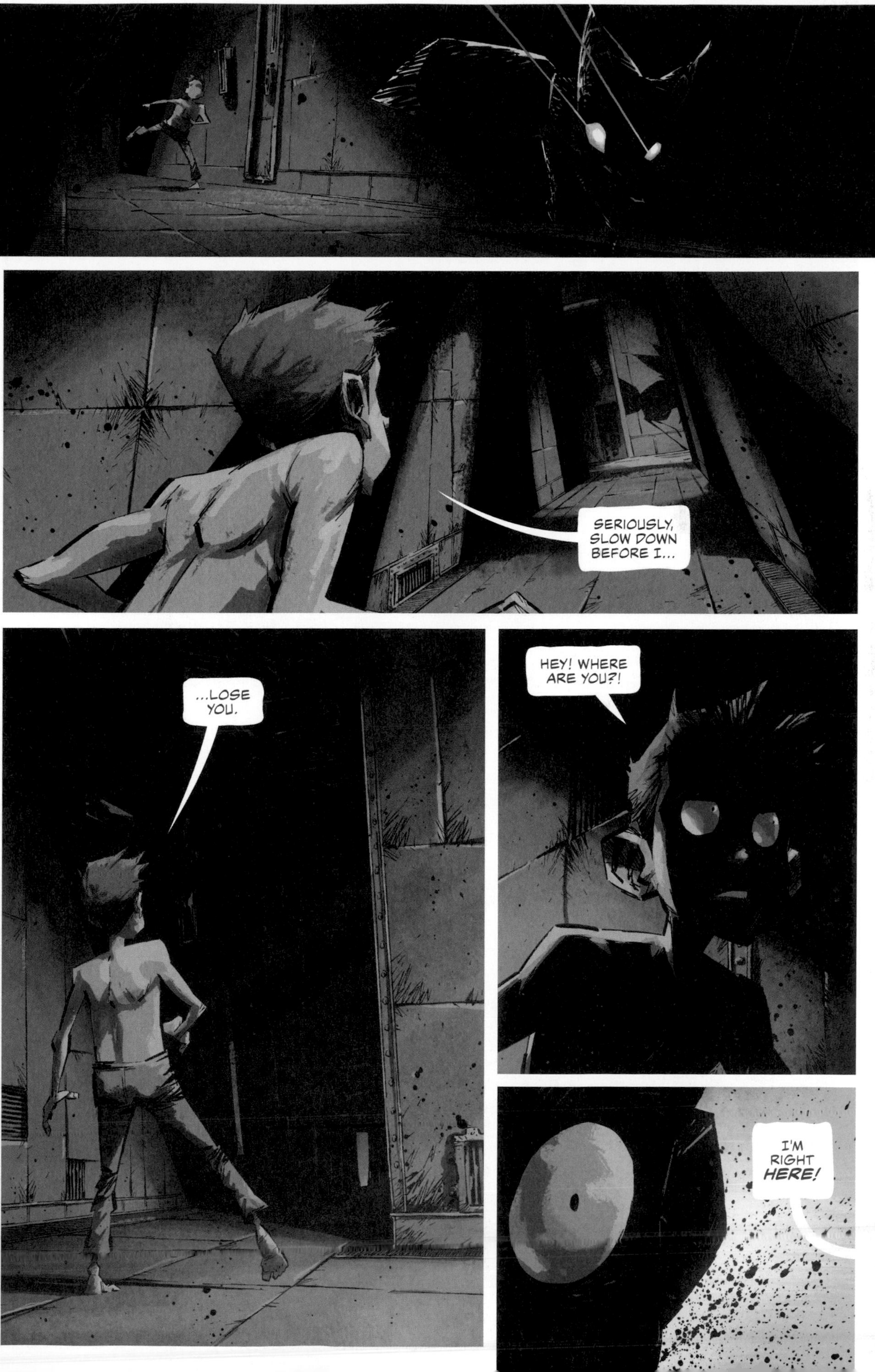
SERIOUSLY, SLOW DOWN BEFORE I...
...LOSE YOU.
HEY! WHERE ARE YOU?!
I'M RIGHT *HERE!*

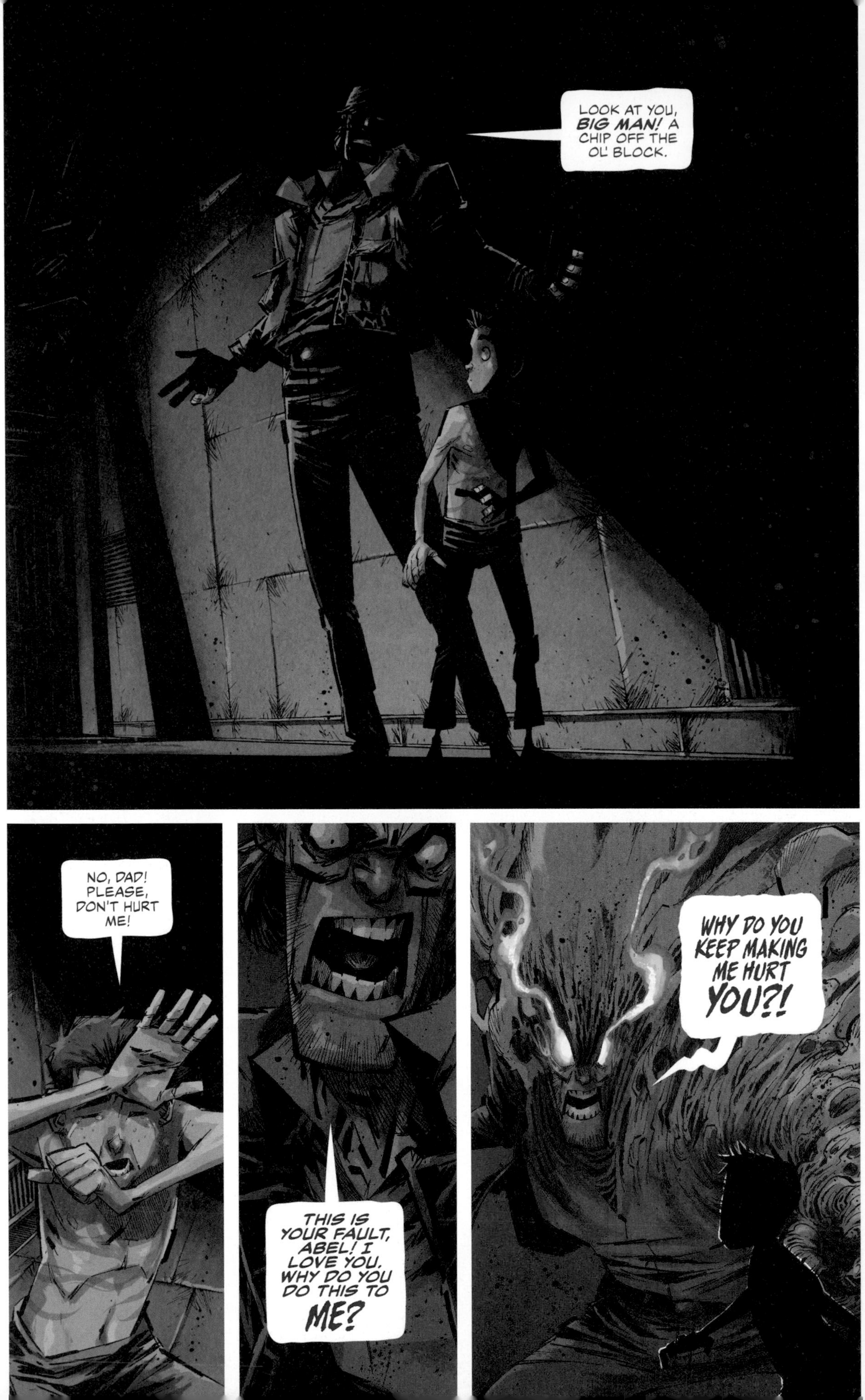
LOOK AT YOU, BIG MAN! A CHIP OFF THE OL' BLOCK.
NO, DAD! PLEASE, DON'T HURT ME!
THIS IS YOUR FAULT, ABEL! I LOVE YOU. WHY DO YOU DO THIS TO ME?
WHY DO YOU KEEP MAKING ME HURT YOU?!

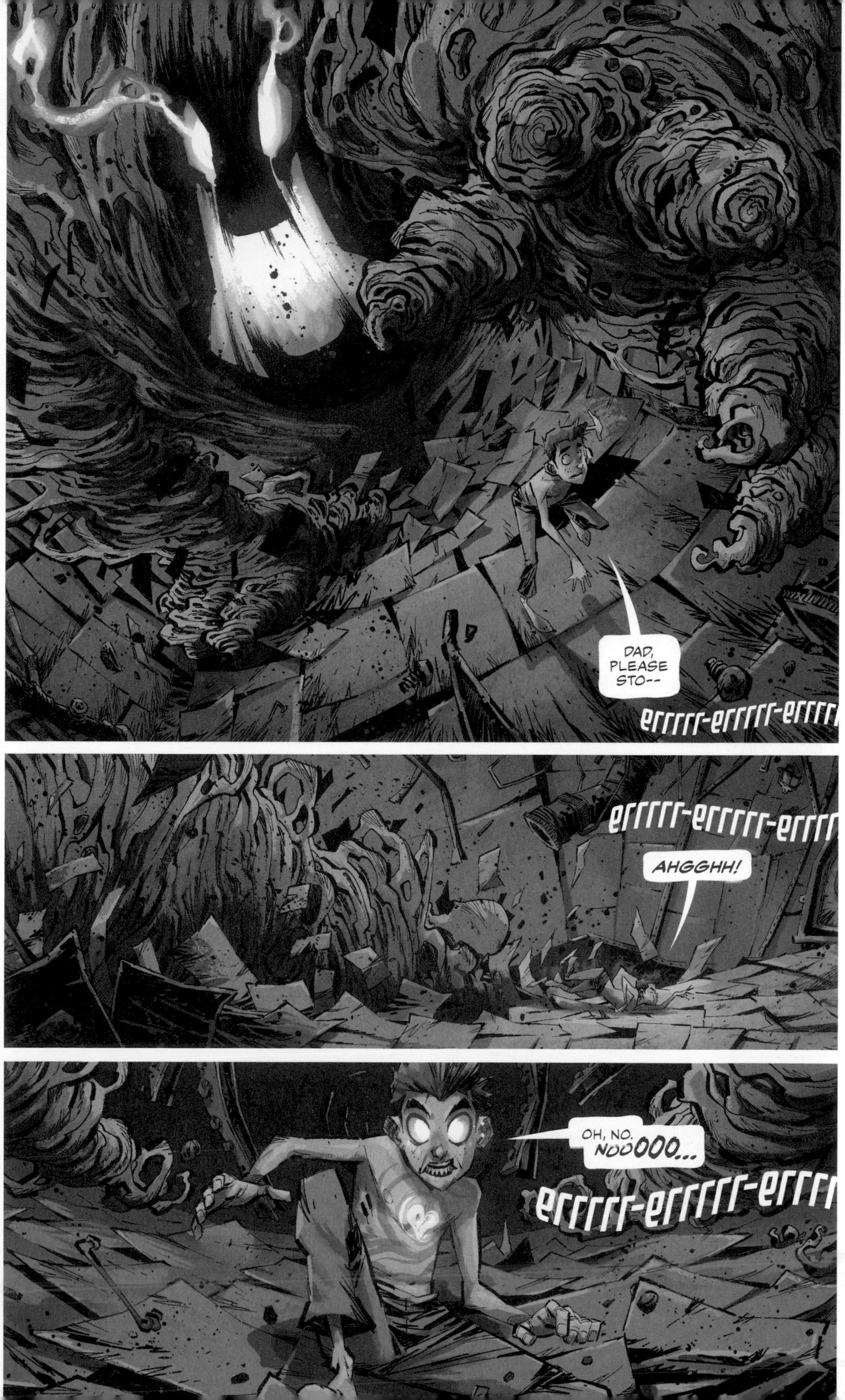
DAD, PLEASE STO--
errrrr-errrrr-errrr
errrrr-errrrr-errrr
AHGGHH!
OH, NO. NOOOOO...
errrrr-errrrr-errrr

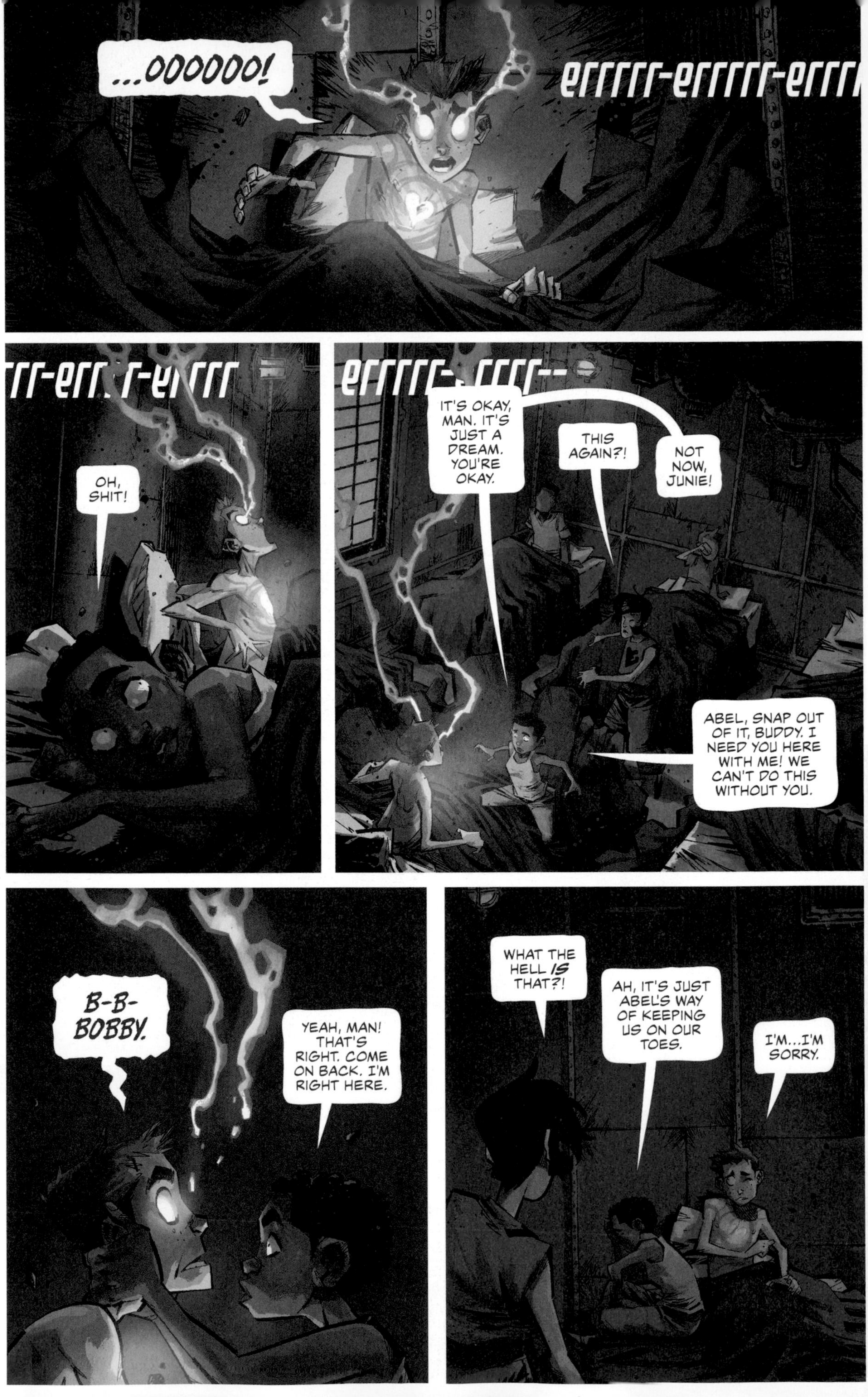

...OOOOOO!
errrrr-errrrr-errrr
rrr-errrr-errrr
OH, SHIT!
errrrr-rrrr--
IT'S OKAY, MAN. IT'S JUST A DREAM. YOU'RE OKAY.
THIS AGAIN?!
NOT NOW, JUNIE!
ABEL, SNAP OUT OF IT, BUDDY. I NEED YOU HERE WITH ME! WE CAN'T DO THIS WITHOUT YOU.
B-B-BOBBY.
YEAH, MAN! THAT'S RIGHT. COME ON BACK. I'M RIGHT HERE.
WHAT THE HELL *IS* THAT?!
AH, IT'S JUST ABEL'S WAY OF KEEPING US ON OUR TOES.
I'M...I'M SORRY.

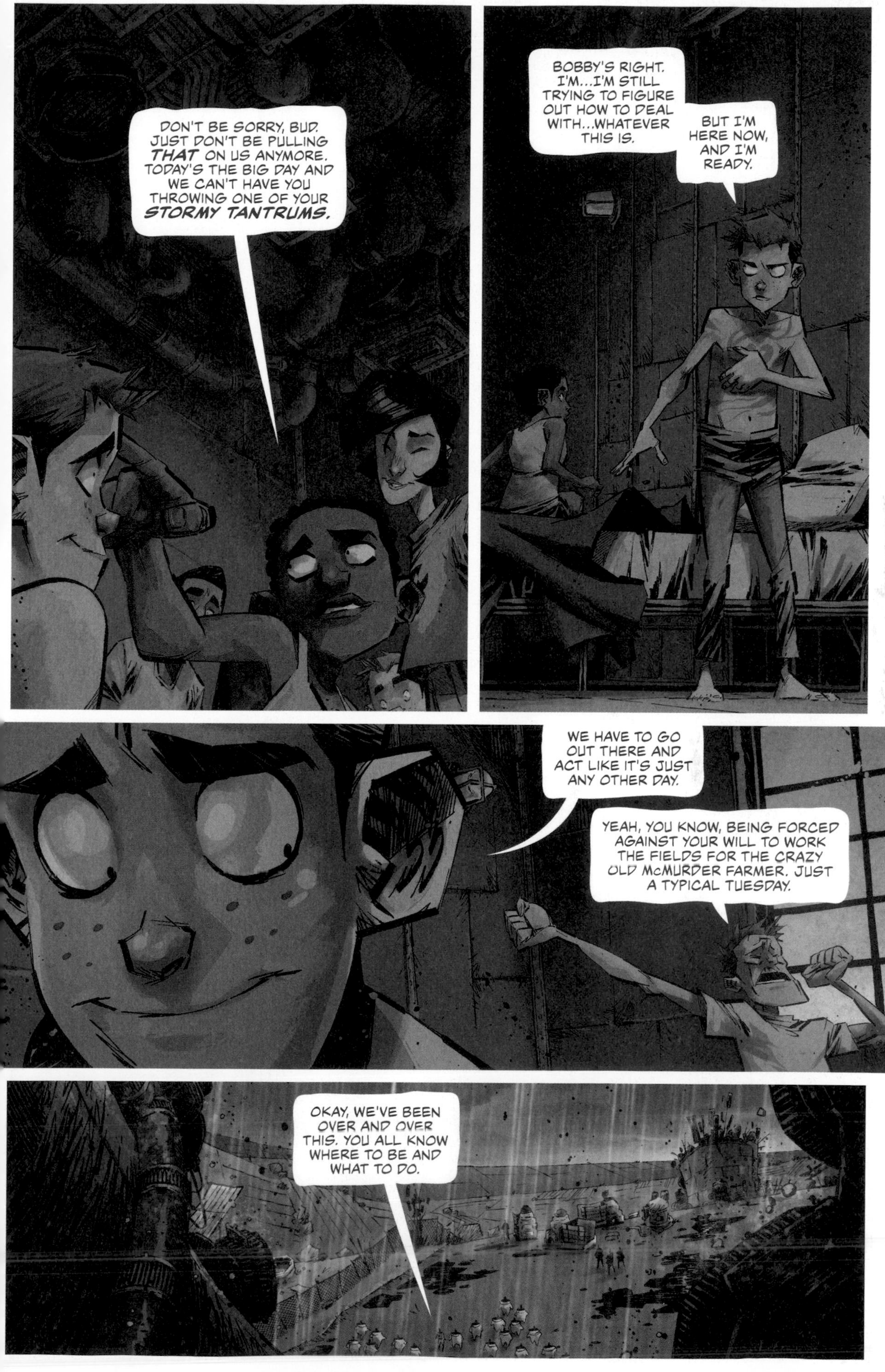
DON'T BE SORRY, BUD. JUST DON'T BE PULLING *THAT* ON US ANYMORE. TODAY'S THE BIG DAY AND WE CAN'T HAVE YOU THROWING ONE OF YOUR *STORMY TANTRUMS.*
BOBBY'S RIGHT. I'M...I'M STILL TRYING TO FIGURE OUT HOW TO DEAL WITH...WHATEVER THIS IS.
BUT I'M HERE NOW, AND I'M READY.
WE HAVE TO GO OUT THERE AND ACT LIKE IT'S JUST ANY OTHER DAY.
YEAH, YOU KNOW, BEING FORCED AGAINST YOUR WILL TO WORK THE FIELDS FOR THE CRAZY OLD McMURDER FARMER. JUST A TYPICAL TUESDAY.
OKAY, WE'VE BEEN OVER AND OVER THIS. YOU ALL KNOW WHERE TO BE AND WHAT TO DO.

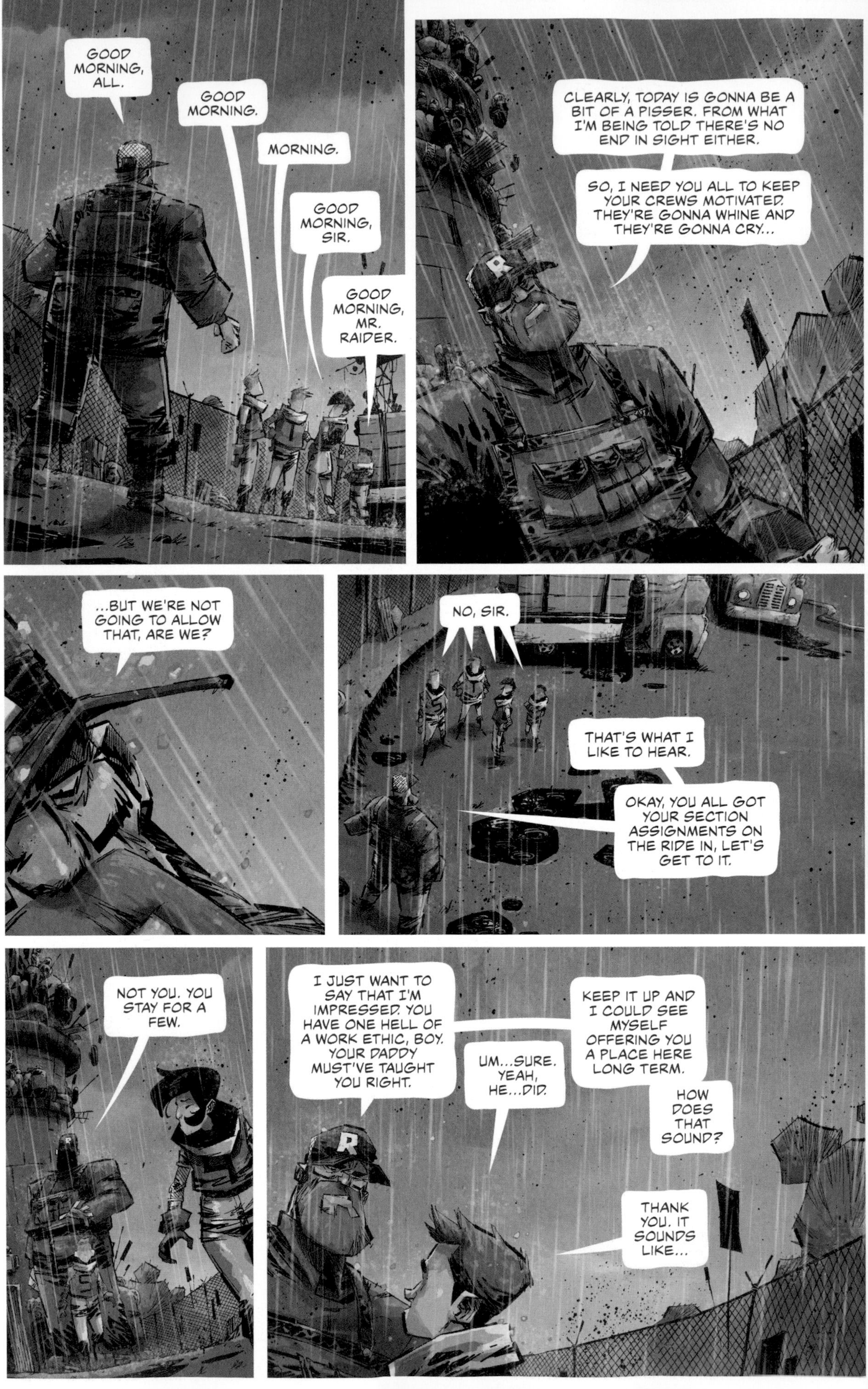
GOOD MORNING, ALL.
GOOD MORNING.
MORNING.
GOOD MORNING, SIR.
GOOD MORNING, MR. RAIDER.
CLEARLY, TODAY IS GONNA BE A BIT OF A PISSER. FROM WHAT I'M BEING TOLD THERE'S NO END IN SIGHT EITHER.
SO, I NEED YOU ALL TO KEEP YOUR CREWS MOTIVATED. THEY'RE GONNA WHINE AND THEY'RE GONNA CRY...
...BUT WE'RE NOT GOING TO ALLOW THAT, ARE WE?
NO, SIR.
THAT'S WHAT I LIKE TO HEAR.
OKAY, YOU ALL GOT YOUR SECTION ASSIGNMENTS ON THE RIDE IN, LET'S GET TO IT.
NOT YOU. YOU STAY FOR A FEW.
I JUST WANT TO SAY THAT I'M IMPRESSED. YOU HAVE ONE HELL OF A WORK ETHIC, BOY. YOUR DADDY MUST'VE TAUGHT YOU RIGHT.
UM...SURE. YEAH, HE...DID.
KEEP IT UP AND I COULD SEE MYSELF OFFERING YOU A PLACE HERE LONG TERM.
HOW DOES THAT SOUND?
THANK YOU. IT SOUNDS LIKE...

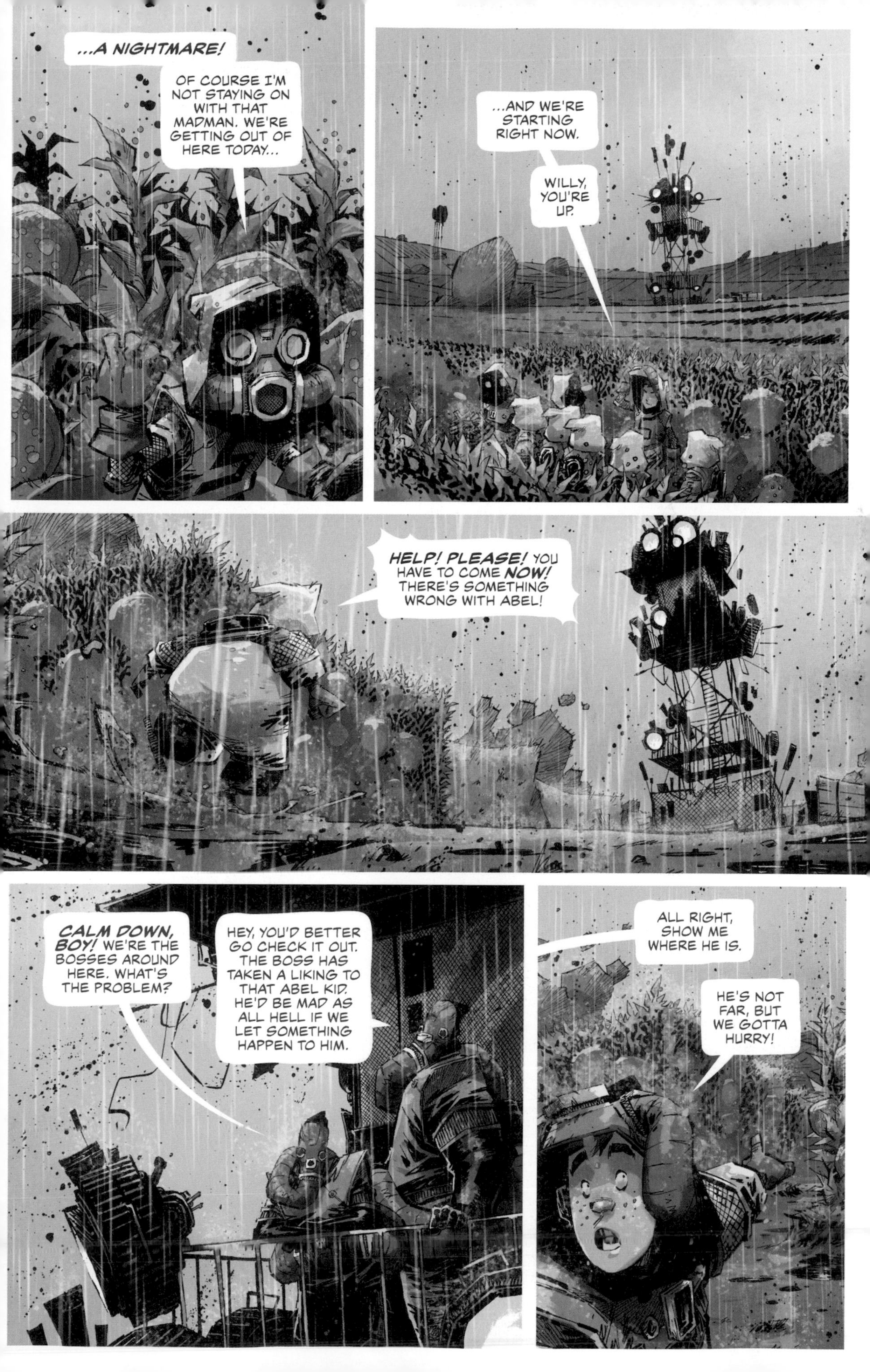
...A NIGHTMARE!
OF COURSE I'M NOT STAYING ON WITH THAT MADMAN. WE'RE GETTING OUT OF HERE TODAY...
...AND WE'RE STARTING RIGHT NOW.
WILLY, YOU'RE UP.
HELP! PLEASE! YOU HAVE TO COME NOW! THERE'S SOMETHING WRONG WITH ABEL!
CALM DOWN, BOY! WE'RE THE BOSSES AROUND HERE. WHAT'S THE PROBLEM?
HEY, YOU'D BETTER GO CHECK IT OUT. THE BOSS HAS TAKEN A LIKING TO THAT ABEL KID. HE'D BE MAD AS ALL HELL IF WE LET SOMETHING HAPPEN TO HIM.
ALL RIGHT, SHOW ME WHERE HE IS.
HE'S NOT FAR, BUT WE GOTTA HURRY!

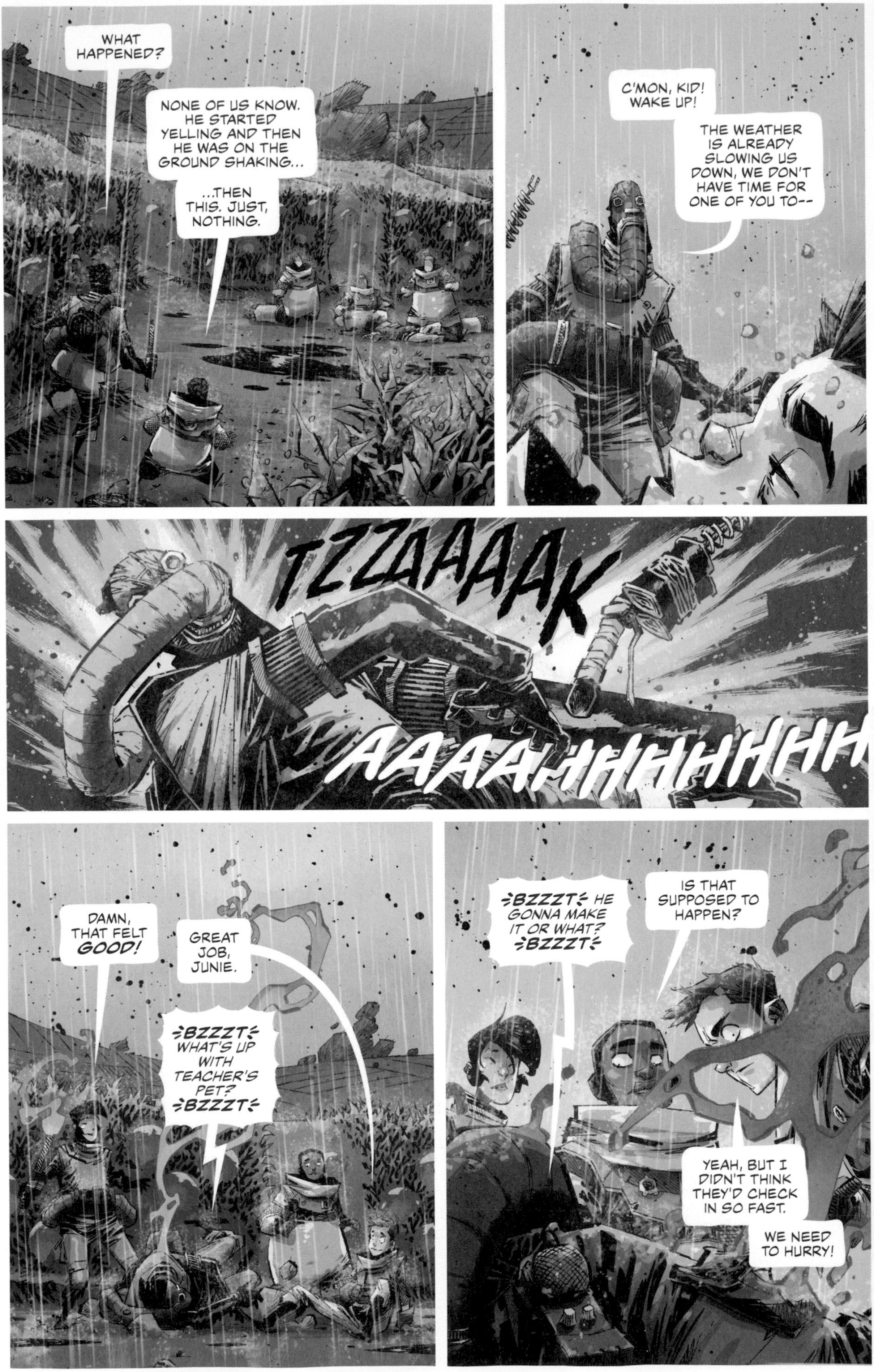
WHAT HAPPENED?
NONE OF US KNOW. HE STARTED YELLING AND THEN HE WAS ON THE GROUND SHAKING...
...THEN THIS. JUST, NOTHING.
C'MON, KID! WAKE UP!
THE WEATHER IS ALREADY SLOWING US DOWN, WE DON'T HAVE TIME FOR ONE OF YOU TO--
TZZAAAAK
AAAAAHHHHHHHH
DAMN, THAT FELT GOOD!
GREAT JOB, JUNIE.
BZZZT WHAT'S UP WITH TEACHER'S PET? BZZZT
BZZZT HE GONNA MAKE IT OR WHAT? BZZZT
IS THAT SUPPOSED TO HAPPEN?
YEAH, BUT I DIDN'T THINK THEY'D CHECK IN SO FAST.
WE NEED TO HURRY!

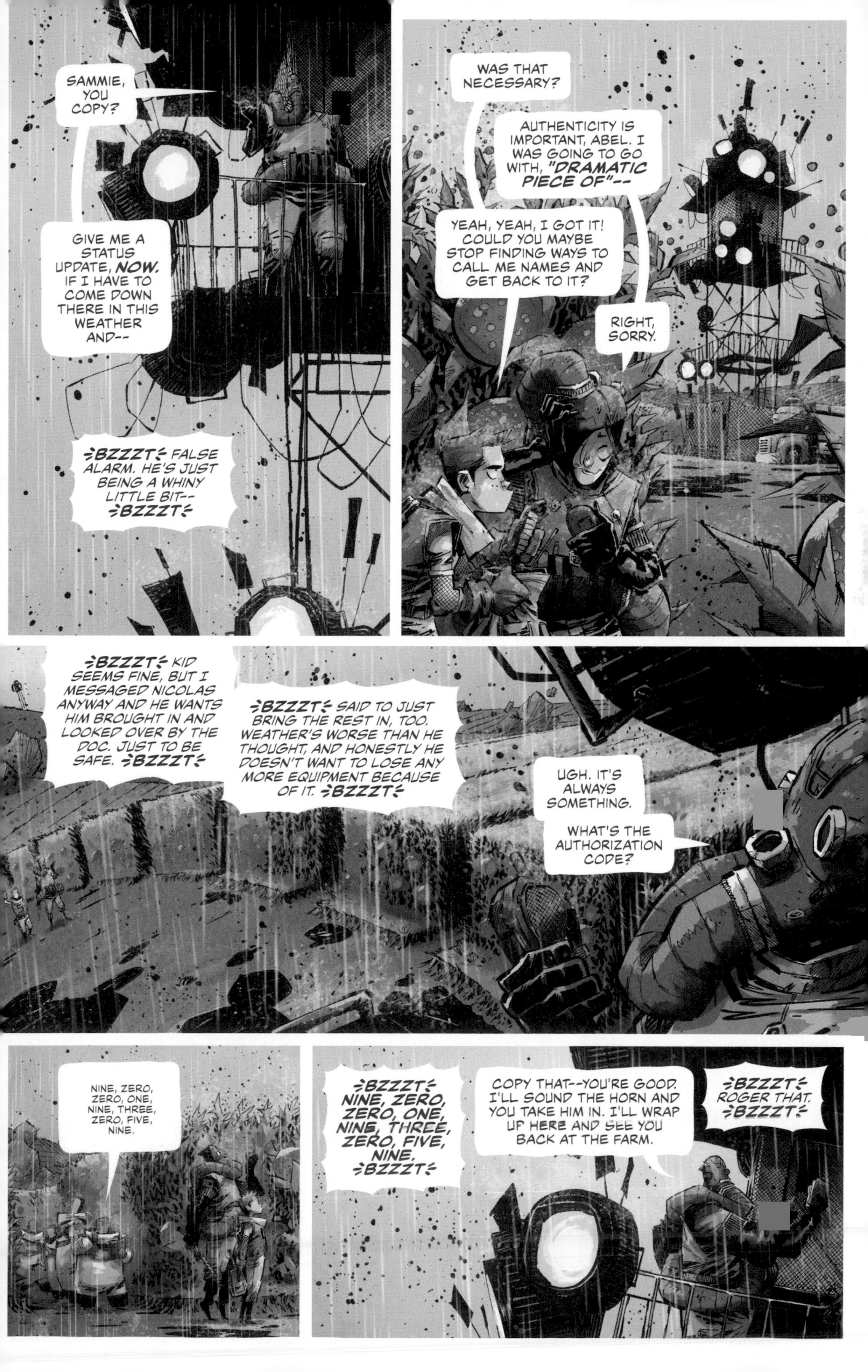
SAMMIE, YOU COPY?
GIVE ME A STATUS UPDATE, NOW. IF I HAVE TO COME DOWN THERE IN THIS WEATHER AND--
BZZZT FALSE ALARM. HE'S JUST BEING A WHINY LITTLE BIT-- BZZZT
WAS THAT NECESSARY?
AUTHENTICITY IS IMPORTANT, ABEL. I WAS GOING TO GO WITH, "DRAMATIC PIECE OF"--
YEAH, YEAH, I GOT IT! COULD YOU MAYBE STOP FINDING WAYS TO CALL ME NAMES AND GET BACK TO IT?
RIGHT, SORRY.
BZZZT KID SEEMS FINE, BUT I MESSAGED NICOLAS ANYWAY AND HE WANTS HIM BROUGHT IN AND LOOKED OVER BY THE DOC. JUST TO BE SAFE. BZZZT
BZZZT SAID TO JUST BRING THE REST IN, TOO. WEATHER'S WORSE THAN HE THOUGHT, AND HONESTLY HE DOESN'T WANT TO LOSE ANY MORE EQUIPMENT BECAUSE OF IT. BZZZT
UGH. IT'S ALWAYS SOMETHING.
WHAT'S THE AUTHORIZATION CODE?
NINE, ZERO, ZERO, ONE, NINE, THREE, ZERO, FIVE, NINE.
BZZZT NINE, ZERO, ZERO, ONE, NINE, THREE, ZERO, FIVE, NINE. BZZZT
COPY THAT--YOU'RE GOOD. I'LL SOUND THE HORN AND YOU TAKE HIM IN. I'LL WRAP UP HERE AND SEE YOU BACK AT THE FARM.
BZZZT ROGER THAT. BZZZT

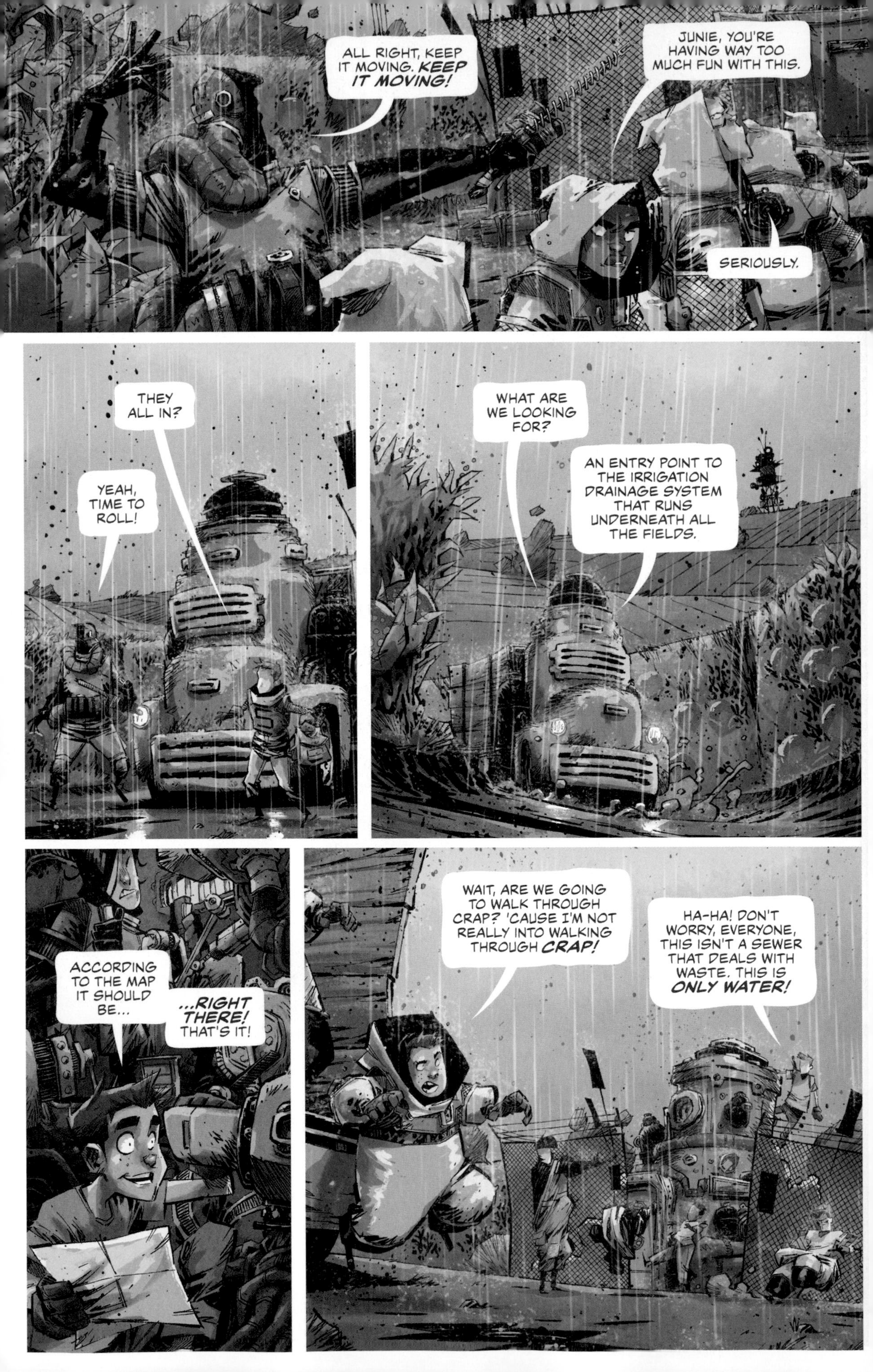

ALL RIGHT, KEEP IT MOVING. **KEEP IT MOVING!**
JUNIE, YOU'RE HAVING WAY TOO MUCH FUN WITH THIS.
SERIOUSLY.
THEY ALL IN?
YEAH, TIME TO ROLL!
WHAT ARE WE LOOKING FOR?
AN ENTRY POINT TO THE IRRIGATION DRAINAGE SYSTEM THAT RUNS UNDERNEATH ALL THE FIELDS.
ACCORDING TO THE MAP IT SHOULD BE...
...RIGHT THERE! THAT'S IT!
WAIT, ARE WE GOING TO WALK THROUGH CRAP? 'CAUSE I'M NOT REALLY INTO WALKING THROUGH **CRAP!**
HA-HA! DON'T WORRY, EVERYONE, THIS ISN'T A SEWER THAT DEALS WITH WASTE. THIS IS **ONLY WATER!**

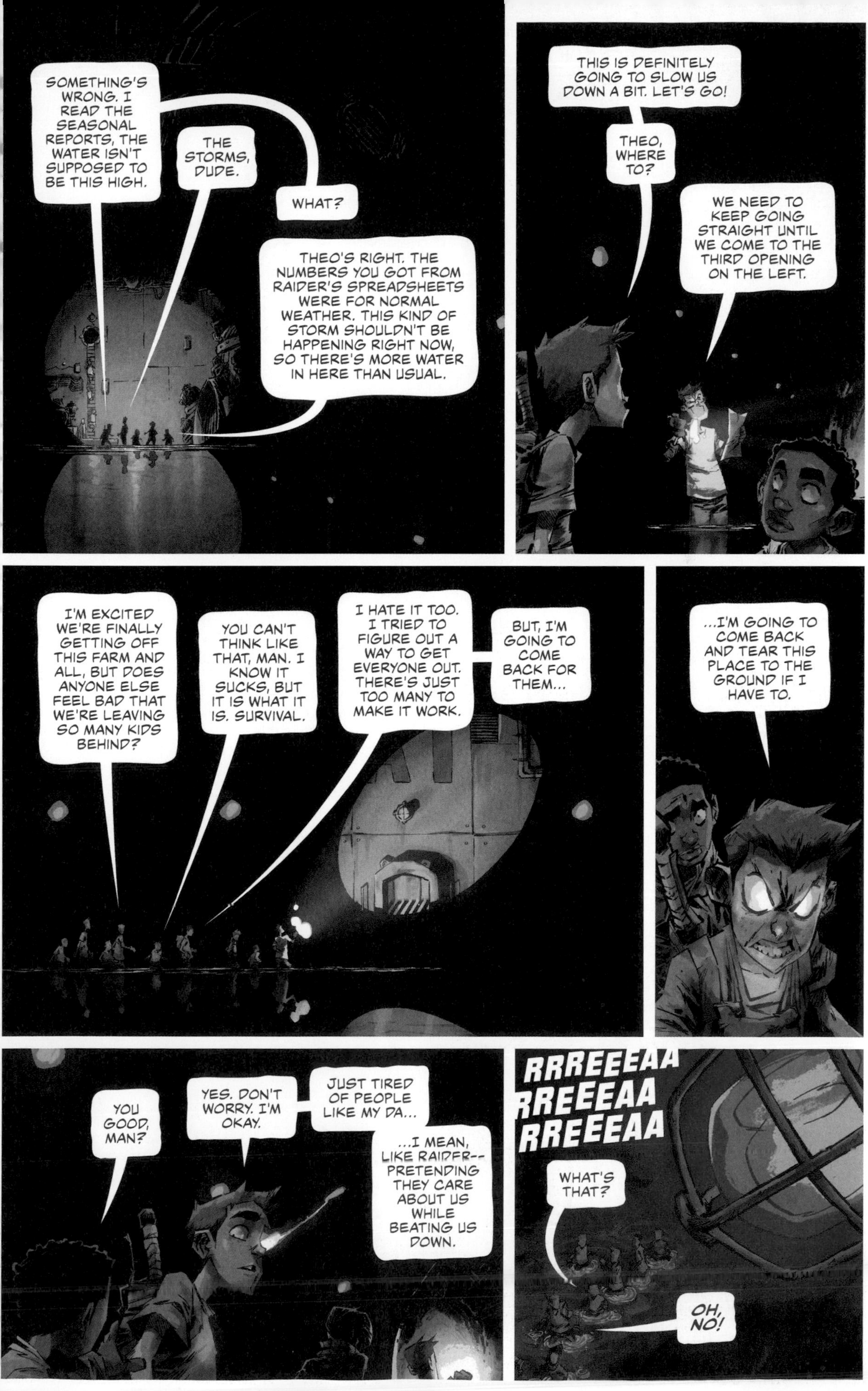
SOMETHING'S WRONG. I READ THE SEASONAL REPORTS, THE WATER ISN'T SUPPOSED TO BE THIS HIGH.
THE STORMS, DUDE.
WHAT?
THEO'S RIGHT. THE NUMBERS YOU GOT FROM RAIDER'S SPREADSHEETS WERE FOR NORMAL WEATHER. THIS KIND OF STORM SHOULDN'T BE HAPPENING RIGHT NOW, SO THERE'S MORE WATER IN HERE THAN USUAL.
THIS IS DEFINITELY GOING TO SLOW US DOWN A BIT. LET'S GO!
THEO, WHERE TO?
WE NEED TO KEEP GOING STRAIGHT UNTIL WE COME TO THE THIRD OPENING ON THE LEFT.
I'M EXCITED WE'RE FINALLY GETTING OFF THIS FARM AND ALL, BUT DOES ANYONE ELSE FEEL BAD THAT WE'RE LEAVING SO MANY KIDS BEHIND?
YOU CAN'T THINK LIKE THAT, MAN. I KNOW IT SUCKS, BUT IT IS WHAT IT IS. SURVIVAL.
I HATE IT TOO. I TRIED TO FIGURE OUT A WAY TO GET EVERYONE OUT. THERE'S JUST TOO MANY TO MAKE IT WORK.
BUT, I'M GOING TO COME BACK FOR THEM...
...I'M GOING TO COME BACK AND TEAR THIS PLACE TO THE GROUND IF I HAVE TO.
YOU GOOD, MAN?
YES. DON'T WORRY. I'M OKAY.
JUST TIRED OF PEOPLE LIKE MY DA...
...I MEAN, LIKE RAIDER-- PRETENDING THEY CARE ABOUT US WHILE BEATING US DOWN.
RRREEEAA
RREEEAA
RREEEAA
WHAT'S THAT?
OH, NO!

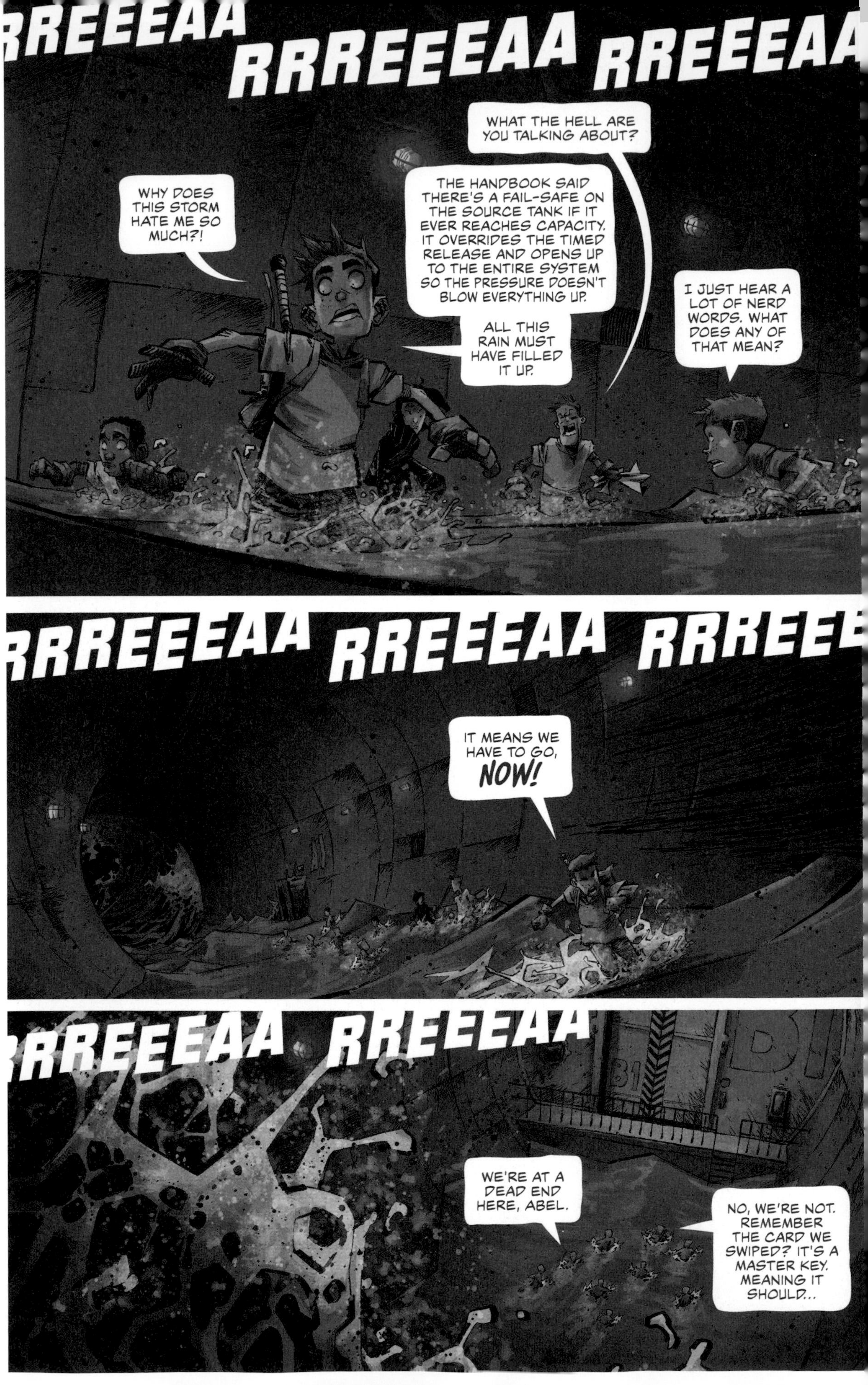
RREEEAA
RRREEEAA
RREEEAA
WHY DOES THIS STORM HATE ME SO MUCH?!
THE HANDBOOK SAID THERE'S A FAIL-SAFE ON THE SOURCE TANK IF IT EVER REACHES CAPACITY. IT OVERRIDES THE TIMED RELEASE AND OPENS UP TO THE ENTIRE SYSTEM SO THE PRESSURE DOESN'T BLOW EVERYTHING UP.
ALL THIS RAIN MUST HAVE FILLED IT UP.
WHAT THE HELL ARE YOU TALKING ABOUT?
I JUST HEAR A LOT OF NERD WORDS. WHAT DOES ANY OF THAT MEAN?
RRREEEAA
RREEEAA
RRREEE
IT MEANS WE HAVE TO GO, NOW!
RREEEAA
RREEEAA
B1
WE'RE AT A DEAD END HERE, ABEL.
NO, WE'RE NOT. REMEMBER THE CARD WE SWIPED? IT'S A MASTER KEY. MEANING IT SHOULD...

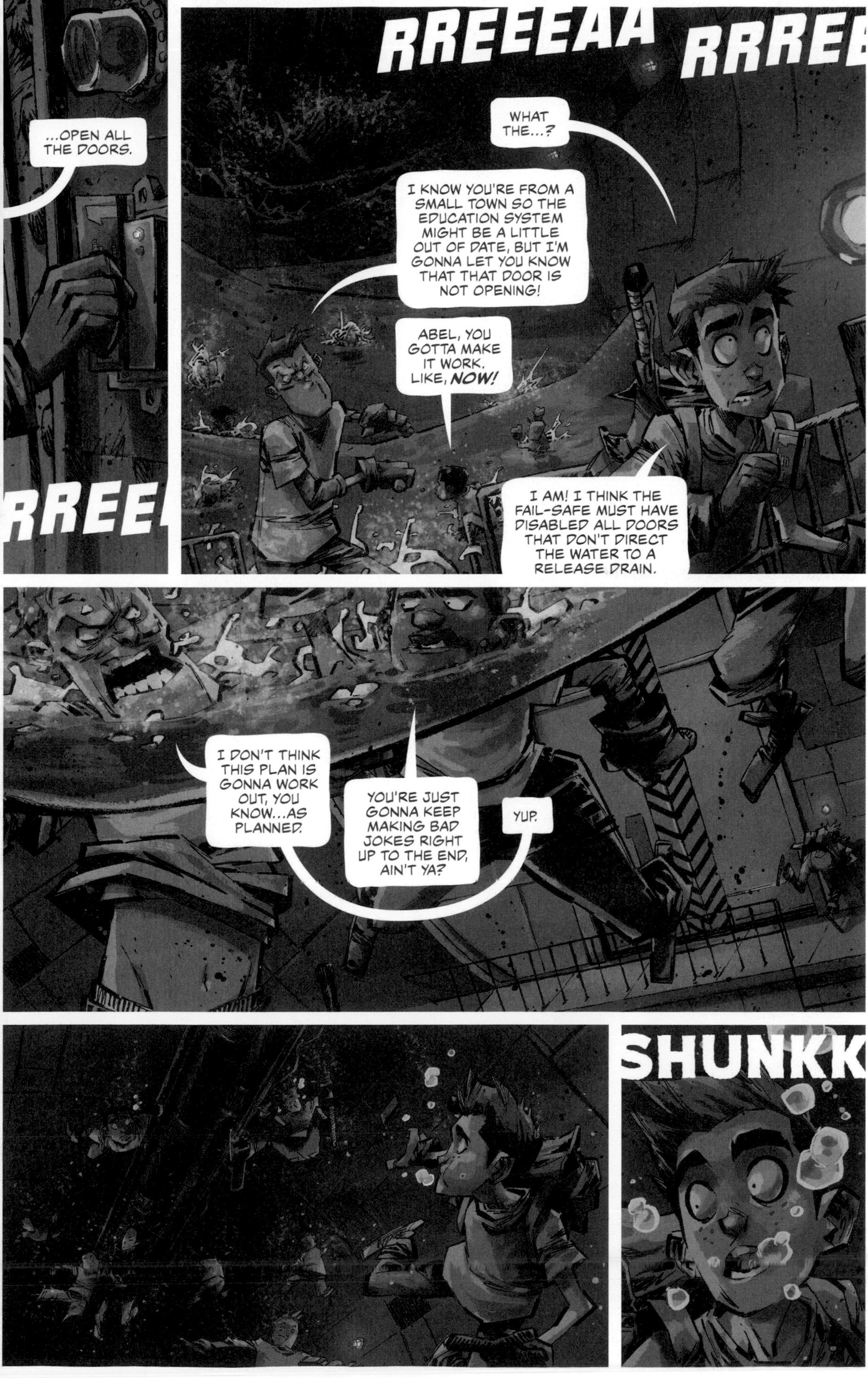
...OPEN ALL THE DOORS.
RRREE
RREEEAA RRREE
WHAT THE...?
I KNOW YOU'RE FROM A SMALL TOWN SO THE EDUCATION SYSTEM MIGHT BE A LITTLE OUT OF DATE, BUT I'M GONNA LET YOU KNOW THAT THAT DOOR IS NOT OPENING!
ABEL, YOU GOTTA MAKE IT WORK. LIKE, NOW!
I AM! I THINK THE FAIL-SAFE MUST HAVE DISABLED ALL DOORS THAT DON'T DIRECT THE WATER TO A RELEASE DRAIN.
I DON'T THINK THIS PLAN IS GONNA WORK OUT, YOU KNOW...AS PLANNED.
YOU'RE JUST GONNA KEEP MAKING BAD JOKES RIGHT UP TO THE END, AIN'T YA?
YUP.
SHUNKK

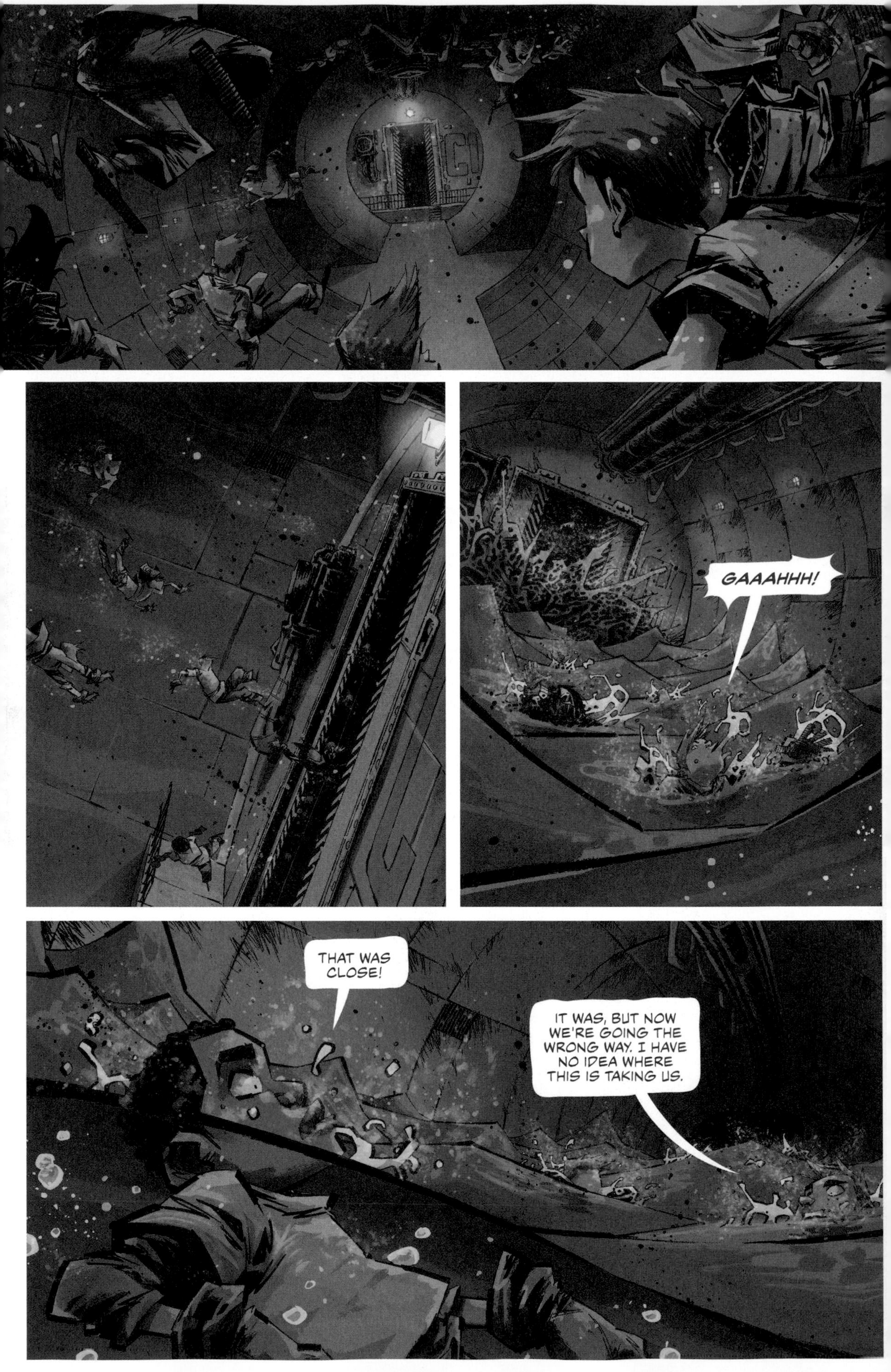
GAAAHHH!
THAT WAS CLOSE!
IT WAS, BUT NOW WE'RE GOING THE WRONG WAY. I HAVE NO IDEA WHERE THIS IS TAKING US.

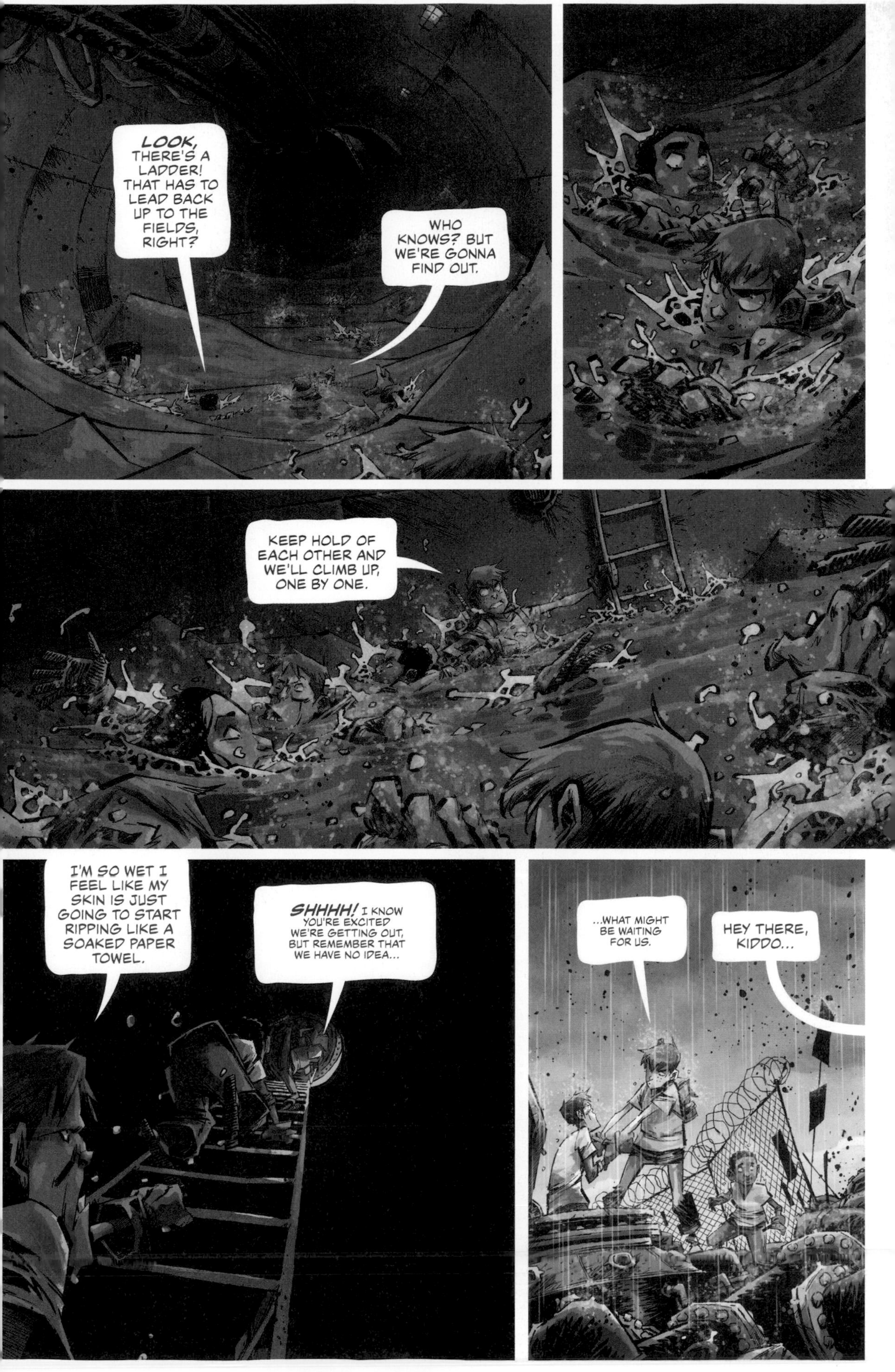
LOOK, THERE'S A LADDER! THAT HAS TO LEAD BACK UP TO THE FIELDS, RIGHT?
WHO KNOWS? BUT WE'RE GONNA FIND OUT.
KEEP HOLD OF EACH OTHER AND WE'LL CLIMB UP, ONE BY ONE.
I'M SO WET I FEEL LIKE MY SKIN IS JUST GOING TO START RIPPING LIKE A SOAKED PAPER TOWEL.
SHHHH! I KNOW YOU'RE EXCITED WE'RE GETTING OUT, BUT REMEMBER THAT WE HAVE NO IDEA...
...WHAT MIGHT BE WAITING FOR US.
HEY THERE, KIDDO...

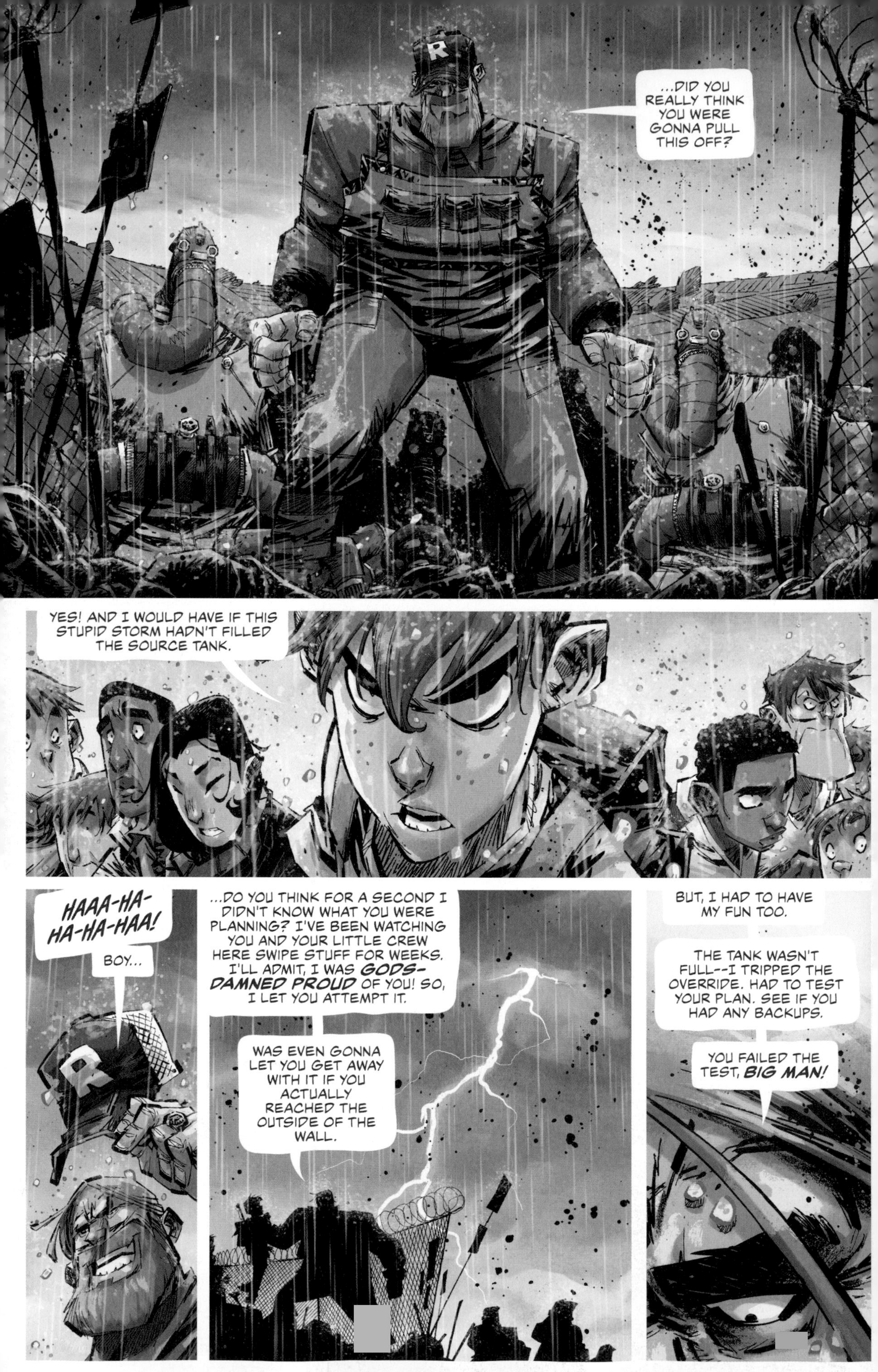
...DID YOU REALLY THINK YOU WERE GONNA PULL THIS OFF?
YES! AND I WOULD HAVE IF THIS STUPID STORM HADN'T FILLED THE SOURCE TANK.
HAAA-HA-HA-HA-HAA!
BOY...
...DO YOU THINK FOR A SECOND I DIDN'T KNOW WHAT YOU WERE PLANNING? I'VE BEEN WATCHING YOU AND YOUR LITTLE CREW HERE SWIPE STUFF FOR WEEKS. I'LL ADMIT, I WAS GODS-DAMNED PROUD OF YOU! SO, I LET YOU ATTEMPT IT.
WAS EVEN GONNA LET YOU GET AWAY WITH IT IF YOU ACTUALLY REACHED THE OUTSIDE OF THE WALL.
BUT, I HAD TO HAVE MY FUN TOO.
THE TANK WASN'T FULL--I TRIPPED THE OVERRIDE. HAD TO TEST YOUR PLAN. SEE IF YOU HAD ANY BACKUPS.
YOU FAILED THE TEST, BIG MAN!

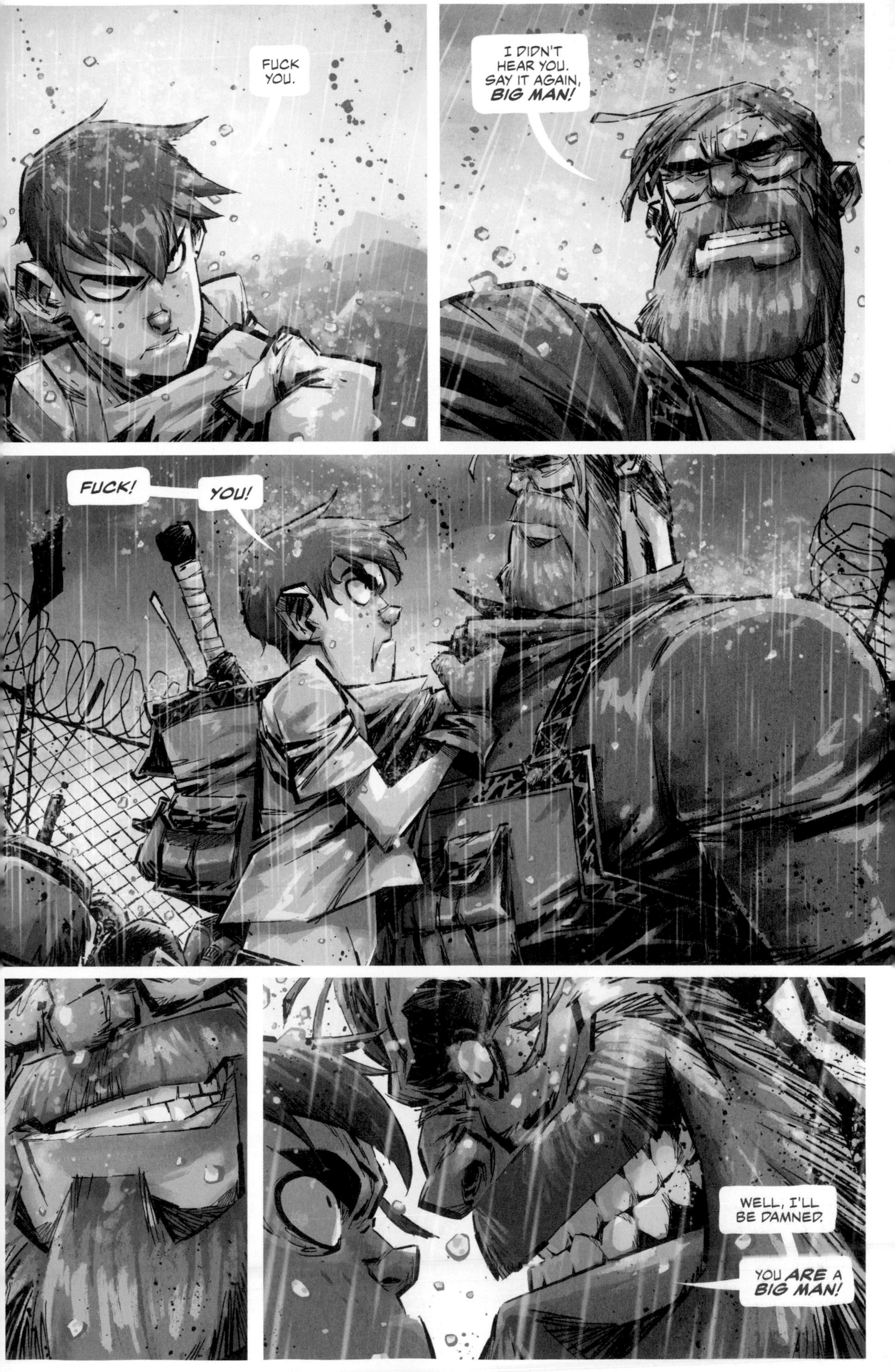
FUCK YOU.
I DIDN'T HEAR YOU. SAY IT AGAIN, BIG MAN!
FUCK!
YOU!
WELL, I'LL BE DAMNED.
YOU ARE A BIG MAN!

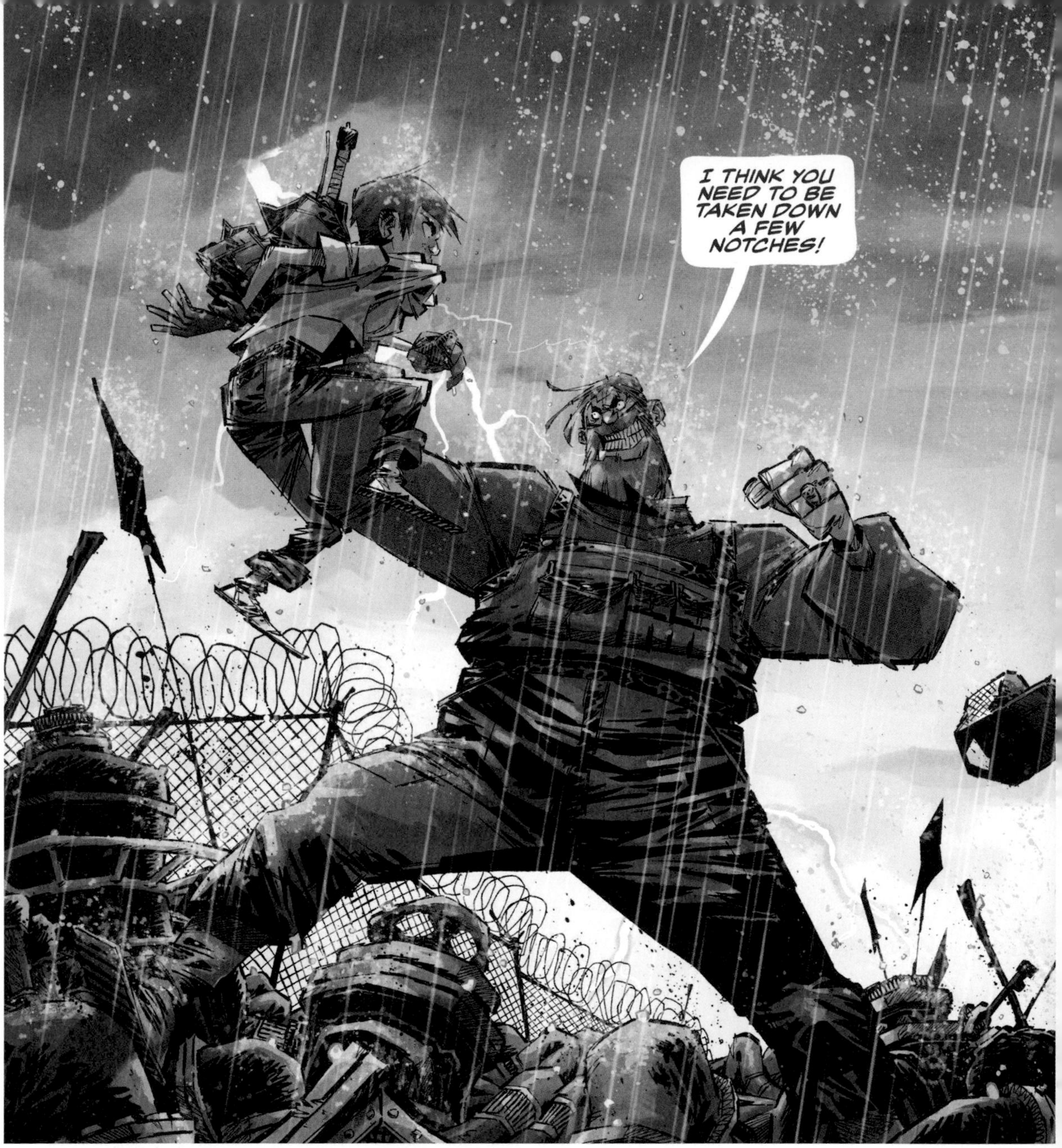
I THINK YOU NEED TO BE TAKEN DOWN A FEW NOTCHES!

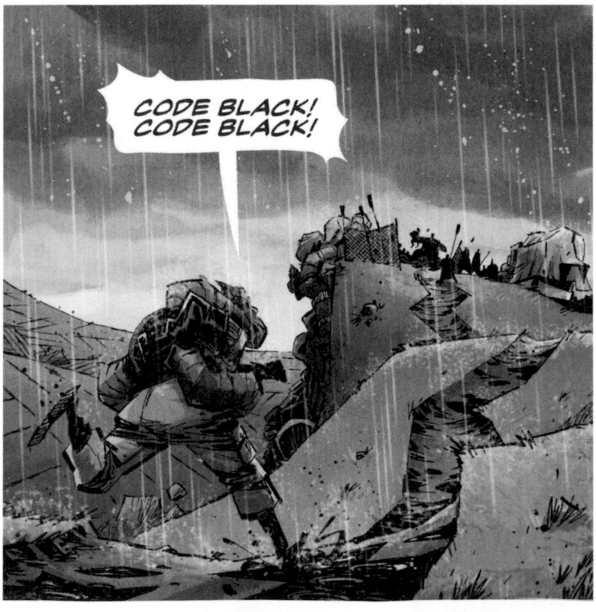
CODE BLACK! CODE BLACK!

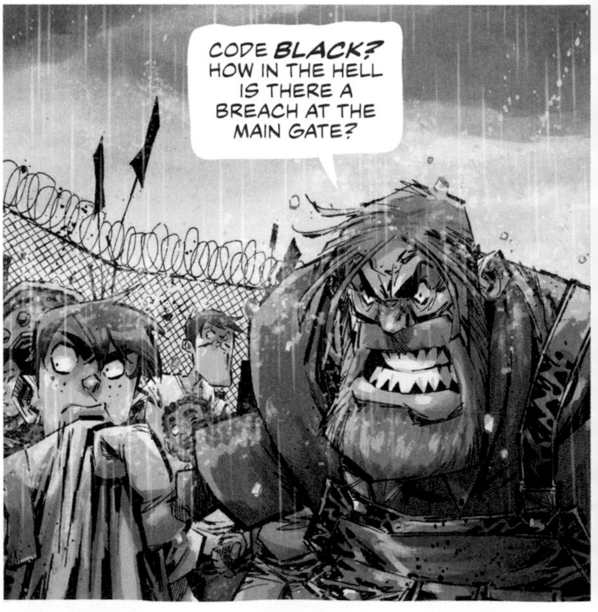
CODE BLACK? HOW IN THE HELL IS THERE A BREACH AT THE MAIN GATE?

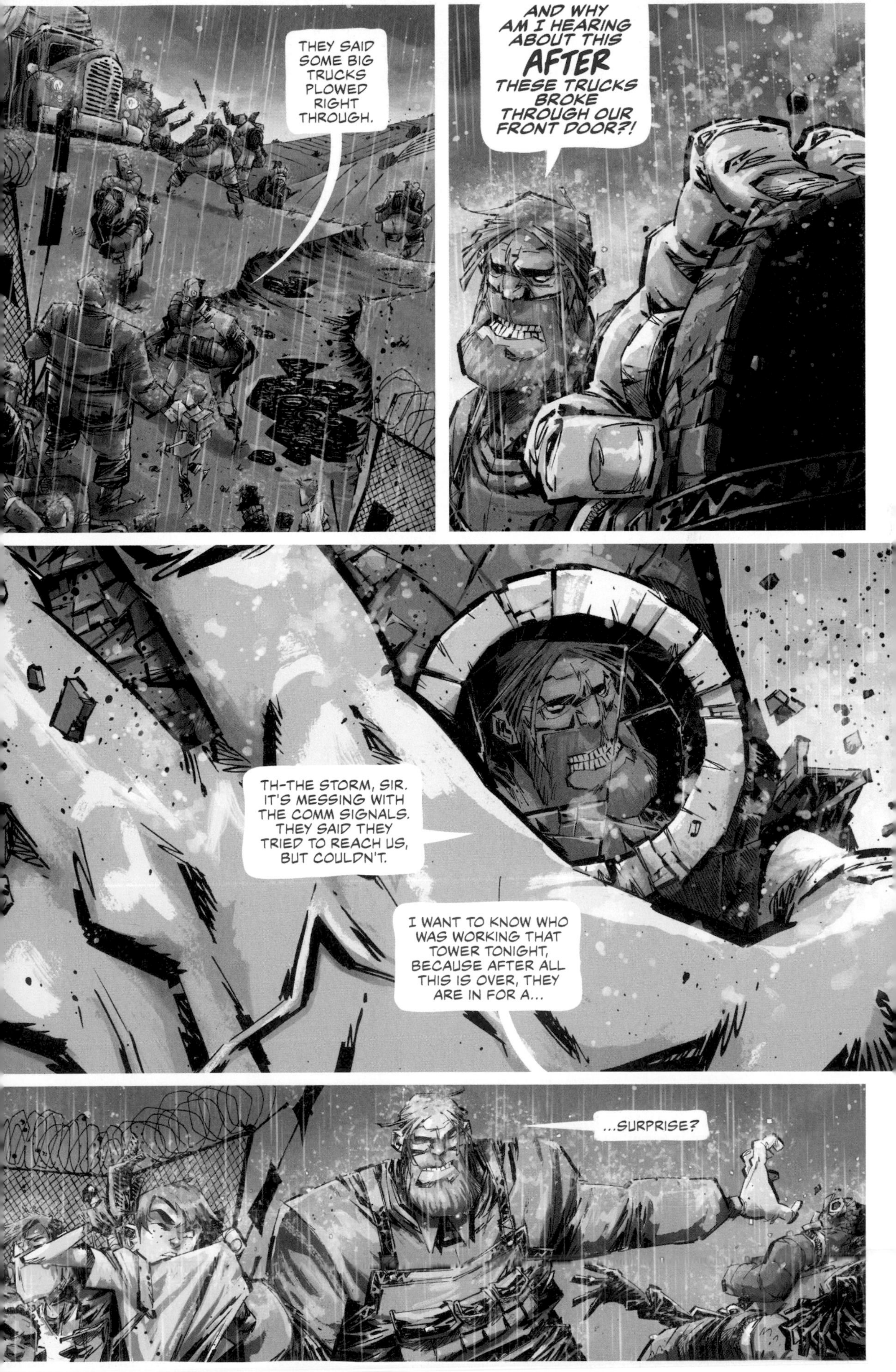
THEY SAID SOME BIG TRUCKS PLOWED RIGHT THROUGH.
AND WHY AM I HEARING ABOUT THIS AFTER THESE TRUCKS BROKE THROUGH OUR FRONT DOOR?!
TH-THE STORM, SIR. IT'S MESSING WITH THE COMM SIGNALS. THEY SAID THEY TRIED TO REACH US, BUT COULDN'T.
I WANT TO KNOW WHO WAS WORKING THAT TOWER TONIGHT, BECAUSE AFTER ALL THIS IS OVER, THEY ARE IN FOR A...
...SURPRISE?

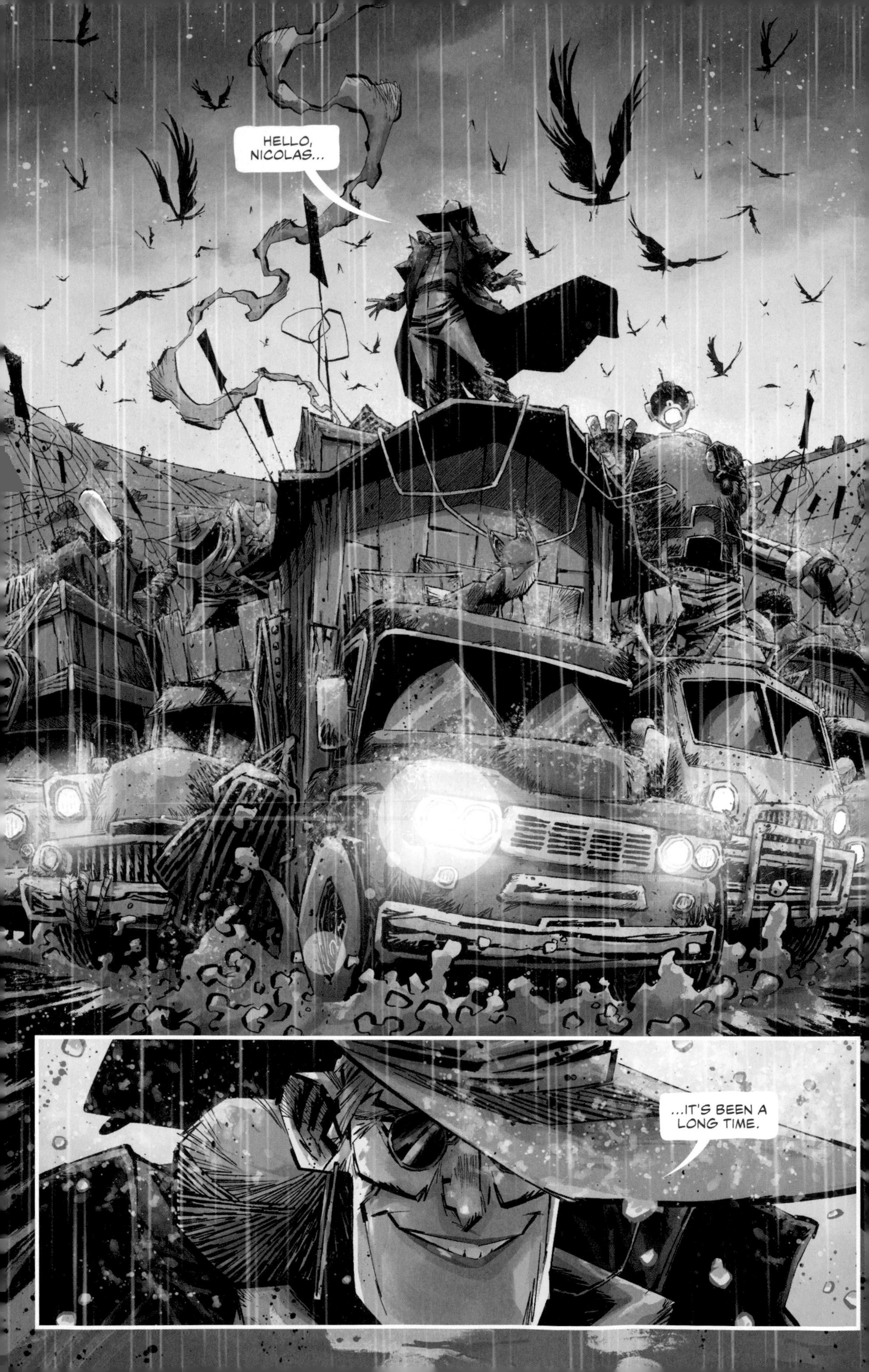
HELLO, NICOLAS...
...IT'S BEEN A LONG TIME.

CHAPTER
SEVENTEEN

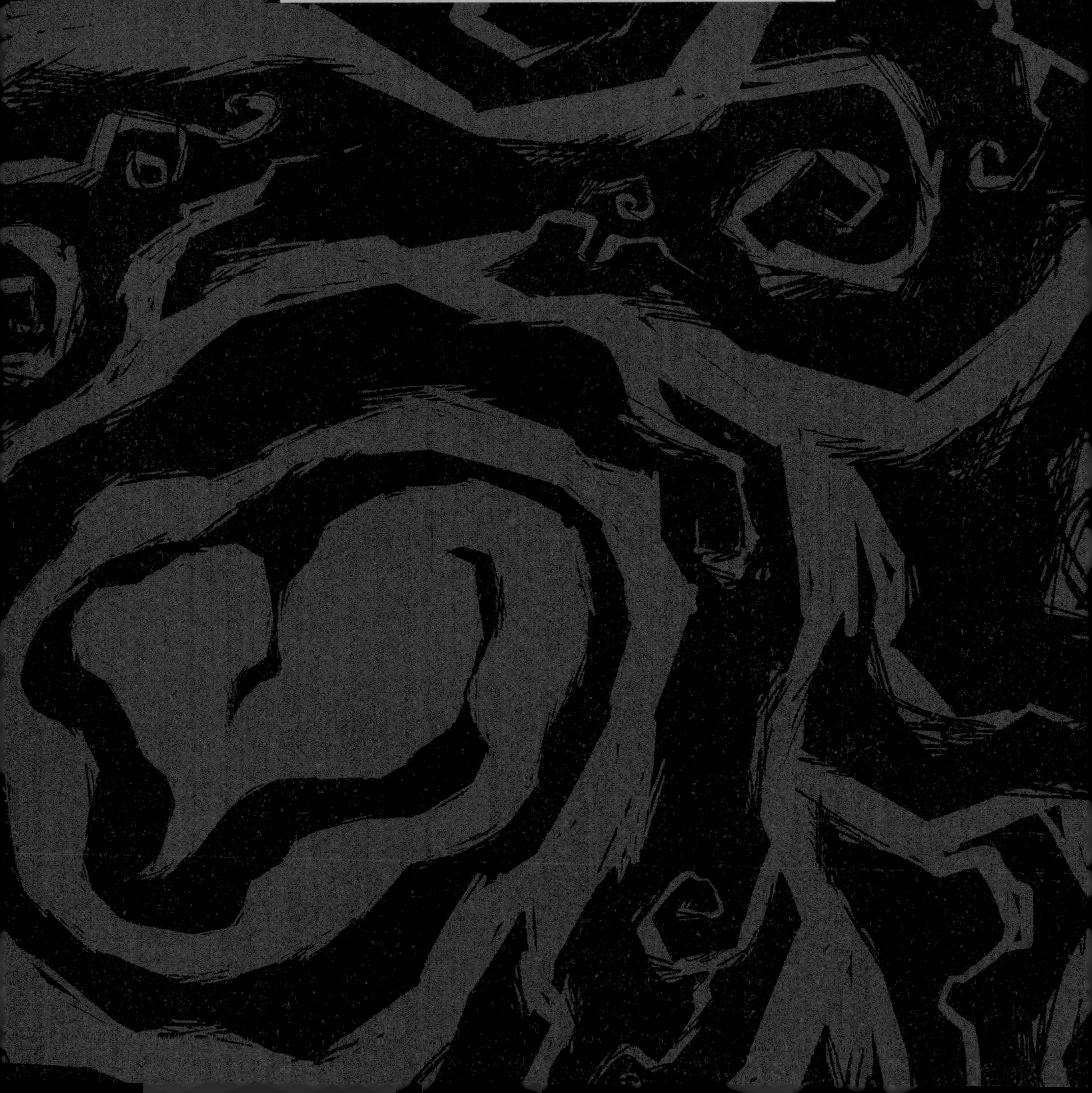

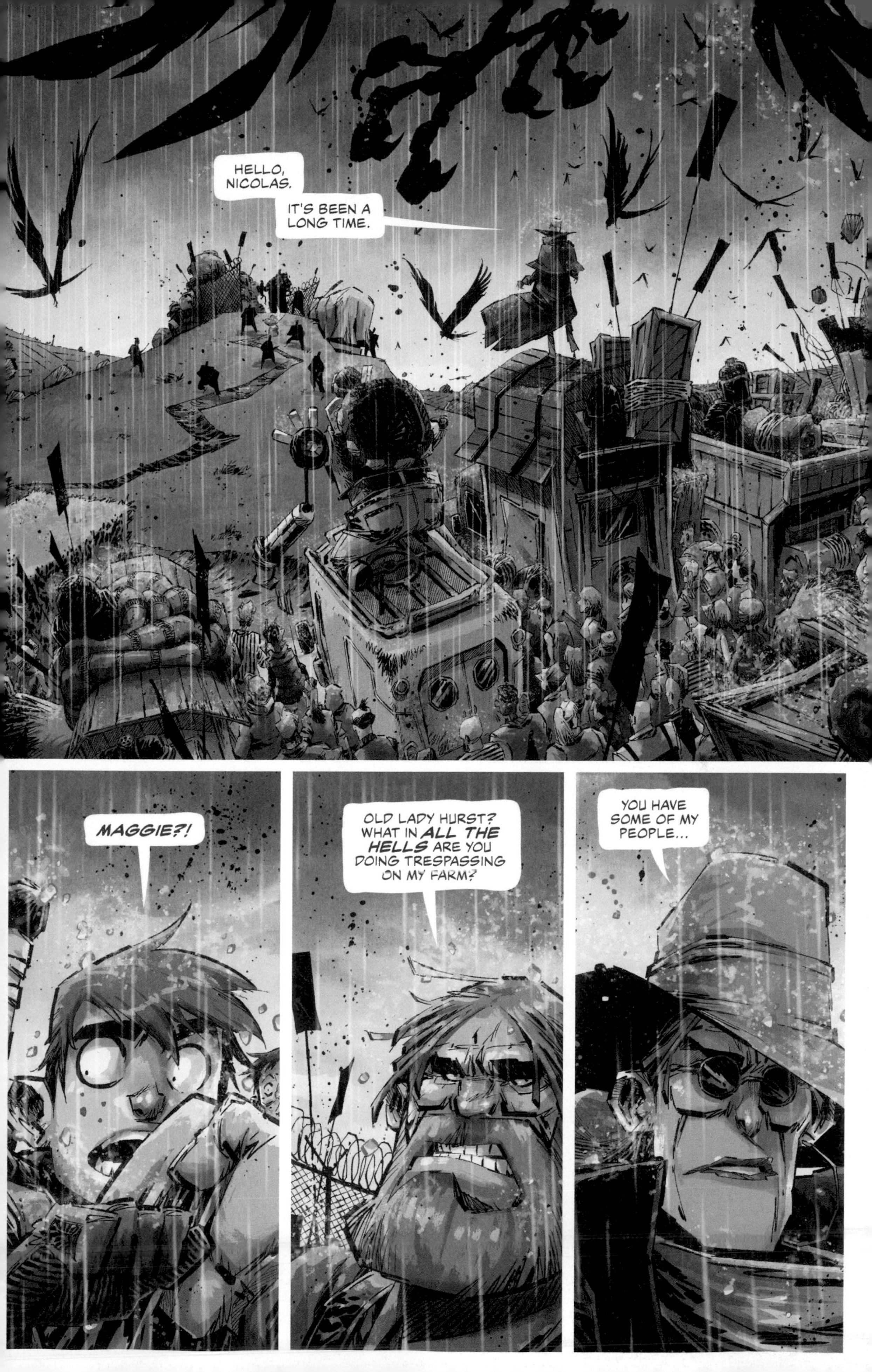
HELLO, NICOLAS.
IT'S BEEN A LONG TIME.
MAGGIE?!
OLD LADY HURST? WHAT IN ALL THE HELLS ARE YOU DOING TRESPASSING ON MY FARM?
YOU HAVE SOME OF MY PEOPLE...

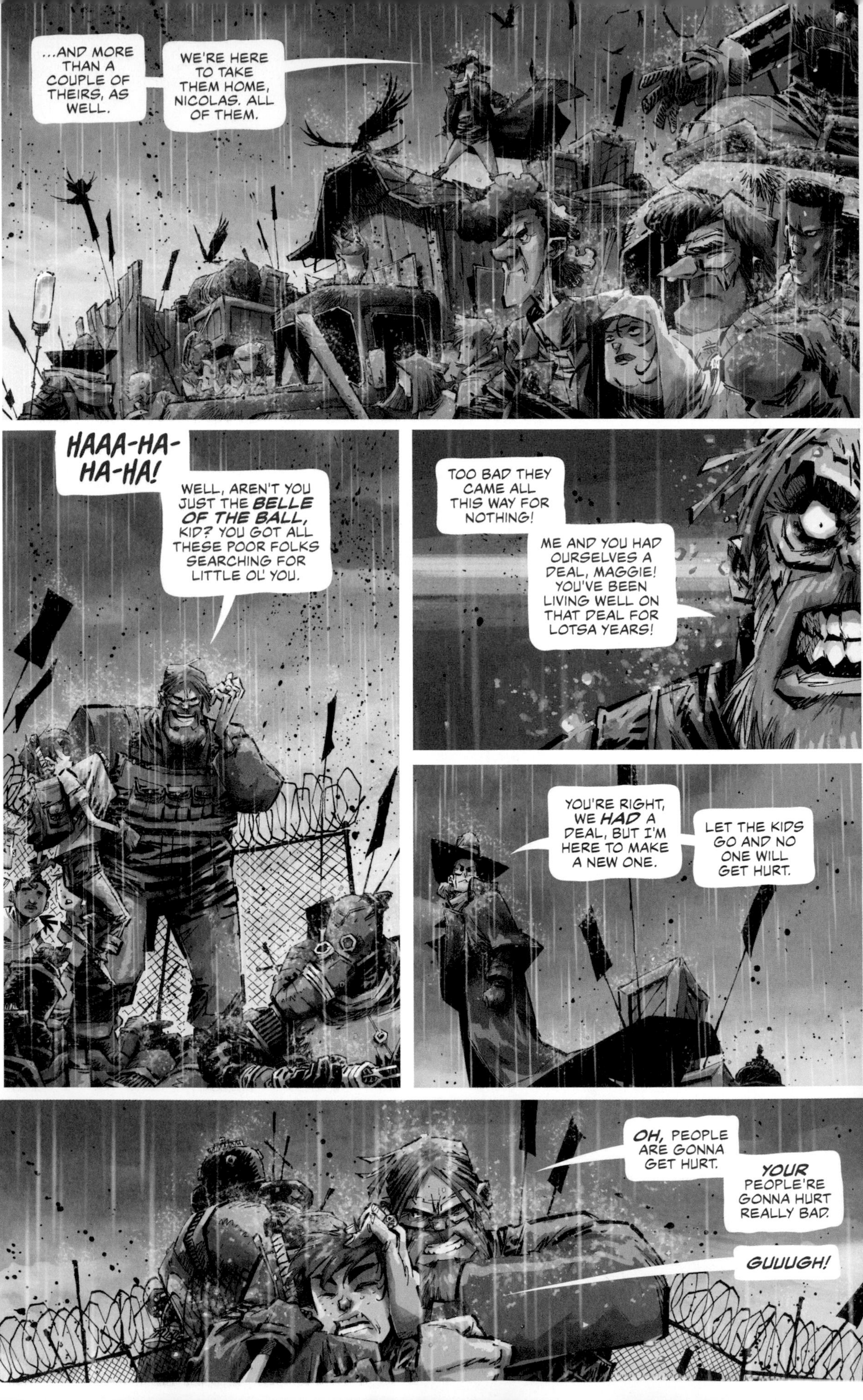
...AND MORE THAN A COUPLE OF THEIRS, AS WELL.
WE'RE HERE TO TAKE THEM HOME, NICOLAS. ALL OF THEM.
HAAA-HA-HA-HA!
WELL, AREN'T YOU JUST THE BELLE OF THE BALL, KID? YOU GOT ALL THESE POOR FOLKS SEARCHING FOR LITTLE OL' YOU.
TOO BAD THEY CAME ALL THIS WAY FOR NOTHING!
ME AND YOU HAD OURSELVES A DEAL, MAGGIE! YOU'VE BEEN LIVING WELL ON THAT DEAL FOR LOTSA YEARS!
YOU'RE RIGHT, WE HAD A DEAL, BUT I'M HERE TO MAKE A NEW ONE.
LET THE KIDS GO AND NO ONE WILL GET HURT.
OH, PEOPLE ARE GONNA GET HURT.
YOUR PEOPLE'RE GONNA HURT REALLY BAD.
GUUUGH!

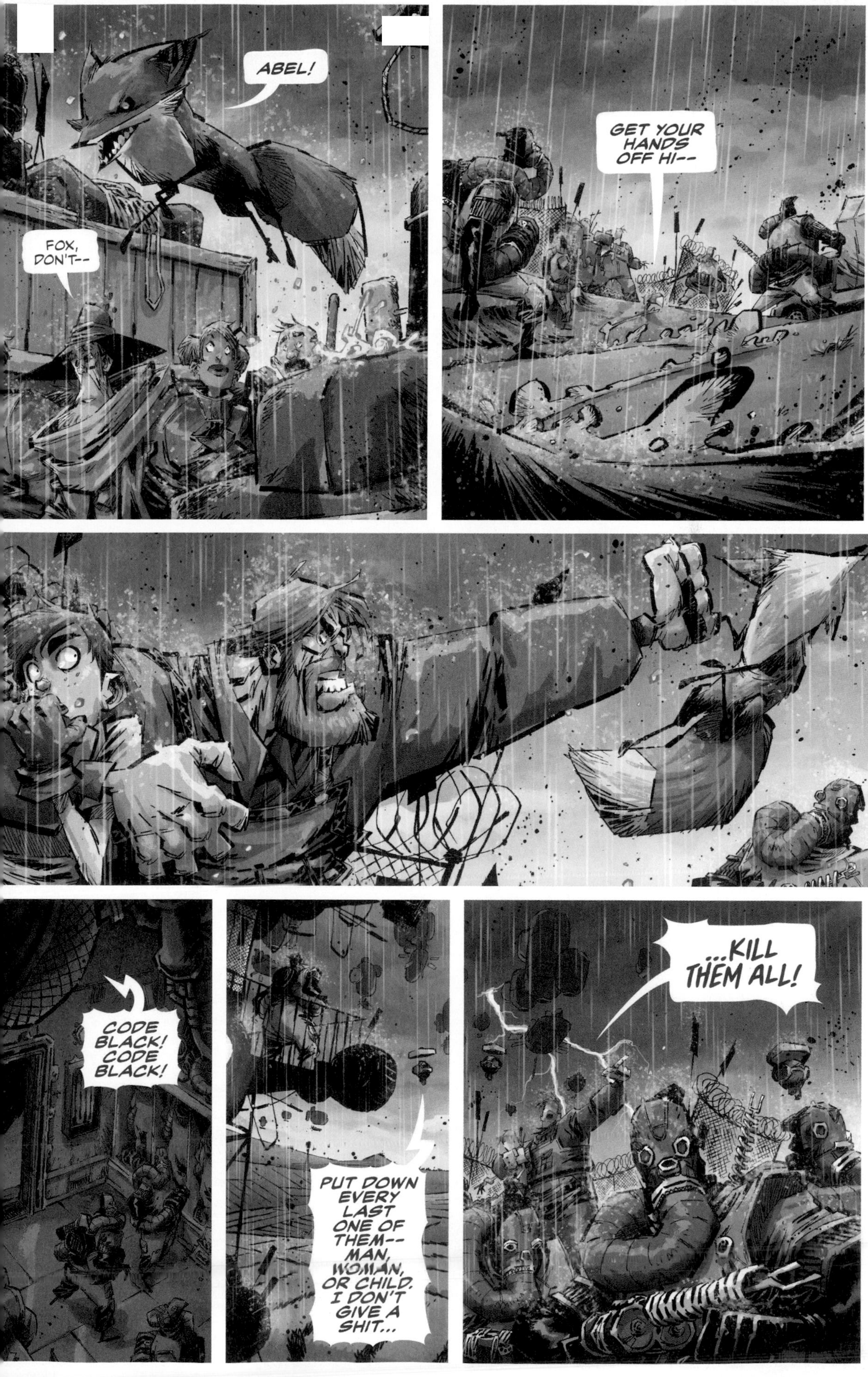
ABEL!
FOX, DON'T--
GET YOUR HANDS OFF HI--
CODE BLACK! CODE BLACK!
PUT DOWN EVERY LAST ONE OF THEM-- MAN, WOMAN, OR CHILD. I DON'T GIVE A SHIT...
...KILL THEM ALL!

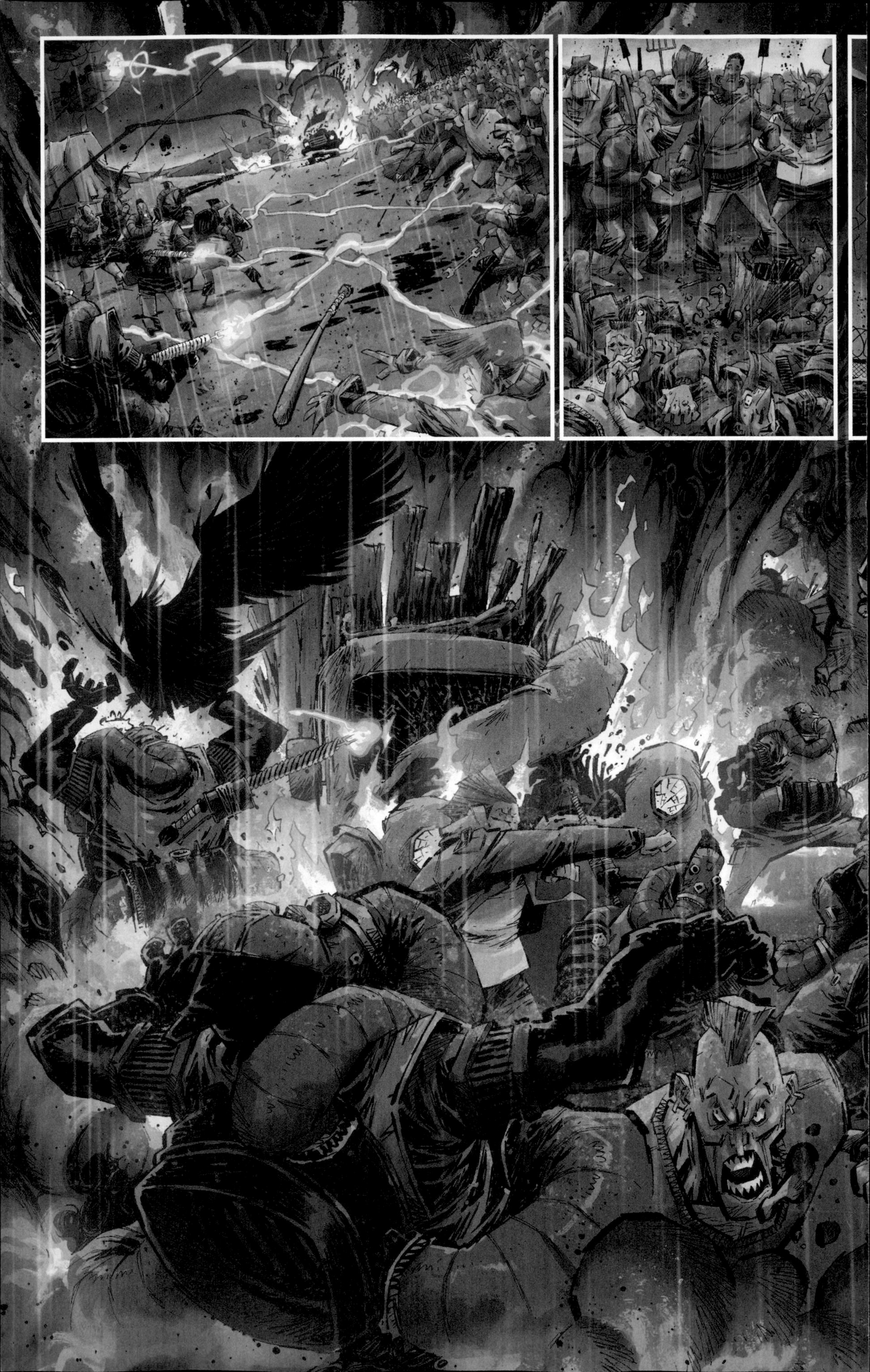

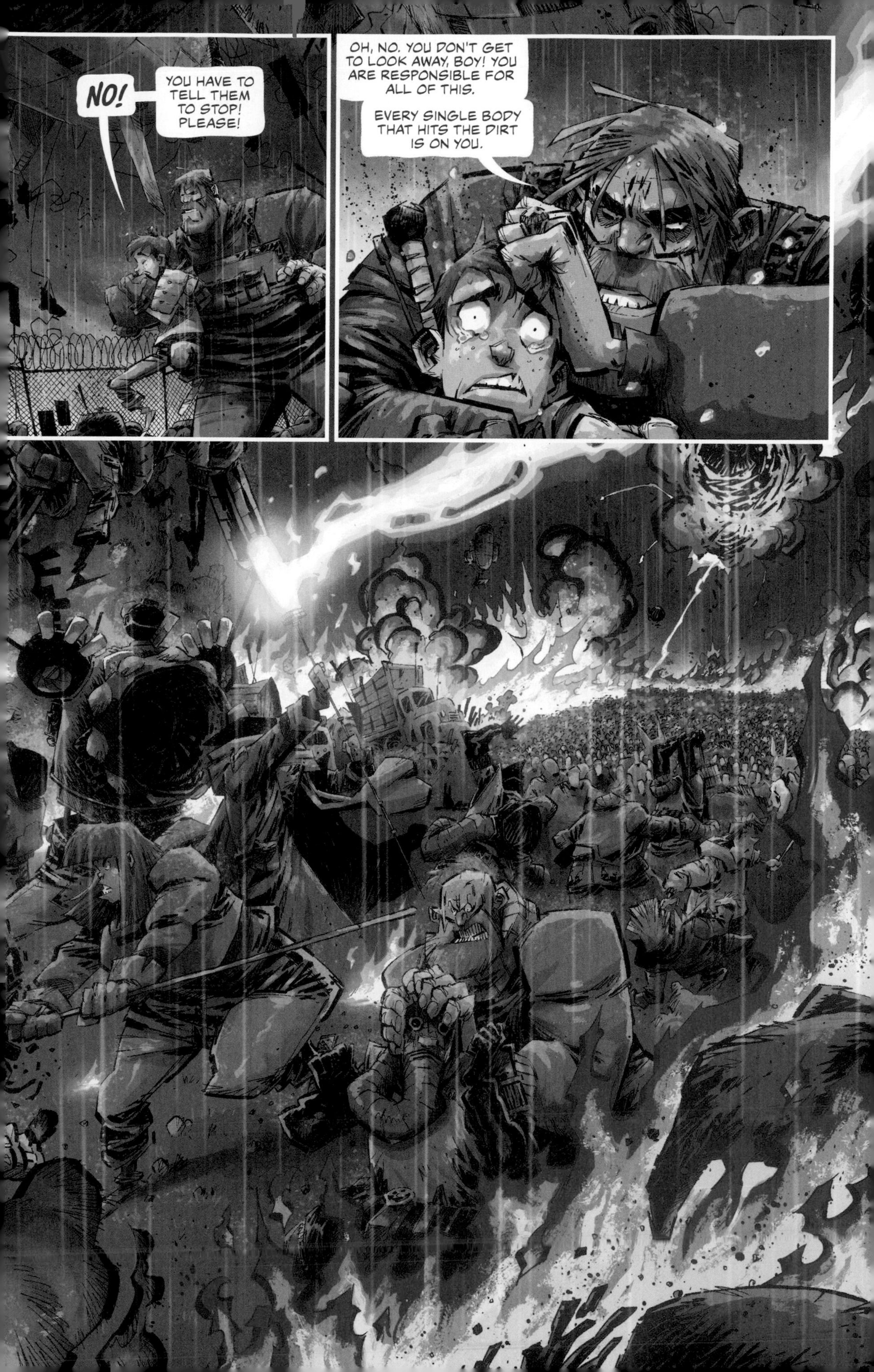
NO!
YOU HAVE TO TELL THEM TO STOP! PLEASE!
OH, NO. YOU DON'T GET TO LOOK AWAY, BOY! YOU ARE RESPONSIBLE FOR ALL OF THIS.
EVERY SINGLE BODY THAT HITS THE DIRT IS ON YOU.

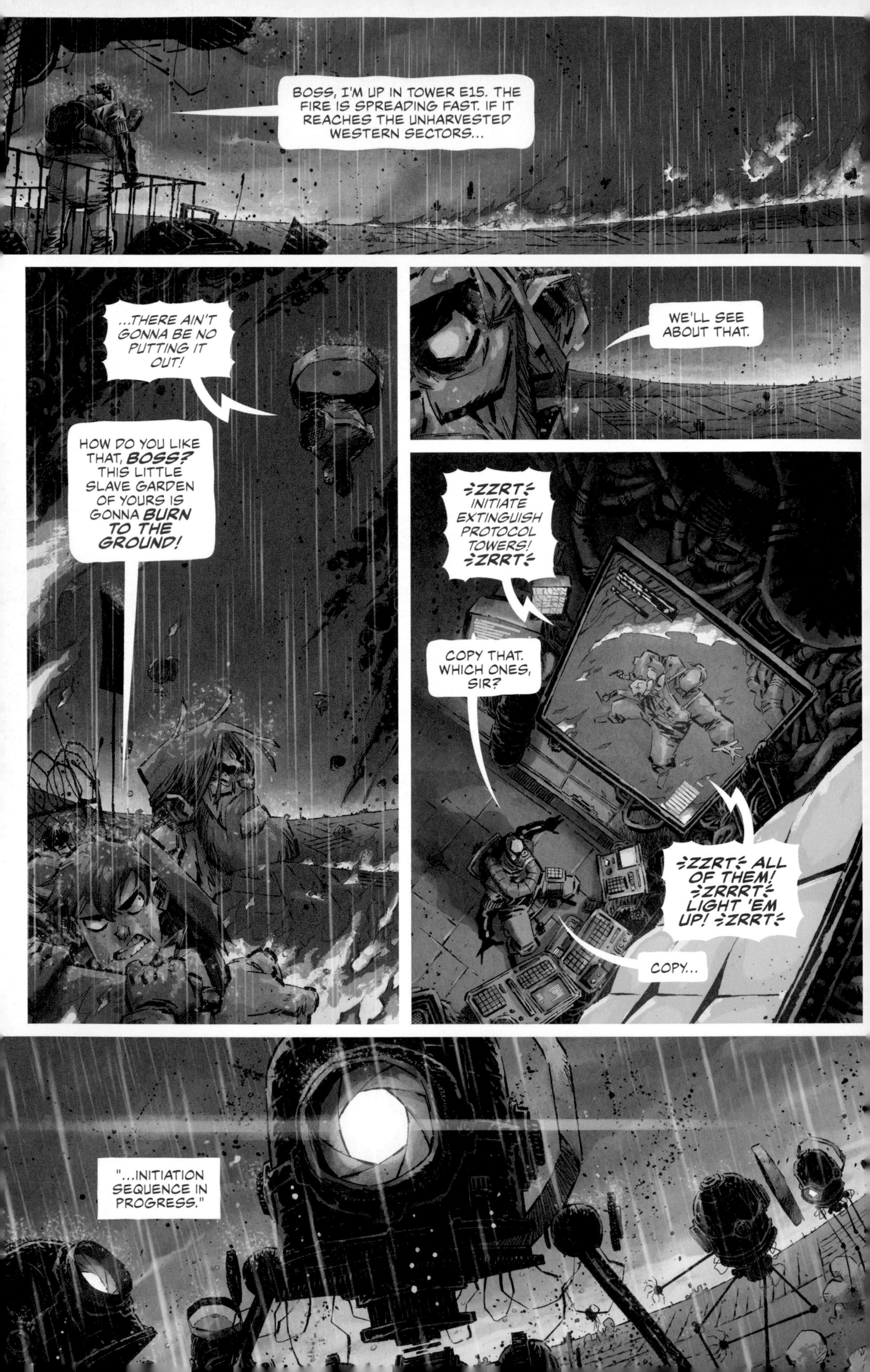
BOSS, I'M UP IN TOWER E15. THE FIRE IS SPREADING FAST. IF IT REACHES THE UNHARVESTED WESTERN SECTORS...
...THERE AIN'T GONNA BE NO PUTTING IT OUT!
WE'LL SEE ABOUT THAT.
HOW DO YOU LIKE THAT, BOSS? THIS LITTLE SLAVE GARDEN OF YOURS IS GONNA BURN TO THE GROUND!
ZZRT INITIATE EXTINGUISH PROTOCOL TOWERS! ZZRT
COPY THAT. WHICH ONES, SIR?
ZZRT ALL OF THEM! ZRRRT LIGHT 'EM UP! ZZRT
COPY...
"...INITIATION SEQUENCE IN PROGRESS."

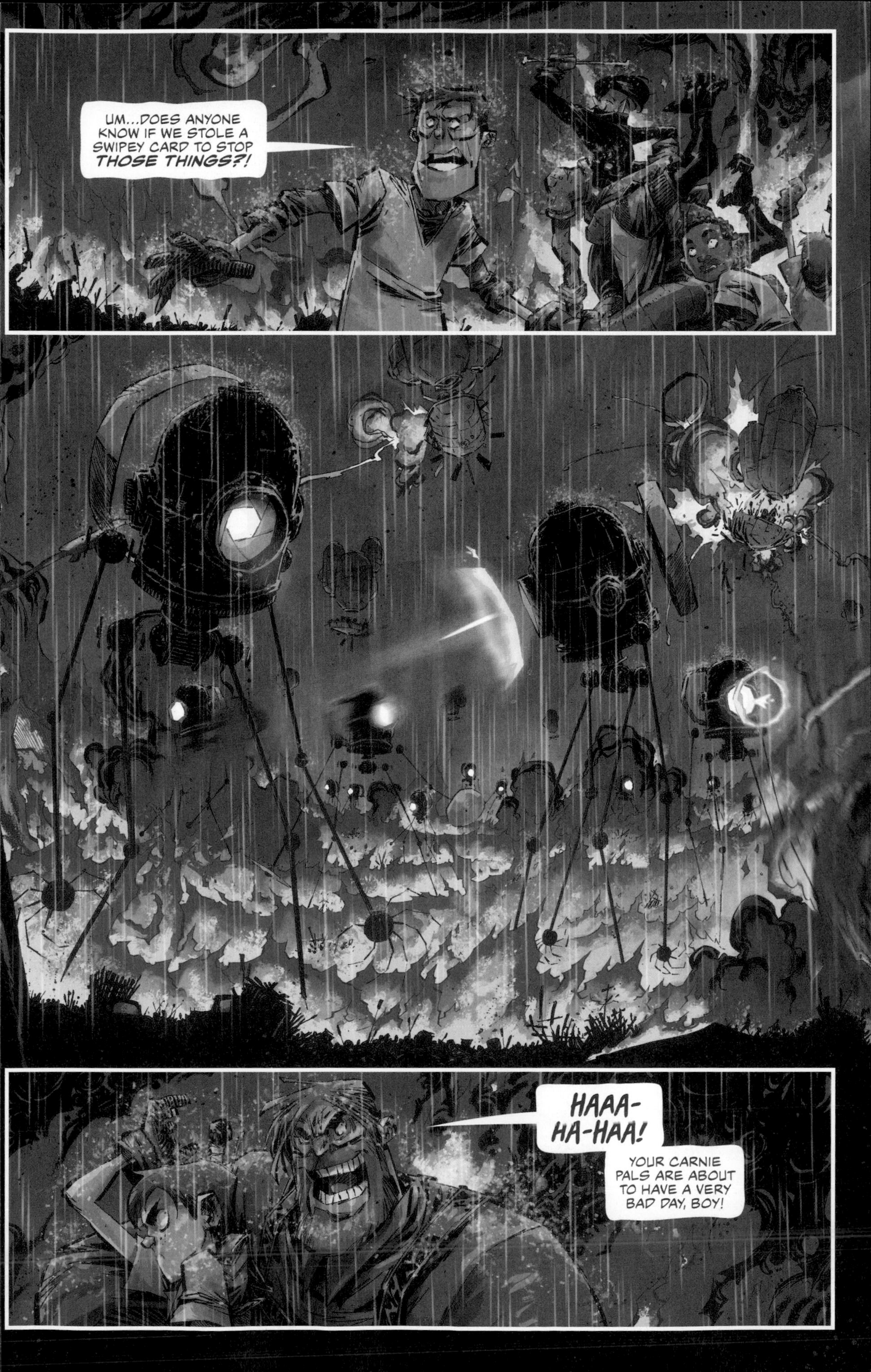
UM...DOES ANYONE KNOW IF WE STOLE A SWIPEY CARD TO STOP THOSE THINGS?!
HAAA-HA-HAA!
YOUR CARNIE PALS ARE ABOUT TO HAVE A VERY BAD DAY, BOY!

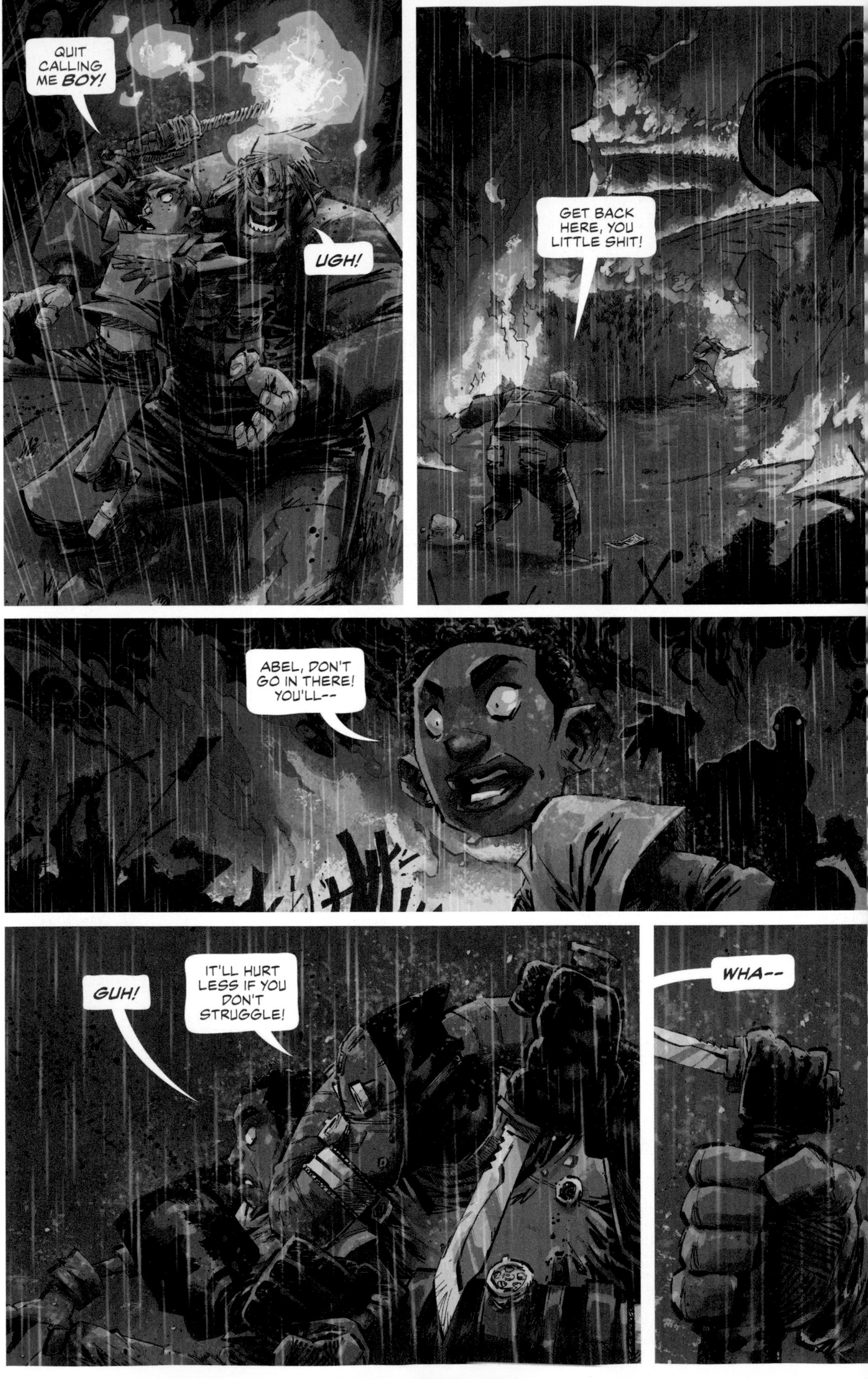
QUIT CALLING ME BOY!
UGH!
GET BACK HERE, YOU LITTLE SHIT!
ABEL, DON'T GO IN THERE! YOU'LL--
GUH!
IT'LL HURT LESS IF YOU DON'T STRUGGLE!
WHA--

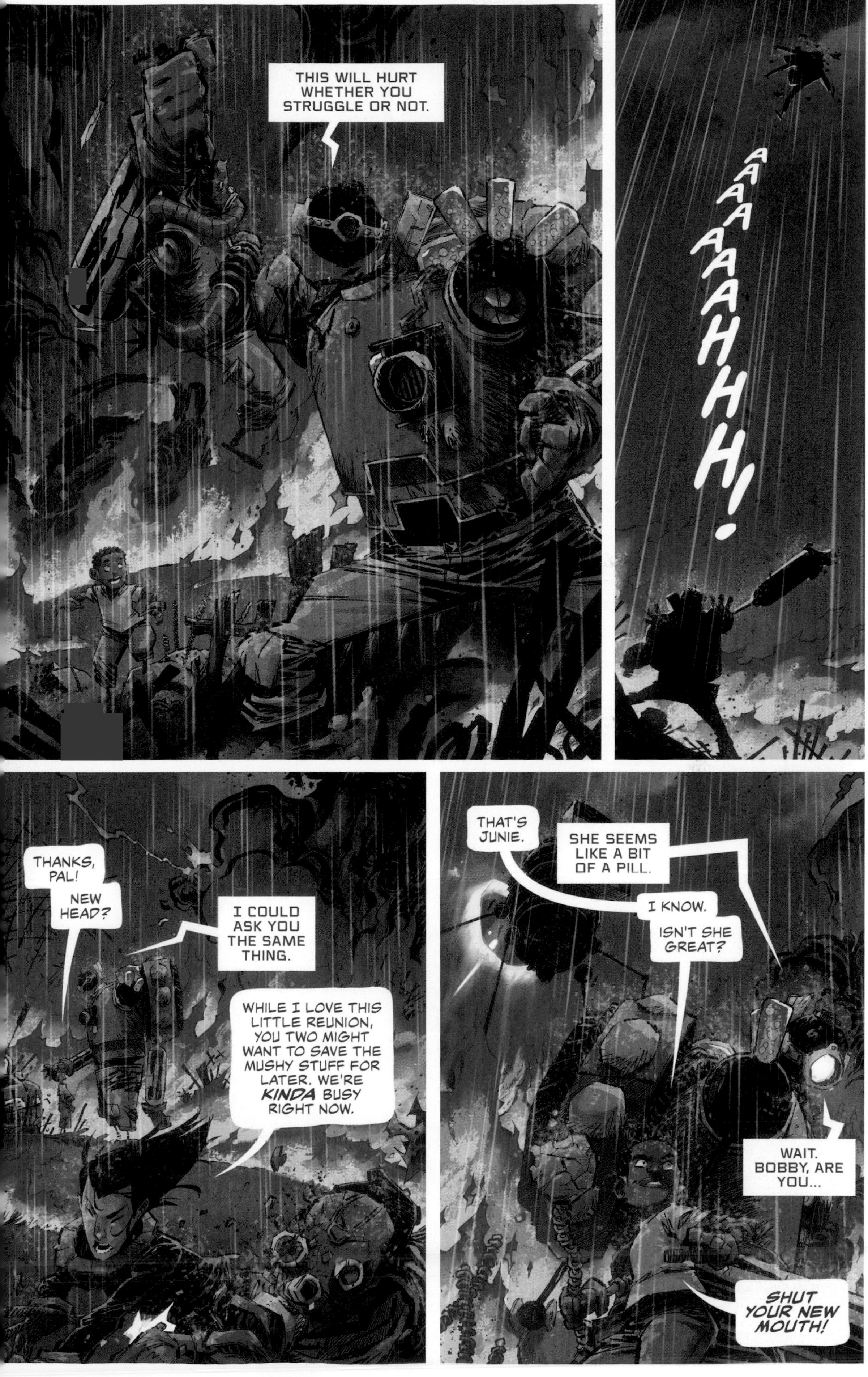
THIS WILL HURT WHETHER YOU STRUGGLE OR NOT.
AAAAAAAHHH!
THANKS, PAL!
NEW HEAD?
I COULD ASK YOU THE SAME THING.
WHILE I LOVE THIS LITTLE REUNION, YOU TWO MIGHT WANT TO SAVE THE MUSHY STUFF FOR LATER. WE'RE KINDA BUSY RIGHT NOW.
THAT'S JUNIE.
SHE SEEMS LIKE A BIT OF A PILL.
I KNOW.
ISN'T SHE GREAT?
WAIT. BOBBY, ARE YOU...
SHUT YOUR NEW MOUTH!

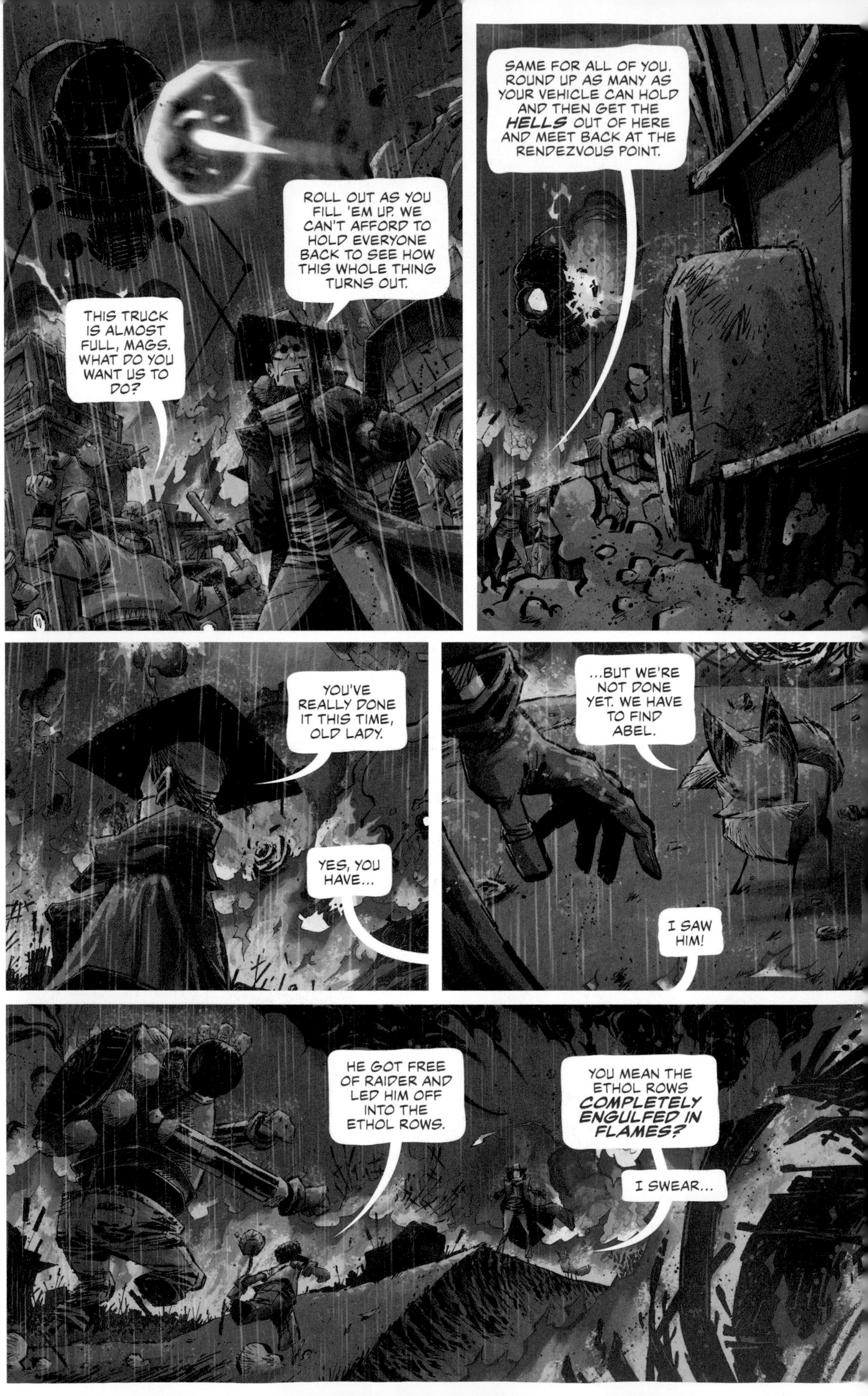
ROLL OUT AS YOU FILL 'EM UP. WE CAN'T AFFORD TO HOLD EVERYONE BACK TO SEE HOW THIS WHOLE THING TURNS OUT.
THIS TRUCK IS ALMOST FULL, MAGS. WHAT DO YOU WANT US TO DO?
SAME FOR ALL OF YOU. ROUND UP AS MANY AS YOUR VEHICLE CAN HOLD AND THEN GET THE **HELLS** OUT OF HERE AND MEET BACK AT THE RENDEZVOUS POINT.
YOU'VE REALLY DONE IT THIS TIME, OLD LADY.
YES, YOU HAVE...
...BUT WE'RE NOT DONE YET. WE HAVE TO FIND ABEL.
I SAW HIM!
HE GOT FREE OF RAIDER AND LED HIM OFF INTO THE ETHOL ROWS.
YOU MEAN THE ETHOL ROWS **COMPLETELY ENGULFED IN FLAMES?**
I SWEAR...

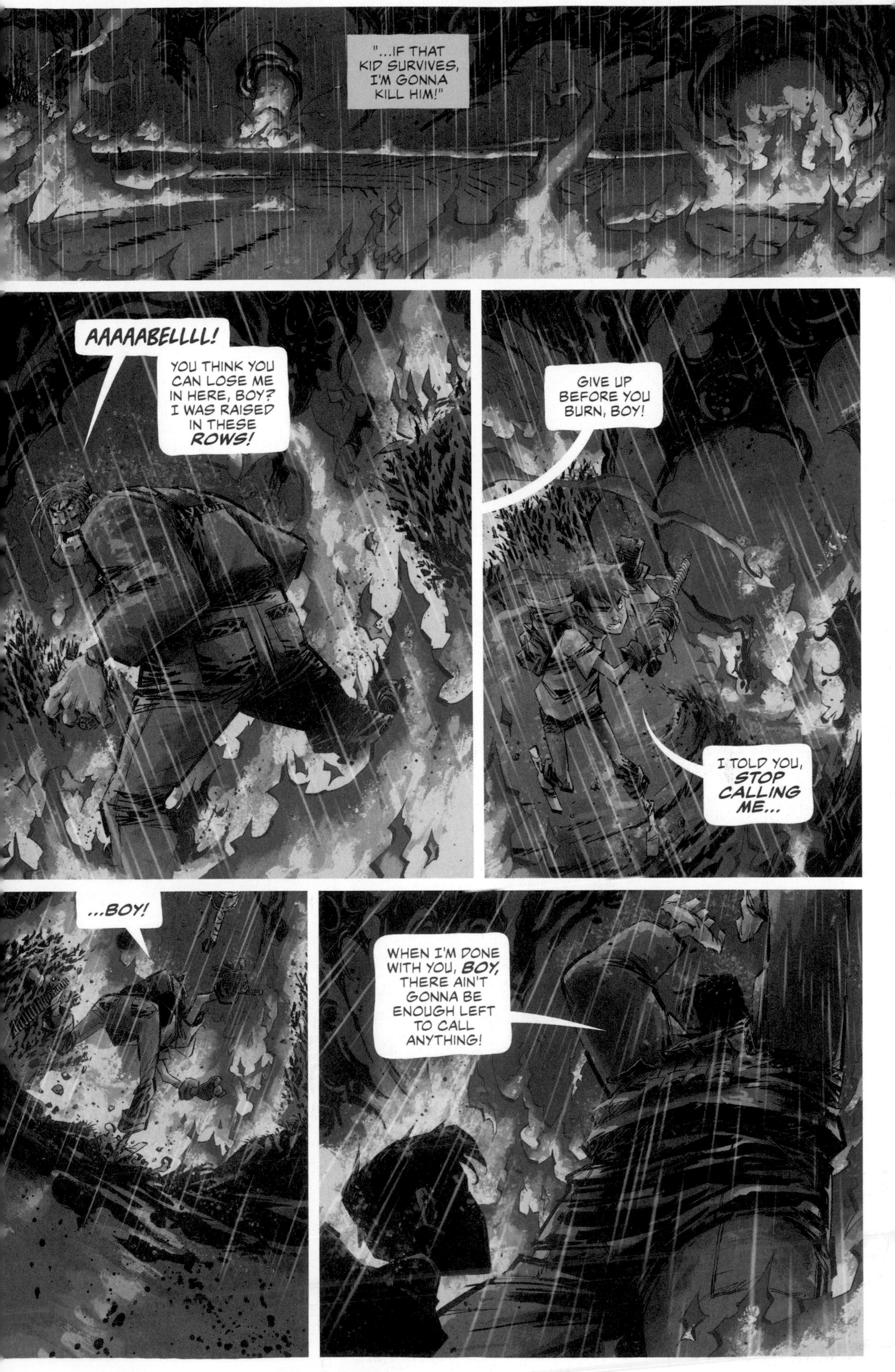
"...IF THAT KID SURVIVES, I'M GONNA KILL HIM!"
AAAAABELLLL!
YOU THINK YOU CAN LOSE ME IN HERE, BOY? I WAS RAISED IN THESE ROWS!
GIVE UP BEFORE YOU BURN, BOY!
I TOLD YOU, STOP CALLING ME...
...BOY!
WHEN I'M DONE WITH YOU, BOY, THERE AIN'T GONNA BE ENOUGH LEFT TO CALL ANYTHING!

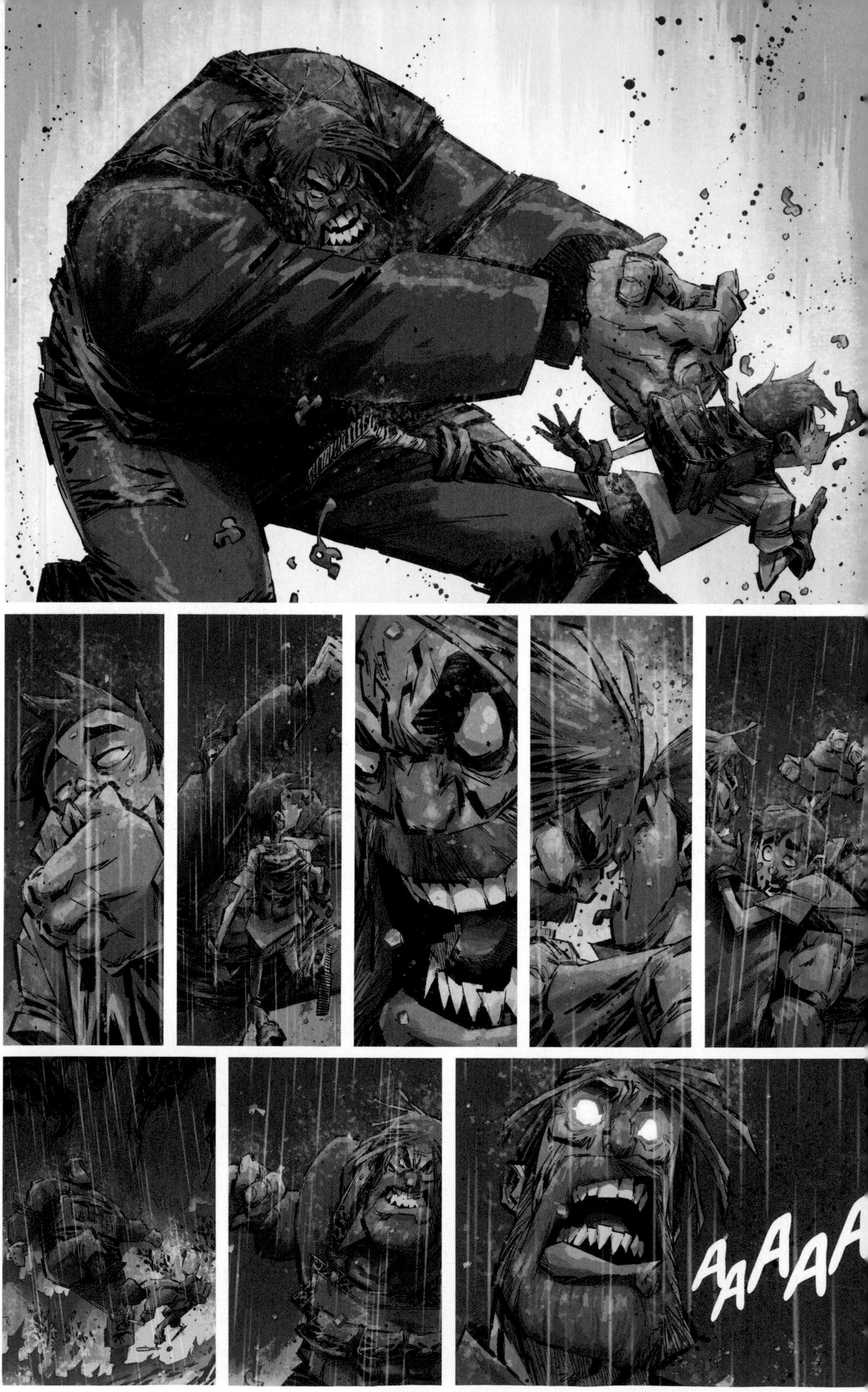
AAAAAA

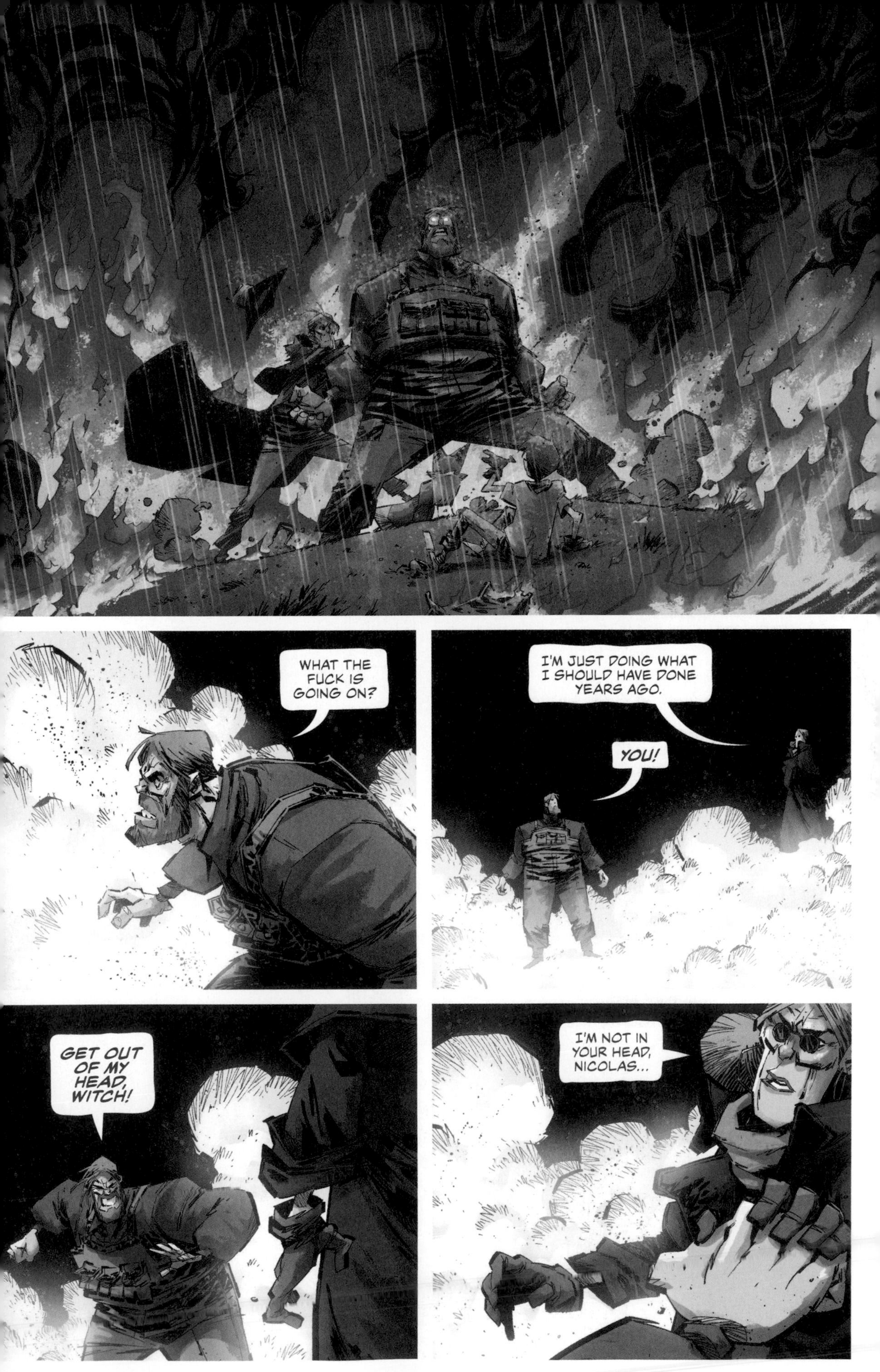
WHAT THE FUCK IS GOING ON?
I'M JUST DOING WHAT I SHOULD HAVE DONE YEARS AGO.
YOU!
GET OUT OF MY HEAD, WITCH!
I'M NOT IN YOUR HEAD, NICOLAS...

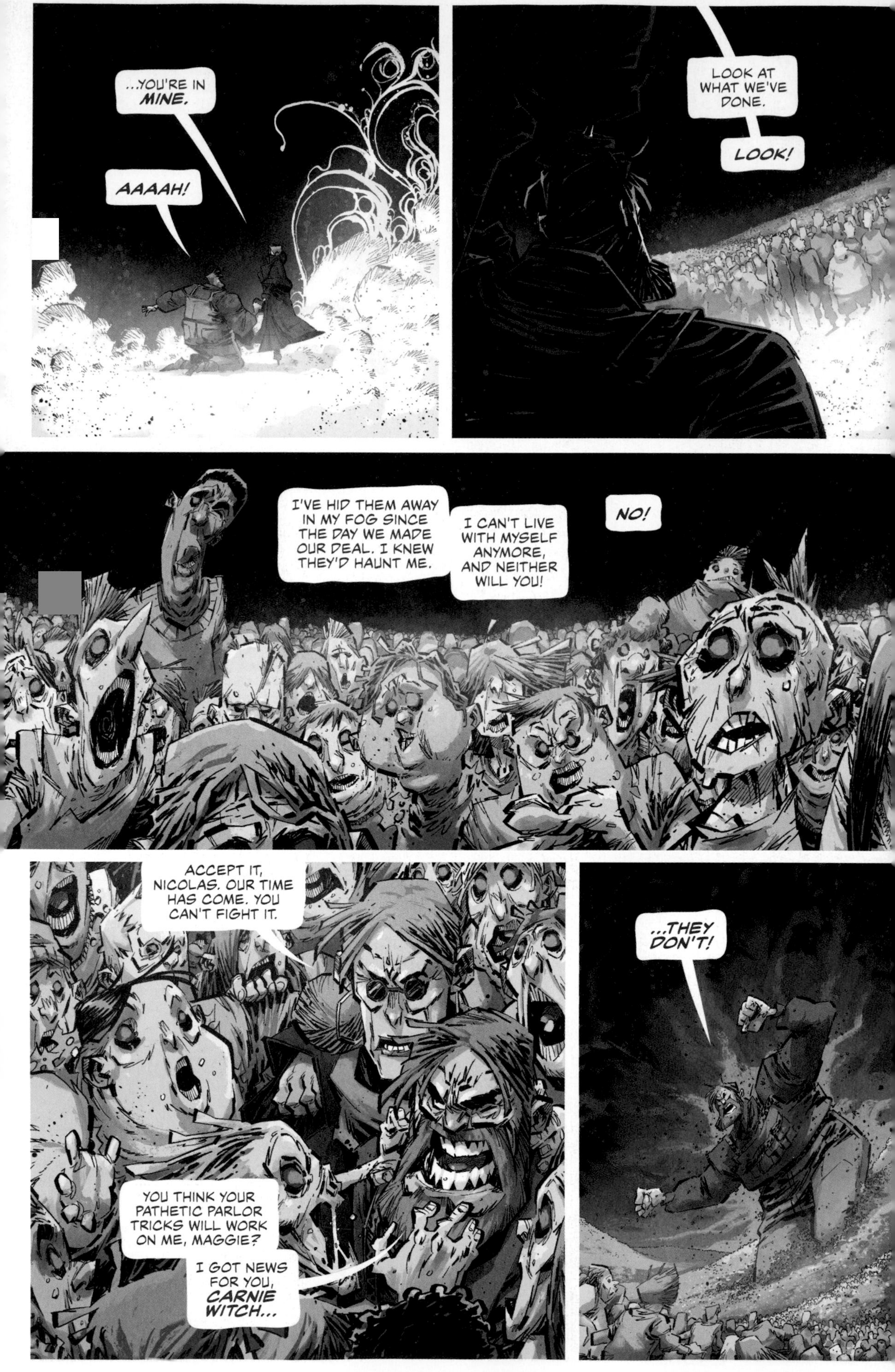

...YOU'RE IN MINE.
AAAAH!
LOOK AT WHAT WE'VE DONE.
LOOK!
I'VE HID THEM AWAY IN MY FOG SINCE THE DAY WE MADE OUR DEAL. I KNEW THEY'D HAUNT ME.
I CAN'T LIVE WITH MYSELF ANYMORE, AND NEITHER WILL YOU!
NO!
ACCEPT IT, NICOLAS. OUR TIME HAS COME. YOU CAN'T FIGHT IT.
YOU THINK YOUR PATHETIC PARLOR TRICKS WILL WORK ON ME, MAGGIE?
I GOT NEWS FOR YOU, CARNIE WITCH...
...THEY DON'T!

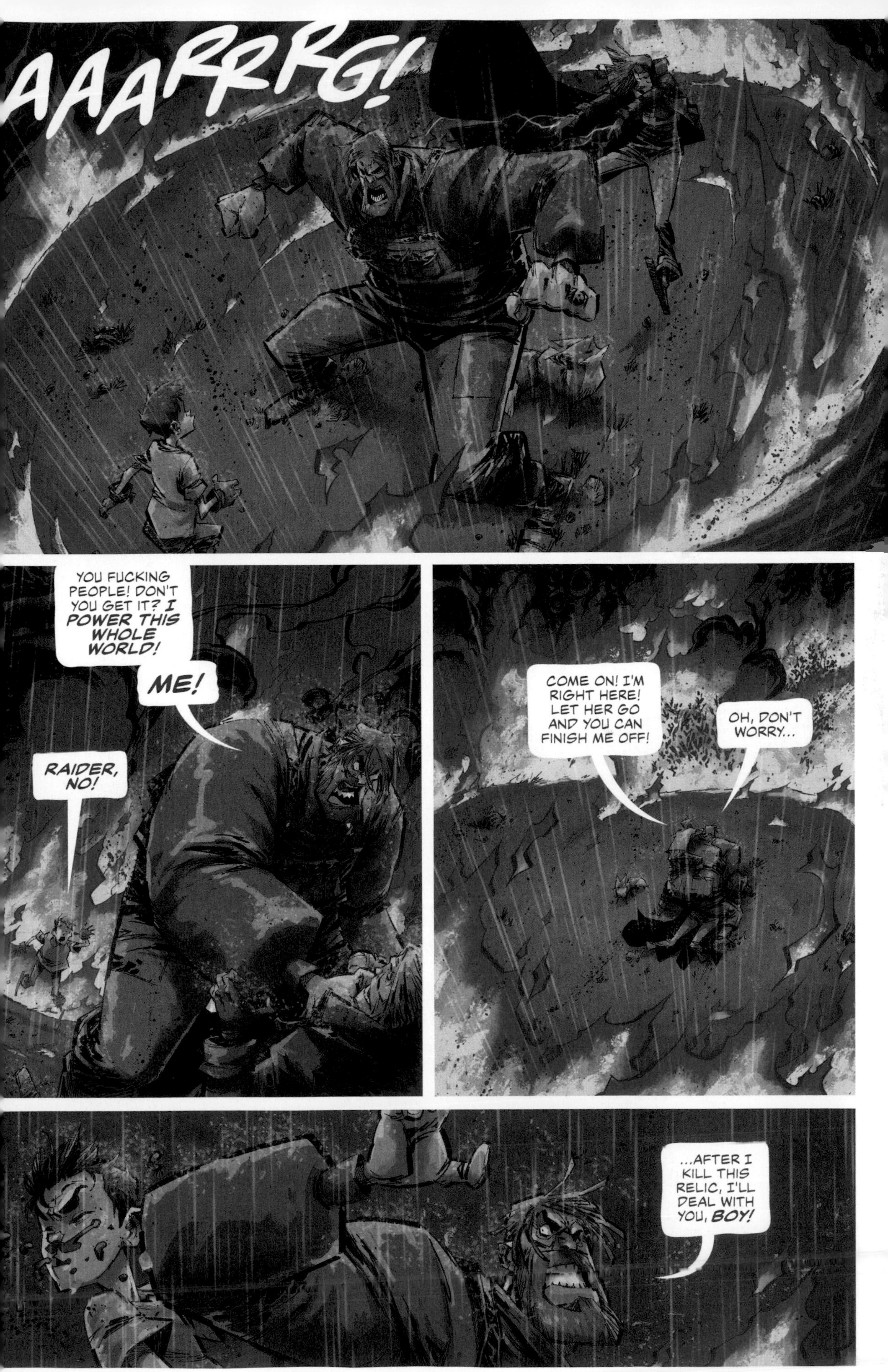
AAARRRG!
YOU FUCKING PEOPLE! DON'T YOU GET IT? *I POWER THIS WHOLE WORLD!*
ME!
RAIDER, NO!
COME ON! I'M RIGHT HERE! LET HER GO AND YOU CAN FINISH ME OFF!
OH, DON'T WORRY...
...AFTER I KILL THIS RELIC, I'LL DEAL WITH YOU, *BOY!*

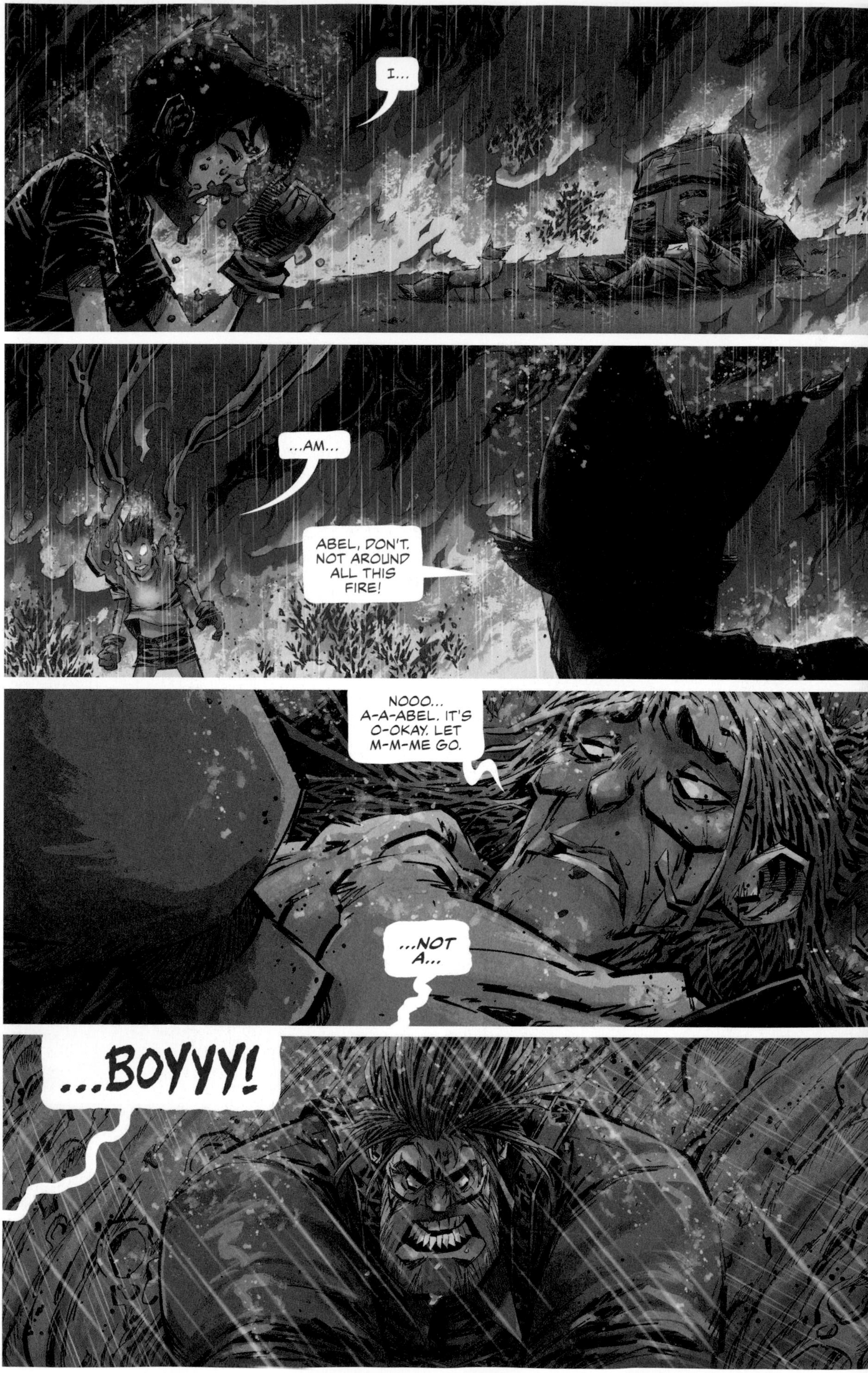
I...
...AM...
ABEL, DON'T. NOT AROUND ALL THIS FIRE!
NOOO... A-A-ABEL. IT'S O-OKAY. LET M-M-ME GO.
...NOT A...
...BOYYY!

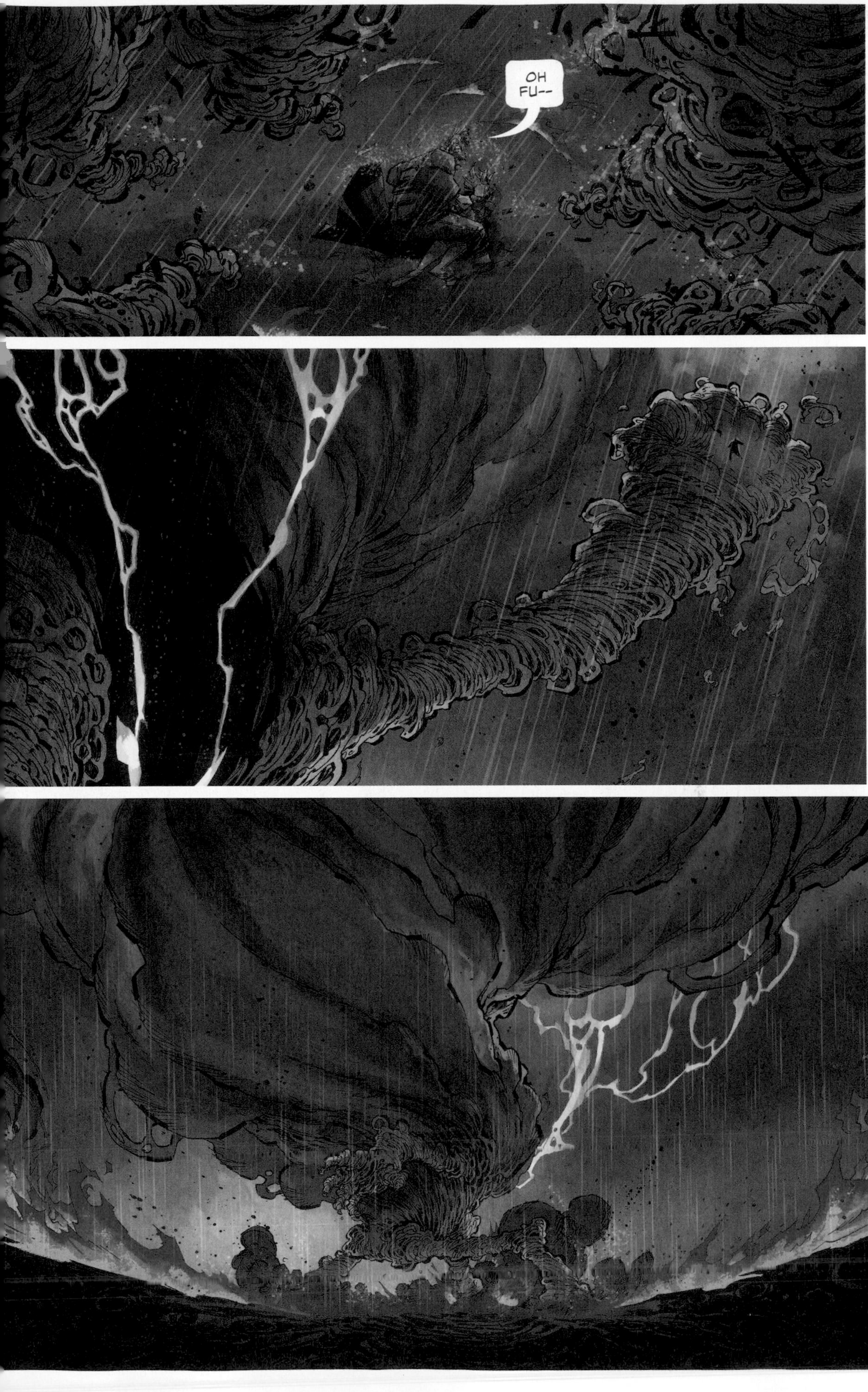
OH
FU--

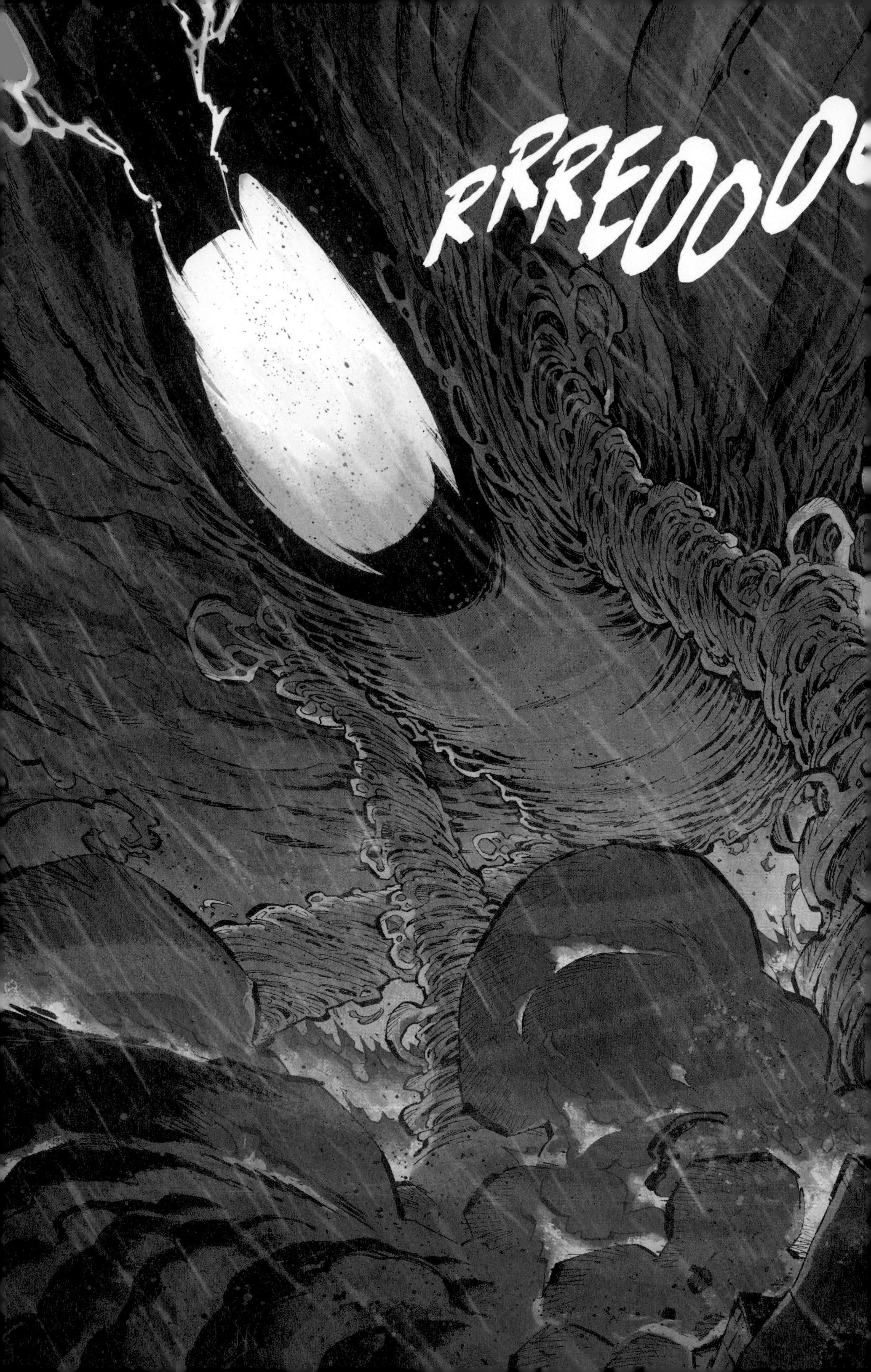
RRREOOOO

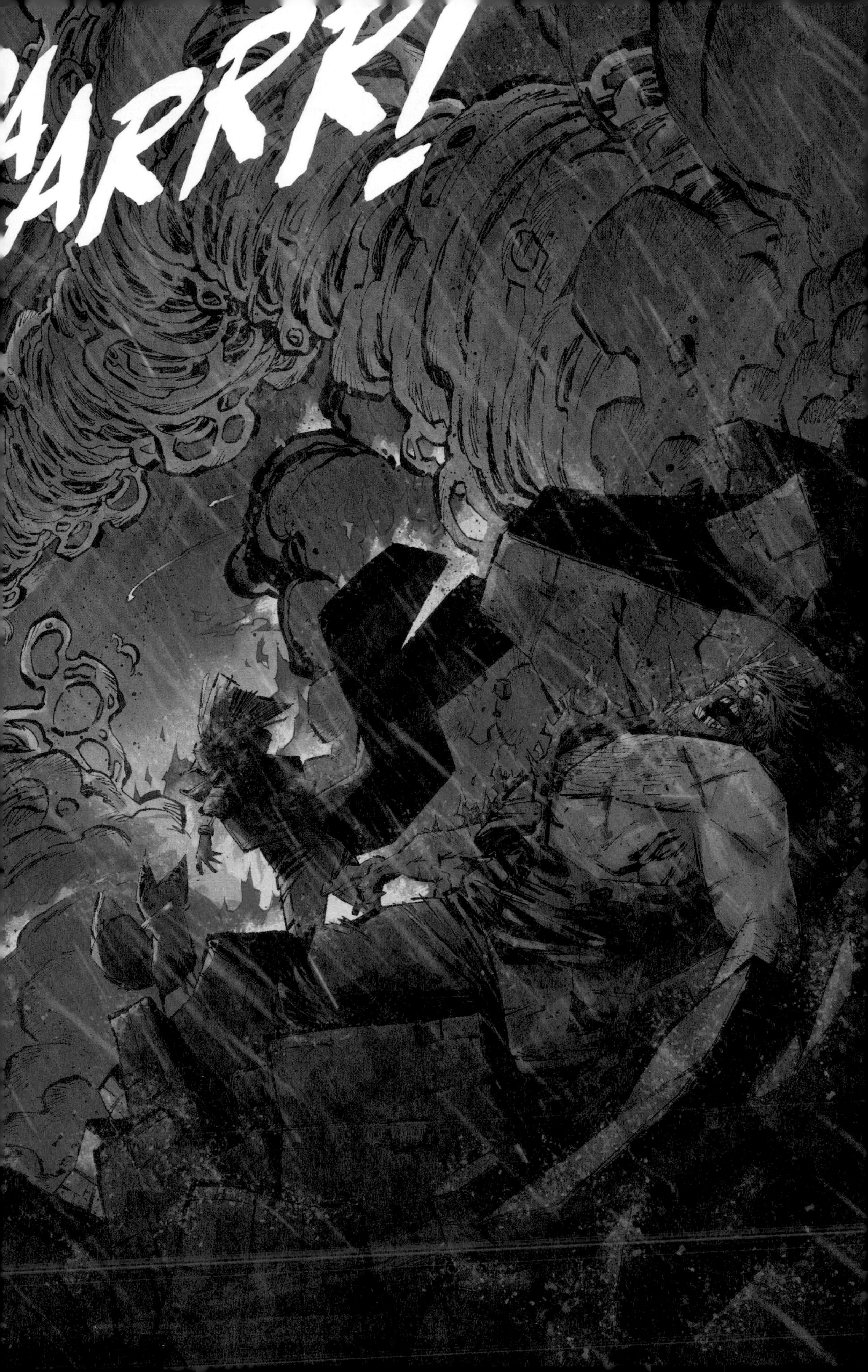
ARRK!

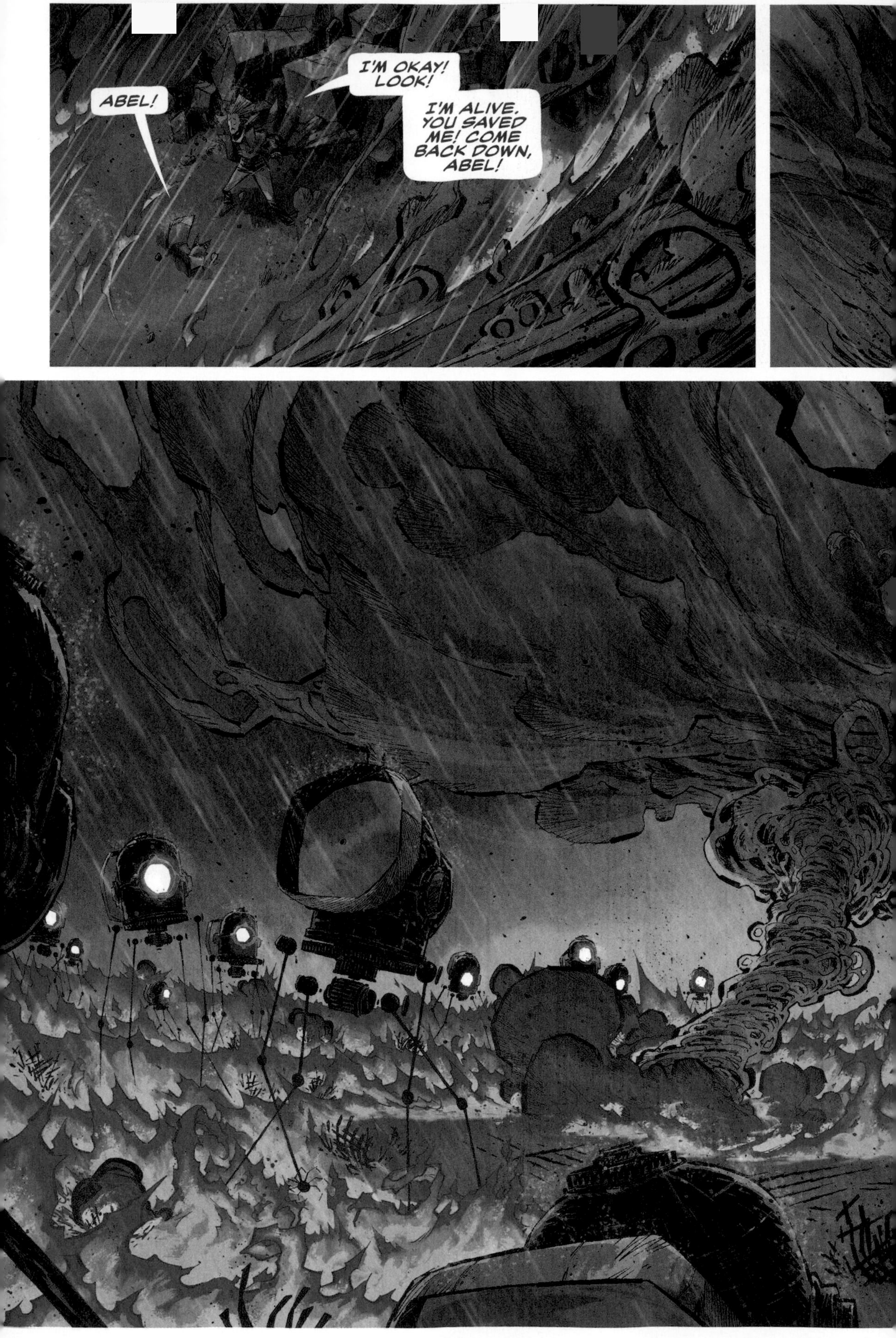
ABEL!
I'M OKAY! LOOK!
I'M ALIVE. YOU SAVED ME! COME BACK DOWN, ABEL!

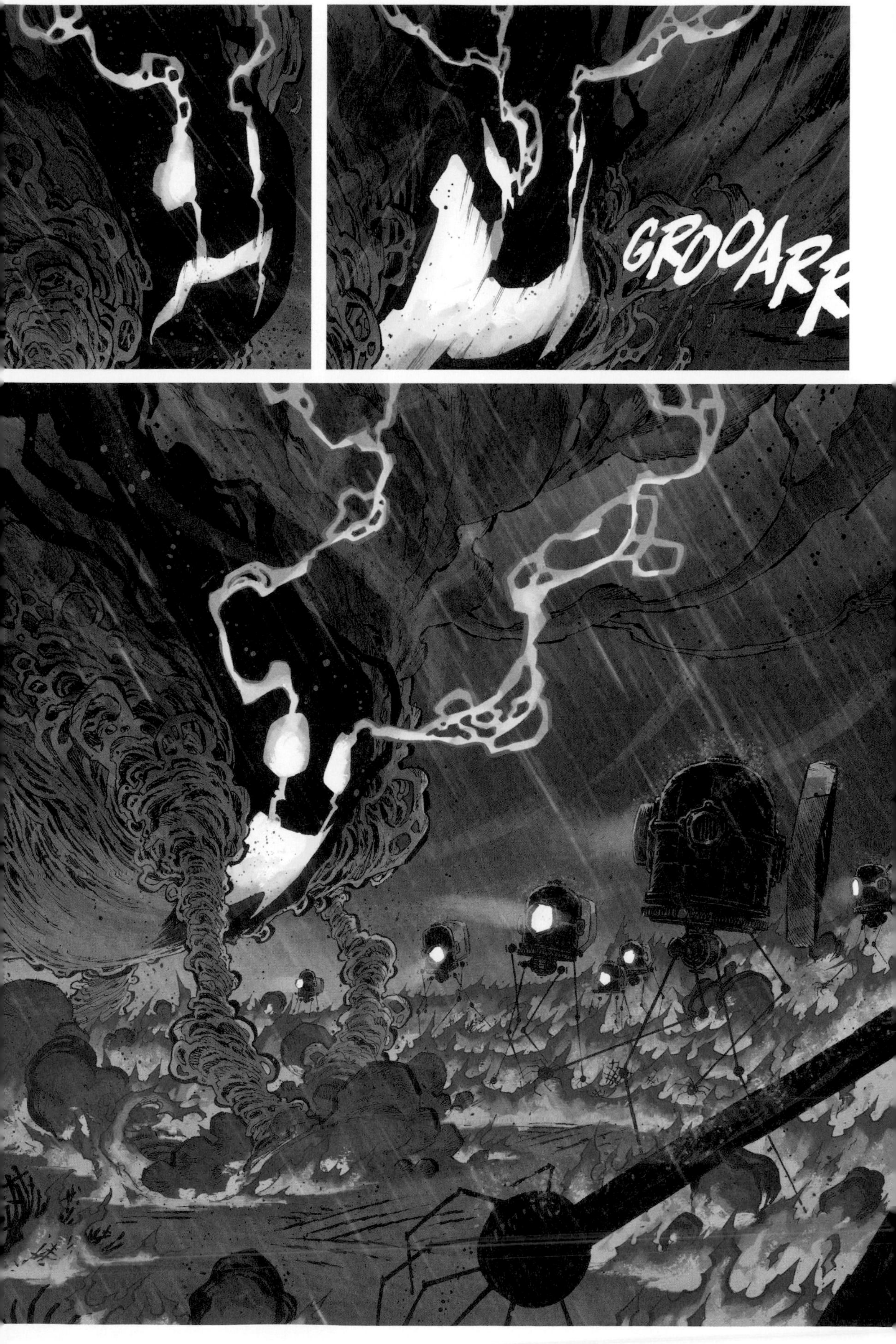
GROOARR

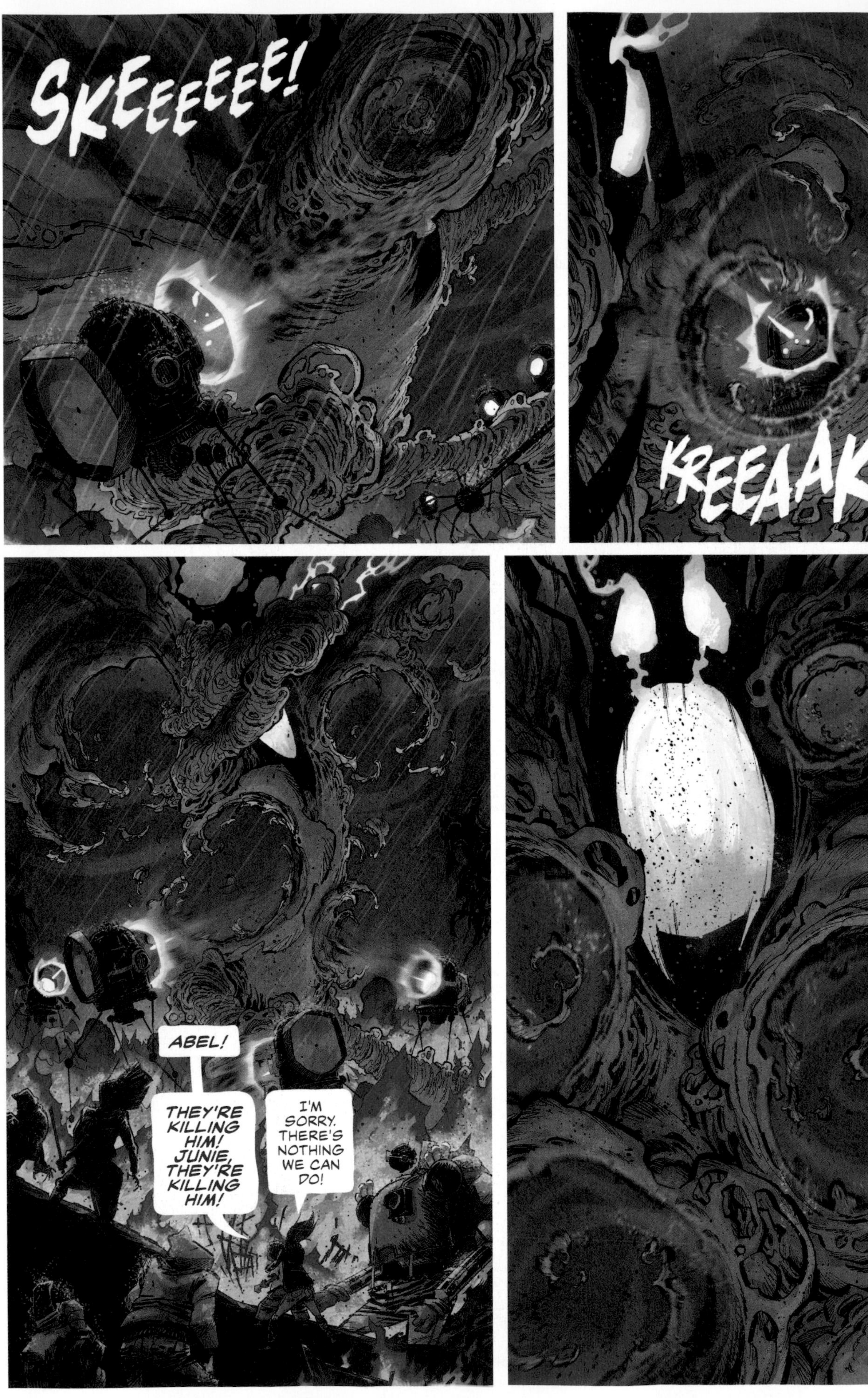
SKEEEEEE!
KREEAAK
ABEL!
THEY'RE KILLING HIM! JUNIE, THEY'RE KILLING HIM!
I'M SORRY. THERE'S NOTHING WE CAN DO!

MY DEAR ABEL, I'M SO SORRY.
WE FAILED YOU.

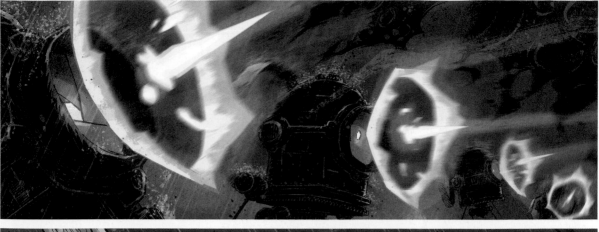

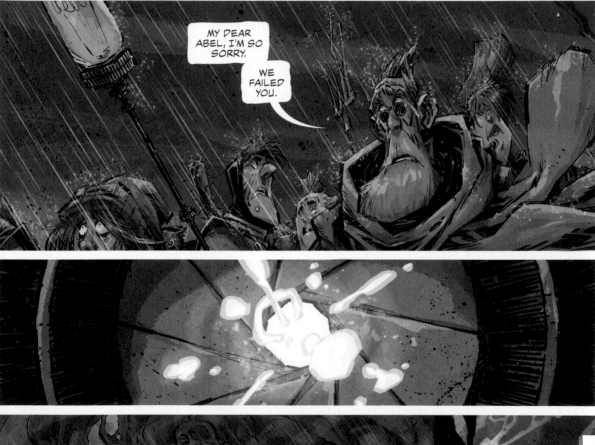

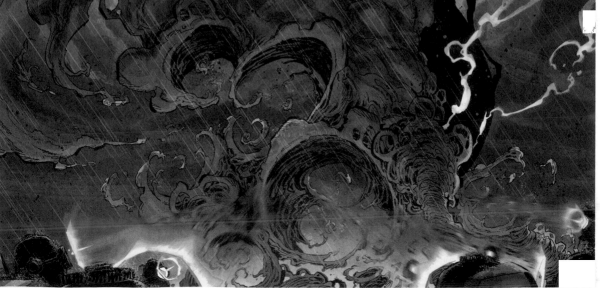

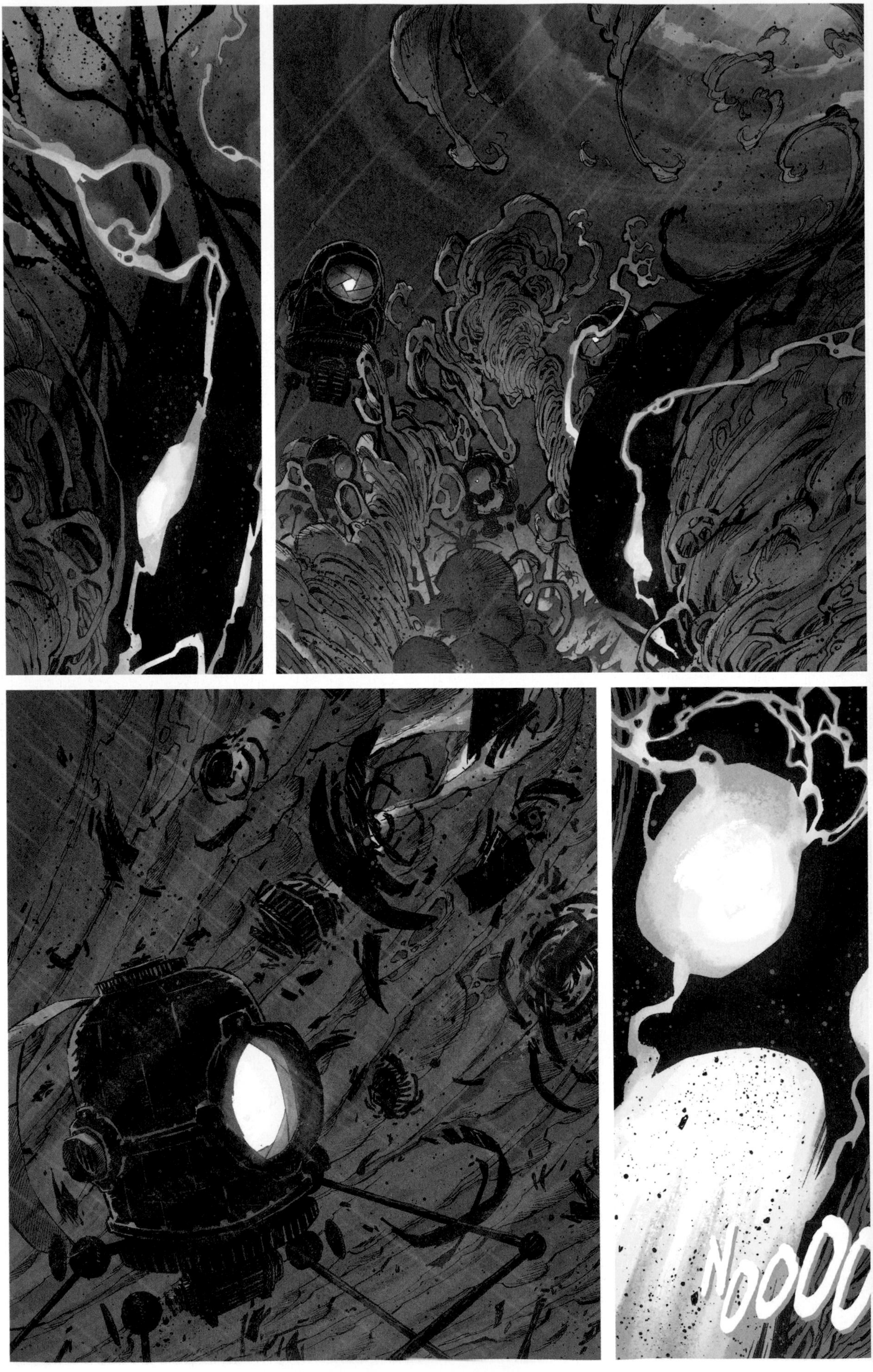

NOOOO

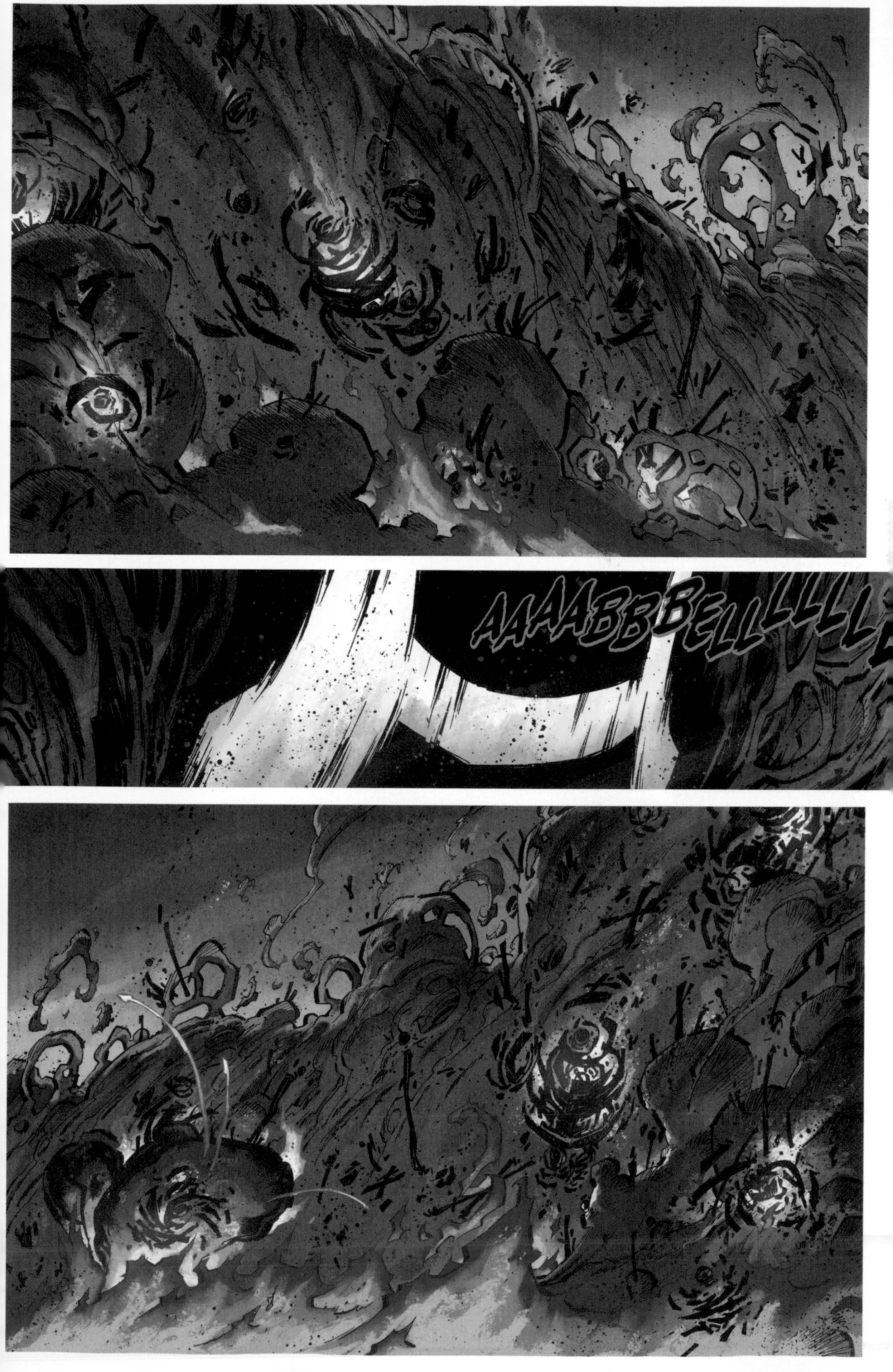
AAAABBBELLLLLL

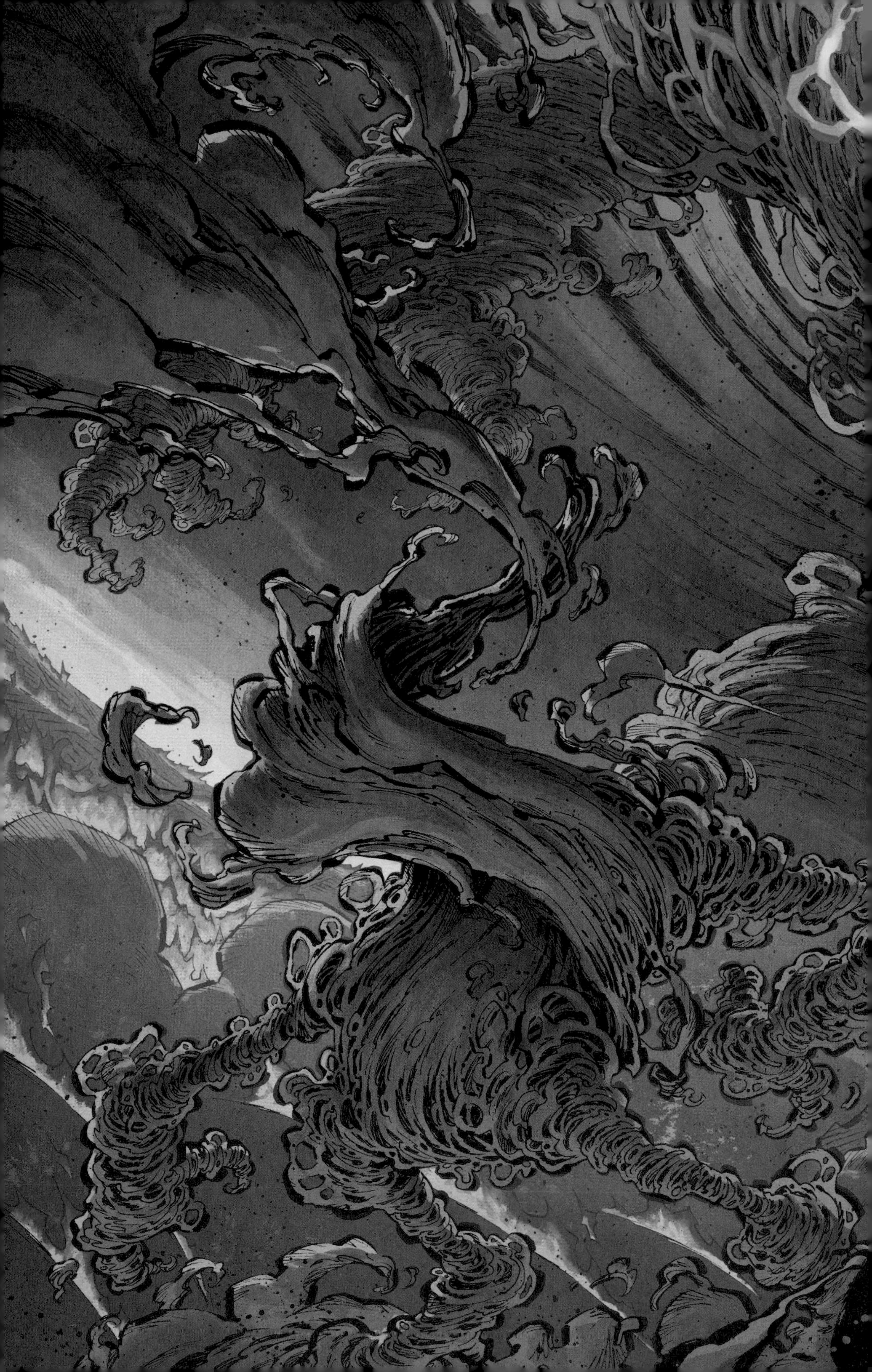

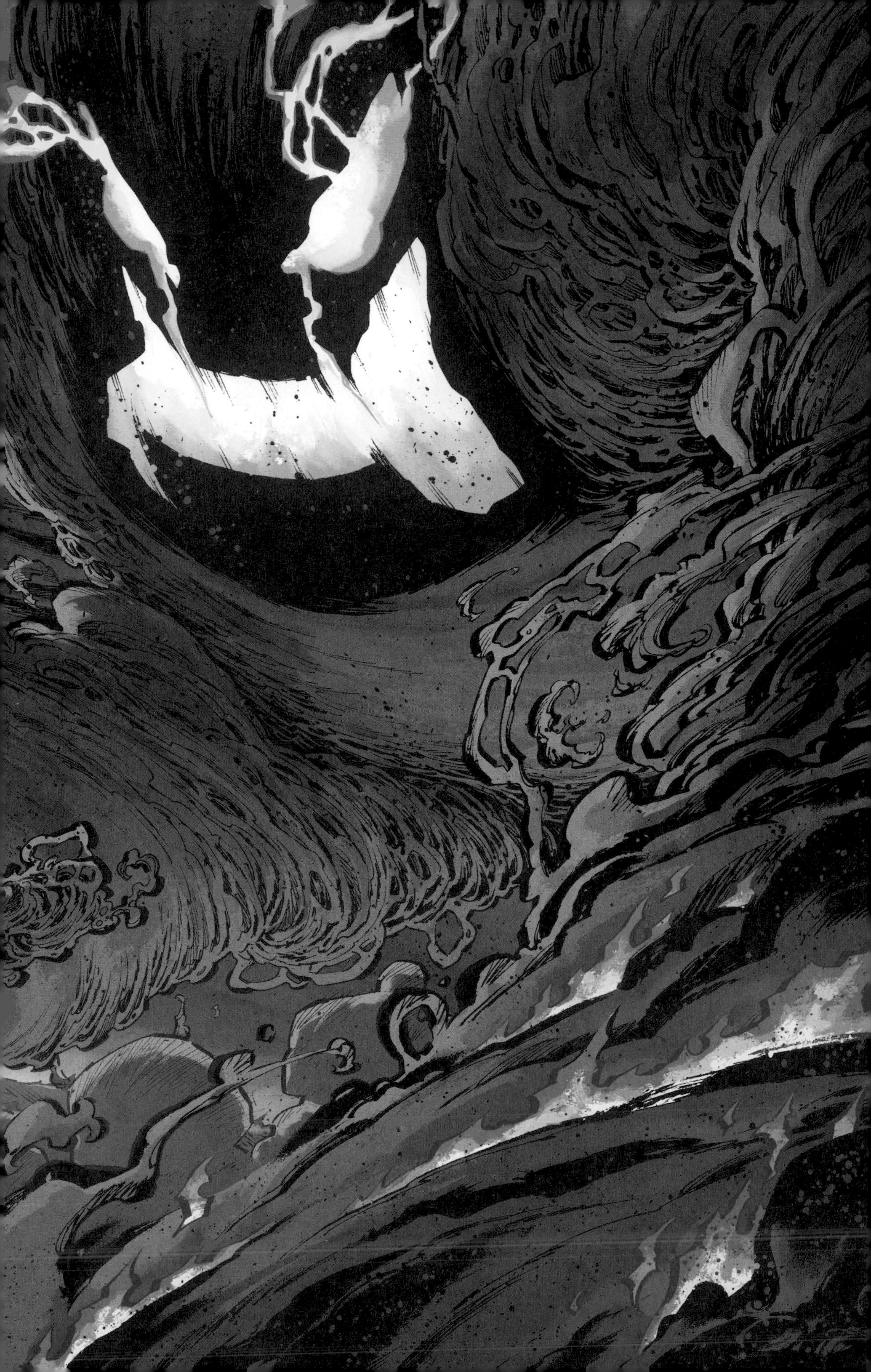

CHAPTER

EIGHTEEN

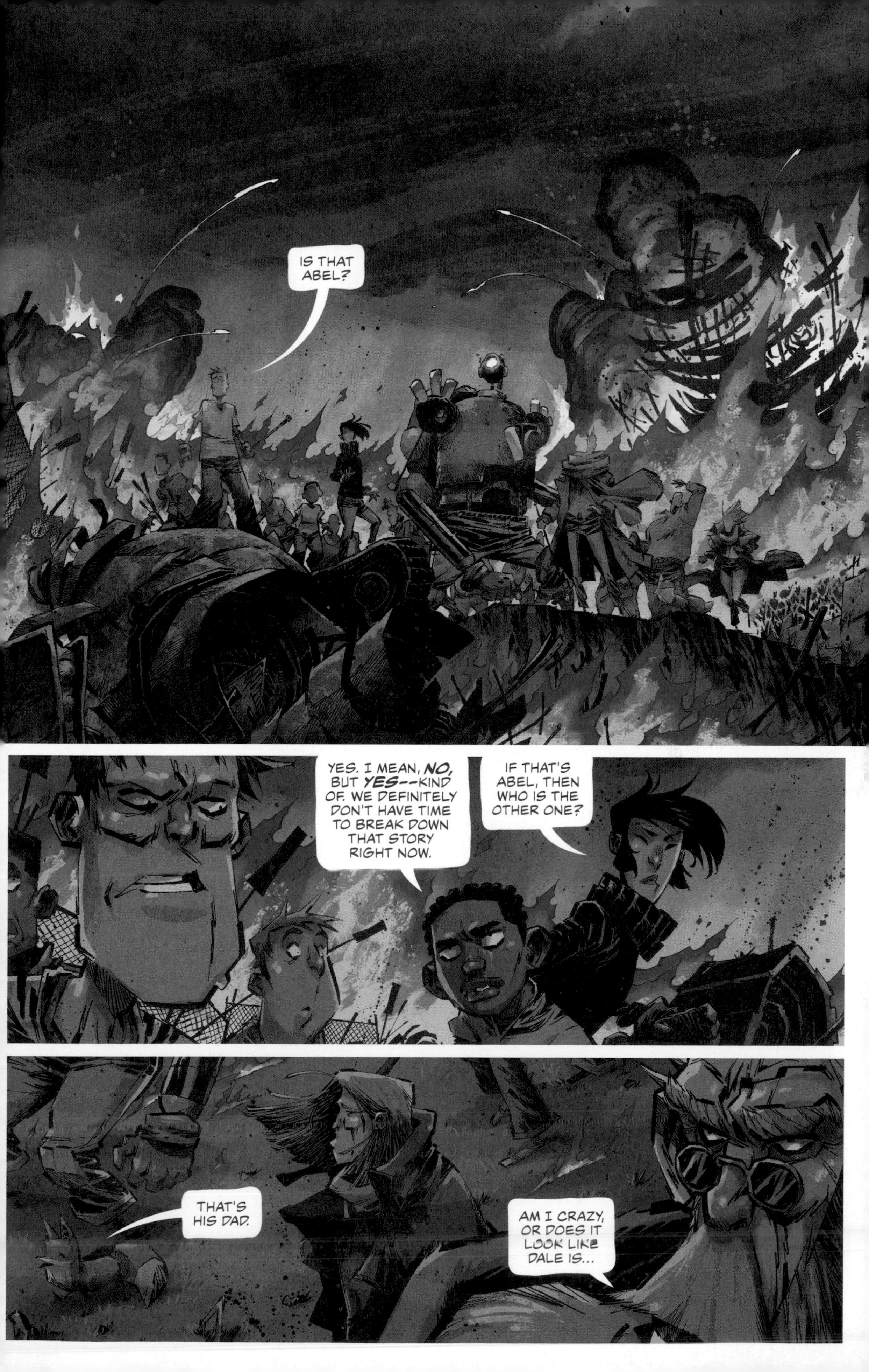
IS THAT ABEL?
YES. I MEAN, NO, BUT YES--KIND OF. WE DEFINITELY DON'T HAVE TIME TO BREAK DOWN THAT STORY RIGHT NOW.
IF THAT'S ABEL, THEN WHO IS THE OTHER ONE?
THAT'S HIS DAD.
AM I CRAZY, OR DOES IT LOOK LIKE DALE IS...

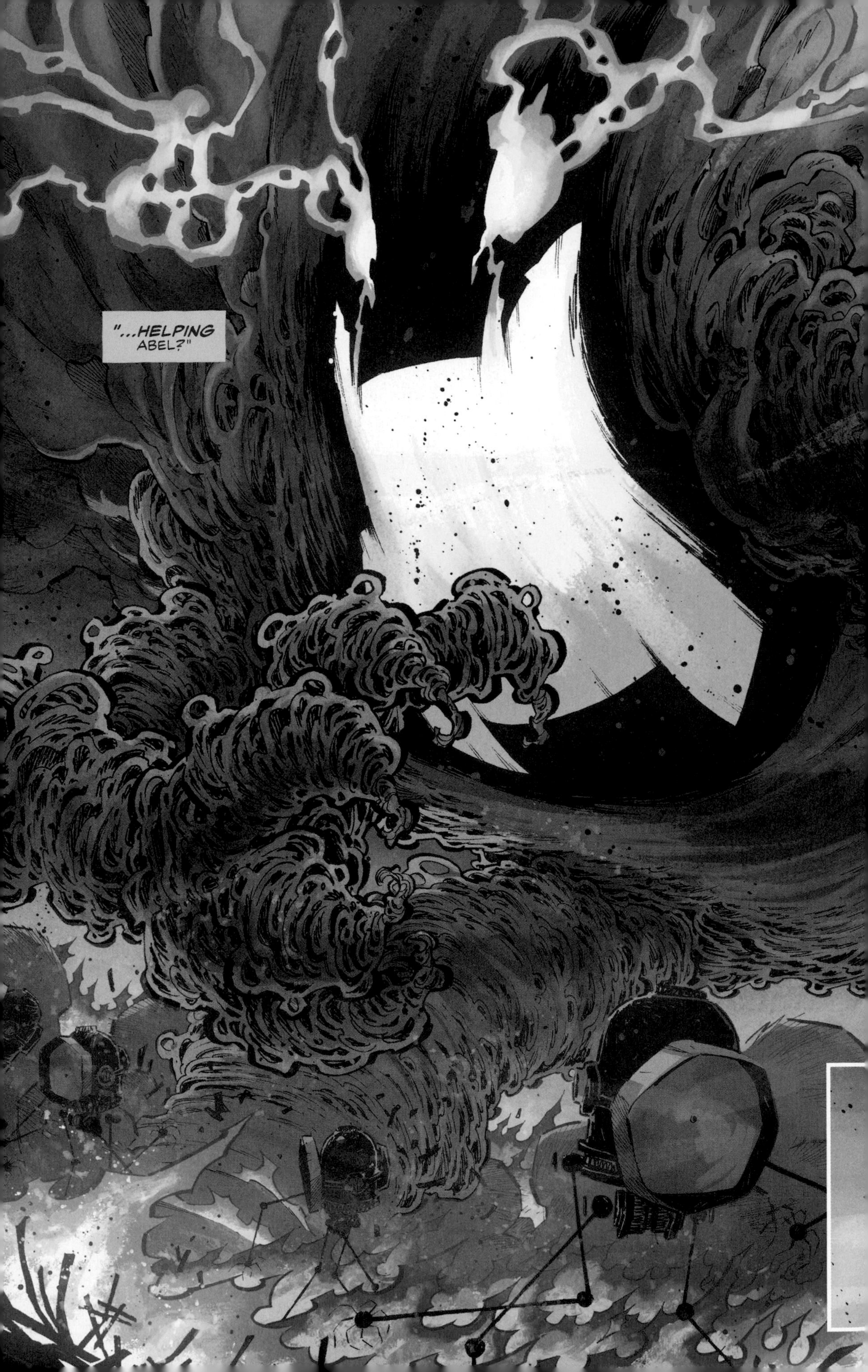
"...HELPING ABEL?"

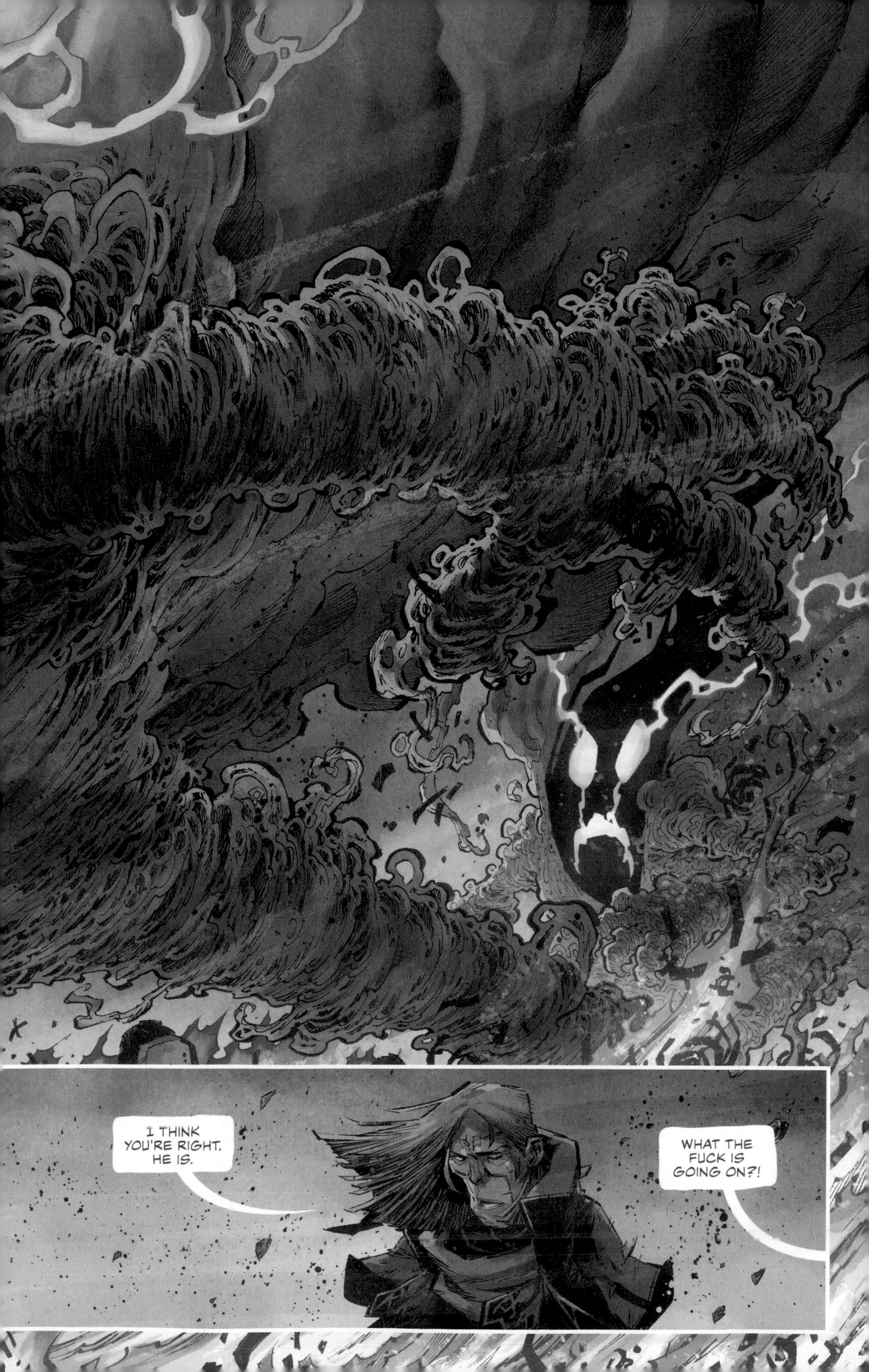
I THINK YOU'RE RIGHT. HE IS.
WHAT THE FUCK IS GOING ON?!

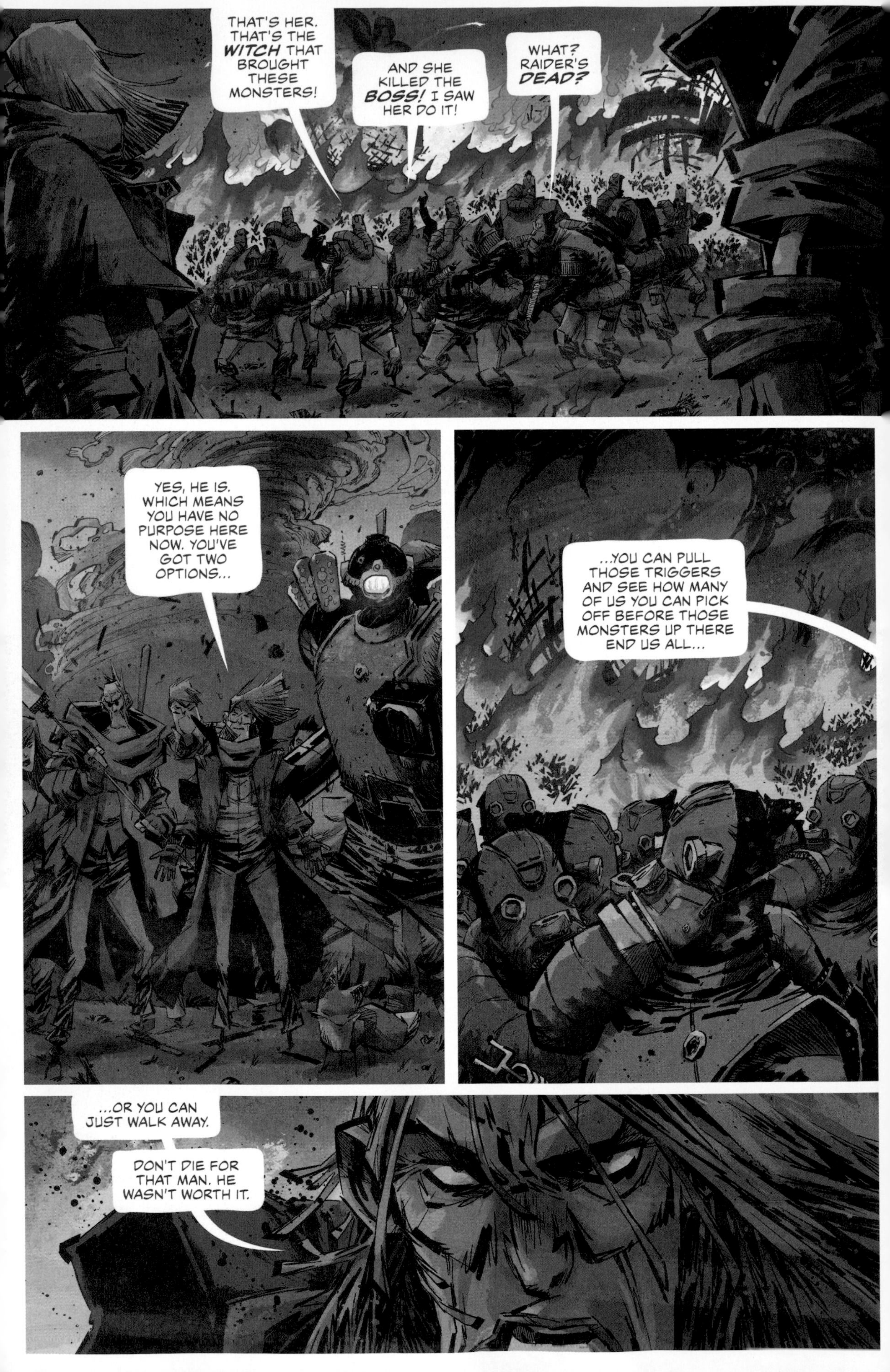
THAT'S HER. THAT'S THE WITCH THAT BROUGHT THESE MONSTERS!
AND SHE KILLED THE BOSS! I SAW HER DO IT!
WHAT? RAIDER'S DEAD?
YES, HE IS. WHICH MEANS YOU HAVE NO PURPOSE HERE NOW. YOU'VE GOT TWO OPTIONS...
...YOU CAN PULL THOSE TRIGGERS AND SEE HOW MANY OF US YOU CAN PICK OFF BEFORE THOSE MONSTERS UP THERE END US ALL...
...OR YOU CAN JUST WALK AWAY.
DON'T DIE FOR THAT MAN. HE WASN'T WORTH IT.

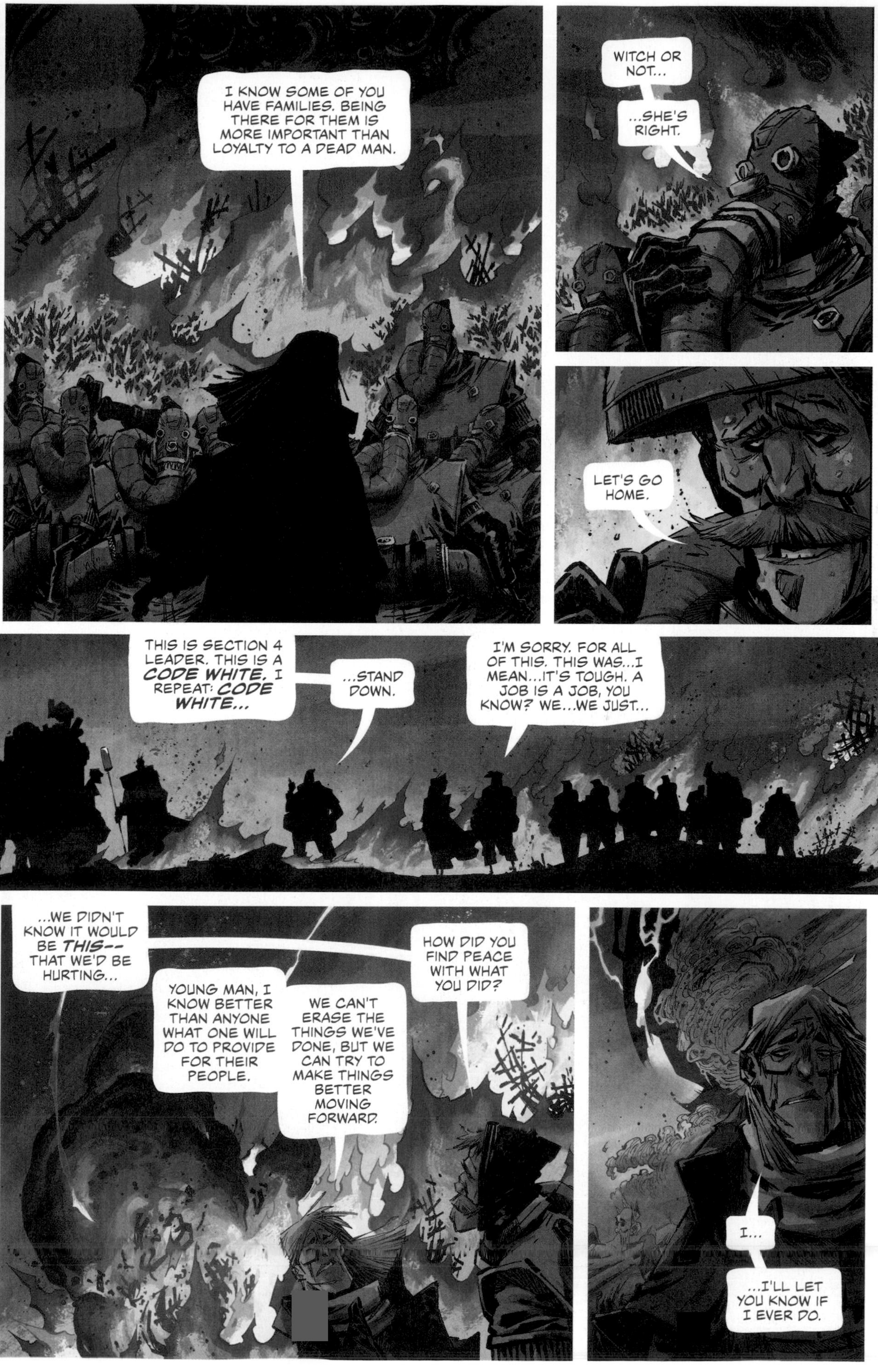

I KNOW SOME OF YOU HAVE FAMILIES. BEING THERE FOR THEM IS MORE IMPORTANT THAN LOYALTY TO A DEAD MAN.
WITCH OR NOT...
...SHE'S RIGHT.
LET'S GO HOME.
THIS IS SECTION 4 LEADER. THIS IS A CODE WHITE. I REPEAT: CODE WHITE...
...STAND DOWN.
I'M SORRY. FOR ALL OF THIS. THIS WAS...I MEAN...IT'S TOUGH. A JOB IS A JOB, YOU KNOW? WE...WE JUST...
...WE DIDN'T KNOW IT WOULD BE THIS-- THAT WE'D BE HURTING...
HOW DID YOU FIND PEACE WITH WHAT YOU DID?
YOUNG MAN, I KNOW BETTER THAN ANYONE WHAT ONE WILL DO TO PROVIDE FOR THEIR PEOPLE.
WE CAN'T ERASE THE THINGS WE'VE DONE, BUT WE CAN TRY TO MAKE THINGS BETTER MOVING FORWARD.
I...
...I'LL LET YOU KNOW IF I EVER DO.

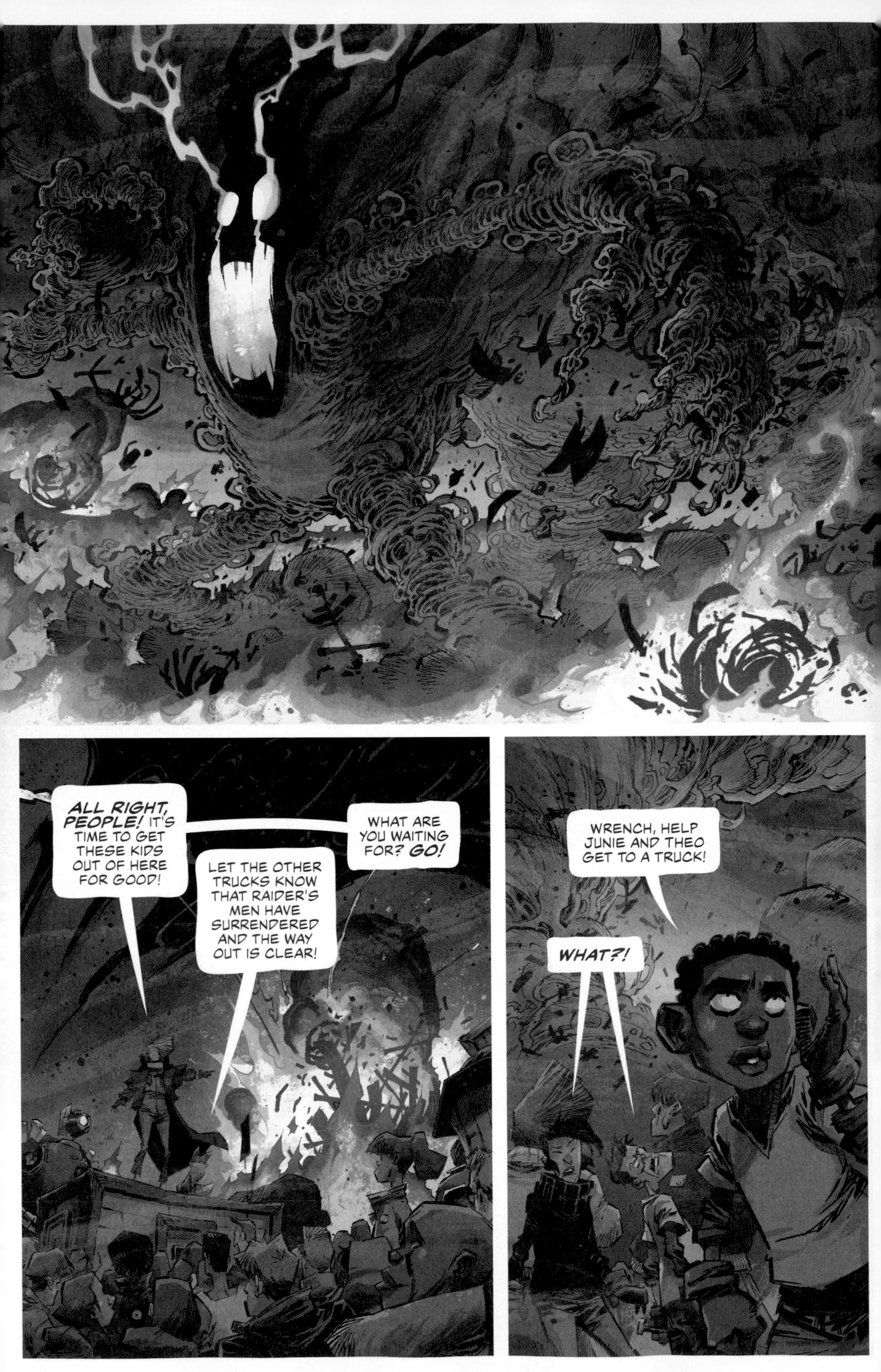

ALL RIGHT, PEOPLE! IT'S TIME TO GET THESE KIDS OUT OF HERE FOR GOOD!
WHAT ARE YOU WAITING FOR? GO!
LET THE OTHER TRUCKS KNOW THAT RAIDER'S MEN HAVE SURRENDERED AND THE WAY OUT IS CLEAR!
WRENCH, HELP JUNIE AND THEO GET TO A TRUCK!
WHAT?!

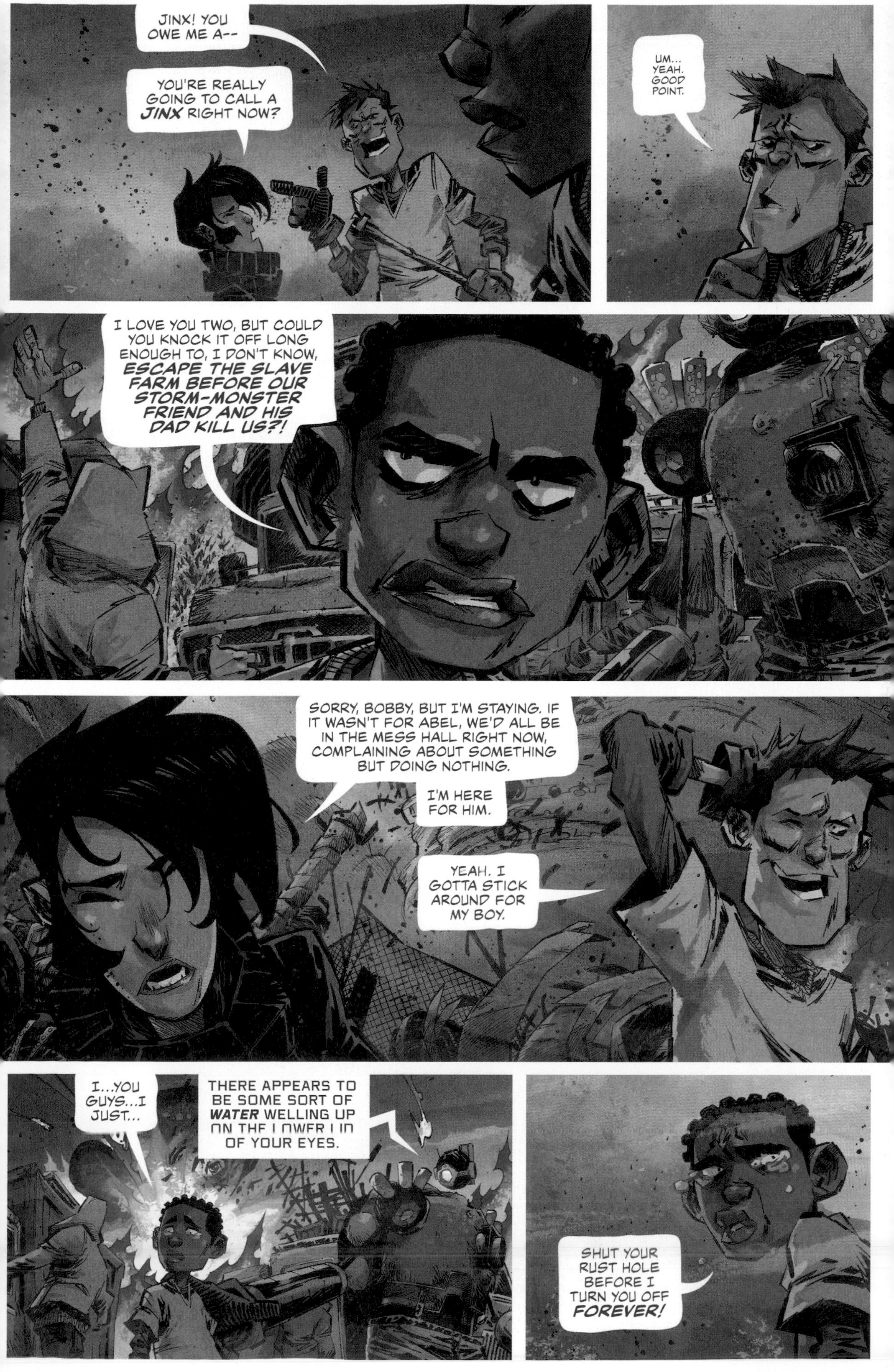
JINX! YOU OWE ME A--
YOU'RE REALLY GOING TO CALL A JINX RIGHT NOW?
UM... YEAH. GOOD POINT.
I LOVE YOU TWO, BUT COULD YOU KNOCK IT OFF LONG ENOUGH TO, I DON'T KNOW, ESCAPE THE SLAVE FARM BEFORE OUR STORM-MONSTER FRIEND AND HIS DAD KILL US?!
SORRY, BOBBY, BUT I'M STAYING. IF IT WASN'T FOR ABEL, WE'D ALL BE IN THE MESS HALL RIGHT NOW, COMPLAINING ABOUT SOMETHING BUT DOING NOTHING.
I'M HERE FOR HIM.
YEAH. I GOTTA STICK AROUND FOR MY BOY.
I...YOU GUYS...I JUST...
THERE APPEARS TO BE SOME SORT OF WATER WELLING UP ON THE LOWER LID OF YOUR EYES.
SHUT YOUR RUST HOLE BEFORE I TURN YOU OFF FOREVER!

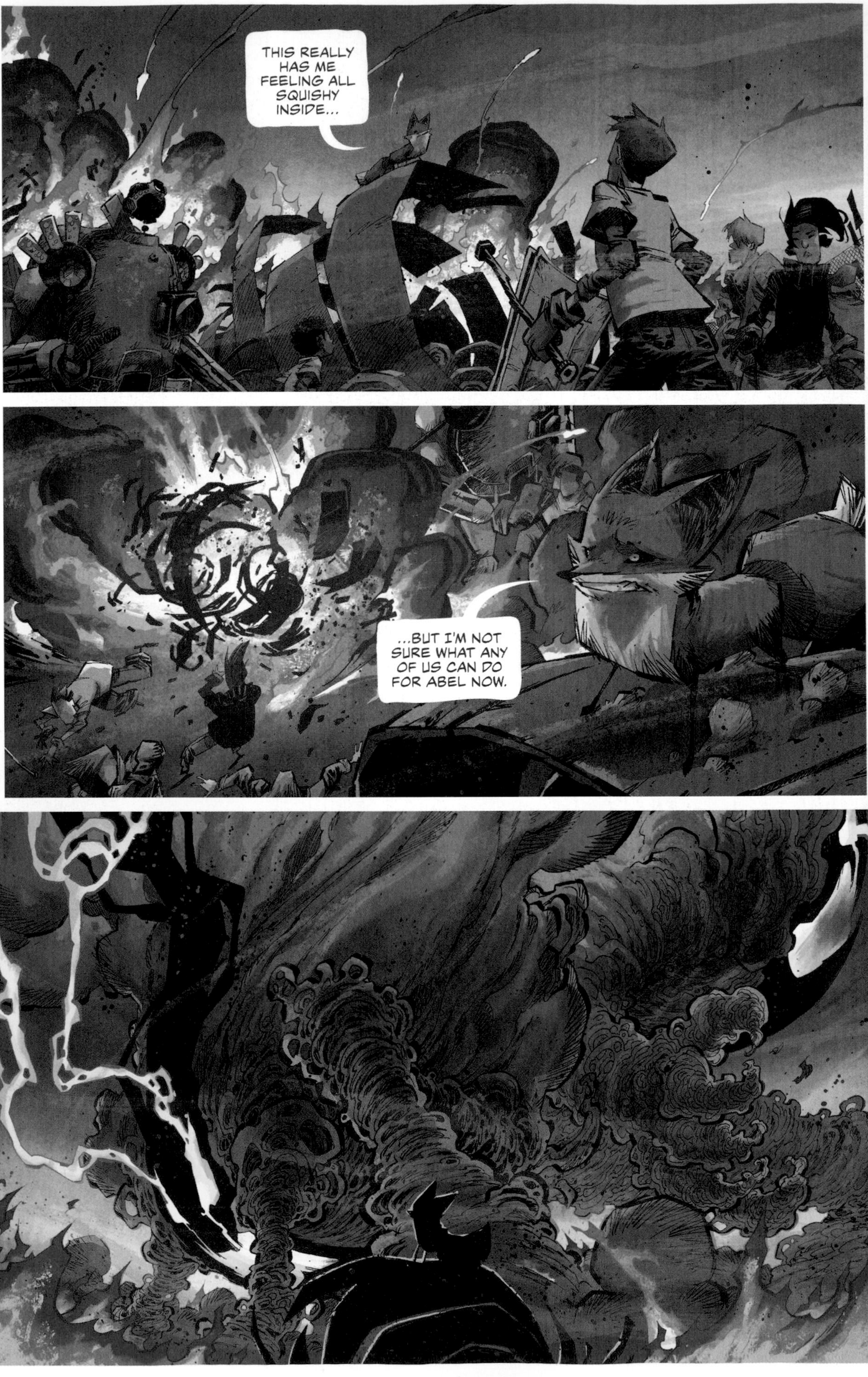
THIS REALLY HAS ME FEELING ALL SQUISHY INSIDE...
...BUT I'M NOT SURE WHAT ANY OF US CAN DO FOR ABEL NOW.

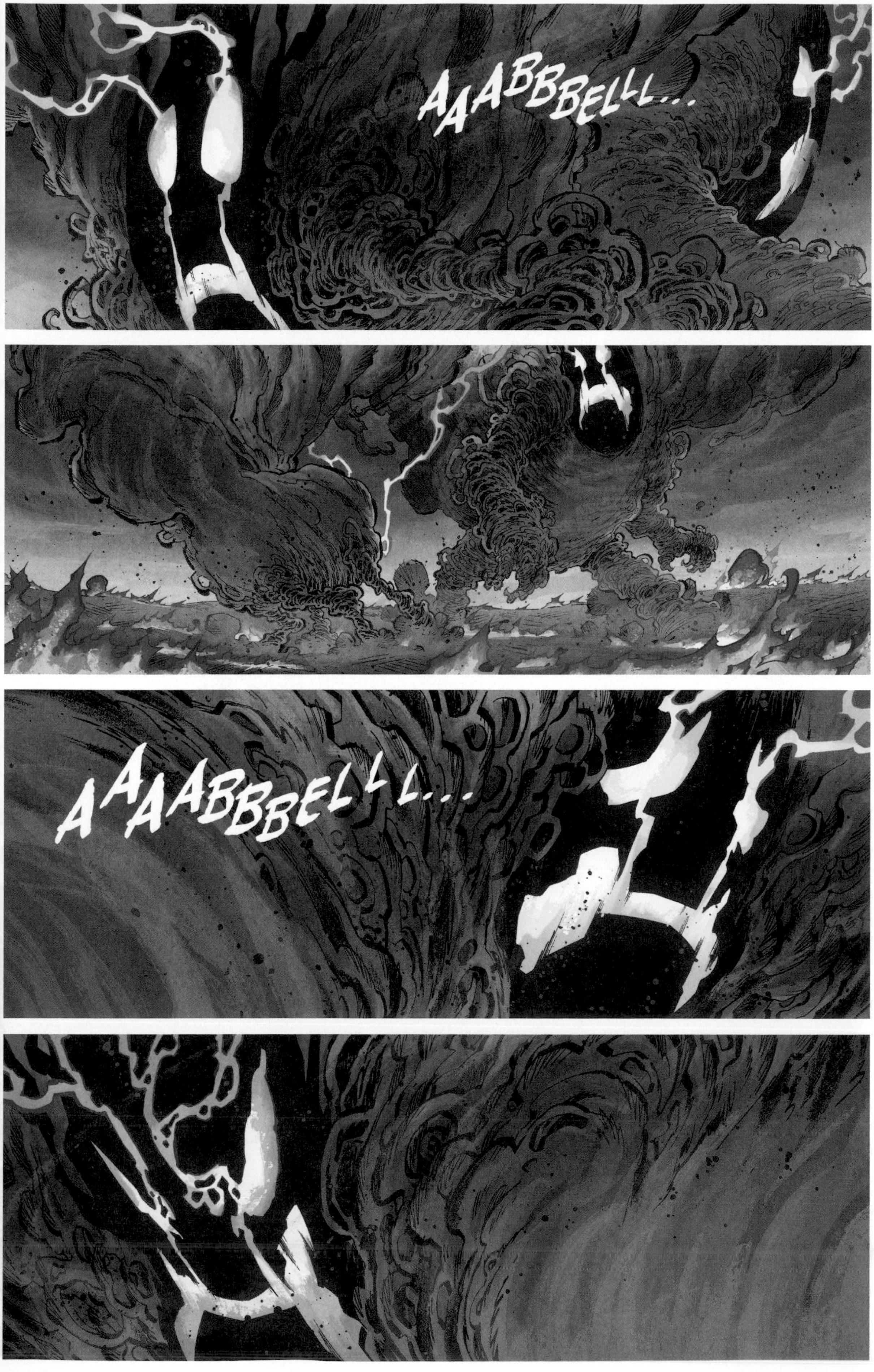
AAABBBELLL...
AAAABBBELLL...

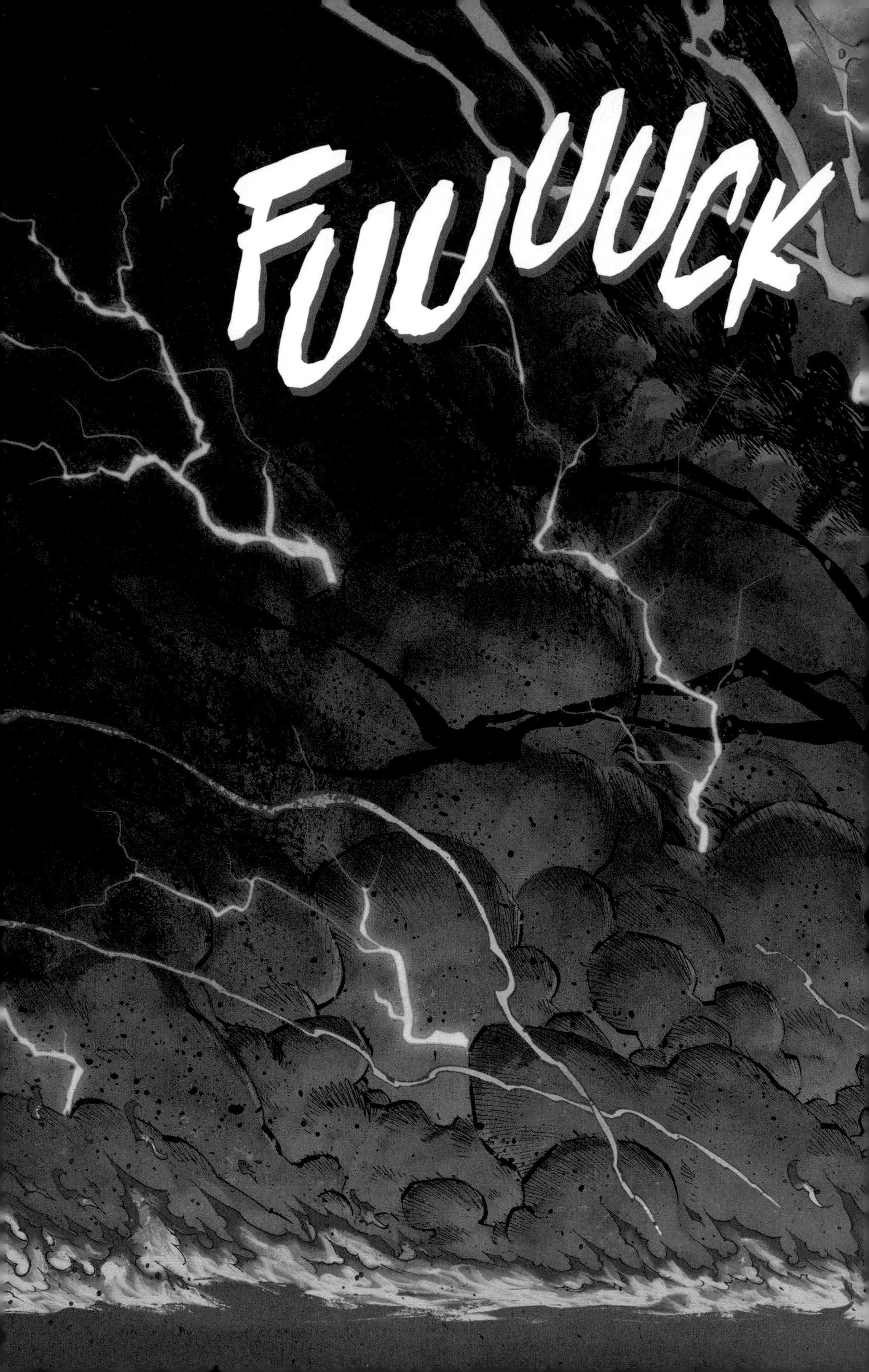
FUUUUCK

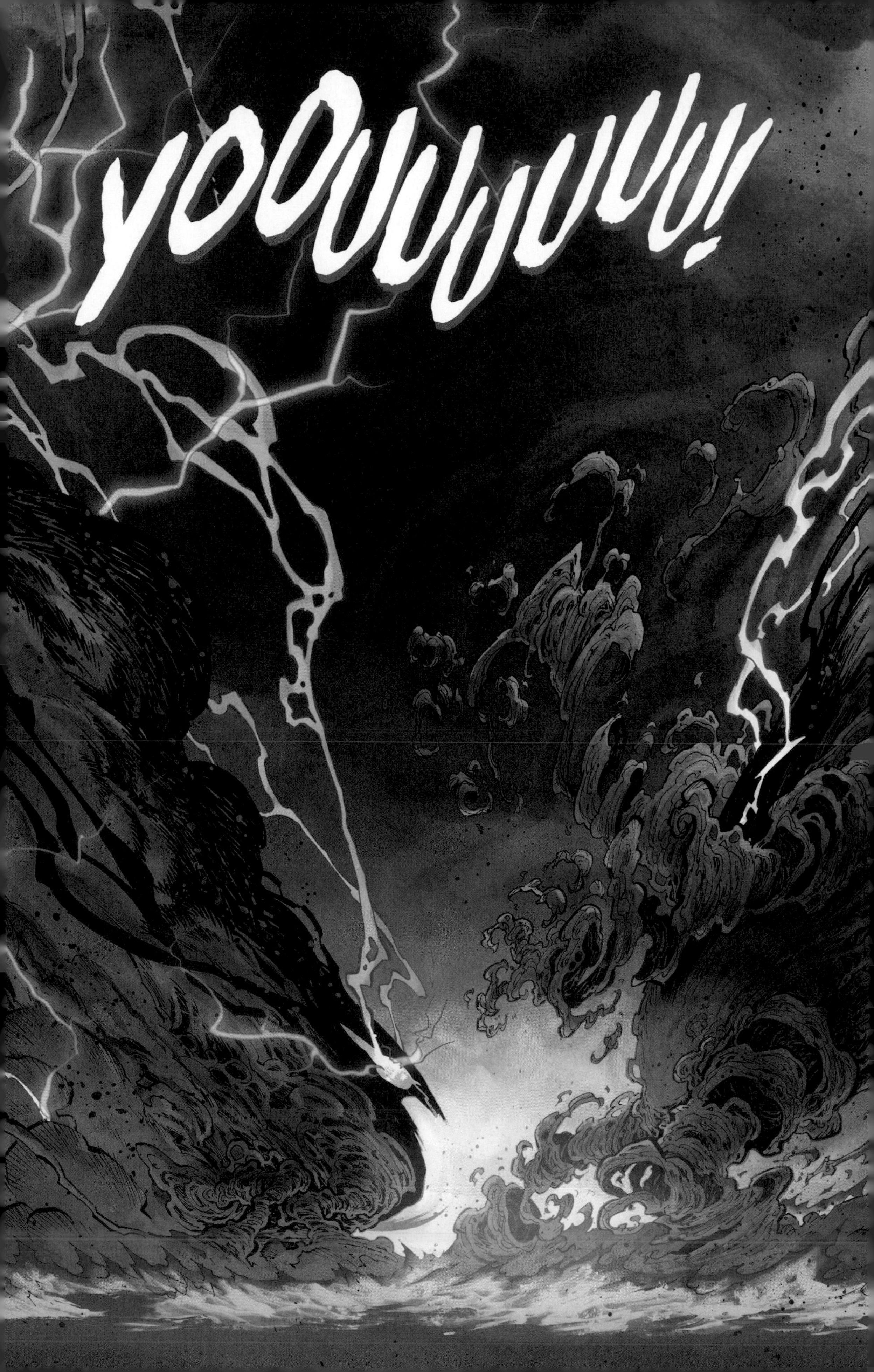
YOOUUUUUU!!

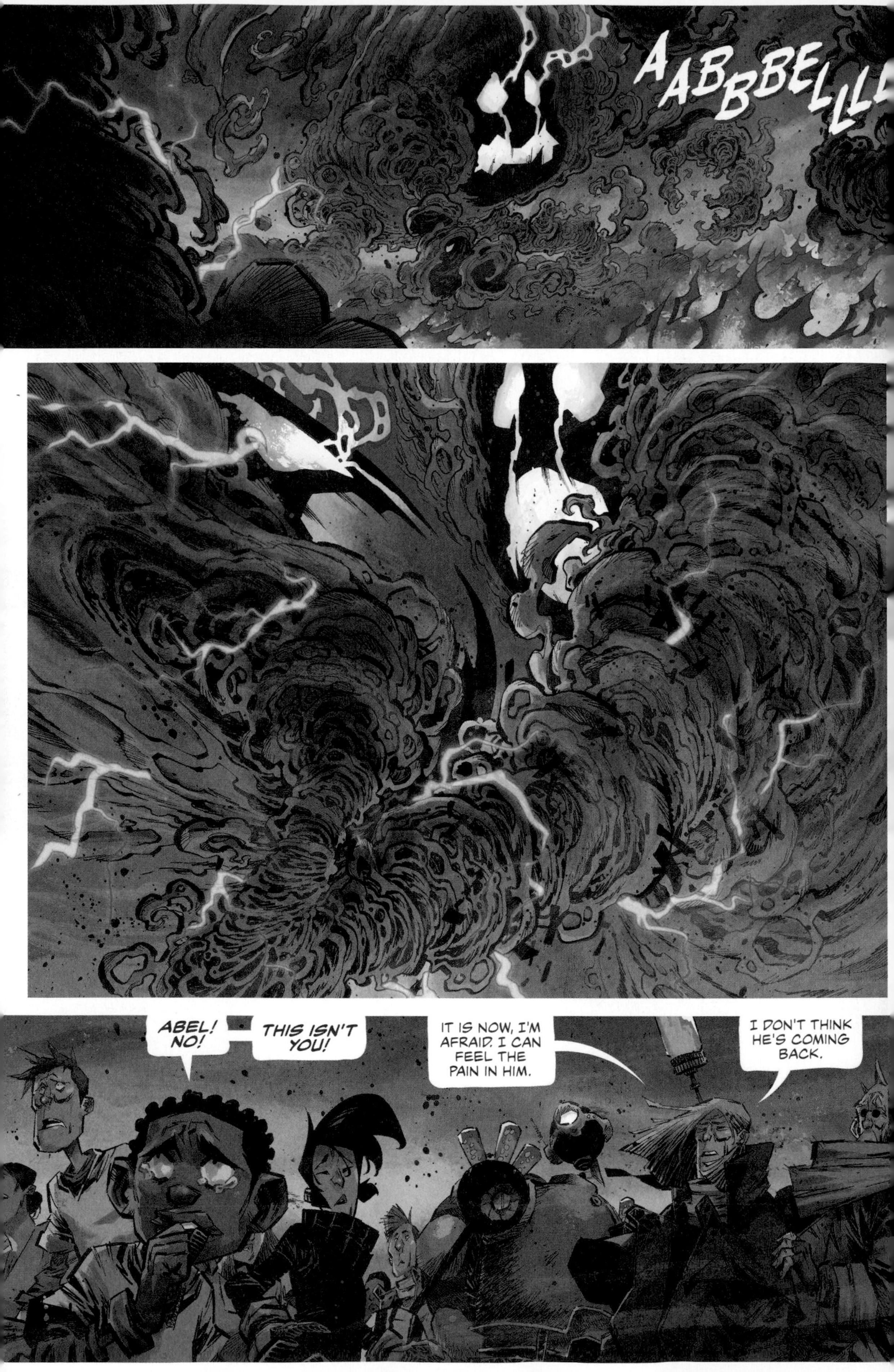
AABBBELLLL
ABEL! NO!
THIS ISN'T YOU!
IT IS NOW, I'M AFRAID. I CAN FEEL THE PAIN IN HIM.
I DON'T THINK HE'S COMING BACK.

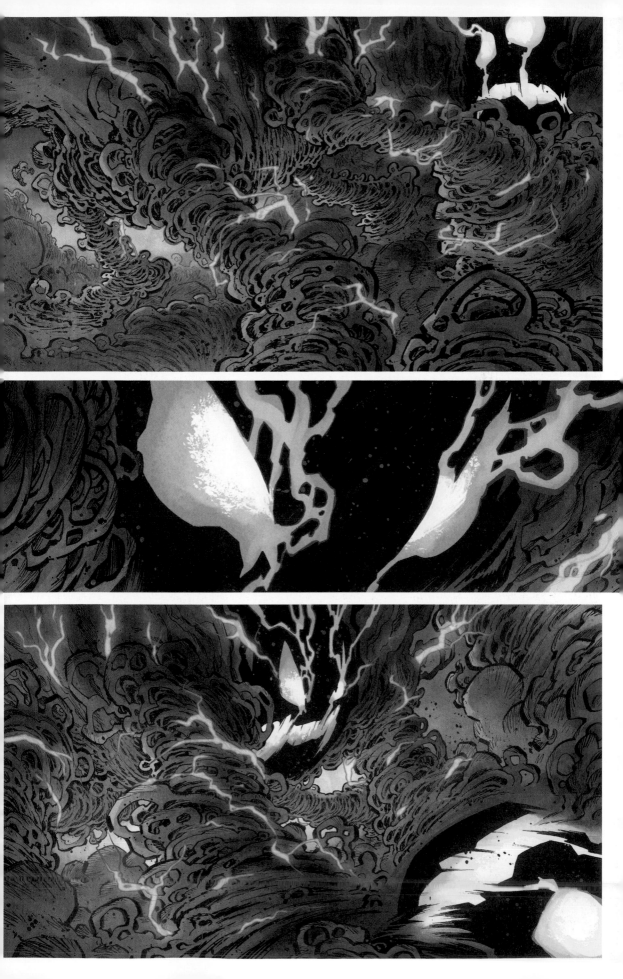

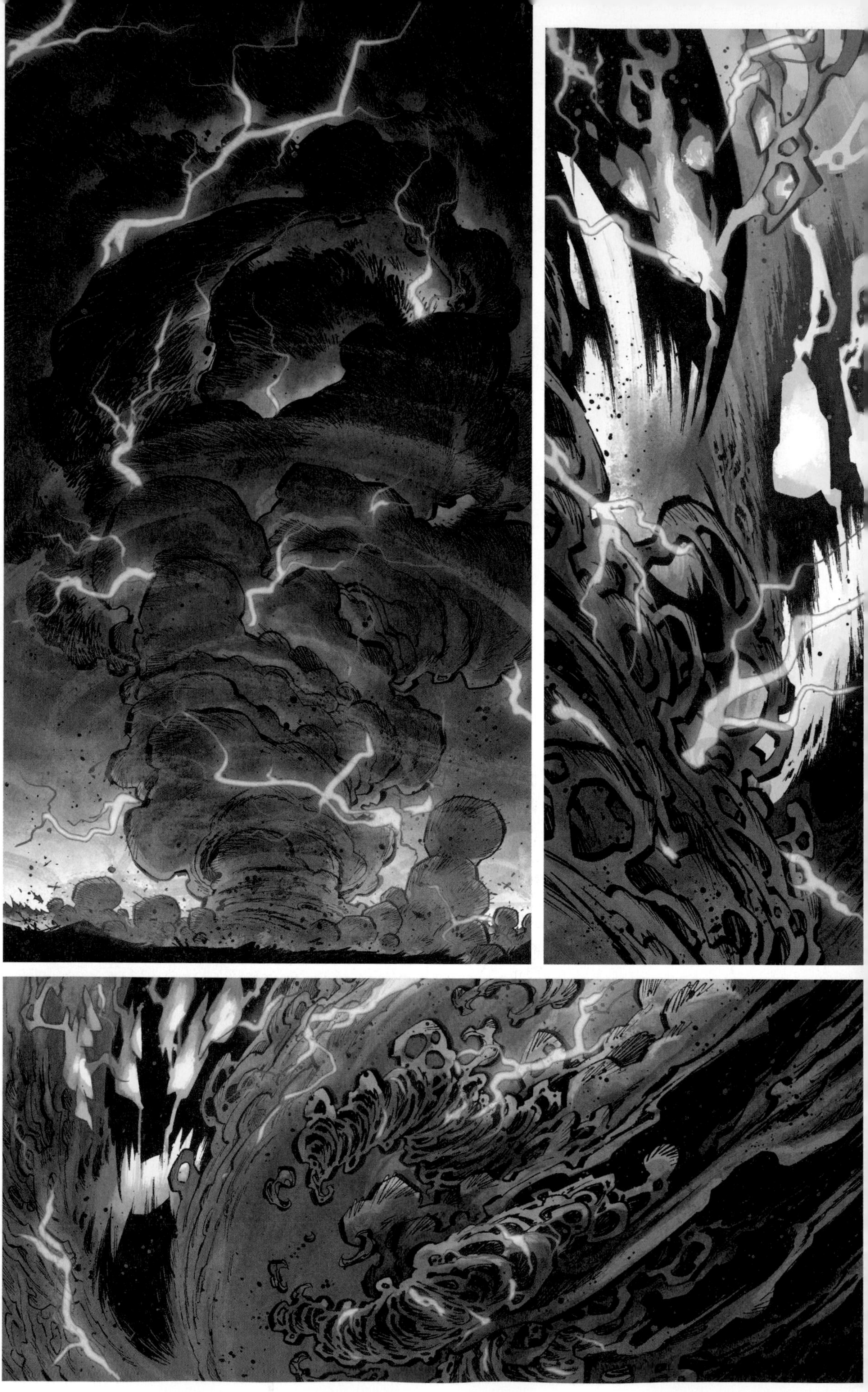

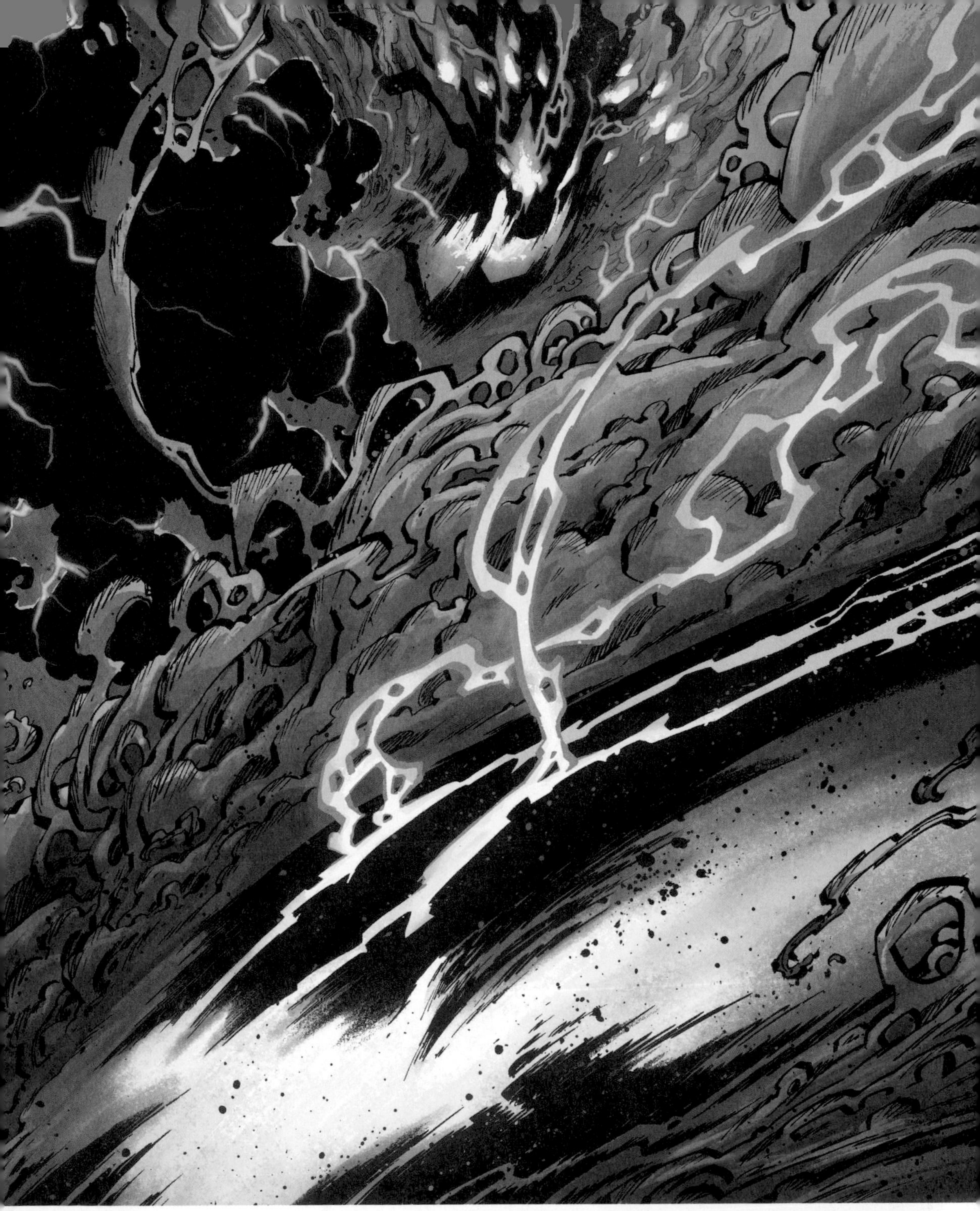

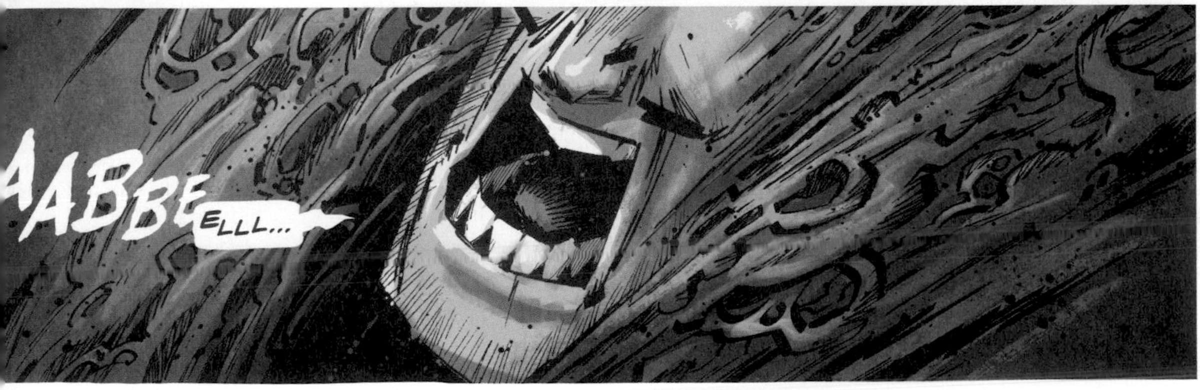
AABBEELLL...

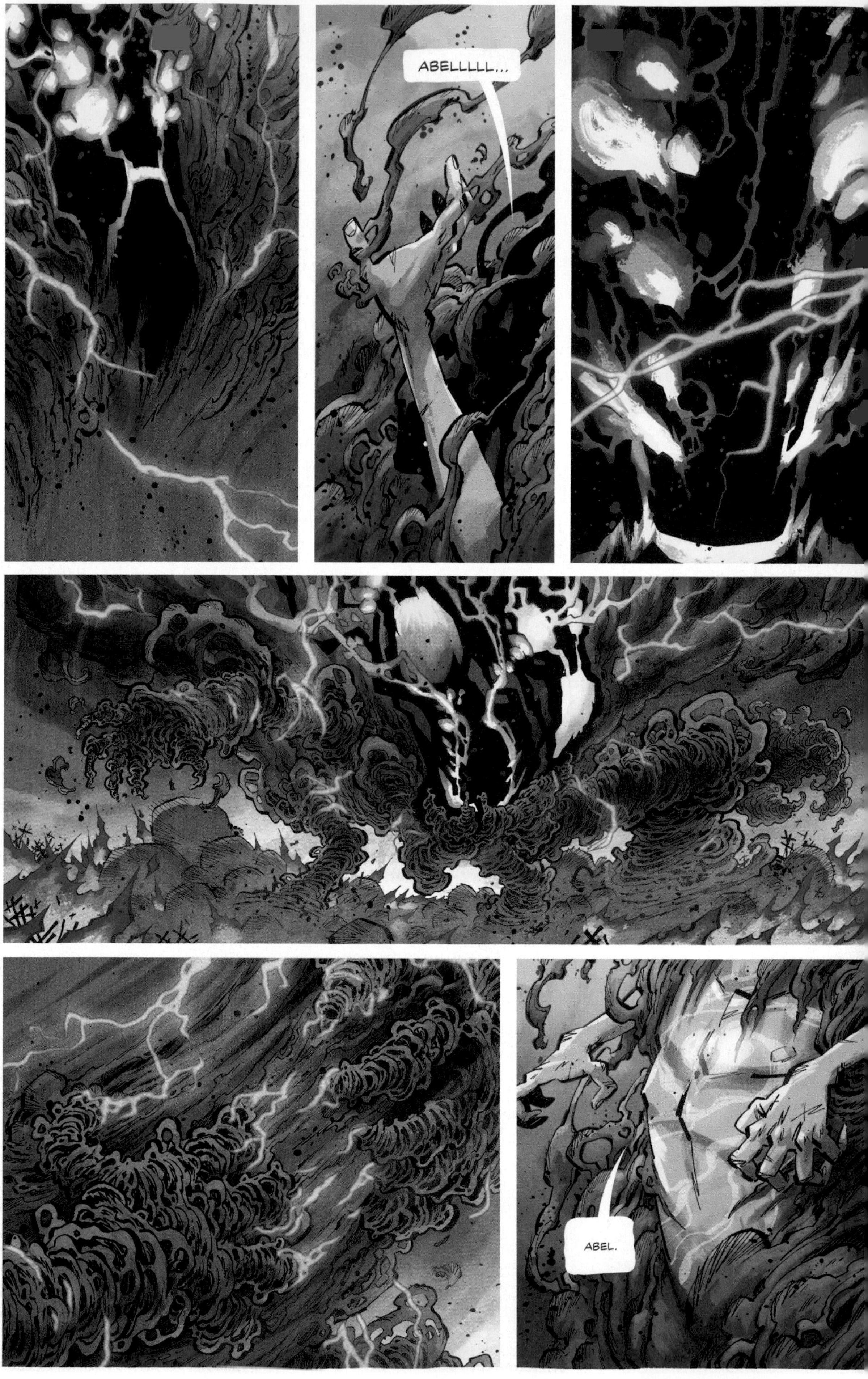
ABELLLLLL...
ABEL.

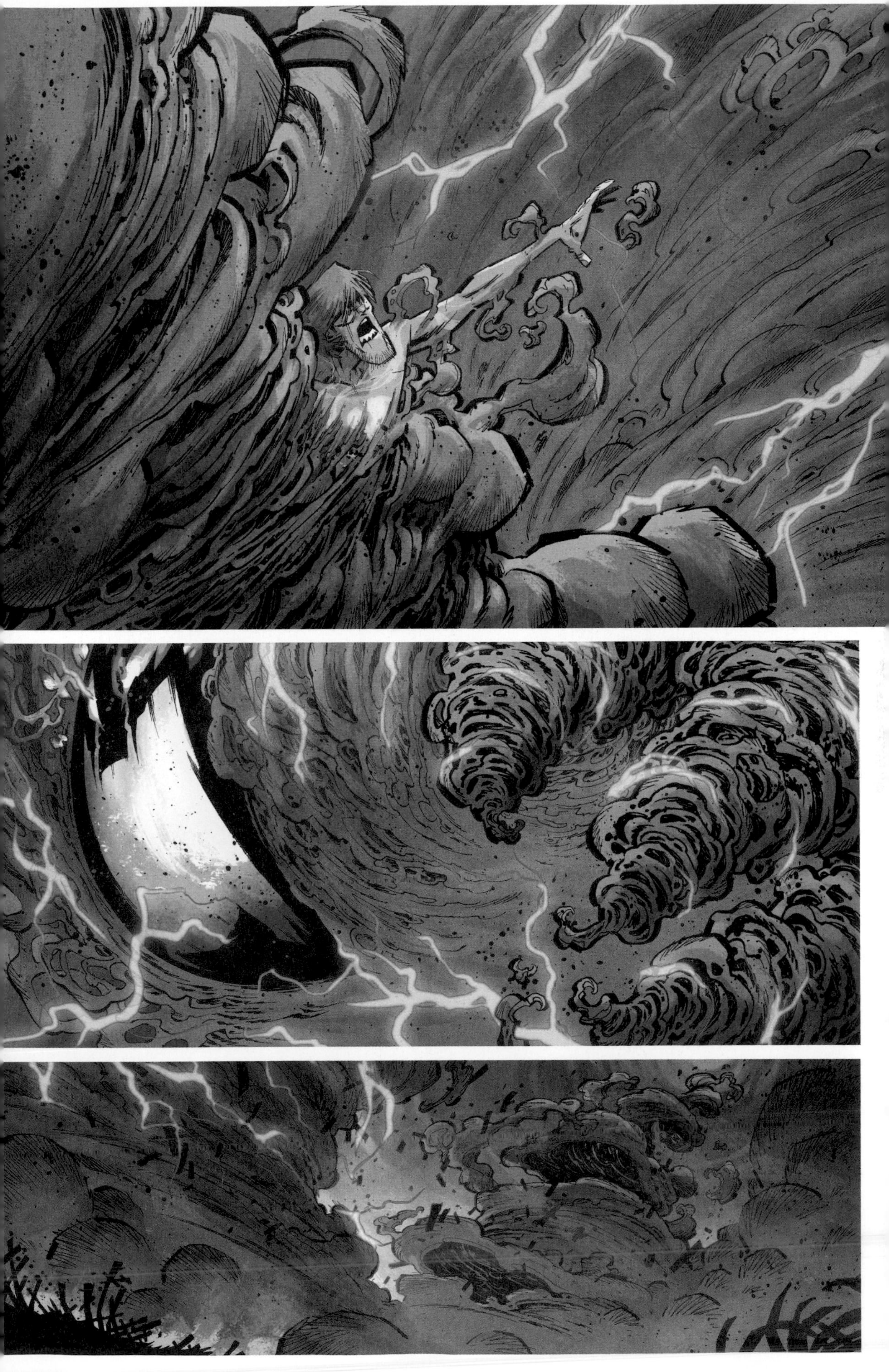

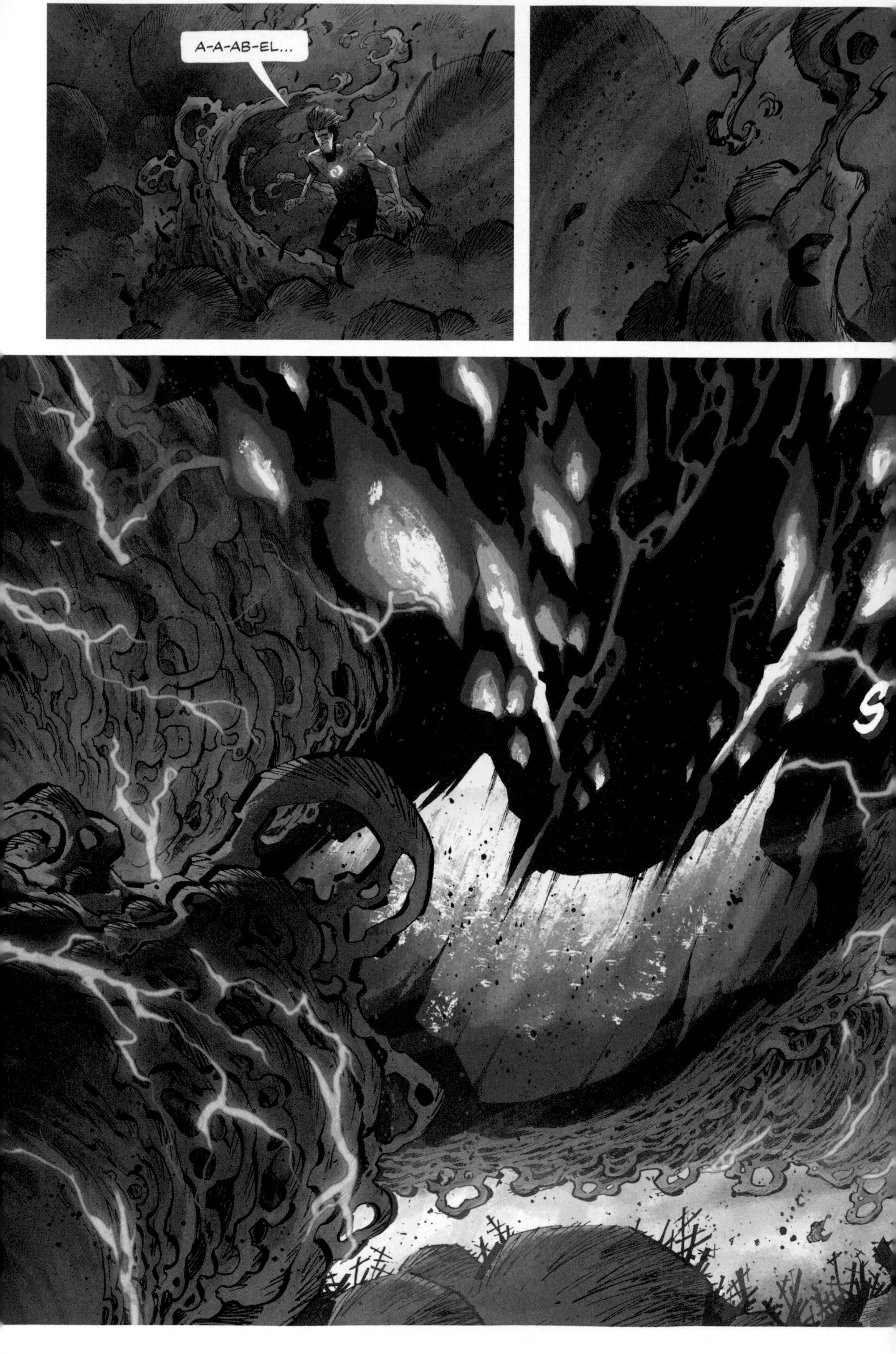
A-A-AB-EL...
S

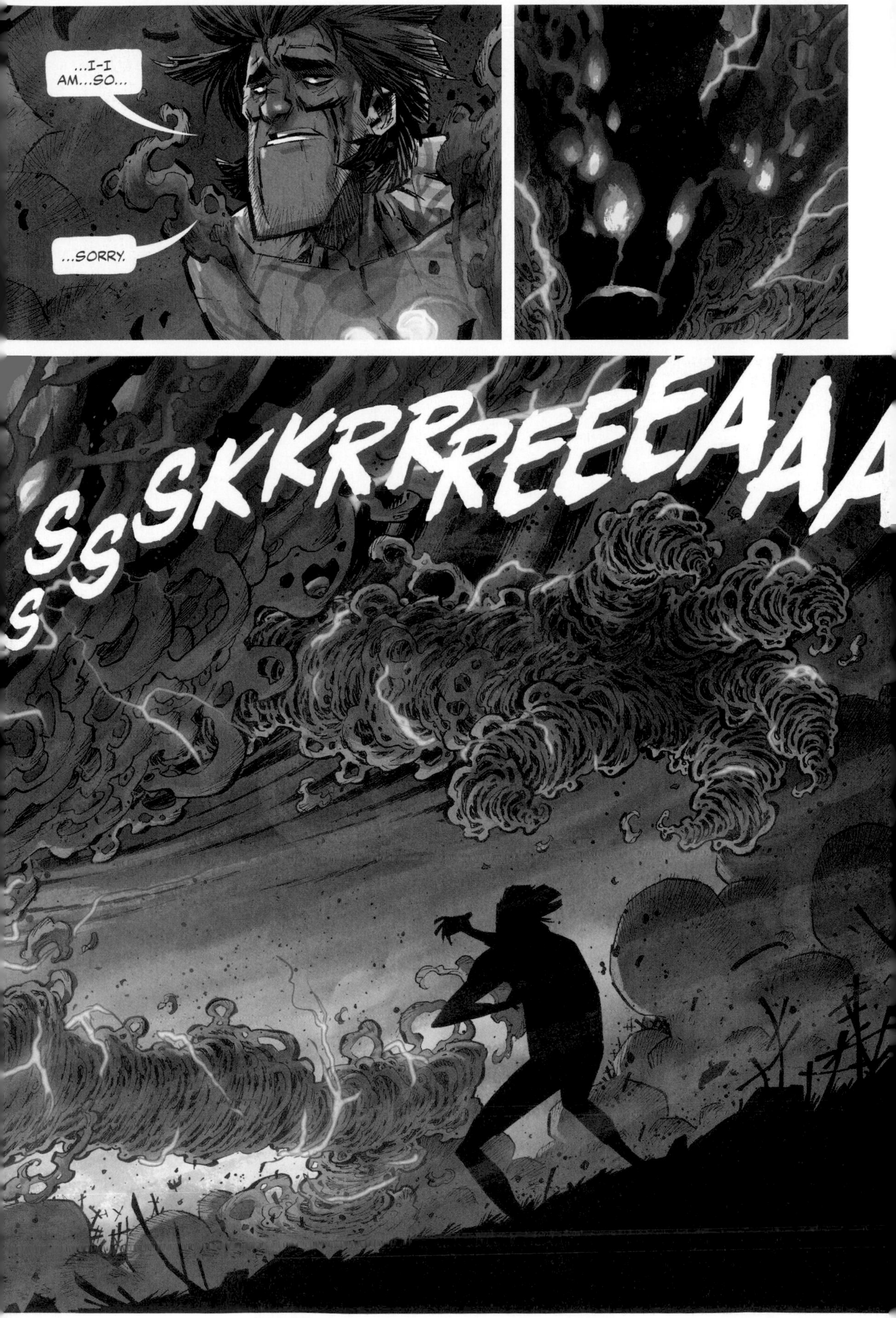
...I-I AM...SO...
...SORRY.
SSSKKRRREEEAAA

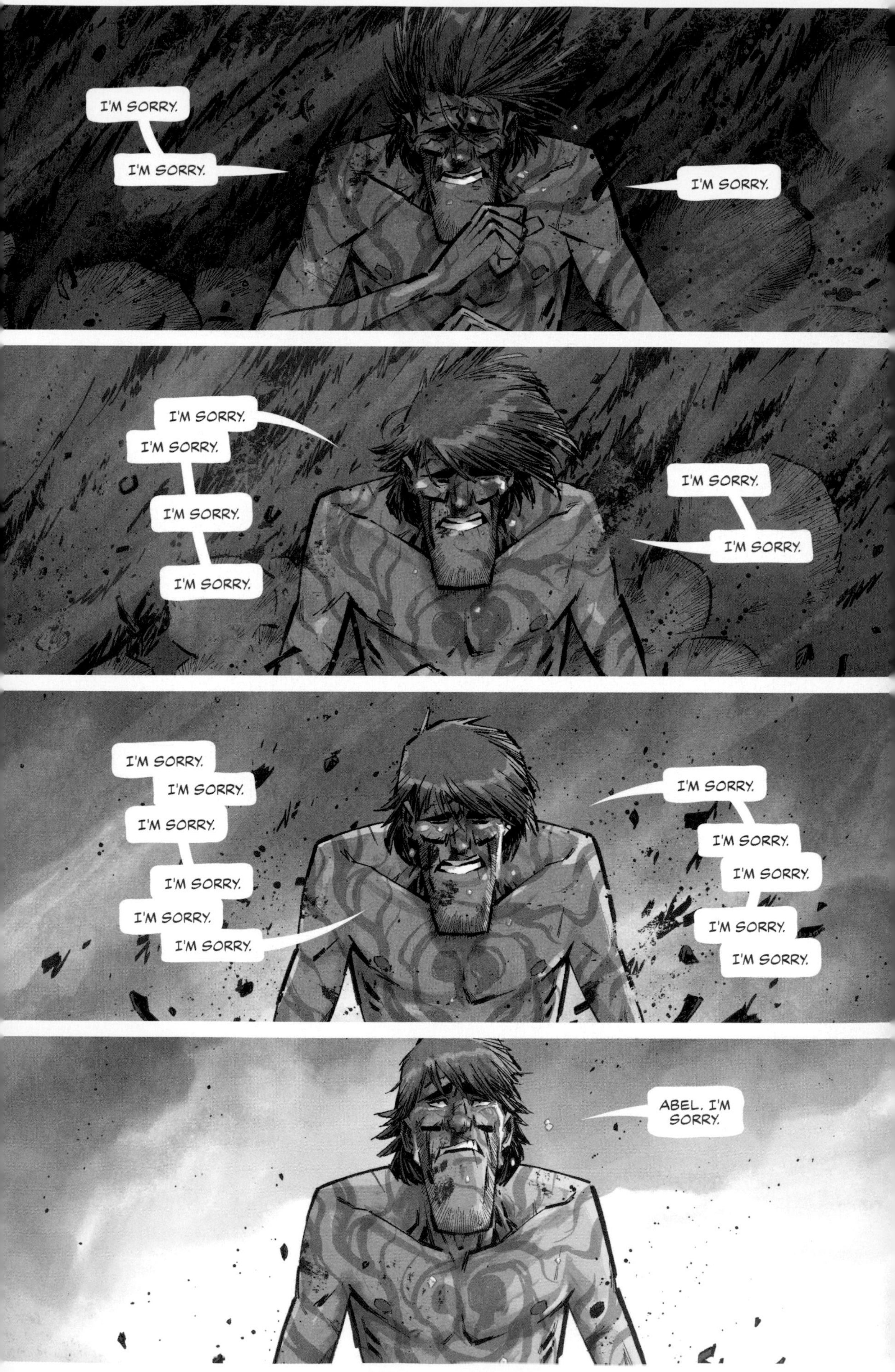
I'M SORRY.
I'M SORRY.
I'M SORRY.
I'M SORRY.
I'M SORRY.
I'M SORRY.
I'M SORRY.
I'M SORRY.
I'M SORRY.
I'M SORRY.
I'M SORRY.
I'M SORRY.
I'M SORRY.
I'M SORRY.
I'M SORRY.
I'M SORRY.
I'M SORRY.
I'M SORRY.
I'M SORRY.
I'M SORRY.
ABEL. I'M SORRY.

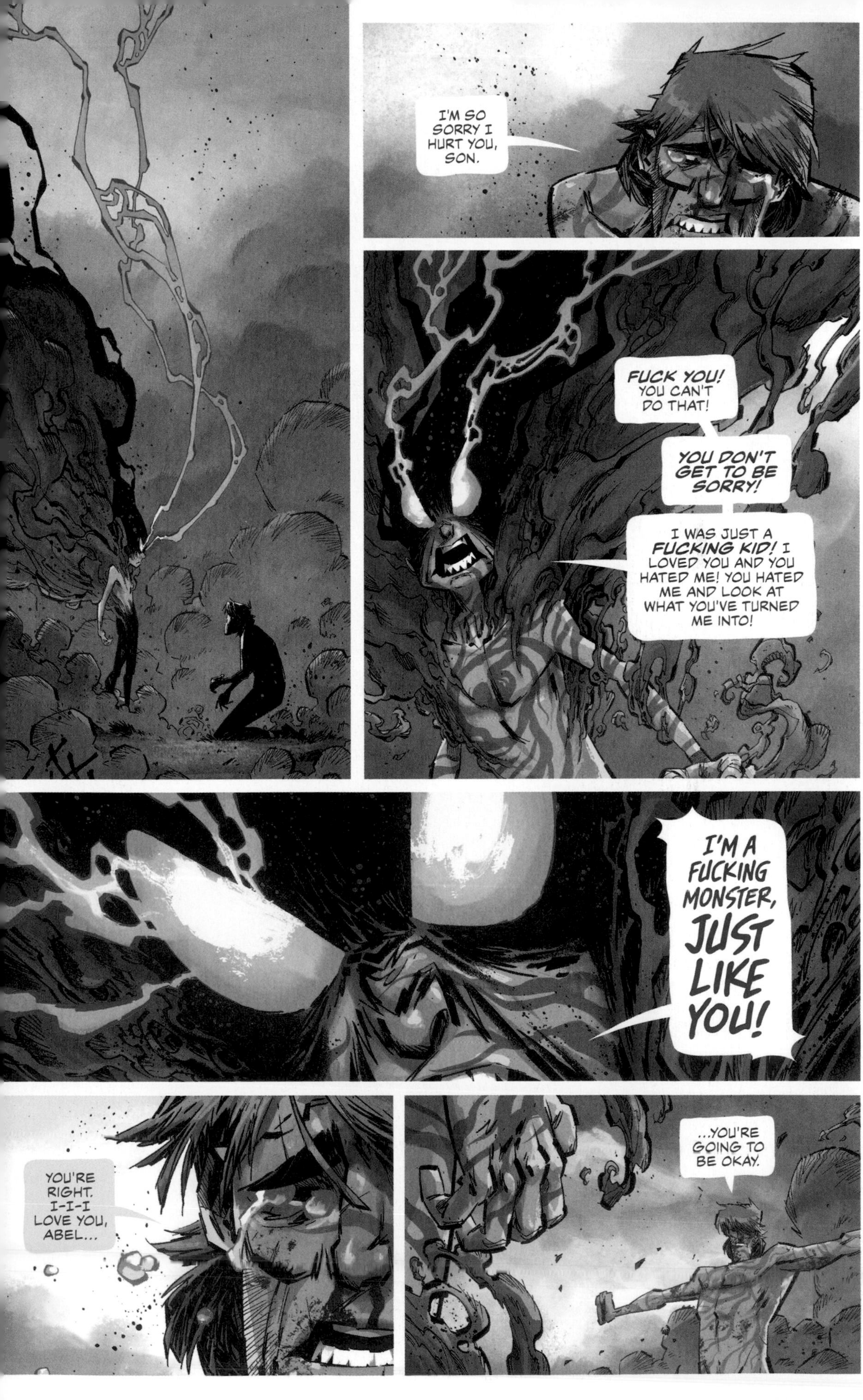

I'M SO SORRY I HURT YOU, SON.
FUCK YOU! YOU CAN'T DO THAT!
YOU DON'T GET TO BE SORRY!
I WAS JUST A FUCKING KID! I LOVED YOU AND YOU HATED ME! YOU HATED ME AND LOOK AT WHAT YOU'VE TURNED ME INTO!
I'M A FUCKING MONSTER, JUST LIKE YOU!
YOU'RE RIGHT. I-I-I LOVE YOU, ABEL...
...YOU'RE GOING TO BE OKAY.

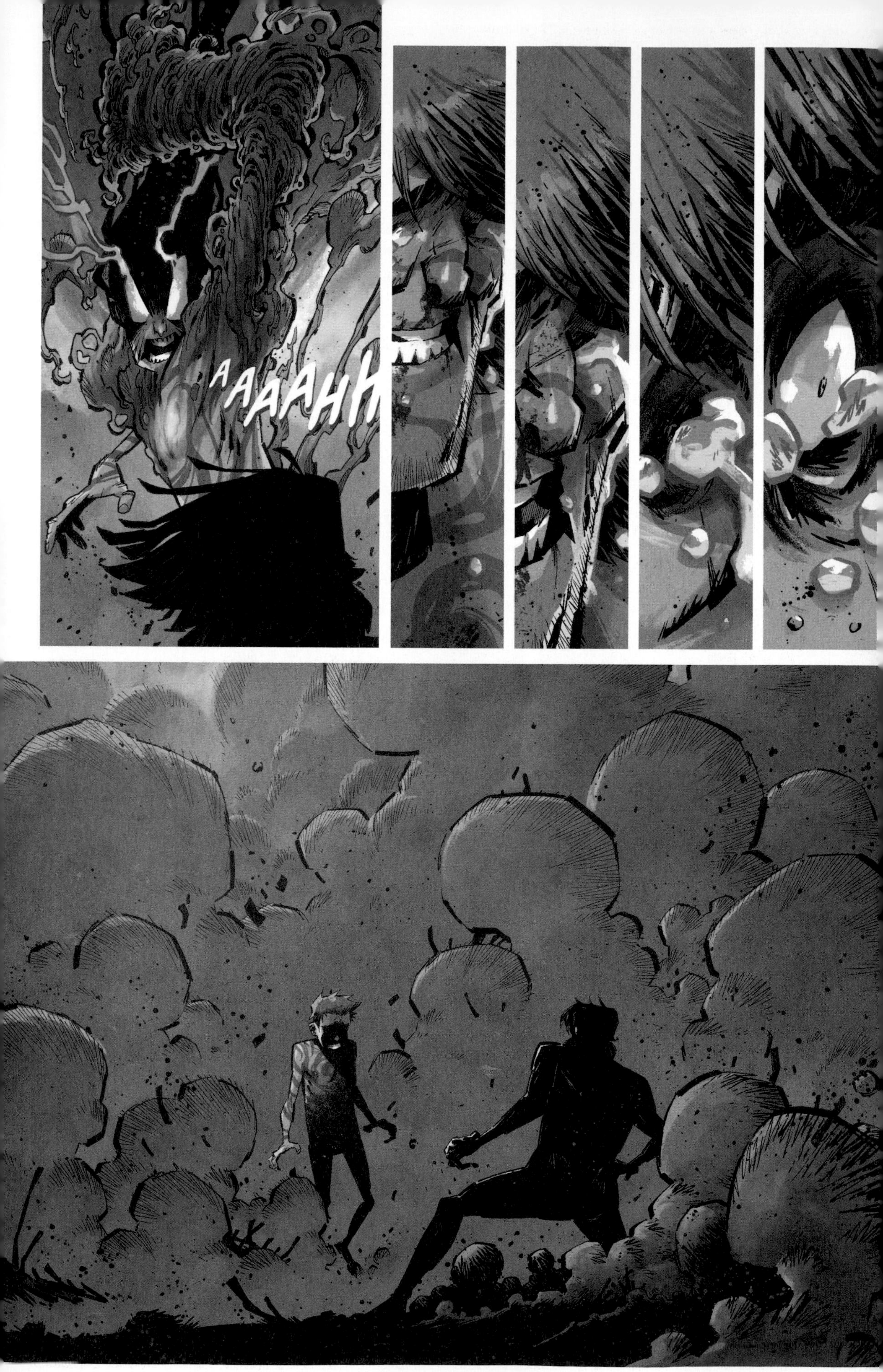
AAAAHH

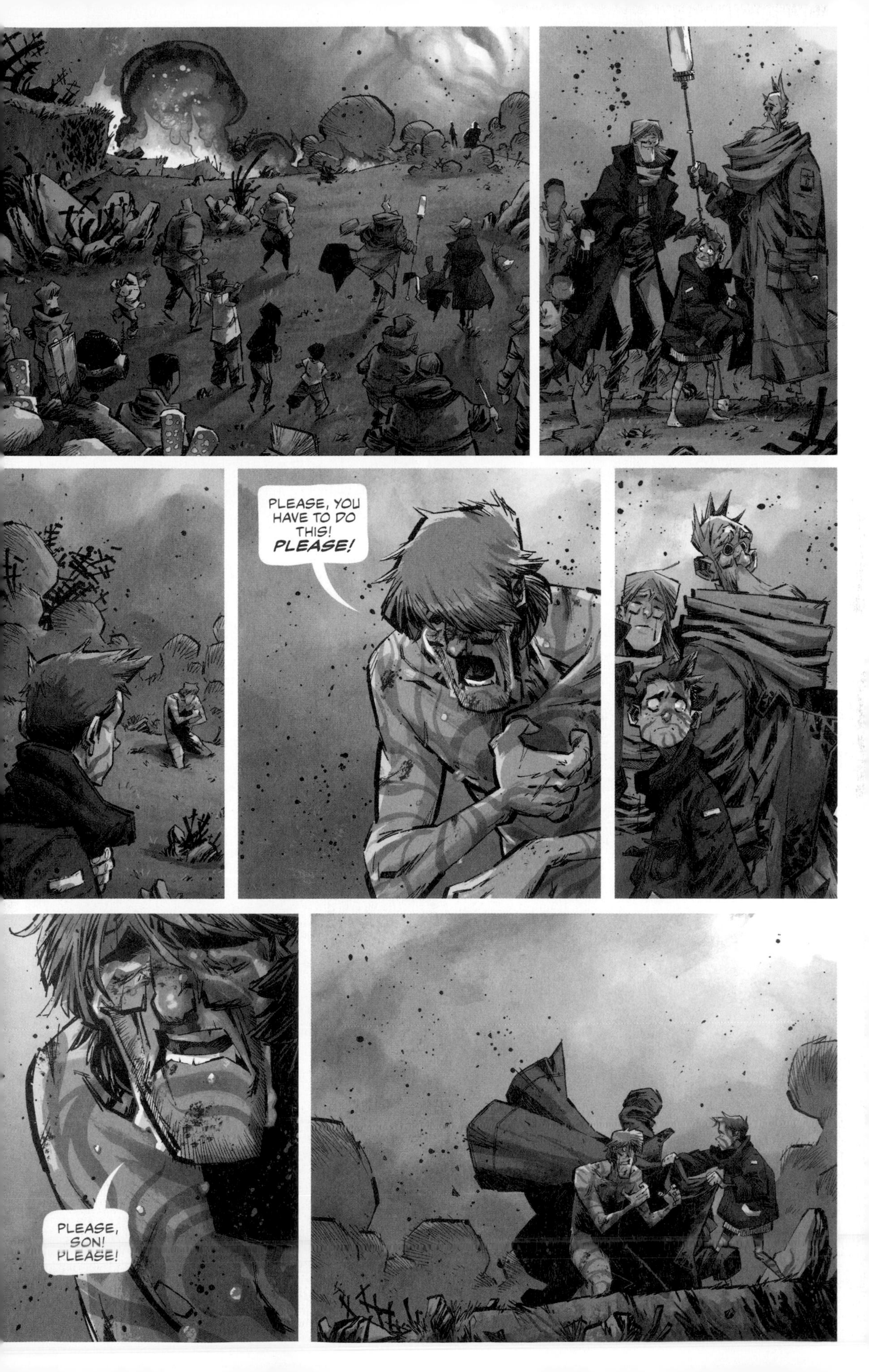
PLEASE, YOU HAVE TO DO THIS! **PLEASE!**
PLEASE, SON! PLEASE!

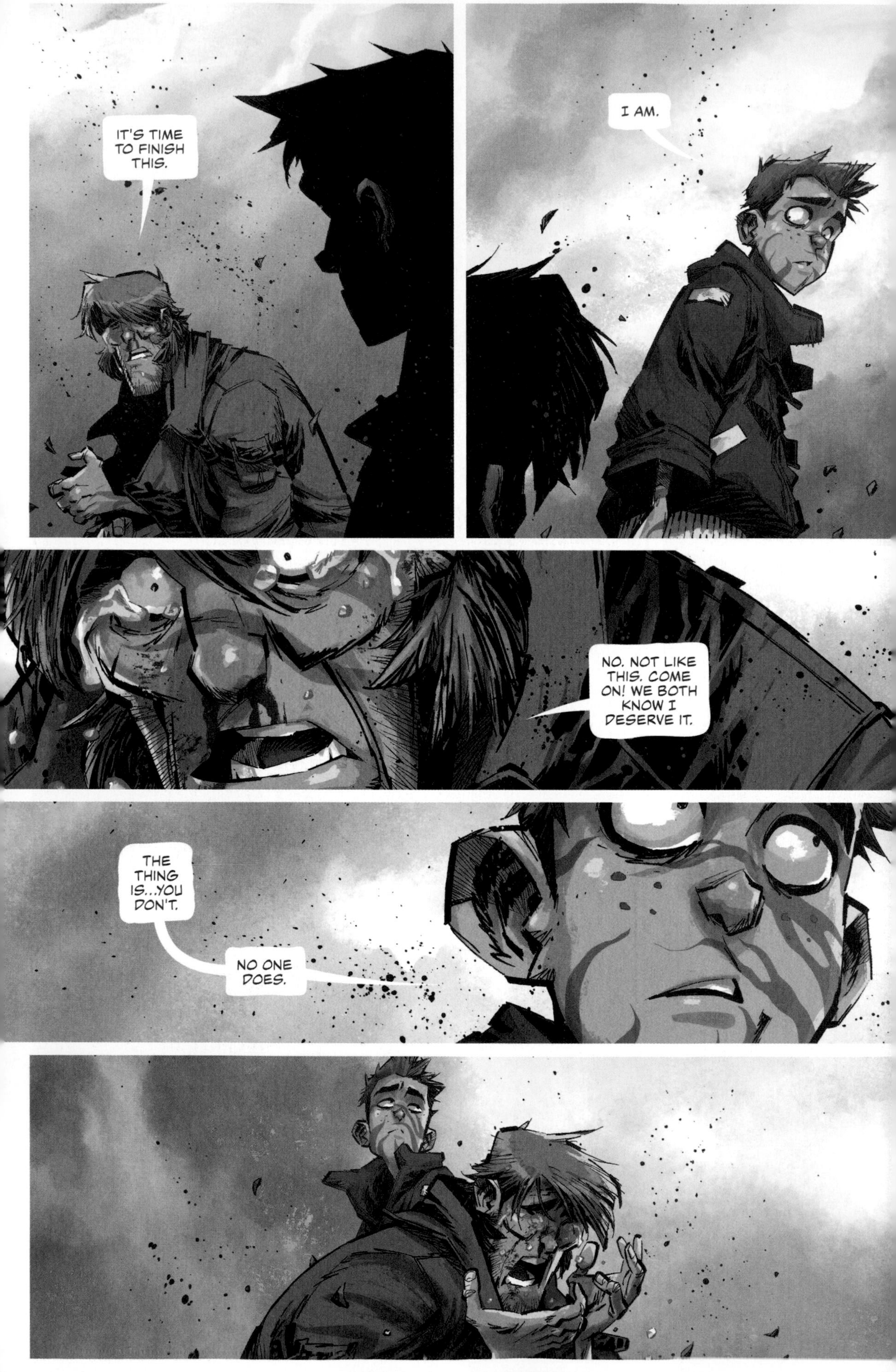
IT'S TIME TO FINISH THIS.
I AM.
NO. NOT LIKE THIS. COME ON! WE BOTH KNOW I DESERVE IT.
THE THING IS...YOU DON'T.
NO ONE DOES.

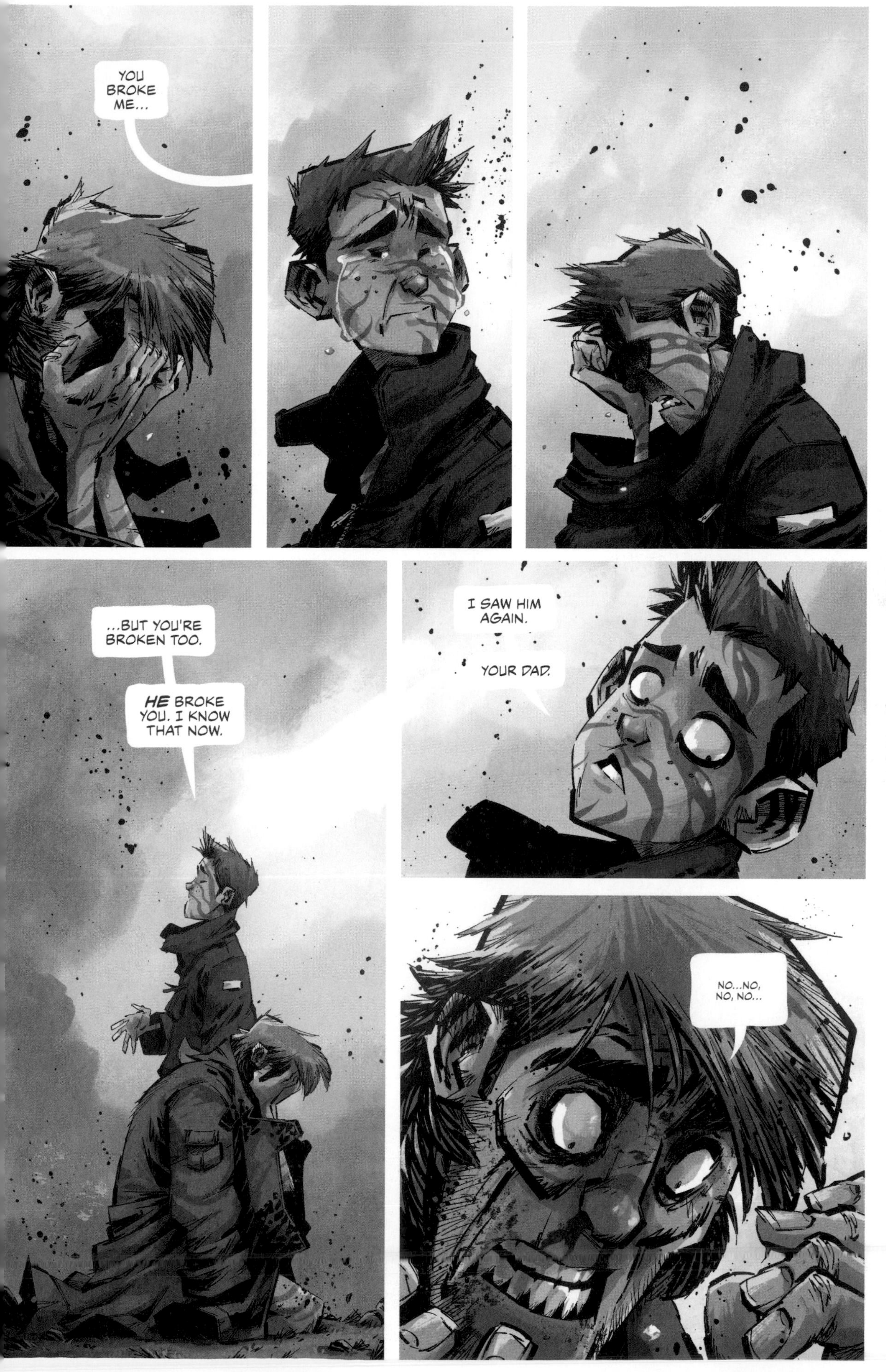
YOU BROKE ME...
...BUT YOU'RE BROKEN TOO.
HE BROKE YOU. I KNOW THAT NOW.
I SAW HIM AGAIN.
YOUR DAD.
NO...NO, NO, NO...

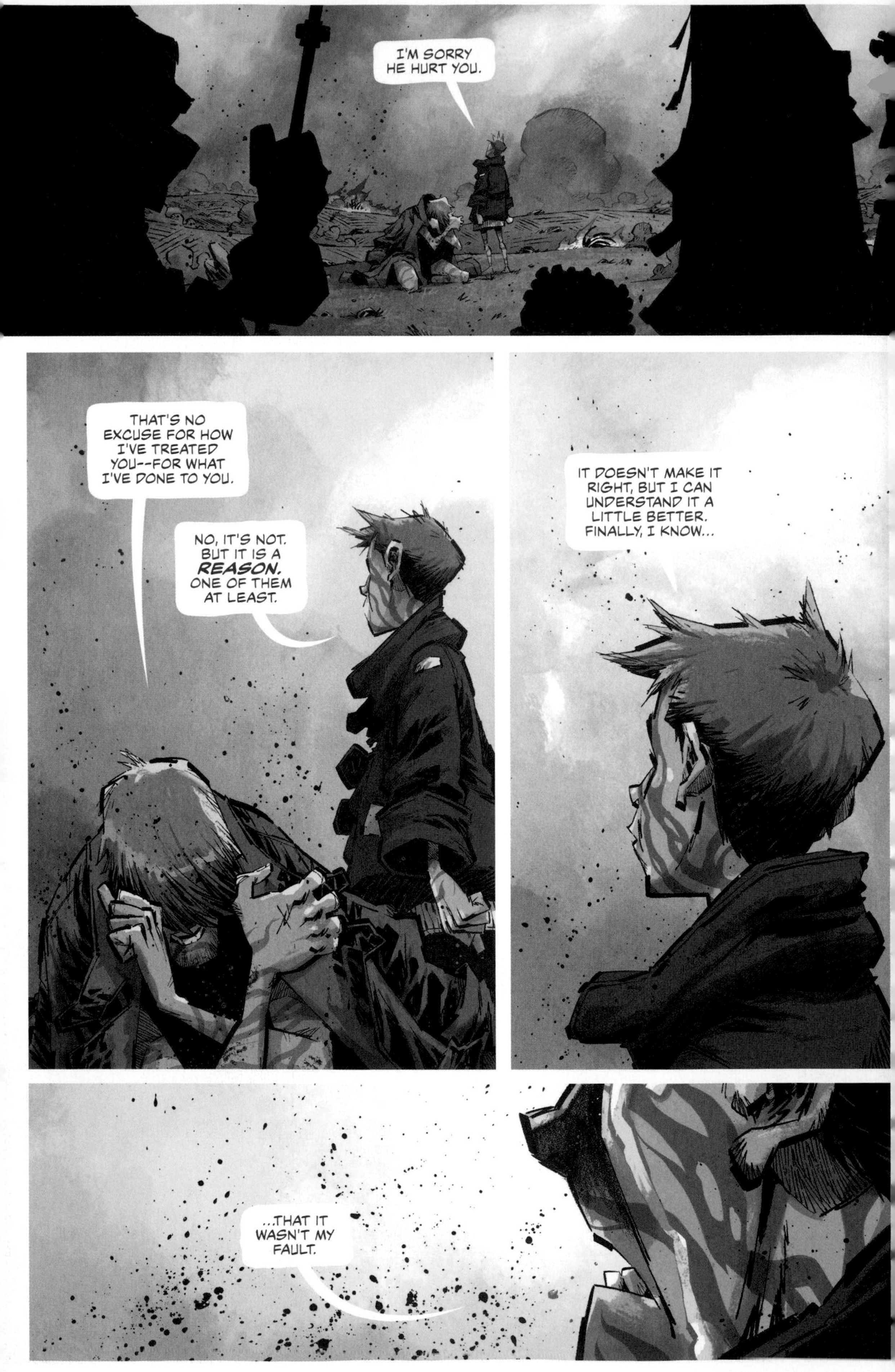
I'M SORRY HE HURT YOU.
THAT'S NO EXCUSE FOR HOW I'VE TREATED YOU--FOR WHAT I'VE DONE TO YOU.
NO, IT'S NOT. BUT IT IS A *REASON.* ONE OF THEM AT LEAST.
IT DOESN'T MAKE IT RIGHT, BUT I CAN UNDERSTAND IT A LITTLE BETTER. FINALLY, I KNOW...
...THAT IT WASN'T MY FAULT.

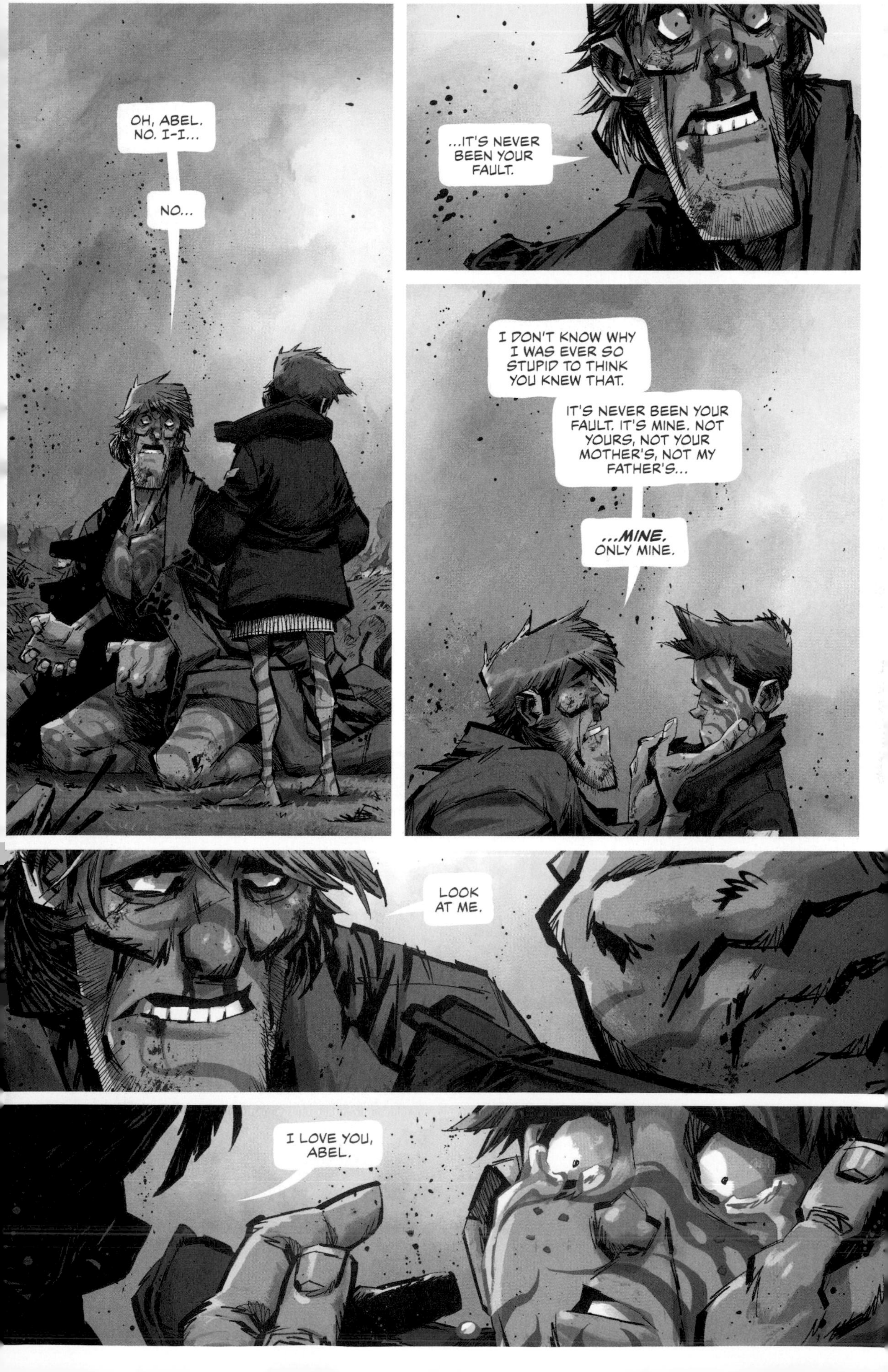
OH, ABEL. NO. I-I...
NO...
...IT'S NEVER BEEN YOUR FAULT.
I DON'T KNOW WHY I WAS EVER SO STUPID TO THINK YOU KNEW THAT.
IT'S NEVER BEEN YOUR FAULT. IT'S MINE. NOT YOURS, NOT YOUR MOTHER'S, NOT MY FATHER'S...
...MINE. ONLY MINE.
LOOK AT ME.
I LOVE YOU, ABEL.

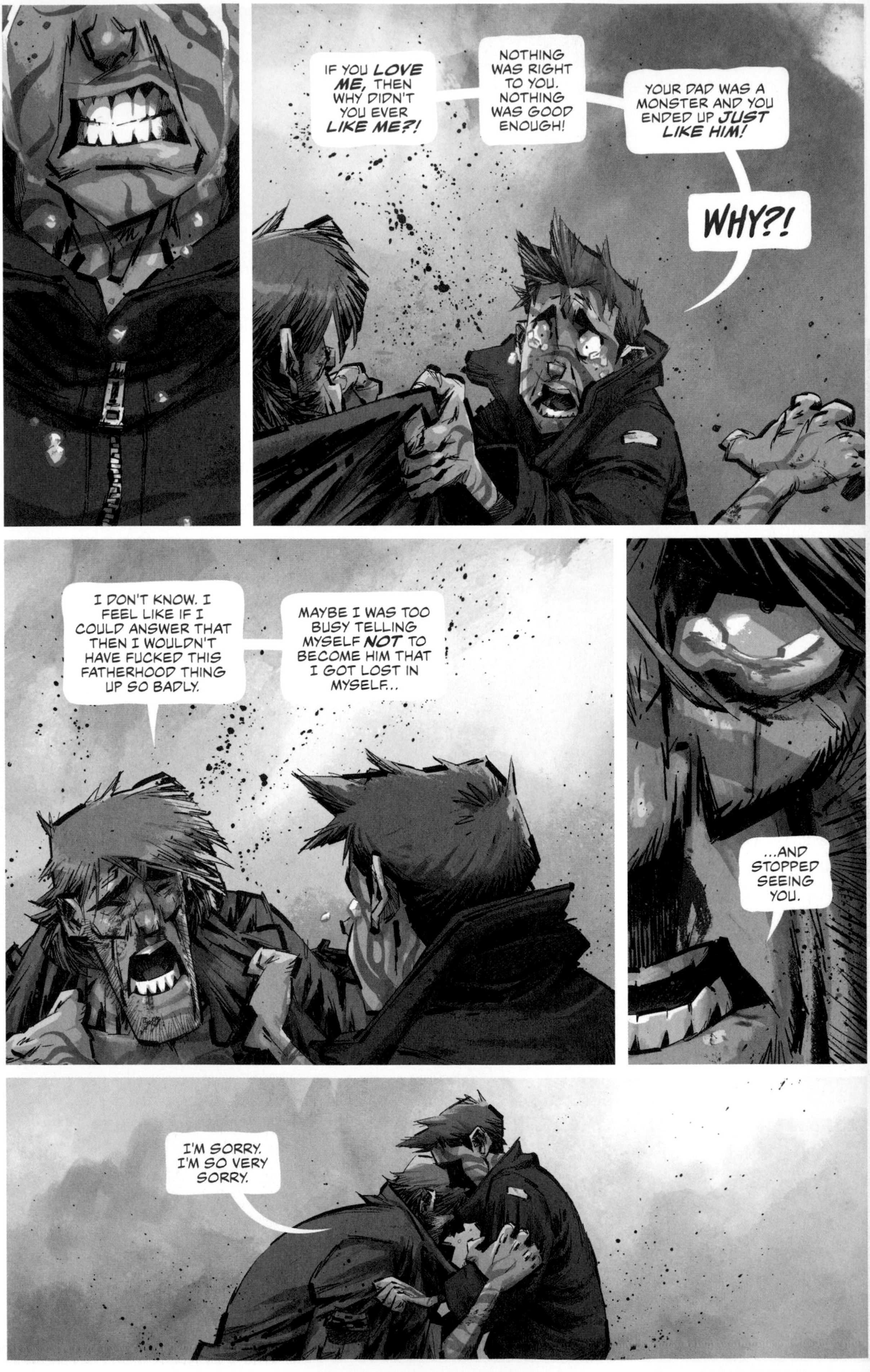
IF YOU LOVE ME, THEN WHY DIDN'T YOU EVER LIKE ME?!
NOTHING WAS RIGHT TO YOU. NOTHING WAS GOOD ENOUGH!
YOUR DAD WAS A MONSTER AND YOU ENDED UP JUST LIKE HIM!
WHY?!
I DON'T KNOW. I FEEL LIKE IF I COULD ANSWER THAT THEN I WOULDN'T HAVE FUCKED THIS FATHERHOOD THING UP SO BADLY.
MAYBE I WAS TOO BUSY TELLING MYSELF NOT TO BECOME HIM THAT I GOT LOST IN MYSELF...
...AND STOPPED SEEING YOU.
I'M SORRY. I'M SO VERY SORRY.

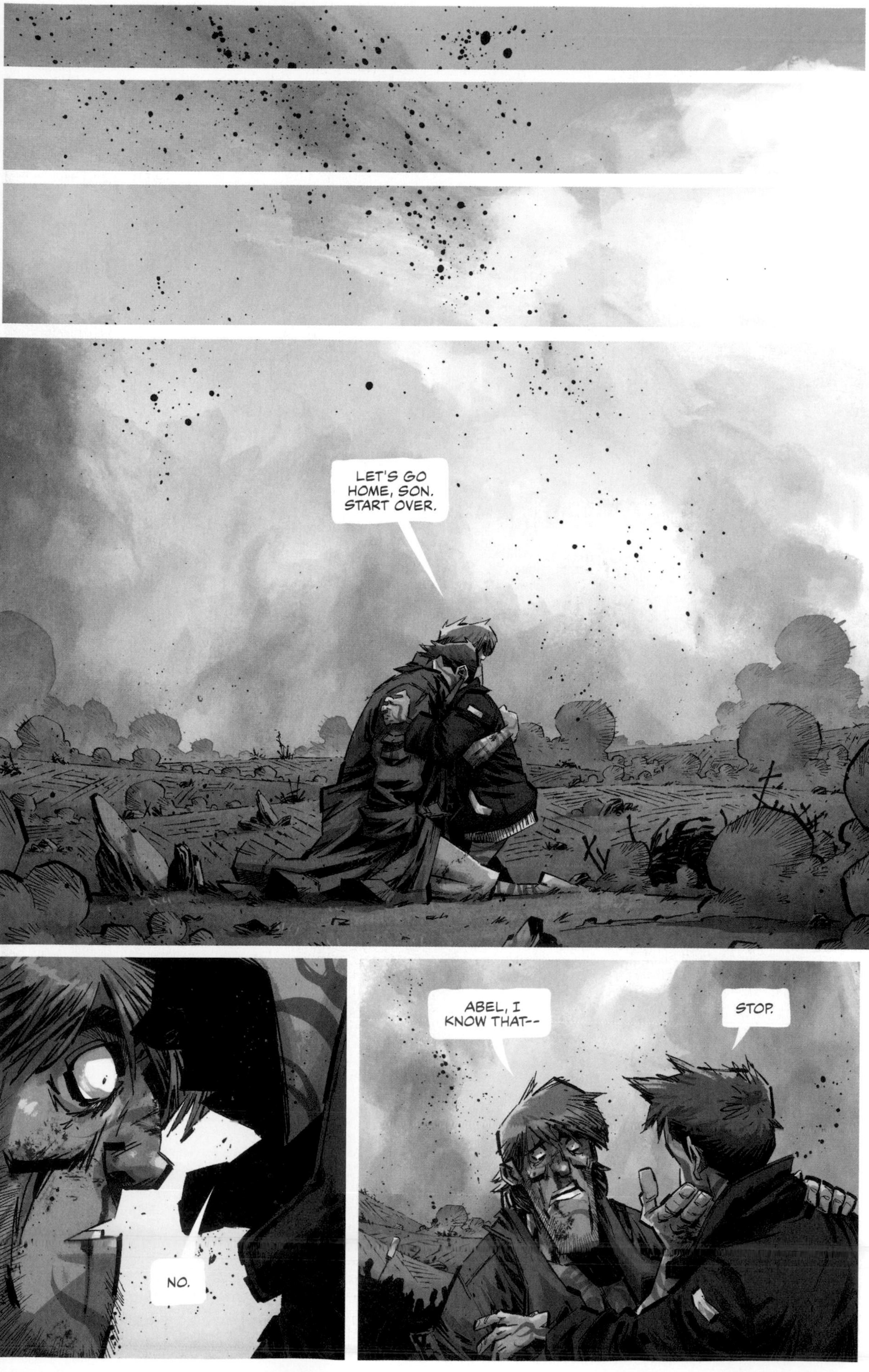
LET'S GO HOME, SON. START OVER.
NO.
ABEL, I KNOW THAT--
STOP.

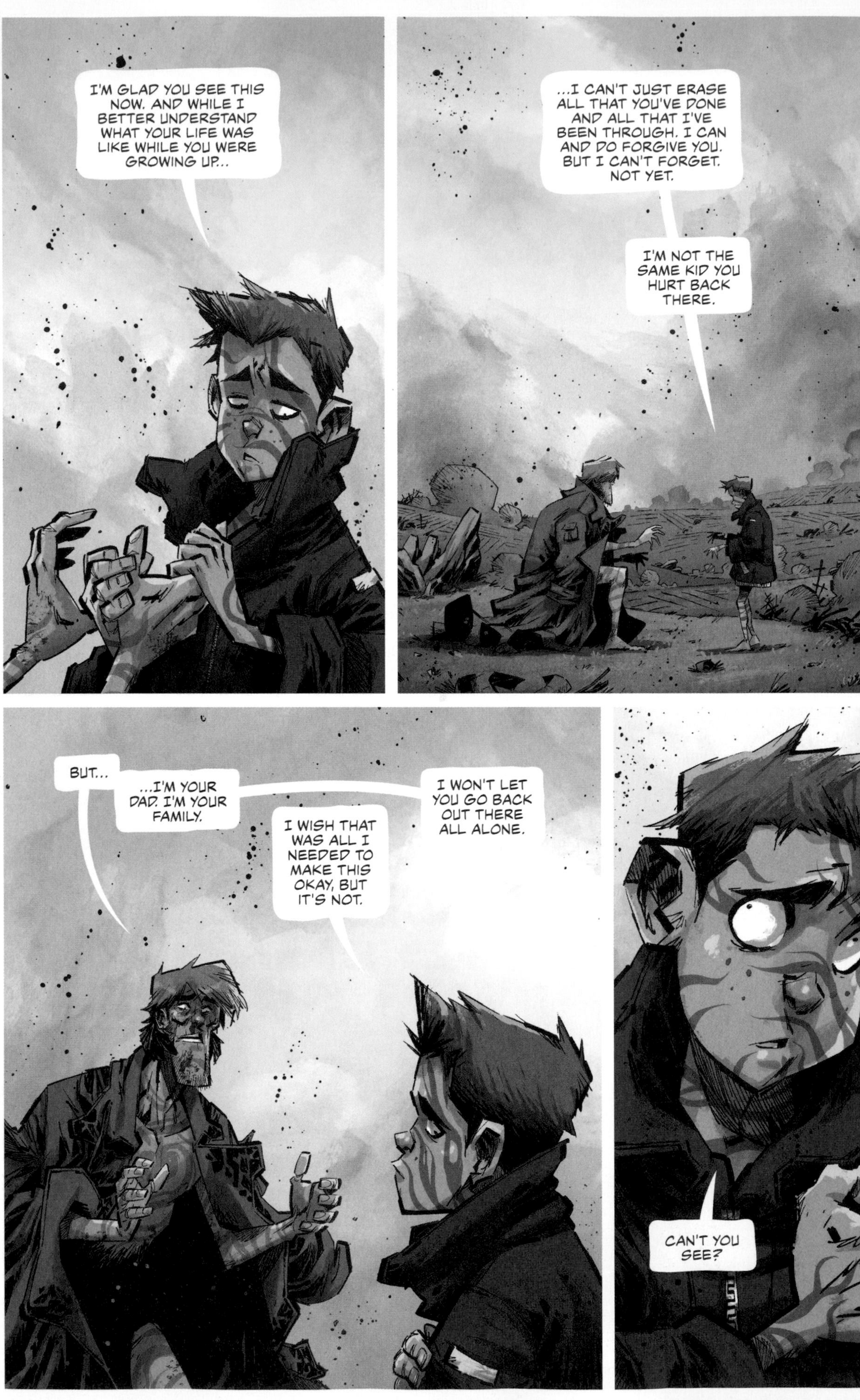
I'M GLAD YOU SEE THIS NOW. AND WHILE I BETTER UNDERSTAND WHAT YOUR LIFE WAS LIKE WHILE YOU WERE GROWING UP...
...I CAN'T JUST ERASE ALL THAT YOU'VE DONE AND ALL THAT I'VE BEEN THROUGH. I CAN AND DO FORGIVE YOU. BUT I CAN'T FORGET. NOT YET.
I'M NOT THE SAME KID YOU HURT BACK THERE.
BUT...
...I'M YOUR DAD. I'M YOUR FAMILY.
I WON'T LET YOU GO BACK OUT THERE ALL ALONE.
I WISH THAT WAS ALL I NEEDED TO MAKE THIS OKAY, BUT IT'S NOT.
CAN'T YOU SEE?

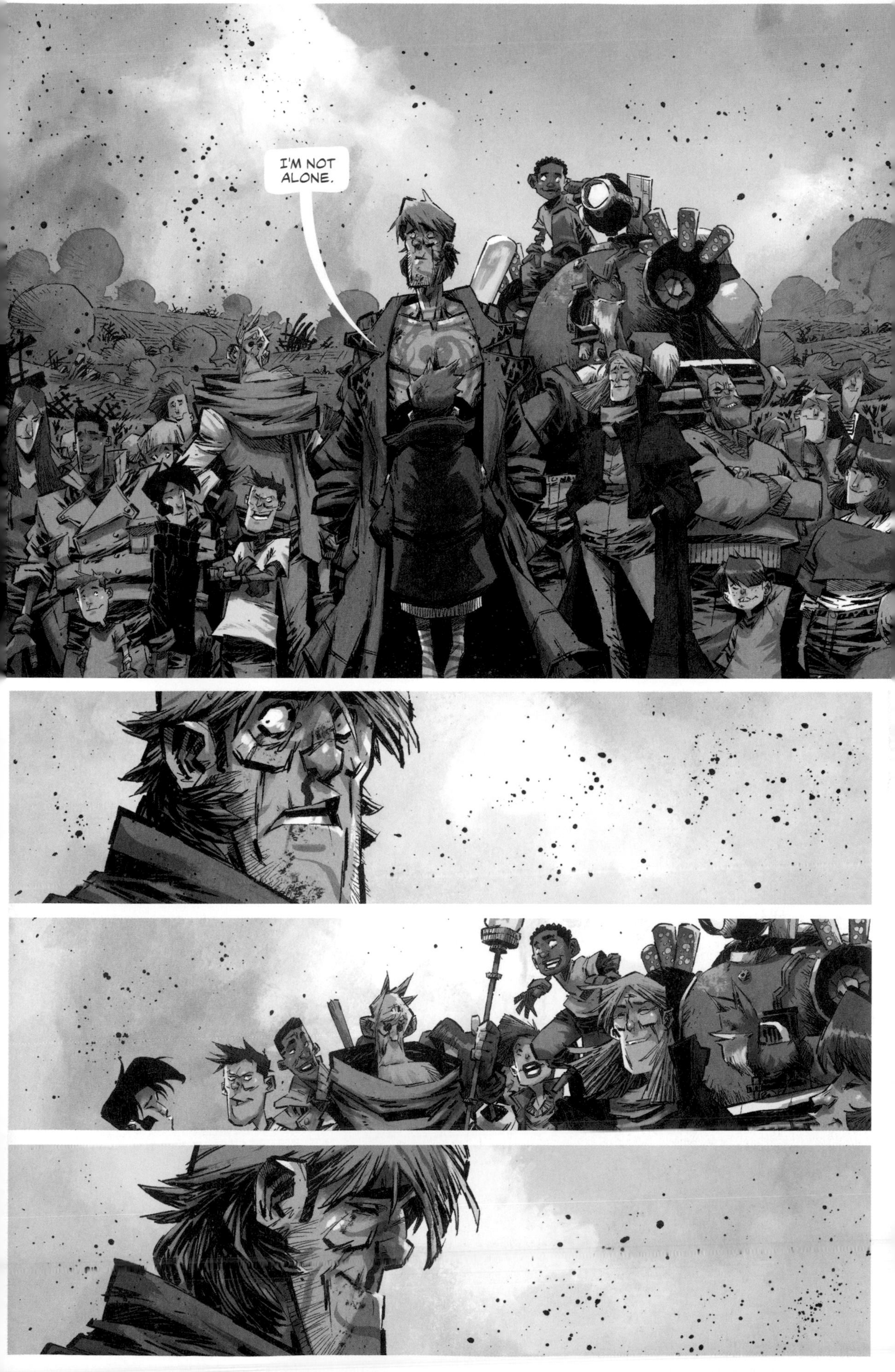
I'M NOT ALONE.

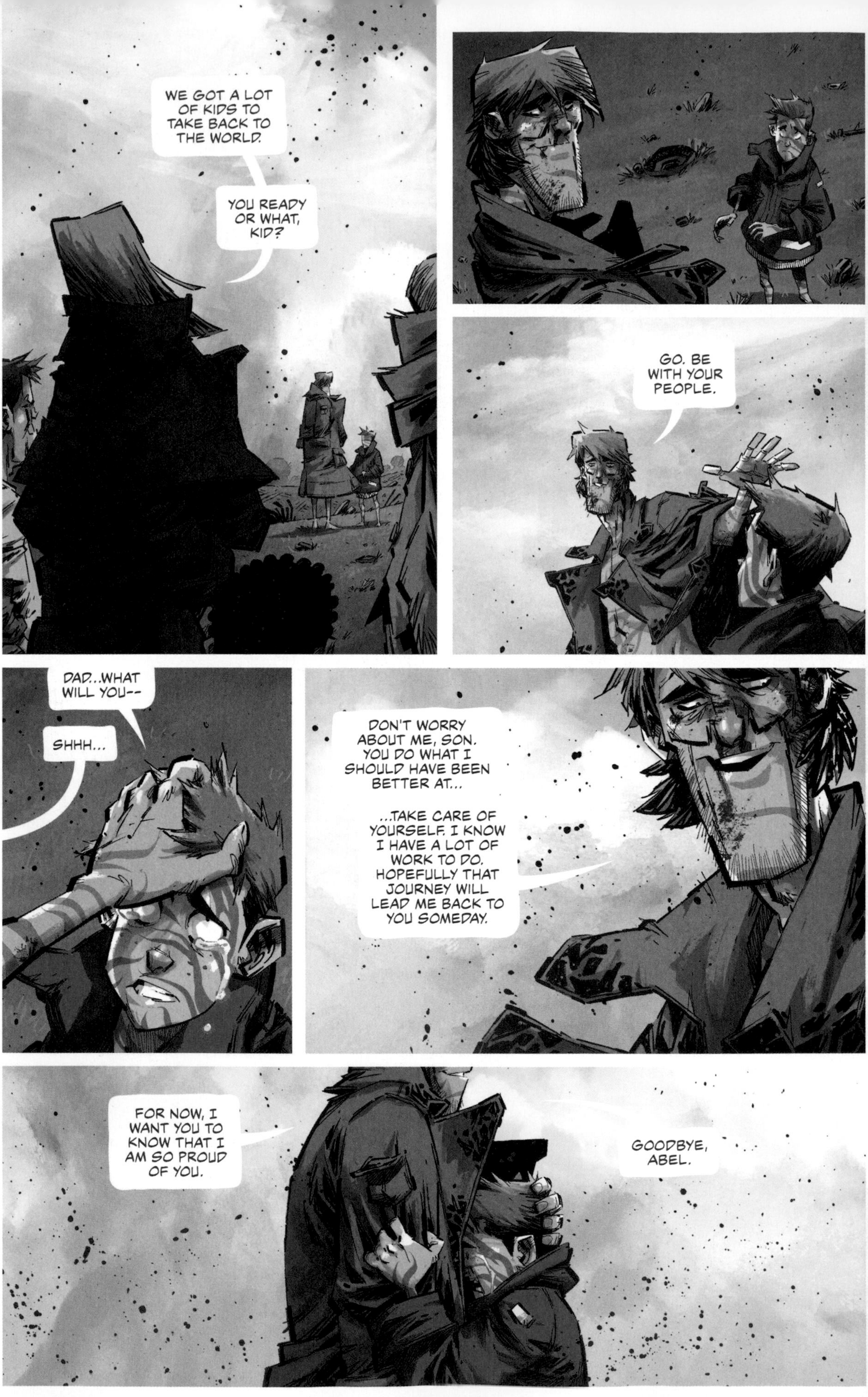
WE GOT A LOT OF KIDS TO TAKE BACK TO THE WORLD.
YOU READY OR WHAT, KID?
GO. BE WITH YOUR PEOPLE.
DAD...WHAT WILL YOU--
SHHH...
DON'T WORRY ABOUT ME, SON. YOU DO WHAT I SHOULD HAVE BEEN BETTER AT...
...TAKE CARE OF YOURSELF. I KNOW I HAVE A LOT OF WORK TO DO. HOPEFULLY THAT JOURNEY WILL LEAD ME BACK TO YOU SOMEDAY.
FOR NOW, I WANT YOU TO KNOW THAT I AM SO PROUD OF YOU.
GOODBYE, ABEL.

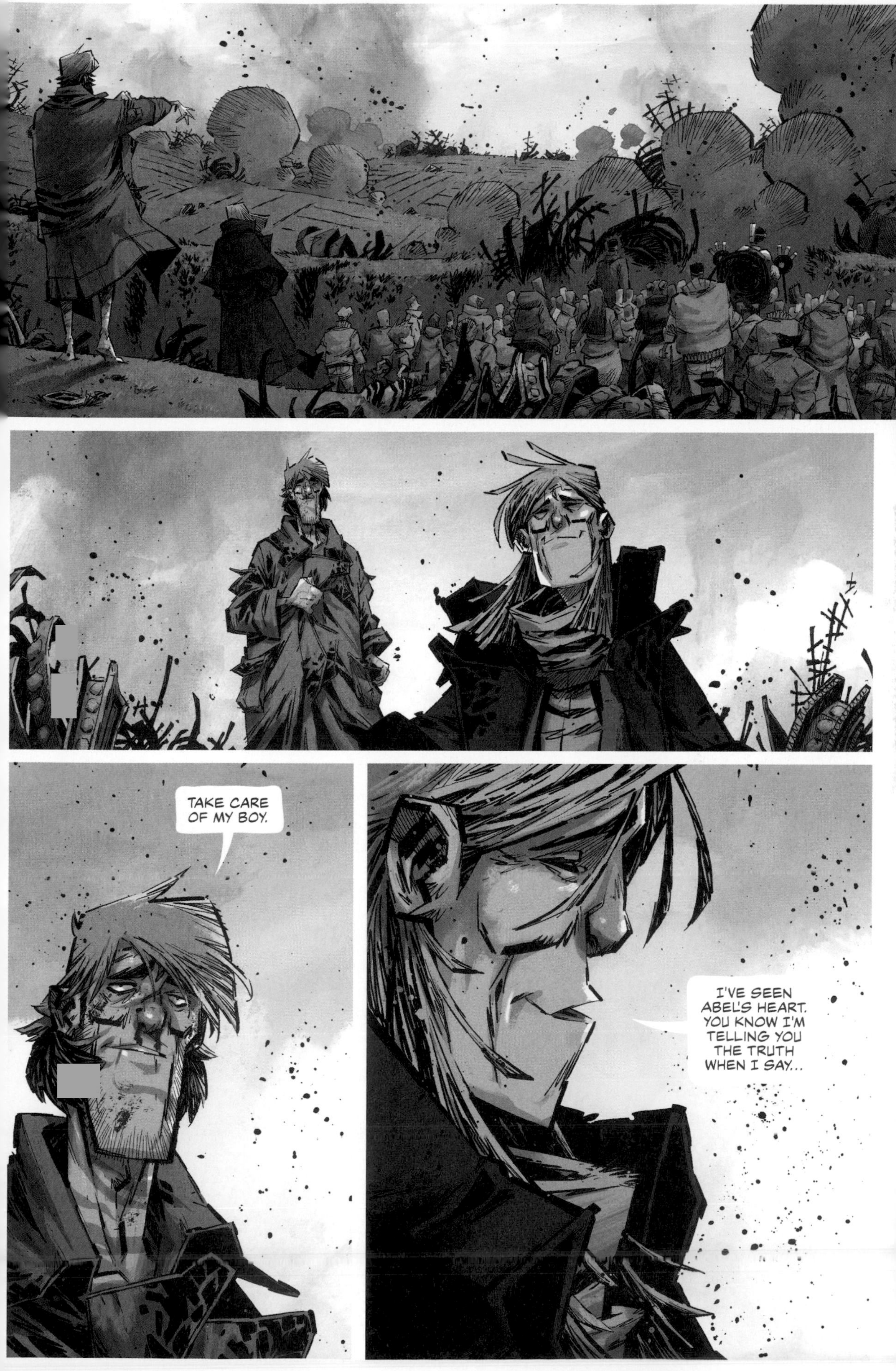
TAKE CARE OF MY BOY.
I'VE SEEN ABEL'S HEART. YOU KNOW I'M TELLING YOU THE TRUTH WHEN I SAY...

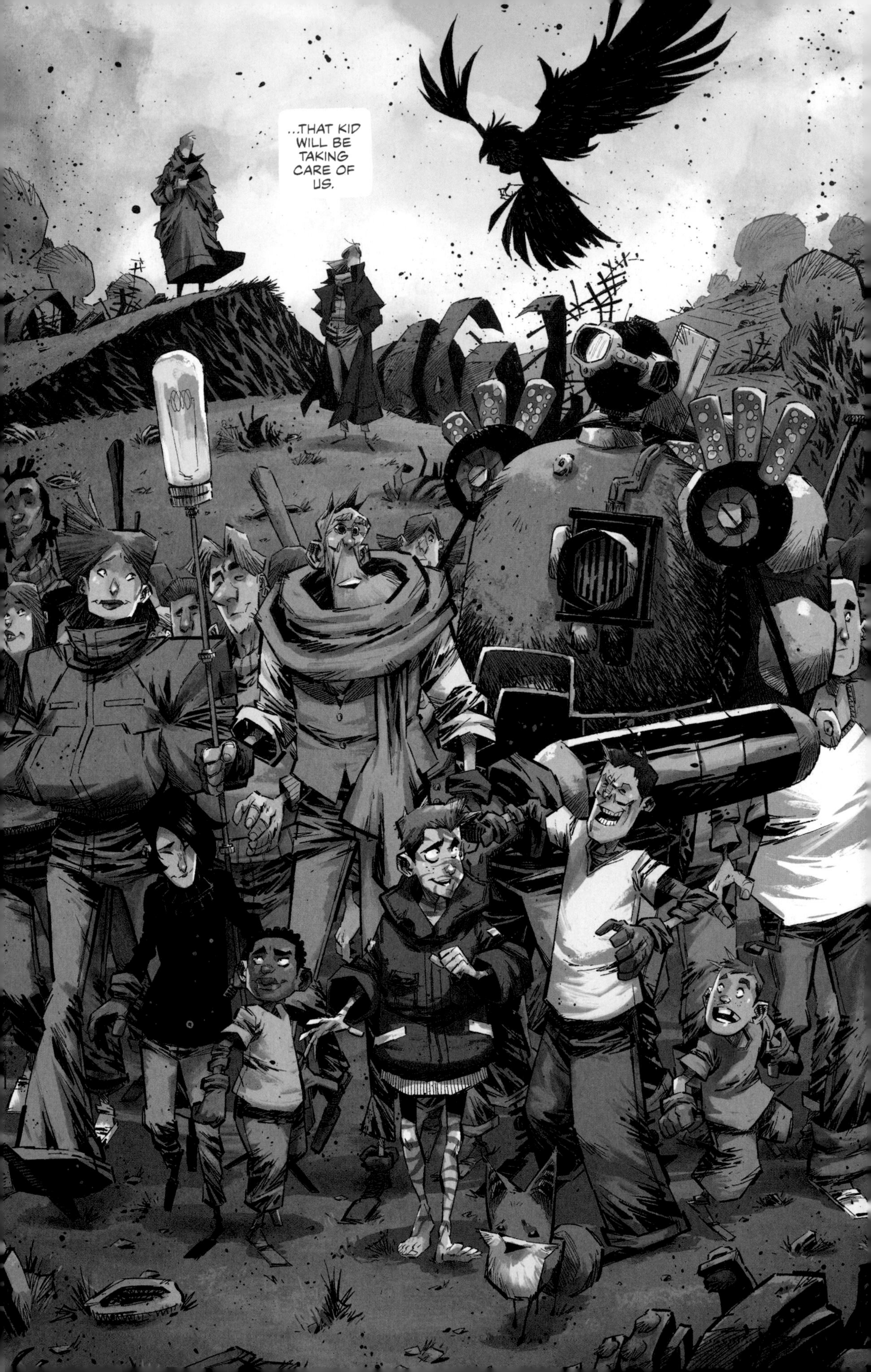
...THAT KID WILL BE TAKING CARE OF US.

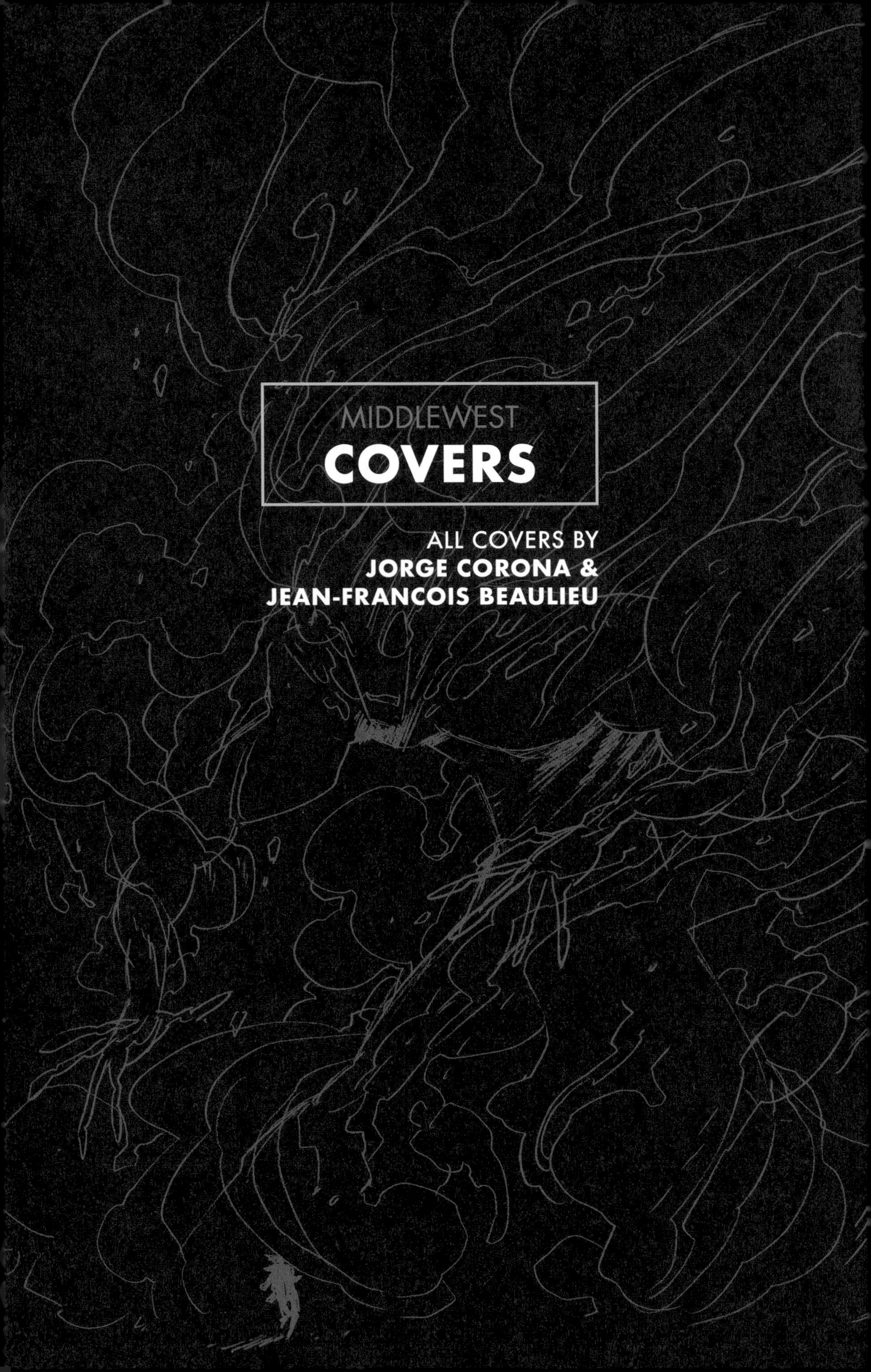

MIDDLEWEST

COVERS

ALL COVERS BY

JORGE CORONA &

JEAN-FRANCOIS BEAULIEU

ISSUE #13

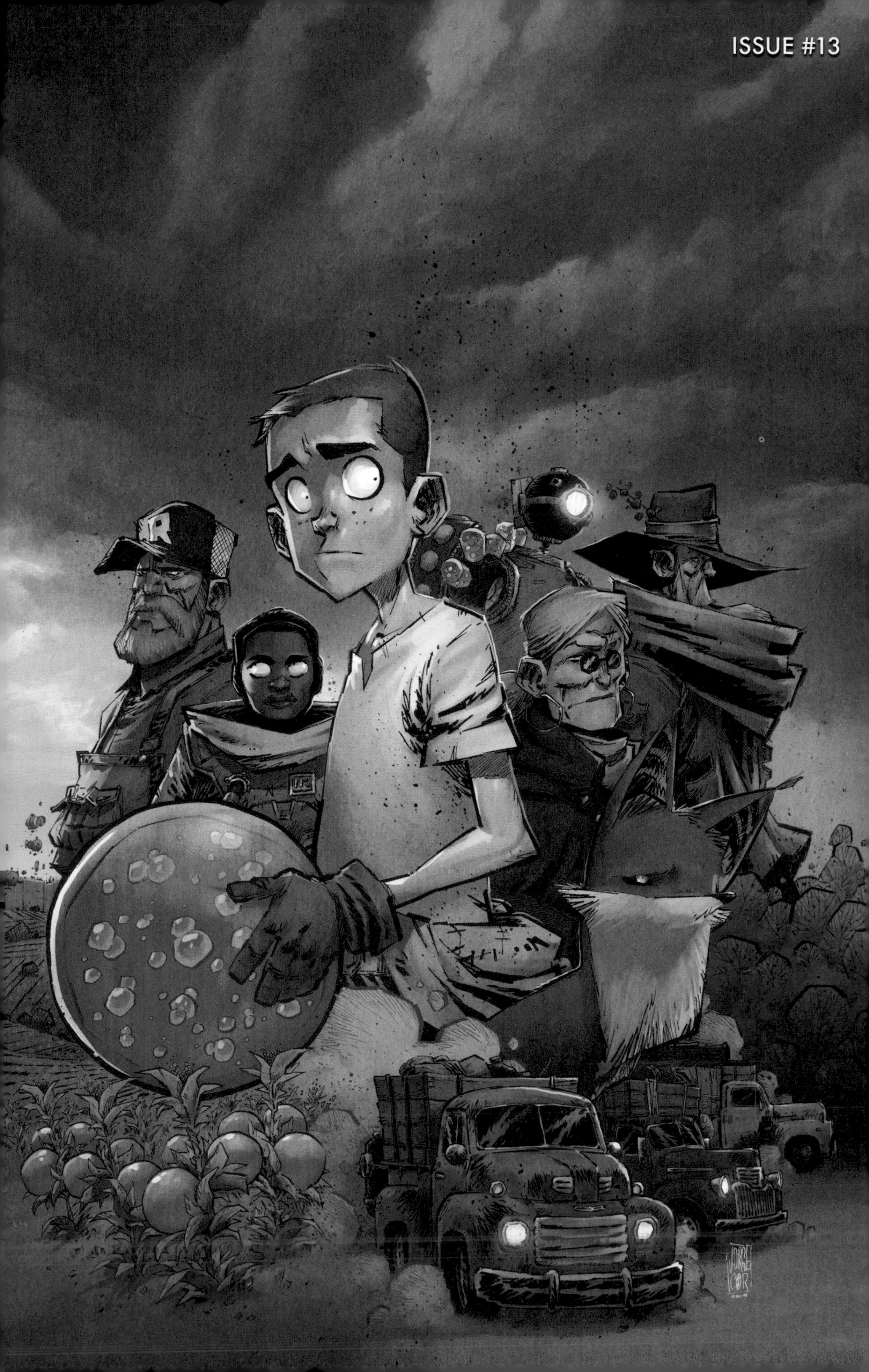

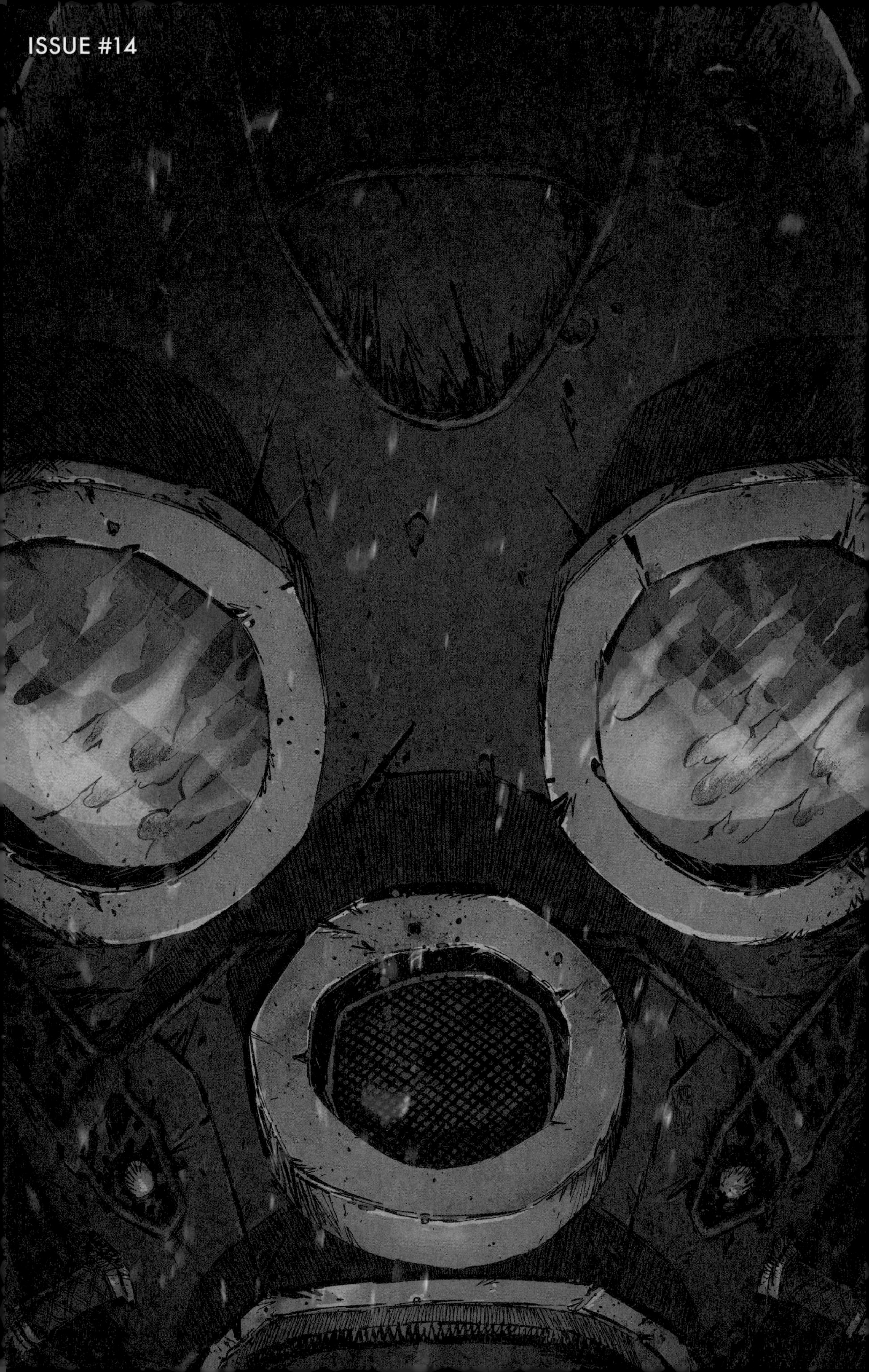
ISSUE #14

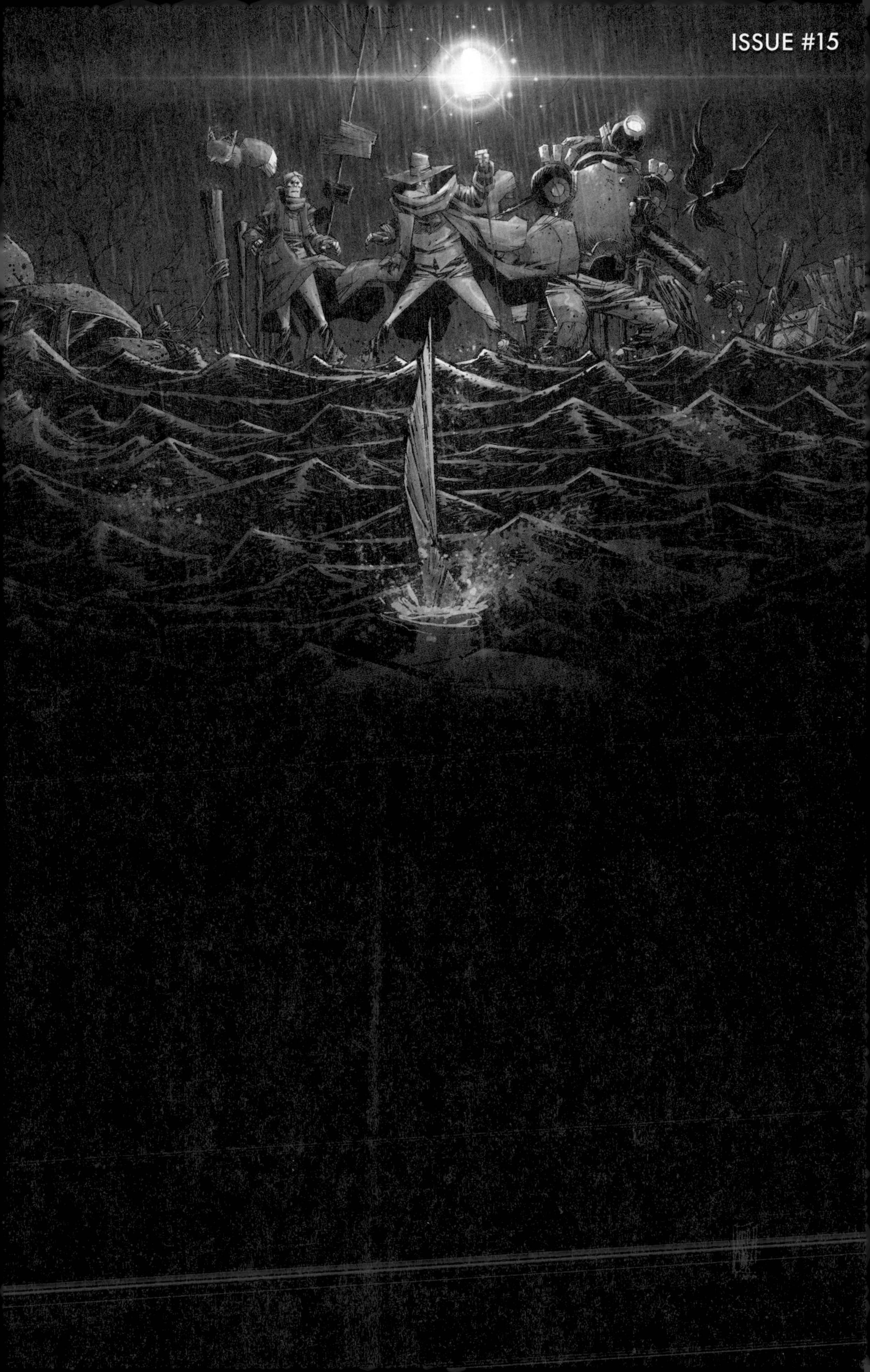
ISSUE #15

ISSUE #16

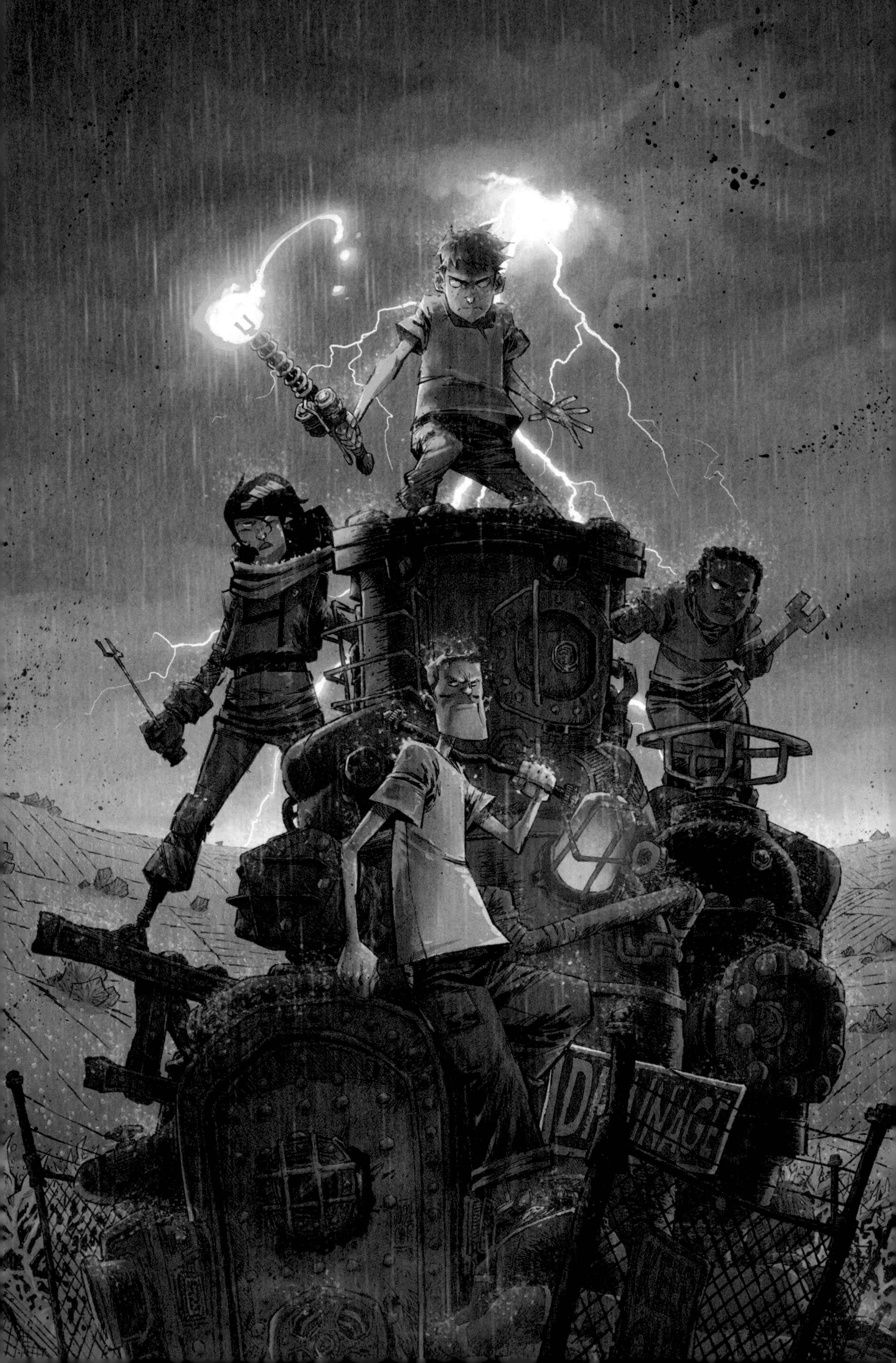

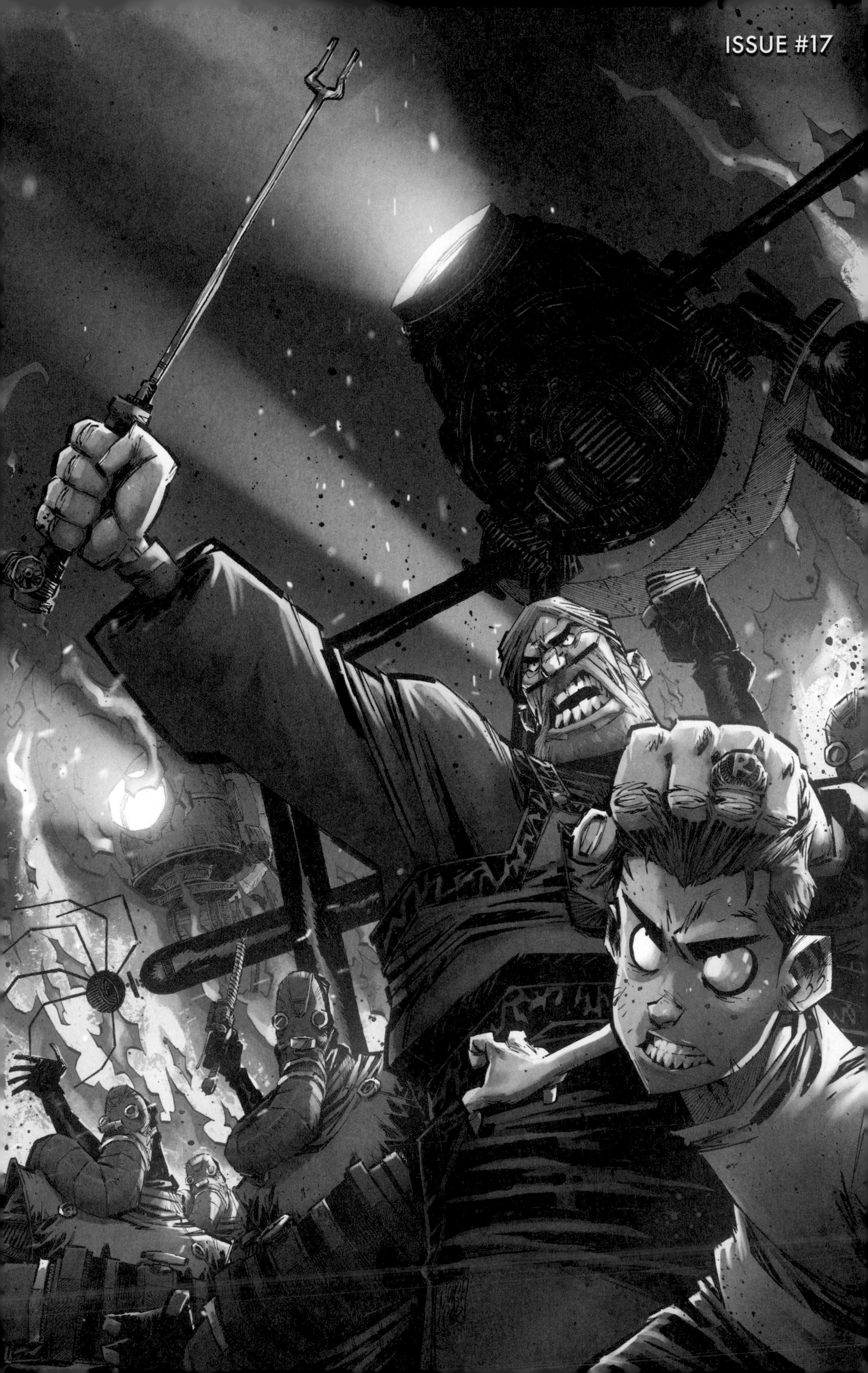

ISSUE #18

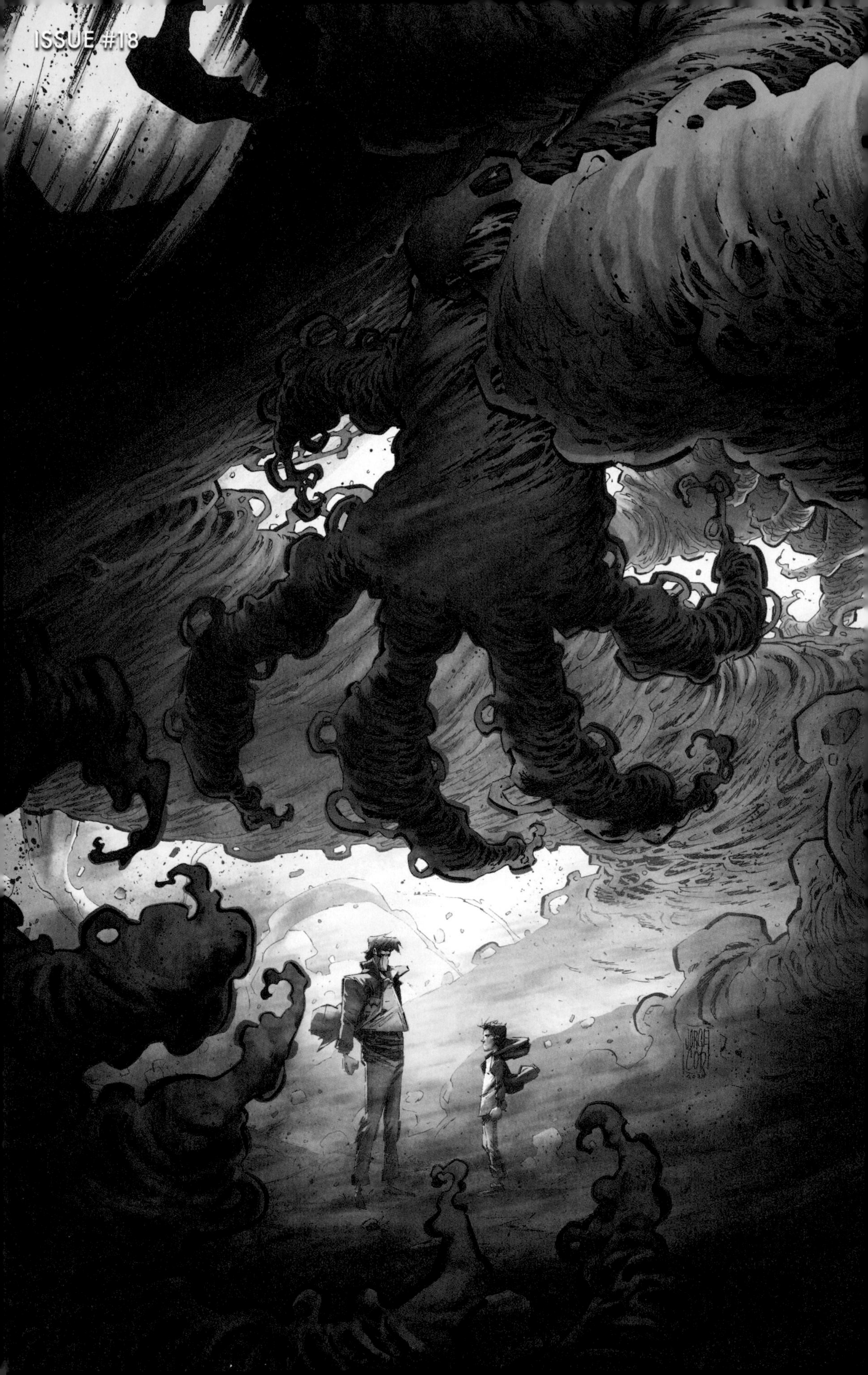

COVER
PROCESS

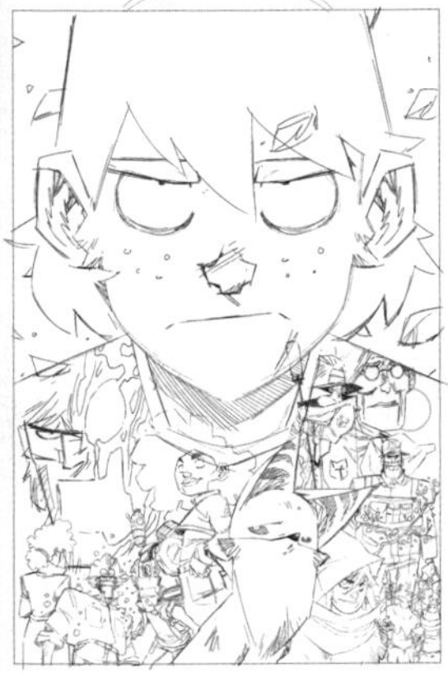
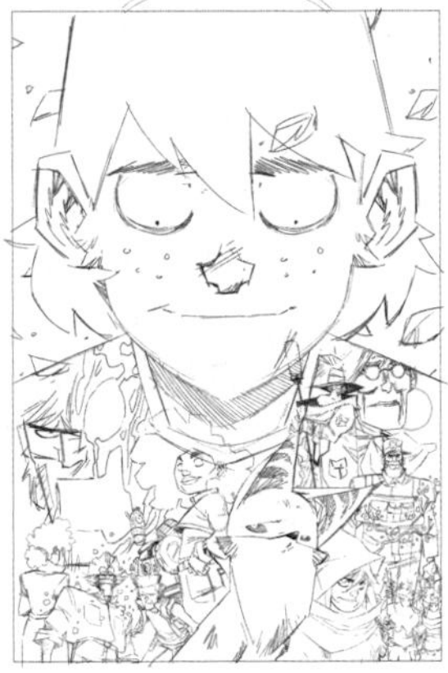
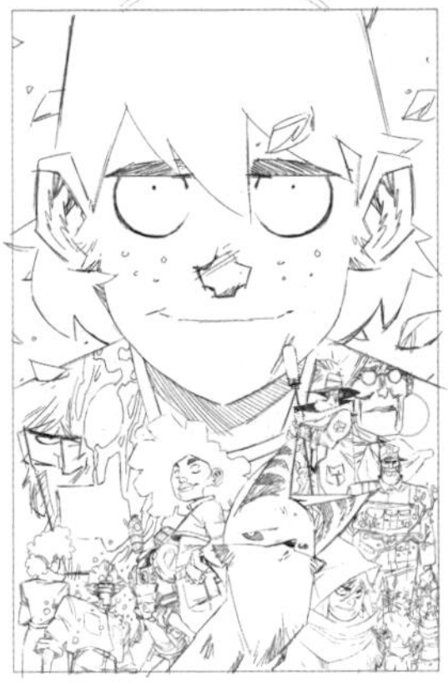
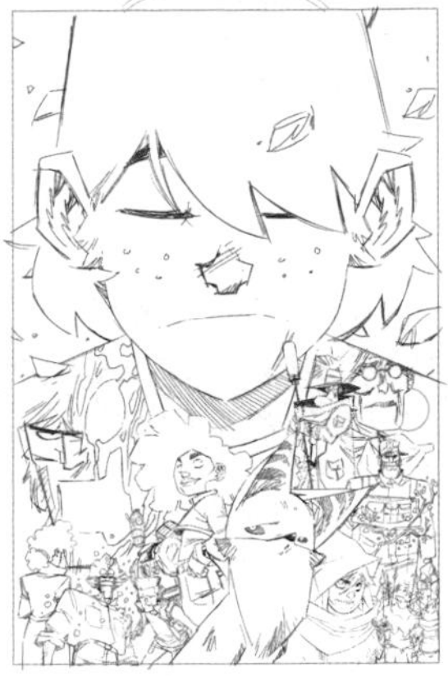
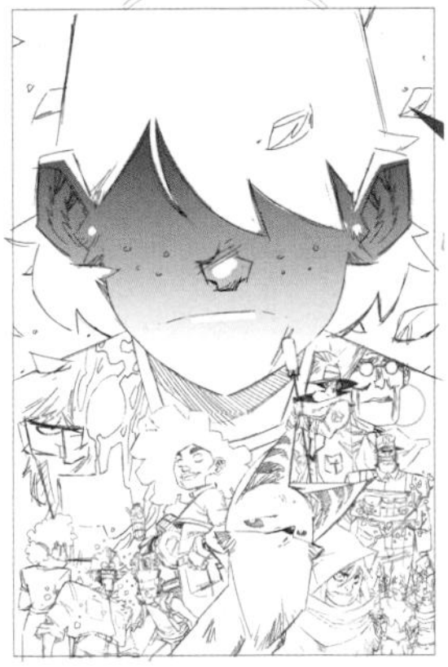
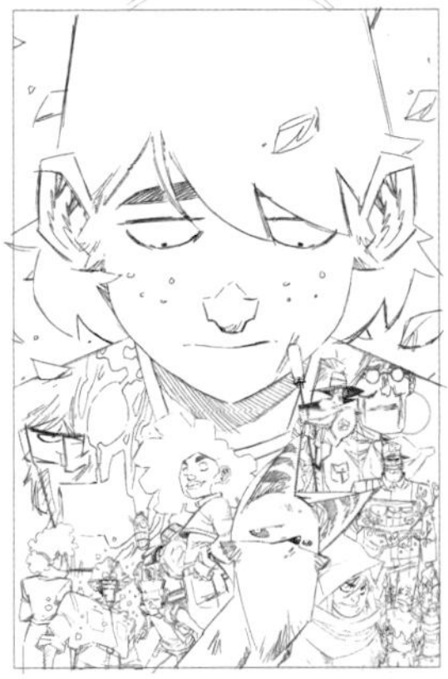
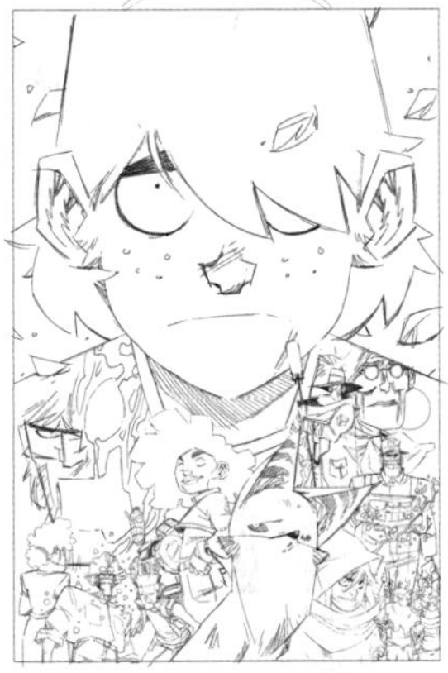
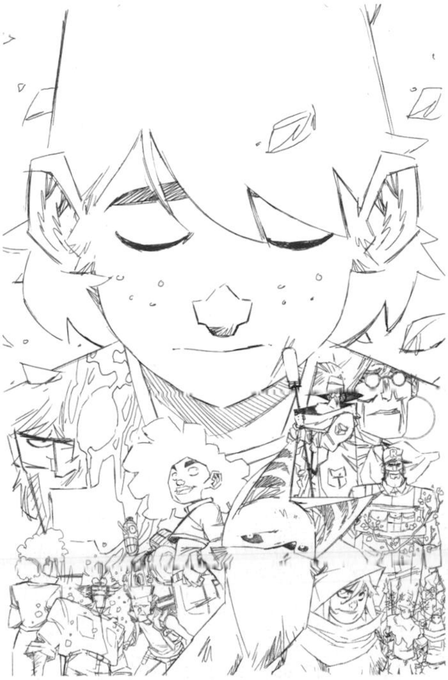
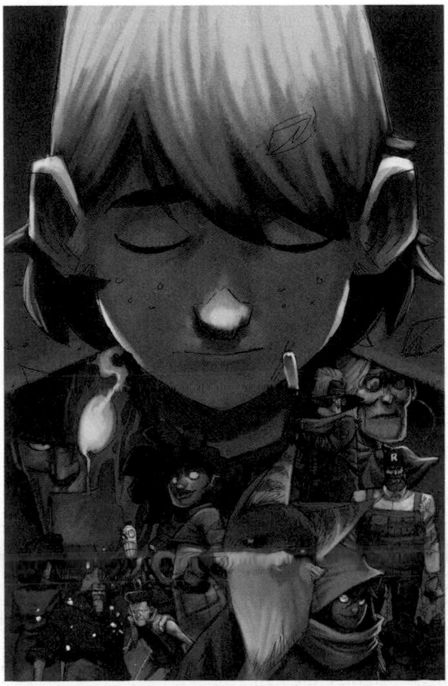

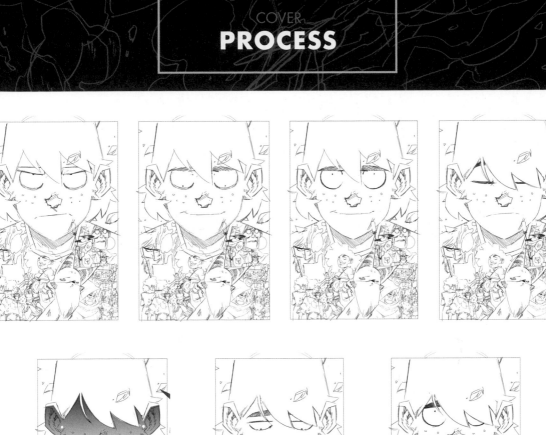

COVER
PROCESS

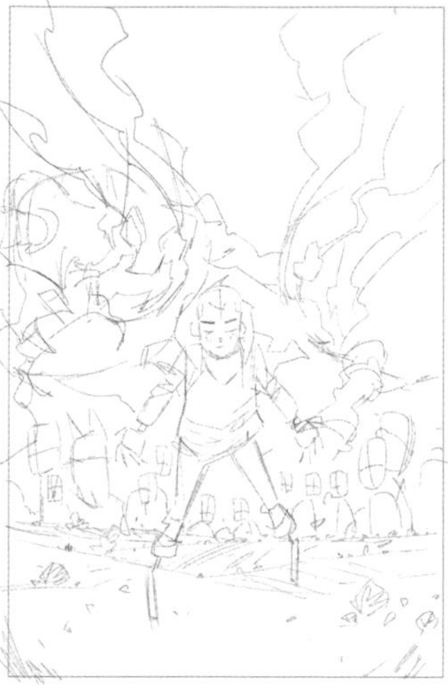

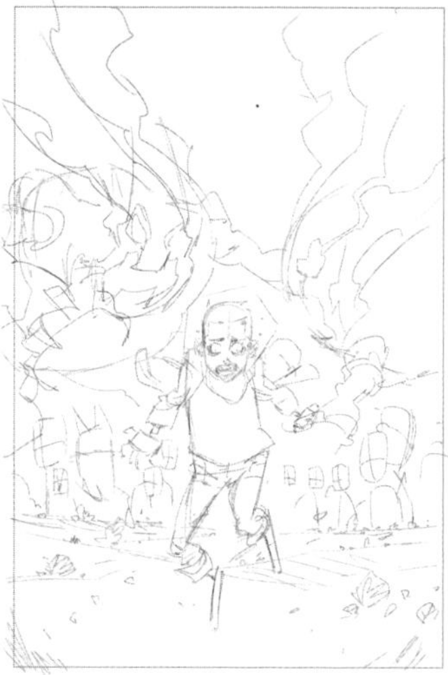

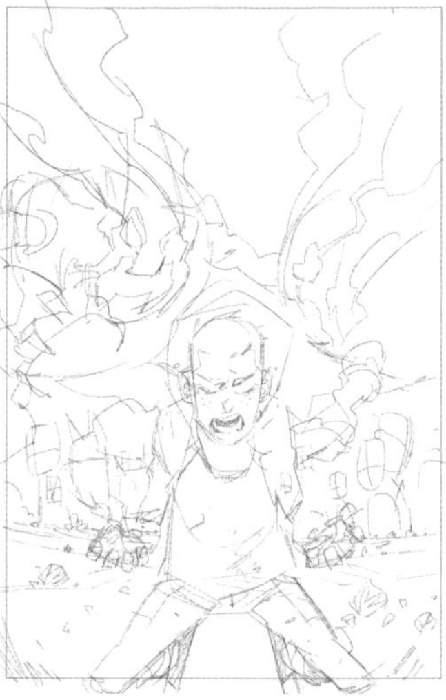

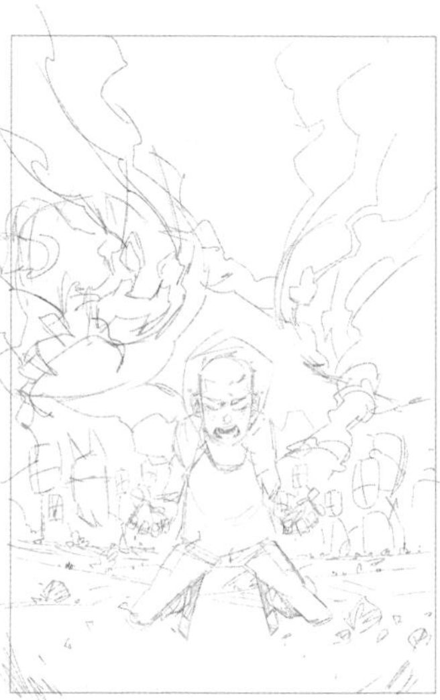

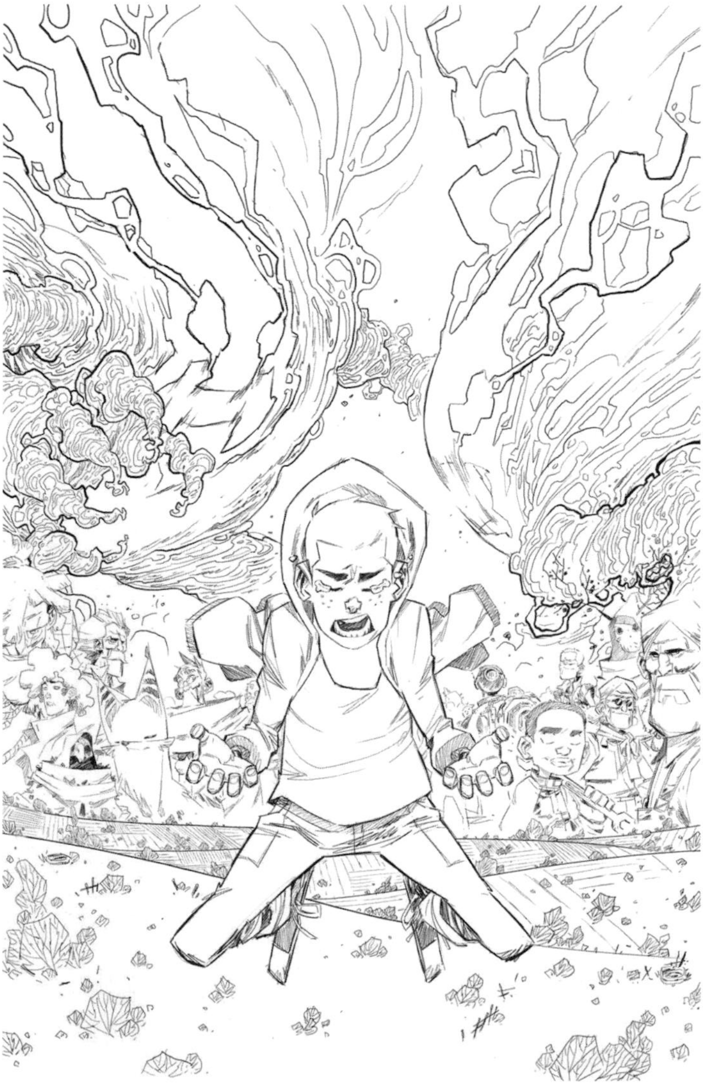

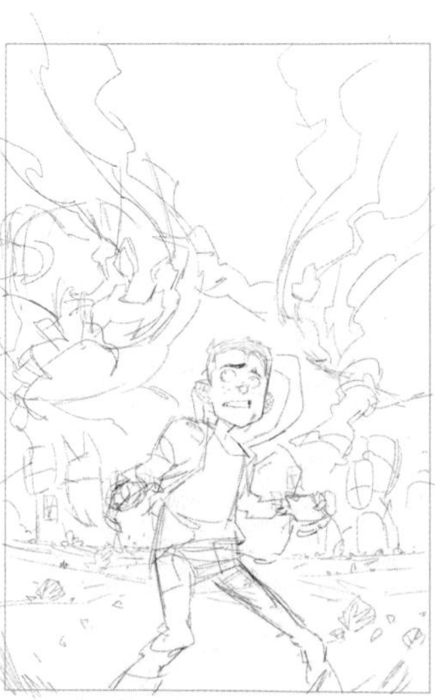

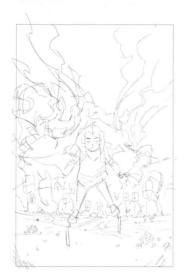

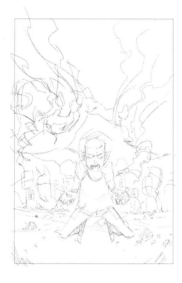

COVER
PROCESS

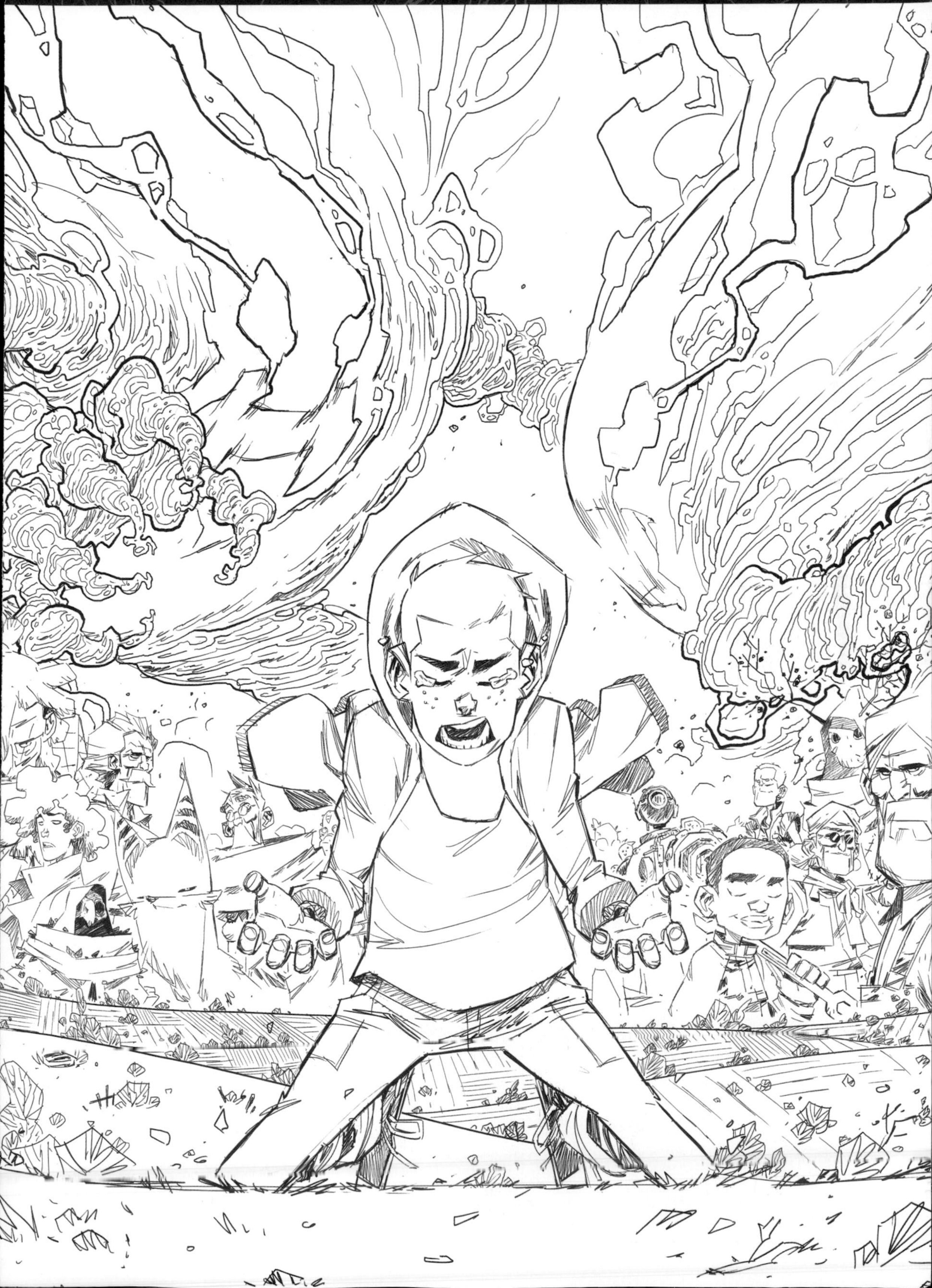

COVER
PROCESS

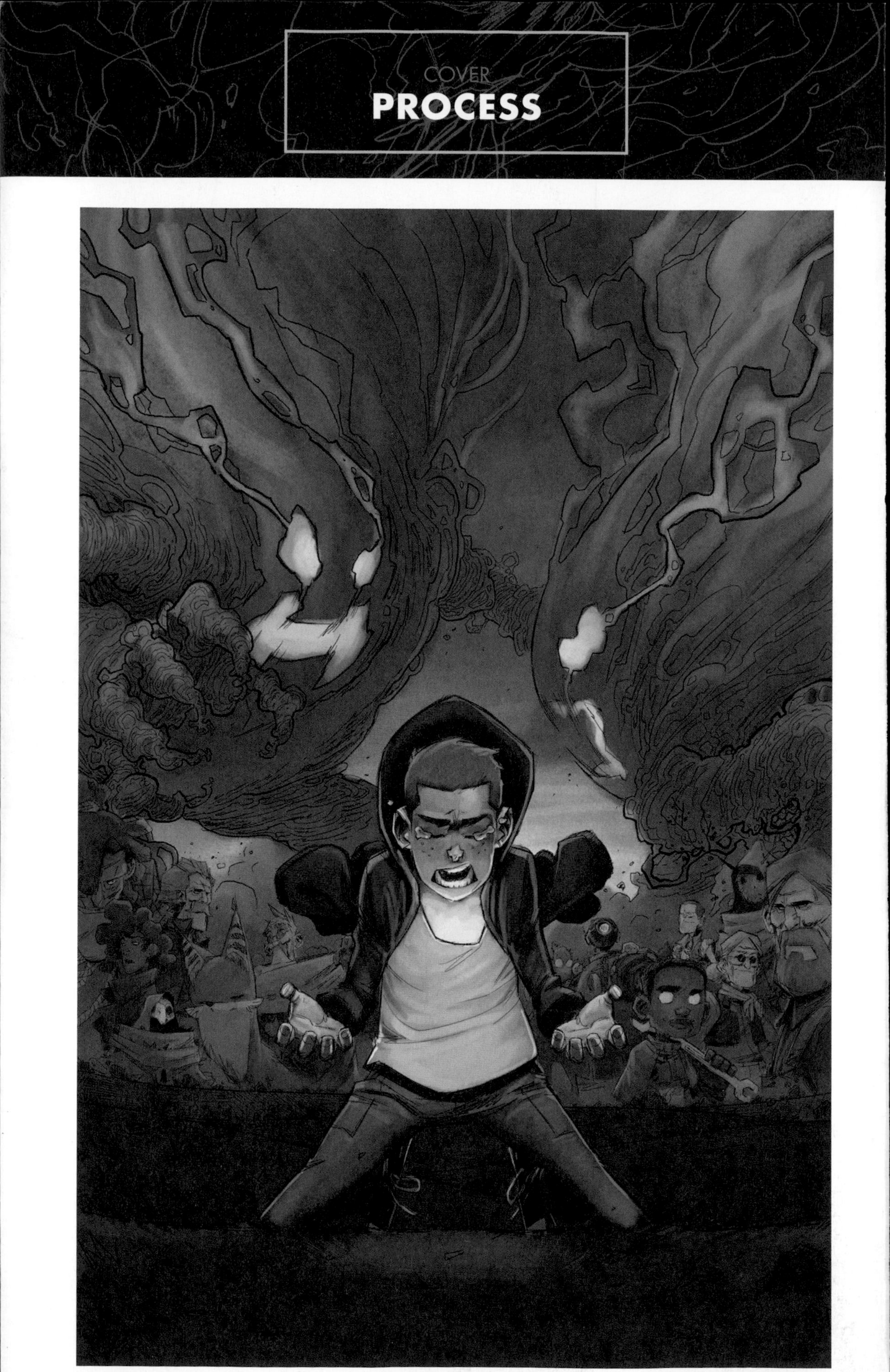